PRAISE FOR FARRAH ROCHON AND
THE DATING PLAYBOOK

"A total knockout: funny, sexy, and full of heart."

—*Kirkus*, starred review

"A rom-com touchdown."　　　　　—*Entertainment Weekly*

"Fun, heartfelt, and totally relatable."

—Abby Jimenez, *New York Times* bestselling author

"Rochon's books are always witty, hot, and engaging."

—BuzzFeed

"Farrah Rochon is one of the absolute best romance writers today. Period."

—Kristan Higgins, *New York Times* bestselling author

THE BOYFRIEND PROJECT

Book of the Month selection
LibraryReads selection
NPR: Favorite Books of the Year
BuzzFeed: Best Books of the Year
Cosmopolitan: Best Romance Novels of the Year
Insider: Best Romance Books of the Year

ALSO BY FARRAH ROCHON

The Boyfriend Project

The DATING PLAYBOOK

♥

FARRAH ROCHON

FOREVER

New York   Boston

Forever

Hachette Book Group

1290 Avenue of the Americas, New York, NY 10104

read-forever.com

twitter.com/readforeverpub

First Edition: August 2021

Forever is an imprint of Grand Central Publishing. The Forever name and logo are trademarks of Hachette Book Group, Inc.

The publisher is not responsible for websites (or their content) that are not owned by the publisher.

The Hachette Speakers Bureau provides a wide range of authors for speaking events. To find out more, go to www.hachettespeakersbureau.com or call (866) 376-6591.

Library of Congress Cataloging-in-Publication Data

Names: Rochon, Farrah, author.

Title: The dating playbook / Farrah Rochon.

Description: First Edition. | New York : Forever, 2021.

Identifiers: LCCN 2021010574 | ISBN 9781538716670 (trade paperback) | ISBN 9781538716663 (ebook)

Classification: LCC PS3618.O346 D38 2021 | DDC 813/.6—dc23

LC record available at https://lccn.loc.gov/2021010574

ISBN: 978-1-5387-1667-0 (trade paperback), 978-1-5387-1666-3 (ebook)

Printed in the United States of America

LSC

Printing 1, 2021

In memory of my big sister and best friend,
Tamara Denise Roybiskie.
You remain forever in my heart.

The

DATING
PLAYBOOK

CHAPTER ONE

A strident clink pierced the crisp, late October evening as Taylor Powell tapped her fork against her champagne flute.

"All right, ladies. Get those glasses in the air!"

She topped off her friends' drinks, then emptied the last of the prosecco into her glass before holding it aloft. Turning to Samiah Brooks, she said, "To you, my kickass friend. May this genius phone app you created set the tech world on fire!"

"Hear! Hear!" the third member of their trio, London Kelley, hailed as their champagne flutes met high above the fragrant Tex-Mex feast on the table.

The light of the setting sun shimmered through the pale yellow wine as Taylor brought the glass to her lips. Its rays, reflecting off the tranquil aquamarine waters of Lake Travis, provided just enough warmth to make their decision to dine on an outside deck commendable instead of foolish. Tonight's celebration warranted a full-fledged dinner at one of Austin's most renowned restaurants.

Its menu prices reflected its prestige, which accounted for the cement block that had settled in the pit of Taylor's stomach.

She shouldn't even be here. After having to choose between

making the minimum payment on her Mastercard or having her Internet disconnected—the Internet won out—Taylor had decided to skip this week's girls' night out. She'd had her excuse primed and ready, but then Samiah texted the news that her new phone app would be featured at some swanky tech conference. She'd asked Taylor and London to help her celebrate. What kind of friend would say no?

A friend who knows she can't afford this shit! That's what kind!

Taylor swallowed another gulp of the pricey wine.

"So I have a question." London gestured to Samiah with the shrimp she'd just plucked from the platter of fajitas. "I don't want to sound like a complete Luddite, but now that your app has been chosen for this fancy-schmancy conference, what does it mean in the real world?"

"It means she's about to make *money* money." Taylor rubbed her thumb over her fingertips.

"It will take some time before I see any real *money* money," Samiah said. "But this is a *big* deal, ladies. Big. Huge."

"Are you purposely quoting *Pretty Woman?*" Taylor asked.

Samiah stuck her tongue out at her. "Always with the jokes," she said. "Seriously, this could be life-changing. The conference chooses only ten candidates from thousands of submissions to present during the Budding Stars Showcase." She directed her attention at London. "It's like a surgical intern being invited to present a paper at the American Heart Association's annual conference."

London straightened in her chair and flicked imaginary dust from her shoulder. "I presented as an intern."

"Of course you did," Taylor said. "You may claim to be a pediatric surgeon, but we all know you're really Wonder Woman."

"Wonder Woman is sitting at this table, but I'm not her."
London held her hand up to Samiah for a high five. "You are
killing it, girl."

Taylor could hardly believe the three had only met three
months ago after learning they were all dating the same guy. It
had been her first and only date with Craig Milton, aka Craig
Walters, aka Craig Johnson—and those were only the aliases
they knew about. An instant sisterhood had formed between
herself, London, and Samiah, and they'd made a pact to spend
some time working on projects that brought them joy instead
of worrying about dating apps or trying to find a man.

Their weekly night out ever since was damn near
medicinal—a heavy dose of much needed support, understanding, and camaraderie none of them had realized they
needed.

Samiah had completed the phone app she'd been working
on for years and, because she was an overachiever, had also
snagged herself a cutie, her coworker turned boyfriend, Daniel
Collins.

"I won't claim success until I've secured funding for the Just
Friends app," Samiah said. "Winning this spot in the showcase
gets me one step closer. What about you?" she directed at
London. "Fill us in on your project's progress."

"I'd rather drink more wine." London signaled their server,
who'd just cleared the table next to theirs. "Can we get another
bottle of prosecco and another order of the combo fajitas?

"I had back-to-back surgeries today," she explained once
the server left. "This is my first meal since the banana I ate
for breakfast."

Equal parts panic and dread clogged in Taylor's throat. She
wasn't the best with numbers, but she could handle simple

math. With another thirty-dollar bottle of wine and forty more for fajitas, tonight's dinner had just crossed the two-hundred-dollar mark. And that was *before* tax and tip. Their practice of splitting the bill evenly meant she was looking at eighty dollars. That was more than her grocery budget for an entire week!

With their six-figure salaries, Samiah and London could easily afford to drop a C-note on a single meal without batting an eye. Meanwhile, Taylor was blocking calls from bill collectors like a thirsty match on Tinder.

"Umm, hello? Taylor!"

She startled at London's fingers snapping just inches from her face.

"Huh? What?" *Shit.* If their concerned frowns were anything to go on, they'd been trying to get her attention for some time. "I'm sorry," Taylor said. "What?"

"I asked about *your* project. How is it going?"

"No," Samiah interrupted. "Before you get to that, you still owe us the full story behind your first and only day at the homeschooling job. And how it ended with you being arrested."

"Oooh, you're right," London said. "Okay, you heard her, lady. Spill it."

Taylor dropped her head back and groaned at the deepening purple sky. She would rather cover their entire dinner bill than talk about her humiliating stint in jail. She'd spent less than three hours behind bars, but that was long enough to convince her that nothing mattered more than her freedom. She felt claustrophobic just thinking about that holding room.

"Didn't we already discuss this?" Taylor asked.

"You haven't told us anything, except that you ran over a

lawn chair with your car," London said. "So what happened? Did one of the kids call you ugly? Talk about your mama?"

"Oh, stop it. It was nothing like that."

"Then what *was* it?" Samiah asked, her words drenched with concern. "When Daniel and I bailed you out of jail, I could tell you were in no mood to talk, so I didn't ask. But I'm asking now. What happened, Taylor? You said yourself that the opportunity to teach that phys ed class was too good to pass up."

Taylor shrugged. "The parents didn't think I was the right person for the job, that's all."

"So you ran over one of their lawn chairs?" Samiah asked.

"That was a misunderstanding."

The server returned with the second bottle of prosecco and another steaming platter of fajitas. Taylor prayed the arrival of more bubbly would steer their attention away from her.

She should have known better.

"Explain the misunderstanding," London said as she topped off their glasses. "How'd things go from 'Sorry, you're just not the right fit for the job' to 'Bitch, you'd better get out of that chair if you don't want tire marks up your ass'?"

Samiah and Taylor both burst out laughing.

"Yeah, it sounds as if we're missing a few details," Samiah said, dabbing at tears of mirth with her dinner napkin. "Didn't you curse out one of the kids too?"

"I never cursed out any kids. However," Taylor continued, "I may have used a few choice words without realizing the kids were just a couple of feet behind me." She raised her hands in defense. "I apologized to the kids! But, of course, little Jack or Ted or whatever his name was went tattling to his mom."

"And the lawn chair?" London asked.

"It was a mistake! I was backing out of the driveway—which was long and winding and not the easiest thing to navigate when you're upset because you've just lost out on a job." Her shoulders sagged. "I didn't even see the chair. I explained it to the police officer, and the parents even backed me up on that. They knew I didn't purposely roll over the chair."

It was just her freaking luck that a police cruiser happened to be driving by as she backed over that stupid piece of lawn furniture.

"Besides, I wasn't arrested because of the chair. I was arrested because my car had an expired license plate tag, and I had a few unpaid parking tickets." More like a dozen, but who was counting? Well, other than the city of Austin.

Now that she thought about it, luck *had* been on her side. She'd gotten off easy, only having to pay a fine along with the unpaid parking tickets. Sure, she'd maxed out her Mastercard, but it was worth it to get out of that stank-ass jail cell.

"I also didn't lose out on the job because I rolled over the lawn chair," she admitted. Taylor sucked in a deep breath and released it. This was the part that left a sour taste in her mouth whenever she thought about it. "They wanted someone with a college degree."

The cement block in her stomach grew heavier.

"The woman who initially offered me the job claimed that it was dishonest of me to withhold that I didn't have a degree, but she never asked! How is it *my* fault that she goes around making assumptions about a total stranger's educational background? I was like, excuse *you*, lady!"

"Well, I can see where she's coming from," London said. "Public school teachers are required to have a degree, so it stands to reason homeschool teachers would as well."

"No, that's just—" Taylor started, but she realized she didn't have a rebuttal. "Whatever. If I'd known they wanted someone with a degree from the very beginning, I would never have gotten my hopes up about the job."

Her face grew fiery as the familiar frustration bubbled to the surface.

She had done everything she could this past year to take her fitness consulting business, Taylor'd Conditioning, to the next level. She'd studied the top Instagram fitness influencers, researching their journeys and trying her best to mimic their success. She just *knew* she would crush it, especially after coming up with the idea to use her background as an Army brat to specialize in boot camp–style workouts. She used all the right hashtags, offered free online fitness classes. She'd even started going live in her InstaStories—something she detested. But she couldn't seem to break free from the pack.

Back in August, someone recorded the confrontation they'd had with Craig, and the video had gone viral. Taylor thought she'd finally hit gold. It wasn't the most ideal way to get her business on the map, but beggars couldn't be choosers and all that.

Alas, her fifteen minutes of fame had barely lasted the full fifteen minutes. After coming out of that viral video debacle with only a handful of new clients, she'd been forced to accept an astoundingly hard truth. Not everyone with an Instagram account or YouTube channel became famous. If she wanted Taylor'd Conditioning to succeed, she would have to do it the hard way.

Her chest tightened. It did that whenever she considered the idea she'd been gnawing on for the past few weeks. Well, for the past year, if she were being honest.

"I think I want to change my goal," she blurted.

"Really?" London asked. "So you *don't* want to grow Taylor'd Conditioning?"

"No, I do! That's always my goal. I just...I guess I want to go about it a different way." She thought about chickening out, but she knew both Samiah and London would hold her accountable. They wouldn't allow her to use the eight hundred reasons she had locked, loaded, and ready to fire at the first hint of fear.

Before she could talk herself out of it, Taylor said, "I'm thinking about going back to school to get my degree in fitness and nutrition."

There. It was out in the universe. No going back.

"Ah, okay. That's cool," London said.

"Good for you," Samiah followed.

That's cool? Good for you? Did they not understand how freaking terrifying this was for her?

Then again, why would they? Neither of them knew about her complicated relationship with school. They were both ridiculously smart women who had probably breezed through high school and college. She doubted they had any concept of the fact that for *some* people, the thought of sitting in a classroom was enough to make one break out in hives.

"This is a big deal," Taylor said. She put a hand to her knee to stop it from bouncing under the table.

"Of course it is," Samiah said. "You'll be working full time while going to school, right? You should try bullet journaling to help organize your schedule. I've heard it helps you stay on track."

"It's not about my schedule. It's about...about the stress of it all. Going back to school would be a *huge* deal for me. It's...Just forget about it," she said.

"We're not going to forget about it. The whole point of this project is to help each other achieve our goals. If your goal is to get your degree, we're going to help you do that."

Taylor wondered how far that offer of help extended. Would they be willing to complete all her assignments and take the tests for her? Because *that's* what she needed from them.

Stop! If you're going to do this, you're going to do it on your own.

Once she decided to do something, she rolled up her sleeves and got things done. A bootstrapper, through and through.

But was this the right move for her?

"I'm still not sure this is something I even *want* to do," Taylor said. "I'm thinking about it, that's all."

"Maybe you should do more than just think about it," London said. "I'm sure I don't have to tell you this, but a degree will open a lot of doors for you. You could find something even better than that homeschooling job."

Taylor knew exactly what she was missing out on because she lacked a college degree. Just days after the homeschooling job had fallen through, she'd been offered her dream job—the kind of position that would elevate Taylor'd Conditioning in a way some stupid viral video never could.

But it, too, had been snatched away.

The server arrived with their bill, and even though London insisted on paying for the fajitas she would be taking home with her, Taylor's stomach still performed a triple backflip when she added her credit card to the leather check holder. This was her emergency credit card. Dining out at a restaurant she couldn't afford did *not* count as an emergency.

No amount of mental gymnastics could justify her irresponsible spending.

Night had completely fallen by the time they made it to

the parking lot. London gestured to Taylor's car. "Will you be okay navigating the twists and turns down this hill in that thing?"

"Hey! Nessie is not a thing," Taylor said, patting the hood of the thirteen-year-old Nissan Sentra she'd inherited from her brother. Her finger caught on a rust patch, but she'd be damned if she showed any sign of pain.

"Why don't you drive ahead of me so that I can keep an eye on you? Just to be safe," Samiah said. She held up a phone. "Give me about five minutes to return Daniel's call."

Taylor knew any argument would be futile when it came to these two. She had to admit, it was nice to know they were looking out for her.

Her hands started to tremble as she slipped behind the wheel of her car, the enormity of what she'd done tonight crashing down on her. Now that she'd shared her intentions about earning her degree, she could no longer come up with a reason not to do it.

Taylor dropped her head on the steering wheel.

"What did you do?" she groaned.

Her head popped up. She knew one thing she'd done: She'd spent a shitload more on dinner than she could afford. She needed to make some money. And fast.

Taylor grabbed her phone and logged in to the Taylor'd Conditioning Facebook page.

Boot camp circuit training pop-up class.

3pm tomorrow.

Zilker Park.

Only $10.

She paid an extra five bucks to boost the post in hopes that it would reach a bigger audience.

"There," Taylor said.

She may be down, but don't ever count her out. In her twenty-eight years on this earth, she had always made a way when there seemed there wasn't one.

Now all she needed was a few people to show up for her class and tonight's dinner would be covered. Who knows, maybe she'd get enough attendees that she would be able to eat something other than ramen for the rest of the week.

It was a big ask, but she liked to stay positive.

CHAPTER TWO

Taylor crossed her arms over her chest and peered out at the group assembled before her. It was a move she learned from her dad when he'd worked with fresh Army recruits.

The eight people who'd signed up for her class resembled her typical clientele, for the most part. There were four college-age women, a couple of Gen-Xers, and a svelte older woman with sensibly coiffed silver hair and flawless skin. A proud Glam-Ma, as she'd informed the class.

There was only one member who gave her pause. Dressed in a black long-sleeved workout tee, with gray shorts over a pair of black running tights, Mr. Hot and Fit had proven to be a bit of a conundrum.

She'd pegged him as a Craighole, the name she'd given to guys who'd sought her out only after her brush with Internet fame. Each had claimed he wanted to get in shape, but what he really wanted was to prove he could succeed where Craig had failed. As if she were the prize in some video game or something. Jerks.

She was more than happy to take the money they paid for one of her classes, but she found most of them couldn't keep up with her intense workout after the first ten minutes.

That hadn't been the case with Mr. Hot and Fit here. He'd breezed through both the warm-up and core exercises. Of course, she had yet to put her foot on the accelerator. Let's see how he handled her high-cardio sequence.

Taylor clapped her hands to get everyone's attention.

"Okay, folks. It's time to get that heart muscle pumping! Now, I understand that fitness levels vary, so you have a choice between burpees and the easier jump squats. I'll show you." She demonstrated both exercises, jumping with her hands stretched toward the sky, before quickly making it to the ground and executing a push-up.

"Do *not* push yourself to do the burpees if you don't think you can handle them," she cautioned. "This isn't a competition. Work at your own fitness and comfort level." She gave them an encouraging smile and a thumbs-up. "Ready? Burpees in three, two, one!"

She was relieved to see the Glam-Ma had opted for the jump squats. She sensed that the older woman had set her sights on the class's lone male participant.

"Keep going," Taylor called out, repeating the burpees again and again and again. "Your heart will thank you for it, but your arms and thighs may not be so happy in the morning."

"Mine aren't happy now!" one woman called.

"Remember to pay attention to your body," Taylor instructed. "Don't push yourself past anything that makes you uncomfortable."

The Glam-Ma inched closer into Mr. Hot and Fit's personal space, "mistakenly" bumping into him as he returned to a standing position.

"Oh, I am so sorry," the woman said in a breathless Scarlett O'Hara–style pant.

"Are you okay?" Mr. Hot and Fit asked, his tone exceedingly patient as he took her by the elbow.

"I am now."

Did she wink at him? Taylor didn't know if she should intervene on his behalf or high-five the Glam-Ma for shooting her shot with a man half her age.

"Let's kick this up a notch," Taylor said, accelerating her pace just to see if Mr. Hot and Fit would follow. He did.

"If you want to...elevate your cardio even more...add some height to your jump," she called.

Of course, Mr. Hot and Fit went for the high jump. He probably thought he could impress her with his stamina.

You think so, boo? Let's see you do this!

"This is only for the most advanced," Taylor said. "If you think you can handle it...put one hand behind your back...and give me an alternating single-arm burpee."

Surprise, surprise. Mr. Hot and Fit was the only one who attempted—and perfectly executed—the most difficult workout move in her arsenal.

Well, damn. What would it take to break this guy?

Sweat poured down his face. His sculpted chest pushed against that expensive high-performance workout tee with each labored breath, but he withstood every challenge she threw his way.

Taylor was about to add on a few four-way lunges when she remembered that this was not a competition between herself and Mr. Hot and Fit. She had other class participants to think about.

Instead, she did one last burpee before instructing, "And rest."

She derived some satisfaction from the fact that the class

show-off looked to be on the verge of collapsing. But so was she. She'd pushed herself close to her own limits.

Not that she would allow *him* to see that.

Shaking out her arms and legs, Taylor pasted on a smile and said, "Do you feel those endorphins rushing through your bloodstream? Doesn't it feel good?"

"My thighs are on fire." This from the college student who had been studying when Taylor and her class of seven gathered for their workout. The girl had pushed her books aside and joined them, paying the ten-dollar fee through Cash App before they got started.

"But is it a *good* burn?" Taylor asked. "The key is to listen to your body and to keep things fun. The more you enjoy your workouts, the more likely you are to stick with it."

She instructed everyone to sit and assume a butterfly pose; then she cued up her favorite cooldown playlist on her phone and guided the class through a series of stretches. She felt good vibes coming from this group. It would be awesome if she landed a few new regulars.

Once they completed the cooldown, she went over to her backpack and grabbed a handful of the overpriced business cards she'd bought when she'd first started Taylor'd Conditioning.

Pro tip: Just say no to embossing. Nobody cares.

"I offer both fitness and nutrition services," she said as she passed out the cards. "I also plan to offer more group classes in the very near future."

As in tomorrow, if she could get them to pay her another ten bucks each. She'd posted this pop-up class to her Facebook page out of sheer desperation. And just like that, her portion of the bill from last night's dinner was covered.

She was unable to mask her smile as she handed cards to

Mr. Hot and Fit and the Glam-Ma, who was now standing so close to him she could probably gauge his body temperature. Taylor had to hand it to the guy, he'd remained a gentleman throughout the older woman's antics.

"Make sure to follow my Instagram account and YouTube channel," Taylor added. "I provide free tips on both platforms."

"Do you offer meal planning?" asked a redhead wearing an I KEEP PRESSING THE SPACE BAR, BUT I'M STILL ON EARTH T-shirt.

"Yes, I do! I offer both meal planning and meal prep—healthy, nutritious, and *fresh* meals. And I tailor them to your lifestyle. Whether you're doing keto, paleo, low-carb, low-sodium, whatever you need."

"I took my great-aunt to her diabetes specialist last week, and he recommended we meet with a registered dietician to work on a low-carb, low-sugar diet. Can you do that?"

"I can," Taylor said. She could do everything a registered dietician could do. But she couldn't lie, even if it was by omission. "Although, I'm not technically a registered dietician," she admitted. "But I can absolutely help you come up with meal plans."

"Oh." The woman frowned. She hunched her shoulders in an apologetic shrug. "I would be more comfortable working with someone who's certified. Thanks for the class, though. It was so much more fun than the exercise classes I've joined at the gym."

"Yes, it was." This from the Glam-Ma. "I travel too much to sign on with a long-term trainer, but I can handle getting sweaty every now and then." She tossed Mr. Hot and Fit a brazen smile.

Taylor bit down on her lip in an effort to contain her giggle.

"Thanks. I'm happy you all enjoyed the class," she replied, trying to keep the disappointment from her voice.

You win some. You lose some.

And sometimes you lose *a lot*. But she wasn't ready to give up. She *never* gave up.

She pulled the elastic ponytail holder from her hair and gathered the flyaway strands. She'd sweated it out again, which meant at least an hour of blow-drying and flat-ironing tonight. She needed her hair braided in the worst way, but the thought of spending two hundred dollars at the salon was laughable. Braids were a luxury she couldn't afford at the moment.

As she watched the class disperse, she noticed Mr. Hot and Fit had finally managed to fend off his new crush. He was now off to the side, performing calf stretches.

Oh, c'mon. Could he be more transparent? He was clearly waiting for the others to leave so *he* could shoot *his* shot.

Taylor rolled her eyes and prepared for the inevitable corny pickup line. She only hoped he was smoother than the Craighole who'd joined her Muay Thai class last week. He'd approached after their workout, stretched the hem of his sweaty shirt toward her, and said, "Feel this. I wore it for you. It's made of boyfriend material."

Okay, so the old Taylor would have *totally* fallen for that line. But she'd changed in the last three months. It would take more than a cute, but still corny, pickup line to get her number these days.

Mr. Hot and Fit was about to learn that lesson.

He did a couple of side bends while the last two members of the class gathered their belongings. As soon as the women walked off, he made his way toward her.

"Thanks for coming out today," Taylor said before he could speak.

"I knew when I signed up that I would get a good workout, but this was incredible. Even better than I anticipated," he replied.

Oooh, he went with flattery. Nice move. It wouldn't work, but she appreciated the tactic.

"I'm Jamar, by the way," he continued.

"I'm happy you enjoyed the class, Jamar. Thanks again for participating." Taylor slung the strap of her backpack over her shoulder and started for the parking lot where she'd parked Nessie.

He followed.

To his credit, he didn't crowd her personal space, but she still didn't want to deal with some kind of awful pickup attempt.

"Hey, umm...you give one-on-one instruction, right?" he asked.

Ah, here we go. The old *Let's have some one-on-one fun together* line. Gah. She *so* was not up for this today.

This was the downside of having to advertise her business on social media. It was all but impossible to avoid the creeps who signed up for her classes with something other than getting in shape in mind. The problem had only gotten worse since that stupid video with Craig.

Taylor stopped and turned. "Look, I appreciate you taking the class and everything, but this is a really shitty way to hit on women. Now, if you'll excuse me, there's a smoothie with my name on it."

"Hey, wait." He put his hands up. "That's not what this is about. I want to hire you as my personal trainer."

Of course he did. So did every other Craighole.

She fought not to roll her eyes. "Look, if you want to schedule a consultation, you should email me or send a message through—"

He pulled at the waistband of his shorts.

Taylor took a step back and braced her legs apart, preparing to deliver a swift kick to his groin. "What in the hell are you doing?"

"Huh? What? No, I'm only getting my phone." He tugged it out of a pocket sewn into the waistband of the tights he wore underneath his shorts.

He swiped his fingers across the screen and then turned the phone toward her.

"I messaged you a couple of days ago through the Taylor'd Conditioning Facebook page, asking about a consultation meeting. See the message from YourFavorite23?" He tapped his chest. "That's me."

She had at least one hundred unread Facebook messages. Including his if he'd only sent it this week. She really needed to get better at checking her inbox.

"I'm sorry, but I'm behind on reading my Facebook messages."

"I was impressed after watching your videos on YouTube, but after this"—he hitched a thumb back toward the soccer fields—"I have no doubt that you're exactly the personal trainer I need."

Taylor couldn't deny that he'd seemed really into their workout. He didn't behave like those jerks who only signed up for her classes because they wanted to hang out with an Internet celebrity.

Okay, so maybe *celebrity* was pushing it, but whatever.

She hefted her backpack higher on her shoulder and crossed her arms over her chest.

"At the risk of stroking your ego, you don't look like someone who needs a personal trainer. Based on how well you kept up in today's class, I'd guess that you know your way around the gym pretty well."

"I'm trying to take my fitness to the next level," he continued. "Look, why don't you let me buy you that post-workout smoothie? I can go into more detail about what I'm looking for in a fitness and nutrition coach, and you can decide if I'm someone you want to work with." His smile, framed by his neatly trimmed goatee, hit Taylor in a way she was *not* expecting.

She gave him a slow and deliberate head-to-toe perusal, making sure he knew that she was sizing him up. How could she be sure he wasn't a Craighole?

So what if he was? Did that mean she would turn down a free smoothie?

"I'll meet you at the food truck park on Barton Springs Road," she said.

His broad shoulders practically wilted with relief. He made a sweeping motion with his hand, indicating she should go ahead of him. "I'll follow you there."

CHAPTER THREE

Jamar Dixon divided his attention between his phone and the ancient Nissan Sentra parked across the street. He stood just to the right of an A-frame chalkboard that listed today's smoothie selections, watching as Taylor Powell sat behind the wheel of her car and stared intently at her phone. Or maybe she was just pretending to be enthralled by the phone while debating whether to start her engine and take off.

Her initial skepticism had caught him off guard, but he could also see why she was suspicious of his motives. He tried not to buy into the notion that all professional athletes were superstitious, but when the Facebook post about that pop-up fitness class had appeared on his timeline this morning, he received it as a sign from the universe. Taylor's no-nonsense training style, along with the right combination of cardio, calisthenics, and a targeted weight-lifting regimen, would get his body back into top physical shape. And if he had any hope of securing one of the coveted spots on an NFL roster next season, he would have to be in the best shape of his life.

Taylor Powell was the answer to his prayers. Now he just had to get her on his team.

Some of the tension in his shoulders receded when Taylor's

car door opened and she slipped from behind the wheel. Jamar tried not to stare as she waited on the other side of the street for two cars to pass, but *damn*! How could he *not* stare? After all, it wasn't her exercise moves that had first drawn him to her.

A couple of months ago, one of his former teammates had forwarded a video of this guy being handed his ass by three women in a local downtown sushi restaurant. The first time he watched it, he'd zeroed in on Taylor.

He hadn't been able to tear his eyes away from her exquisite cheekbones or her full lips. He remembered the way those lips had curved upward in a triumphant grin and how she'd sauntered from the table, her head held high after tearing that Craig guy apart. She'd worn her hair in thick braids that day. He liked it now but kinda missed the braids.

Someone had posted a link to her workouts on YouTube in the comments section of the video from the sushi restaurant, and Jamar had immediately watched every one. From one athlete to another, he understood the discipline it took to reach that level of fitness. That was when he realized, if he had to choose between pursuing her as a potential hookup or his potential kick-ass fitness trainer, there was only one option.

Still, it was damn hard not to stare.

"Sorry about that," she said as she approached the food truck. "I had an emergency call from a client."

"Not a problem," Jamar said. "It's good to know you're always on call."

"Being on call costs extra."

"Again, not a problem. As I was saying at the park—"

"Nah-uh." She cut him off. "Smoothie first, then we talk." She walked up to the window and tapped on it before the person inside had a chance to slide it open. "Hi, can I get the super fruit blend with extra acai berries and two scoops of whey? And add a banana to it." She turned to Jamar. "You want something?"

Jamar shook his head and gestured for the guy to go ahead with her smoothie.

She turned to him and crossed her arms over her chest, giving him another of those head-to-toe looks that made Jamar want to flex his abs and puff out his chest.

"So how exactly did I get on your radar?" she asked.

Before he could answer, the window on the food truck opened and the guy called out, "Super fruit smoothie with extra acai, whey, and a banana."

As Jamar handed the smoothie truck operator a twenty, he saw the guy's eyes light up. He braced himself for what he knew would follow.

"Hey, you're Diesel Dixon, right?" The guy angled his lanky frame out the window, extending his hand to Jamar's. "How's it going, man? Damn, I miss seeing you in burnt orange and white."

"Yeah, I miss those days too," Jamar said, because that's what he was expected to say in situations like this. He waved the guy off when he tried to hand him change from the twenty.

"Thanks, Diesel," the guy said before sliding the window closed.

Taylor looked from him to the truck and then back again. She pointed at the truck. "Okay, what was that all about? Who's Diesel?"

"I'll explain everything after you agree to work with me," Jamar said.

She held up a hand. "Pump the brakes, Twenty-Three. *If* I decide to work with you."

Jamar lowered his voice, even though the food truck park was relatively empty. "Look, Taylor, it's obvious you don't know who I am."

"Am I supposed to know who you are, Twenty-Three? Or is it Diesel?"

"It's Jamar."

"Ah, so we're still going with Jamar?"

He hitched his chin toward her phone. "Why don't you Google Jamar Dixon?"

With her bullshit meter obviously on full blast, Taylor started typing with one thumb. Jamar leaned forward to get a better look at her screen. He noticed the way her forehead scrunched when the search results popped up.

"'Starting running back for the Texas Longhorns for three years,'" she read. "'First-round draft pick of the Chicago Bears.'"

"You forgot the most important one—the Katy High School Tigers."

She rolled her eyes. "I will never understand this weird relationship Texas has with high school football."

"It's a religion," he said with a laugh, feeling even better about his chances. She was joking with him. That had to be a good thing.

"Here's what I don't get." She tipped her head to the side, her brow creasing with a perplexed frown. "If you're Mr. Hot Shot Football Star, why do you need me? The NFL has some of the top trainers in the world. I didn't even grow up in the States and I know being a player for the Chicago Bears is a huge deal."

"*Former* player. And that's where you come in," Jamar said.

He glanced over his shoulder to make sure they were still relatively alone. In a lowered voice, he said, "I want to work with someone who isn't attached to the League, and the training I need requires someone who knows what they're doing. It's one thing to be in shape, but it's entirely different to be in the kind of shape it takes to play professional football."

"Is that your goal?"

He peered over his shoulder again before giving her a quick nod.

"And you think I can get you ready for the football field?" Taylor asked. "I mean, not that I can't. *I* know that I can, but what makes you so sure?"

"Because your teaching style is exactly what I need, someone who will push me and won't be afraid to call me out when I start to complain."

"A drill sergeant," she said.

Jamar nodded. "A drill sergeant."

A hint of amusement drew up one corner of her mouth and Jamar was struck again by how damn lovely she was. Not for the first time, he found himself wishing she wasn't so good at her job.

But she was. She'd proven that the moment she added one-armed push-ups to those burpees. His physical attraction to Taylor Powell would have to take a back seat.

Lizzo's "Good As Hell" blasted from her phone.

She looked at the screen. "Oh, shit. Can you hold this?" She shoved her smoothie at him and used both hands to peck at the phone. "Sorry, one of my regulars needs to move up our training session." She slipped her phone into a side pocket on her camouflage-print workout leggings and lifted her smoothie from his fingers. "I need to go."

"What about what we just discussed? Are you willing to take me on as a client?"

"Are you for real?" she asked. "I mean, *for real* for real?"

"Do you know how many gyms I passed on my way down here, just to take your class?" he said. "I promise, I'm for real."

"All the way down from where?"

"Georgetown."

She grimaced. "Okay, yeah, I wouldn't drive all the way out from Georgetown just to hit on someone." She gave him another of those quick perusals. "You don't look that desperate."

"For a date? No. For a trainer I believe in? Yes, I'm desperate."

"Be careful there, Twenty-Three. My rate is based on a sliding scale. The more desperate you are, the more that price slides upward," she said in a teasing voice. She pulled her phone from her pocket and looked down at it again. "I really have to go. Can we talk about this another day?"

"Tomorrow?" he asked. "I need to start training as soon as possible. Should we meet here? I can buy you another smoothie."

"You said you're up in Georgetown, right?" she asked. Jamar nodded. "I've been meaning to make an IKEA run. How about I meet you halfway? There's a Starbucks at the outlet mall in Round Rock that's near IKEA. Does that work for you?"

If he wrote up a list of places where he would run into the most Texas Longhorns fans, Texas Memorial Stadium would be at the top. A Starbucks near an outlet mall would be second.

"Would you mind if we met someplace else? There's a little café not too far from the outlet mall." He held up the business card she'd handed him back at Zilker Park. "Is this a good number to text you with the name and directions to the café?"

She nodded, but then her eyes narrowed once more. "You'd better be legit, Twenty-Three. I don't want you wasting my time."

"I won't," he said. "I don't have any time to waste, yours or mine."

He walked back to the smoothie truck and rapped on the window. He handed the guy a ten this time. "She'll take another smoothie to go." He turned back to Taylor. "I'll see you tomorrow."

CHAPTER FOUR

Taylor pulled into a parking spot next to a sky-blue minivan parked at the far end of the aisle, a good distance away from any other vehicle. She got out of her car and met a grinning Melonie Phillips standing at the rear of the minivan.

"I see you're taking advantage of some of the tips I taught you," Taylor said in greeting. "Did you even look for a closer parking space?"

"Nope." Melonie held up her wrist, showcasing the fitness tracker she'd purchased at Taylor's insistence when they began working together this past summer. "I upped my daily goal to twelve thousand. It's not as easy to get in those extra two thousand steps as I thought it would be. I've had to get creative."

"You'd be surprised at how many steps you can get in by adjusting your routine just a little bit here and there. One of my favorite tips is to keep the TV remote next to the TV instead of on the couch or bedside table. I can almost guarantee you'll get another few hundred steps going back and forth to flip channels." Taylor gestured toward the grocery store and rubbed her hands together. "Let's get to shopping. I'm excited to see what you've come up with as a sensible meal plan."

Once in the store, she followed Melonie to the produce department, observing as she loaded up on leafy greens, colorful bell peppers, and broccoli. When she reached for a bag of russet potatoes, Taylor stopped her.

"If you're going to have potatoes, which I recommend limiting as much as possible, go for sweet potatoes."

"Really? I would have thought sweet potatoes had more sugar."

"They do, but they're also much higher in vitamin A. With your family's history of eye disease, they're the smarter choice. Better yet," she said, reaching for a butternut squash, "go half sweet potatoes, half squash, whether you're roasting or mashing them. It will lessen the carbs and sugar and you won't be able to tell the difference."

A grateful smile lit up Melonie's face. "This is the kind of advice I was hoping for when I hired you. It's all so much to keep track of, especially with three kids to run after. I swear, Taylor, you have been a godsend."

Melonie's praise was the kind of validation Taylor's battered ego had been thirsting for. Screw all those people who thought she needed a degree to do her job. She had as much fitness and nutrition knowledge as anyone she'd come across. She studied her ass off, making sure to learn as much as she could, determined to provide her clients with the most up-to-date advice.

"That's what I'm here for," Taylor said. "Remember, this is a partnership. How much weight have you lost since July?"

"Twenty-two pounds." Melonie preened. "I cannot wait for my ex and his new fiancée to drive down from Omaha in a couple of weeks to pick up the kids. I bought a new pair of jeans that make my ass look amazing. I want him salivating."

"Now *that* is the kind of vindication I live for." Taylor held her hand up for a high five. "Gimme some!"

They slapped palms, then migrated to the meat department, picking out lean cuts of beef and protein-rich salmon. By the time they were done shopping, Taylor couldn't stop herself from beaming like a proud mama.

"You did a great job, Mel. You ready to do it again next week?"

"That would be wonderful, but..." Melonie trailed off, her lips tilting downward in an apologetic frown.

A sinking feeling immediately settled in the pit of Taylor's stomach. "But...?" she asked.

"I found out last week that Avery, my middle daughter, needs braces. I have to sacrifice something to cover the dental bill, and unfortunately, that something is having a private fitness and nutrition coach."

No! God, please. She couldn't lose one of her few steady clients.

"Are you sure?" Taylor asked. "Maybe we can negotiate a new rate?"

"You've been a great help, Taylor, but I just can't justify this expense any longer."

Taylor knew she shouldn't allow her disappointment to show, but dammit, this sucked.

Melonie placed a hand on her forearm. "I'm forever grateful for everything you've taught me. It's been priceless."

Actually, it *did* have a price. Sixty dollars per session, to be exact. She'd already earmarked the two hundred forty dollars she'd expected to earn from Melonie Phillips this month. Guess her car insurance wasn't getting paid.

"I understand," Taylor said. Because she did. If she

understood anything at all, it was having to sacrifice to make ends meet. "We can always start the sessions again if your circumstances change."

She gave Melonie a hug and helped her load her minivan with the groceries she'd purchased; then she got in her car and tried her hardest not to burst into tears. Her dad loved to bring up that old adage *When it rains, it pours*. Well, Taylor was in the midst of a freaking downpour that refused to let up for a single second. She wasn't sure how much more of this she could take before she cracked under the deluge of pressure.

Once home, she found an empty plastic storage container propped against the door, a thank-you note taped to the lid. It was from Rob, her downstairs neighbor.

She baked when she was stressed—and not any of that healthy stuff like chickpea blondies or chocolate cake made with black beans that she encouraged her clients to eat. Give her all the sugar and butter. But, because she didn't want the temptation of sweets around, she often shared the baked goods with Rob.

She unlocked her front door and made her way inside, dropping her backpack on the couch. She went into the kitchen and grabbed a bottle of elderberry kombucha from the fridge. She'd become addicted to this stuff, but a couple of weeks ago she'd started limiting herself to a half bottle per day.

Sacrifices.

She returned to the living room and plopped down on her couch. It felt as if the walls were closing in on her, as if no matter what she tried, nothing could get her out of this financial mess.

"*You* can get yourself out of this. You always do," she said. But her voice didn't hold the same conviction it usually did. She felt ... defeated.

She *despised* this feeling. She'd made a promise to herself a long time ago that she would never allow defeat to enter her mind again. Because once you gave that insidious notion just the smallest bit of leeway, it took over. She could not allow that to happen.

She jumped up from the couch and returned to the kitchen, grabbing the bag of flour and canister of cocoa from the tiny pantry. She opened the refrigerator to retrieve a couple of eggs, but then she shut it.

"You do *not* need brownies." And neither did Rob. The way things were going, they would both end up diabetic if she didn't turn her life around.

Instead of baking, Taylor reached for her cell phone. A group video chat would get her mind off her problems without the added sugar rush of brownies.

London was the first to answer. She was on her desktop.

"What's up, chica?" she said, the bright yellow walls of her office at the hospital serving as her backdrop. It was decorated with cute stick figure drawings and photos of smiling kids.

"Nothing much," Taylor said. "I was just calling to check in."

"You started looking at colleges yet?"

Taylor should have known London would bring this up. "It's on today's to-do list," she lied.

A second later, Samiah appeared. Her face was scrubbed clean and her hair was in a sloppy ponytail. It was a bit jarring. Samiah was always so put together.

"Hey, ladies, what's up?" she greeted. "What are we talking about?"

"The twist on Taylor's new project," London supplied as she tilted her computer screen up. "Oh, just an FYI, I can't stay on for too long. I have rounds in another fifteen minutes and I need to return my stepmom's call before the end of my break." She shoveled in a forkful of salad.

"Well, since you have to leave us soon, why don't we talk about *your* project," Samiah said. "How is your search for a hobby going?"

London had decided that finding a way to disconnect from her stressful career was what she needed the most. Becoming a renowned pediatric surgeon had consumed her every waking minute since medical school.

London put up one finger as she continued chewing. She swallowed, then said, "The hobby search is...Yeah, it's going nowhere. I tried Googling hobbies, but when I typed the *H* in the address bar, my previous search on hepatoblastoma came up, and I got distracted."

"Who has to Google hobbies?" Taylor asked.

"Me," London said. "How about if I make sitting on Samiah's couch and drinking wine my new hobby? I'm so good at that."

"Ha ha," Samiah deadpanned. "Joke's on you, because that's actually close to one of my suggestions. I just read about this shuttle that takes you from Austin to several of the wineries in the Hill Country. We can make a weekend of it and stay at one of the cute bed-and-breakfasts out there. Should I book it for next Friday?"

"Wait! I can't!" Taylor blurted. Sweat instantly pebbled along her hairline. "I—" She briefly closed her eyes. "I'm not sure I can go on vacation right now. I have to consider my clients."

"Can't you reschedule?" Samiah said. "It's just a couple of hours away."

"I just..." Taylor started. *Shit.* This conversation had taken the wrong damn turn. "The truth is, I've hit a bit of a rough patch. Financially." Understatement to end all understatements. "I honestly can't afford to do anything extra, even a short weekend." She shrugged. "I'm trying to look on the bright side. I could be living out of my car," she said with a shaky laugh. "Of course, there's a pretty good chance I *will* be living out of my car if I can't pay my rent this month."

London's fork stopped halfway to her mouth. "What are you talking about?" she asked, leaning in closer to her computer screen.

"That's my question too," Samiah said.

Well, this had gone sideways in a hot-ass second.

Taylor massaged her temple with her free hand. Was there anything she regretted more than making this phone call? Maybe stealing Skittles from the commissary back when they lived at Baumholder Army Base in Germany. Or that time when she used bleach to dye her own hair when she was in the seventh grade.

Okay, so she'd made her fair share of effed-up decisions in the past, but this group call definitely ranked up there.

Yet...

If her friends were willing to play the part of sounding board, why not go ahead and let them? She was tired of shouldering all of this on her own.

"Taylor?" Samiah said.

"I'm broke," she admitted. "That's it in a nutshell. I made a bunch of dumb moves while trying to find new clients, and now I can't pay my rent."

"What kind of dumb moves?" Samiah asked.

"And exactly how broke are you?" London added.

After weighing each question, she determined Samiah's was the least demoralizing of the two. Addressing that one first, Taylor told them about the discount coupon site she'd signed up for in an attempt to drum up business for Taylor'd Conditioning.

"I use those websites all the time," London said. "It's how I discovered my favorite bakery."

"Yeah, well, those deals work just fine for bakeries because people like cupcakes and scones. They're more likely to become repeat customers. Most of the people who bought my coupon were the same people who join a gym on New Year's Day and stop going by the second week of January."

"Guilty," Samiah said with a shrug.

"I'd hoped to keep at least a *few* on as clients." She shook her head. "Instead, I've been working my ass off for seventy-five percent less than my normal fee, and I haven't been able to make a dent in the mountain of debt I've been sitting on."

"I'll ask again, how broke are you?" London said.

"If I say it out loud, I'm going to throw up."

"Come on, Taylor," Samiah said. "I have some money put away. I can make you a loan."

"No. No way." She shook her head. "I knew you would say that. I am *not* borrowing money from you. From either of you."

"I didn't offer any," London said. She put both hands up. "Not that I wouldn't. I just have to make my student loan payment first."

"It doesn't matter, because there will be no loans," Taylor said. "Seriously, who goes around offering to loan someone they met just a few months ago twenty thousand dollars?"

She clamped a hand over her mouth. *Shit.*

"Um, wow," London said. "Twenty thousand, huh?"

"I'm not sure I can send that much through Apple Pay," Samiah said, not missing a beat. "But maybe I can send half through Apple and the other half through Cash App? I'll do that once we end the call."

"Stop it! I'm not taking any more money from you!" She still owed Samiah the eighty-dollar booking fee from her stint in the city jail. Taylor dropped her head back and sighed up at her apartment's water-stained ceiling. "Look, I appreciate the offer, but I got myself into this mess. I'll figure a way out of it."

"Will you figure it out before or after you get a crick in your neck from sleeping in your car?"

"If you angle your head just right, you won't get a crick in your neck," she retorted.

"This isn't funny, Taylor," Samiah warned.

Who was she telling?

"I know," Taylor said. "But I think I've found a solution. Maybe." She paused for a moment before asking, "Have either of you ever heard of Jamar Dixon?"

"The football player?" Samiah asked.

Taylor sat up straight. "Wait, you *know* about him? How? You don't even watch football."

"Actually, I do watch when Daniel is here on a Sunday afternoon, but being from Houston means I can't escape high school football even if I tried. Jamar Dixon went to Katy High. He was one of the top recruits in the country his senior year. He went pro, but I can't remember which team."

"The Bears," Taylor provided. "He was injured during his rookie season. Apparently he did a lot of rehab after surgery, but I guess the Bears thought he was still too much of a liability to keep him."

"How do you know all of this about him?" Samiah asked.

"He signed up for the boot camp workout I held in Zilker Park earlier today. He wants to hire me to be his personal trainer."

"Wow," Samiah said. "Fancy."

"Are you sure that's *all* he wants?" London asked.

Taylor laughed. "My self-esteem is as healthy as the next chick's, but even *I* don't think I'm worth going through that much of a hassle." She shrugged. "He said he needs a personal trainer and nutrition coach, so I'm going to take him at his word. I'm meeting him at a café in Round Rock tomorrow. If we decide to work together, I can at least use his fee to start paying down my debt."

"Text us when you get there, when he shows up, when he leaves, and when you get back home," London said.

"Sure, Mom. I'll do just that," Taylor said, rolling her eyes.

"Don't be upset that people care about you, Taylor Marie."

"Oh my God, now you *do* sound like my mother. And it's Taylor Renee," she said. "And, don't worry, I promise to call you both as soon as I'm done speaking with the hot football player."

"Is he hot?" London asked.

"Oh yeah," Samiah said. "He's too young for me, but *so* damn fine. You should Google him."

"I'll do that after my shift. I need to go," London said as she shut the plastic lid on her salad container. "Oh, shit! I was supposed to call my stepmom. Forget it, she'll just have to call my mom if she needs to bitch about my dad."

"Wait," Taylor said. "Your stepmother actually calls your dad's ex-wife to complain about him?"

"All the time," London said. "My mom loves to tell her

that he's her problem now." She shook her head. "It's a strange relationship, but surprisingly healthy." She stood and threaded her arms through the sleeves of her white coat. "Talk to you guys later," she said before clicking out of the call.

"I need to go too," Samiah said. "But my offer still stands. If you need to borrow rent money, all it takes is a phone call. No sleeping in the car."

"Thanks," Taylor said, even though she knew she wouldn't take her up on it.

After saying goodbye to Samiah, Taylor pulled up the browser on her phone. She did another web search for *Jamar Dixon*, clicking until she reached web hits that she had yet to read. She knew as much about football as she knew about botany or hieroglyphics, but based on the numerous sports blogs she read, Jamar had been one of the most promising running backs to make it to the NFL in a generation.

He'd also made it onto a number of Hottest Players in the NFL lists and Pinterest boards. She couldn't refute that. The man was hot.

"Yeah, you're fine and all," Taylor said. "I just hope you're legit."

CHAPTER FIVE

Taylor hadn't realized just how tense she was until her fingers relaxed their grip on the steering wheel. Seeing Jamar Dixon's fancy SUV parked in one of the slots facing the café eased a smidgen of the worry that had taken hold since Melonie dropped that atomic bomb on her yesterday afternoon. Taylor wanted to play it cool with Jamar and not come across as too eager. But with the way she was shedding clients, she feared she would fall at the man's feet and beg him to hire her the moment she saw him.

Please, don't do that. You're a professional.

A professional in desperate need of some business, but still a professional.

She waited for a Subaru Outback to back out of a spot near the entrance before guiding Nessie into the space. As she approached the entrance to the café, the door opened and Jamar walked out. Her brain stuttered at the sight of him.

She had a type. She liked her men lean but toned. Height didn't matter, but she gravitated toward those who were a bit taller than her five-foot-four frame. Dreadlocks were a plus. Add in a nose ring and a couple of tattoos and her panties started to melt away.

Basically Lenny Kravitz. Just give her Lenny Kravitz.

Jamar Dixon was no Lenny, but maybe she should add sculpted shoulders and a goatee to the list of qualities on her DTF list.

Stop it! You want him as a client, not someone you're down to fuck!

She gave the horny little devil on her shoulder a stern warning as she got out of her car.

"Hey there," Taylor said.

"Hi," he replied. "Glad you could make it." He smiled as he held the door open for her.

"Are you hungry?" Jamar asked, pointing to the counter. "It's my treat."

Taylor ordered a jackfruit and black bean burrito, carrot juice, and a vegan brownie that would absolutely be her dinner tonight. Jamar added an orange juice to the order.

"You mind if we sit back there?" Jamar asked once they'd collected their food. "It's a little more private."

She looked around, wondering why it would make a difference in the virtually empty café. "Um, okay."

As they made their way to the table, Taylor took the opportunity to size him up from the back. She decided she now had two types: Lenny Kravitz and any man with a firm butt. She was pretty sure if she flicked Jamar's ass, she would break her finger.

Oh my God. Stop!

If she was going to work with him, she had to get her filthy mind off his world-class ass. Well, except when it was time to work his glutes. That was the *only* context in which she would think about his ass. It was a muscle. A very shapely, ridiculously firm muscle that was worthy of her attention and appreciation as a fitness professional.

Taylor tried not to attack her food as soon as they sat down, but once the aroma of the sautéed onions hit her senses, there was no holding her back. She'd been so caught up in binge-watching her missed episodes of *Real Housewives of Atlanta* that she'd skipped breakfast this morning.

"So what exactly do you have in mind?" Taylor asked as she finished her first mouthful.

"Full immersion," he said. "I need to go all in with my workouts." He glanced around as if he expected the CIA to come bursting through the doors at any moment. "I have a fitness goal that I'd like to reach by the end of December," he said in a lowered voice. "I've been trying to do it on my own, but my results just won't cut it. I need you to create a blueprint that will jump-start my fitness regimen."

"What does your normal workout look like?"

Jamar filled her in on his typical day—a six- to eight-mile run, weights, more cardio. "I'm looking to up my training to between four and five hours a day, five days a week. The doctors said I only have a twenty percent chance of ever playing professionally again, but the way I see it, twenty percent is still twenty percent. I've spent too much time focusing on the eighty. I don't want to do that anymore. I want to move forward."

Taylor pushed her lunch to the side and brought her elbows up on the table. "So what's your goal in terms of this blueprint you want me to create?"

"How much do you know about college football?" Jamar asked.

"About as much as I know about dairy farms. And I ain't from Wisconsin."

His lips tipped up in a half grin. "Actually, California has the most dairy farms."

"Are we trying out for *Jeopardy!* or coming up with a workout regimen?"

"The second one," he said. He brought his elbows up on the table as well and folded his hands. "There's this weeklong scouting event in college football called the Combine. College players who hope to make it onto an NFL team are given a battery of tests, both mental and physical. It's their chance to show NFL scouts what they're made of. My goal is to be within the top five best times in each test that's used at the Combine."

"What kind of tests?"

"Things like the forty-yard dash, bench press, vertical jump. There's a long list of evaluations and each will require me to be in top form. I can run the forty in seven-point-four-nine seconds, but I need to shave at least one-point-five seconds off that number if I want to have a chance."

"That's insane," Taylor said.

He shrugged. "Welcome to the NFL."

Taylor sat back in her chair and crossed her arms over her chest. She studied him, taking in the determined set to his strong jaw. He was serious about this.

"I'll be honest," she said. "I don't get why you would hire someone you saw in a YouTube video. There are trainers out there who would kill for the opportunity to work with you."

"Are you saying you're not one of those trainers?"

"I'm not saying that at all. I'm just trying to understand your motives here. Why me?"

"I already told you. I like your training style. That hardcore, in-your-face approach is what I need to kick me into high gear."

The more he explained, the more she was convinced that he really was legit.

Taylor decided to be up front about her lack of a degree. The one thing she did not need right now was to get excited about this job and then have him back out of the deal because she hadn't graduated from some fancy university.

"Before we go any further, you need to know that I'm not a certified dietician," she said. "Actually, I don't even have a degree."

He regarded her with a quizzical frown. "So you *are* trying to talk me out of hiring you?"

"No! No, I just don't want there to be any confusion here." She picked up a potato chip and tossed it back into the basket. "Not too long ago, I was promised a position—one that I am one hundred percent qualified for, I might add. But when the people who wanted to hire me learned that I didn't go to college, they backed out of it."

His perfectly shaped lips pressed into a thin line as he studied her.

Taylor braced herself for the blow she knew was coming. She was pissed she hadn't gotten a second brownie out of him before the inevitable end of their nonexistent partnership.

"Is that you in those videos on YouTube?" Jamar finally asked.

"Yes," she answered slowly.

"And are you the trainer all those Yelp reviewers were raving about?"

She nodded.

He shrugged. "Then why do I care if you have a college degree? Bill Gates didn't have a college degree when he started Microsoft."

She'd been so busy mentally preparing herself for disappointment that it took a moment for his words to register. He still wanted to hire her?

Taylor tried to contain the squeal threatening to explode from her mouth. Jamar Dixon would never understand the gift he'd given her with those words. Growing up surrounded by people who collected degrees the way some people collected baseball cards, her refusal to go to college had only added to her odd-duck status in the Powell household.

Having Jamar as a client could turn her entire business around. His endorsement could lead to legions of his fans clamoring to work with the fitness consultant who put their beloved favorite football player back in the game.

"I realize that what I'm asking you to do is pretty intense," he continued. "I'll pay you fifteen thousand dollars if you'll work exclusively with me for the next two months."

Thank God she hadn't chosen that moment to take a sip of her carrot juice, because it would be all over the table right now.

"I looked up the average charge for personal trainers," Jamar continued, as if he hadn't just blown her freaking mind. "According to most of the websites I researched, trainers charge between forty and seventy dollars per hour session. I figure you average around five clients a day, so that would be three hundred fifty dollars per day. Am I right?"

"Umm..." was all she managed. Her brain was still stuck on fifteen thousand dollars.

"Do you see more than five clients a day?"

"I..." She shook her head. This was banana pants.

"I should mention my one caveat," he said. "And, before you ask, it's something I'm not willing to compromise on."

Unease trickled down her spine as she took in his intent, resolute stare.

"What is it?" Taylor asked.

"No one can know we're working together."

CHAPTER SIX

As he sat across from her, Jamar tried to come up with the most accurate word to describe the look on Taylor Powell's face. Horrified? Maybe some confusion. Possibly a bit of indignation.

"What do you mean no one can know I'm working with you?" she blurted.

Definitely indignation.

"If we're going to work together, we have to keep it under wraps."

"But...but why?"

As if on cue, an older woman in a Texas Longhorns sweatshirt walked up to their table and asked, "Excuse me, but aren't you Diesel Dixon?"

Jamar nodded and pasted on a good-natured smile. "Yes, ma'am, I am."

"I knew it! I told Barry, 'That's Diesel.'" She pointed to the man sitting a couple of tables over, and then she went on for a solid five minutes, regaling them with stories of legendary home games she'd witnessed and a list of Longhorns greats she'd watched play over her thirty years as a season ticket holder.

"I would put you in the same category as Ricky Williams

and Cedric Benson," she said. "Some of the best running backs to ever wear the burnt orange and white."

"That's fine company to be in," Jamar said. "Thank you for stopping by—"

"You should think about coaching for them now that you have that busted knee," she said. "The Longhorns would be lucky to have you."

"I'll tell that to Coach Green when I visit the team in a couple of days," he said.

Jamar prayed she'd walk away. If he had to maintain this smile a second longer, his face would break.

"Well, I'll let you get back to your meal," she said, patting him on the shoulder. "I just had to come over when I saw it was you."

"Thanks for stopping by," he said again, his shoulders slumping in relief when she finally returned to her table. He looked at Taylor and said, "*That's* why I don't want anyone to know we're working together."

Her brows scrunched in genuine incredulity. "So you have fans who recognize you. It still doesn't explain why no one can know we're working together. People work with personal trainers all the time."

"I'm not most people, Taylor. You can work out with your other clients at a local gym and no one would bat an eye. If people see *me* working out with you—especially with the type of intense workout my training will require—that's when the speculation starts."

He fidgeted with the buckle on his watchband as he grappled with how much he should divulge. She hadn't agreed to work with him yet, but he couldn't make this kind of demand without giving her at least some explanation.

Other than Taylor, he wasn't planning to tell anybody about his plans. Even the people he trusted most. *Especially* the people he trusted most. Because those were the people he was most afraid of disappointing if this attempt to reenter the League didn't work out.

No! He wouldn't let his mind go there. He refused to even entertain thoughts that his plan wouldn't work. It *would* work. It *had* to.

He owed it to Silas.

Jamar's football career had ceased being solely his own the moment his best friend's motorcycle collided with a pickup truck on a rain-slicked stretch of Highway 99 their senior year of high school. From the moment they'd put Silas in the ground, fulfilling the dream he and Silas had held since elementary school—to one day make it into the NFL—had become Jamar's singular goal.

"When I got hurt last year, there was endless chatter over whether I'd play football again. Every blogger had an opinion, and not a single one gave me a chance. I want to prove them all wrong."

"Which is why you should want them to see that you're working with a trainer."

"No." He shook his head. "Look, if I go through months of conditioning and I'm still unable to get back into the League, then it will prove them right."

"Don't do that," she said. "You're setting yourself up for failure if you're thinking that you may not succeed before we even get started. When it comes to physical fitness, it's ninety percent mental."

"I know all about mental toughness, Taylor. I've played through sore muscles, the flu, just about every injury that didn't need hospitalization, and it was all because of mental toughness."

"Okay, explain this to me," she said. "How are we supposed to train without anyone knowing?"

"My personal home gym has the same equipment you'd find in a regular gym."

"Your personal home gym? Really? You expect me—a woman who met you for the first time *yesterday*—to now work with you at your home? Alone? And I can't let anyone know I'm there?" She snorted. "Yeah, that's not happening."

Well, damn. When she put it that way...

To use one of his mom's favorite sayings, Taylor didn't know him from Adam. Why did he think she would feel comfortable training him alone at his private gym?

Shit. He pressed his lips together, trying to come up with a solution that would work for both of them.

"How about this? I'm okay with you confiding in a couple of trusted family members or friends, but only a couple. And they have to promise not to say anything."

"Do you want them to sign an NDA or something?" She said it as a joke, but he wouldn't be opposed to it. "Oh, c'mon," she said. "Is it really *that* serious?"

"It is to me. Look, Taylor, your friends don't have to sign an NDA, but you have to understand how important it is that this doesn't get out. I know it sounds over the top, but I've put up with a lot this past year. If this doesn't work out..." He shook his head. "I don't want to face any more ridicule. Honestly, I can't."

He could feel heat rising up the back of his neck as he sat there under her silent scrutiny. After several torturous moments, she slapped her hands on the table and said, "Okay, enough with this defeatist attitude. I do not tolerate that shit from my clients."

Jamar's muscles went weak as pent-up tension ebbed from his body. He wasn't a big fan of hyperbole, so it wasn't an exaggeration to say that his career hinged on her answer. He'd tried going at this alone for months, but his discipline level was at an all-time low. He needed someone like Taylor to break through whatever was holding him back.

"So your answer is yes?" he asked. He had to make sure he hadn't misinterpreted her response.

"Yes." She nodded. "I would be a fool to pass up this kind of money and the opportunity to work with a potential NFL star." She held up both hands. "However, I have my own caveat."

Jamar braced himself. "Go on."

"If— No, when," she corrected. "*When* you make it back to the NFL, you have to agree to endorse Taylor'd Conditioning. And you have to recommend me to your footballer buddies."

He huffed out a laugh. "Footballer buddies, huh?"

"The NFL is like one big fraternity, isn't it?"

"Close to it," he answered.

"I figured it was like the military in that way. So yes, that's my requirement. Once you're playing again, I expect you to sing my praises to all your teammates." She arched her eyebrows. "So do we have a deal?"

Jamar held out his palm. "Deal," he said when she clasped his proffered hand.

"Okay, so if I'm going to get you in tip-top shape in just two months, we have to get started right away."

"I'm ready right now," he said.

"Whoa, whoa. Slow your roll, Twenty-Three. I didn't mean this very minute. I don't have any gear, and I will not go to your house without first letting my friends know where I am."

Before he knew what she was doing, she lifted his phone from his hand and held it up to his face, unlocking it.

"Hold on. What are you—"

"Just give me a minute," she said. Her fingers moved swiftly across the screen. Then she smiled, snapped a selfie, and handed the phone back to him. A second later, her phone rang. She turned it to face him and Jamar saw his name on her phone. "I added my number to your contacts and now I have yours. Smile," she said, then snapped a picture of him. She frowned. "Ugh. No. There are way better pics of you online. I'll just download one of those."

She set her phone down. "Okay, so we meet tomorrow. What time do you want to get started?"

"I'm up at six every morning."

"No amount of money is getting me out of bed before the *Today Show* theme music starts playing." She wrapped the uneaten portion of her burrito back in the foil and pushed it to the side. "And speaking of money, that's another discussion we need to have before we leave this restaurant." She folded her hands on the table. "Now, my clients usually pay me per session, but as you pointed out, you're not like my other clients."

Jamar couldn't help but laugh at the way she'd used his words against him. It was such a boss move.

"That's true. I guess we need to come up with some sort of payment schedule." He did the math in his head. "I'll pay you eighteen hundred per week, for the next eight weeks."

"Wait a minute." She held up a finger before grabbing

her phone. She tapped on the screen a few times before she said, "That's only fourteen thousand four hundred. You'll still owe me another six hundred dollars. *And* if I'm driving to your home every day, I'll need compensation for gas and mileage."

She had a point.

"Okay, I'll pay you two thousand a week for the next eight weeks."

"Deal," Taylor said.

The way she'd finessed that extra grand from him was pretty impressive. Maybe his agent, Micah Hill, should talk to her about joining Hill Sports Management.

"Does nine a.m. work for you?" she asked.

"If you say nine a.m., I'll be ready at nine a.m. You're the boss."

Her mouth curled up in a smile. "I like the sound of that."

CHAPTER SEVEN

Taylor pulled to the side of the narrow asphalt road, convinced the GPS had guided her in the wrong direction. There was no way Jamar Dixon lived in this wooded area, which was better suited for a scene in a B-rated horror flick than the home of a former NFL player. She understood wanting peace and quiet, but this was tiptoeing into recluse territory.

Samiah and London had made her promise to text when she arrived at his house and once every hour that she was there. They really were as bad as her mother at times, except they didn't give her side-eye when she had more than one alcoholic beverage at dinner.

Taylor tossed the phone onto the passenger seat and rubbed her hands together.

"Okay, Taylor Renee. Time to earn that money."

Capturing the braids she'd had done last night—thank God for a stylist willing to take her at the last minute and work past midnight—she gathered them in a scrunchie, then pulled back onto the road. After another mile and several winding turns, she rounded a bend and a gorgeous, sprawling mansion with two-story windows and a curved cobblestone driveway came into view. A four-car garage flanked one side of it, while a smaller structure—probably a pool house—occupied the other. Towering cedars cocooned the area, enclosing the massive home in its own little oasis.

"Well, damn," she muttered.

She drove underneath the portico and pulled to a stop behind a mocha-colored Range Rover. A deep orange Audi was parked about five yards ahead of the SUV.

Why have a four-car garage if you're going to keep your cars parked outside? Unless he had six cars...

Taylor grabbed her duffel from the passenger side floorboard, got out of the car, and started for the front door. It was gorgeous: the beveled glass, iron, and wood materials were typical of what was found on other homes in this part of Texas, but the design was more elaborate. A dark figure, distorted by the glass's myriad angles, appeared on the other side of the door. A moment later, it opened and Jamar stepped outside wearing gray sweatpants and a white Texas Longhorns T-shirt.

She had to stop herself from releasing a low whistle. That smile and those broad shoulders were pretty devastating on their own, but the gray sweatpants transformed him into a living, breathing thirst trap. She would take a minute to appreciate the view, but now that he was her client, she could not think of Jamar and his fantasy-worthy body as anything other than what he was—her ticket out of debt.

Besides, Taylor had learned the hard way that mixing business with pleasure was insanely foolish, and she'd vowed never to do it again. Once you crossed that line, guys no longer considered you their paid trainer. You became the chick they're sleeping with who gives them free fitness advice.

She was *not* going there with Jamar Dixon. She was here

to earn that sixteen-thousand-dollar fee and to secure his future endorsement for Taylor'd Conditioning. That was it. Nothing else.

"Did you have any issue on your way out here?" he asked as she approached the base of the steps he'd descended.

"You mean other than wondering if I was still in the state of Texas?"

His megawatt grin beamed bright against his rich dark skin. Yeah, she could appreciate that smile.

"So does this place have its own zip code?" Taylor asked.

"No, I share it with the family on the other side of the San Gabriel River." After a moment, he said, "That was a joke." And then he chuckled, probably at the stunned look on her face.

She rolled her eyes. "You need to work on your delivery. Dave Chappelle you are not."

He only laughed harder. "C'mon," he said, tilting his head toward the door.

Taylor followed him into the house and, for the first time in her life, knew what it felt like to have her jaw literally drop.

Holy. Shit.

Polished marble floors spanned the massive foyer, a large round table with an intricate, wrought-iron pedestal base occupying its center. It was topped by a lush floral arrangement that emitted a soft, soothing fragrance. If she closed her eyes, she would swear she was standing in a field of fresh flowers. The curved staircase to her immediate right ascended to a second-story interior balcony that branched out on both sides of the entrance.

Who lives like this?

Even as she told herself to shut up and keep walking, Taylor heard herself say, "Okay, hold on a minute."

Jamar turned. "What's wrong?"

Just stop talking.

"Before we go any farther, I need to ask a very rude question." She really needed to work on her impulse control.

He grimaced, his brow dipping with his wary frown. "This is going to be about money, isn't it?"

"Well, I did say it was rude," Taylor pointed out. "I just...I mean...*look* at this place! According to Wikipedia, you're only twenty-five years old, and you only played one year of professional football. How much do they pay football players if you can afford a house like this after playing for only one year?"

"You really don't know much about football, do you?"

"Other than the fact that it always causes an argument between my dad and brother on Thanksgiving? No, I don't know jack."

"I have a very good agent who managed to secure me a nice amount of guaranteed money. It's a good thing, too, because I was injured before I could earn any of the performance incentives."

"Performance incentives?"

"Yeah. I could have earned another six hundred grand my rookie season if I'd gotten more than ten touchdowns and rushed for more than twelve hundred yards."

"Hmm, maybe we should add performance incentives to my contract."

A quick grin flashed across his face. "Too late. You know, I think you missed your calling. You've got mad negotiation skills."

"If that was the case, I would be earning a performance incentive," she returned with an eye roll.

He gestured to her duffel bag. "Do you need somewhere to change?"

"Eventually. First, we should discuss the workout regimen I came up with for you. We need to make sure it's targeting everything you think we need to target." She looked around. "Let's walk and talk. You can give me the grand tour of this palace you live in."

"Twenty bedrooms are required in order to qualify as a palace. This house only has seven."

She looked at him. "Another joke?"

"Was that one better than the last one?"

"No."

His eyes crinkled at the corners, and Taylor had to stop herself from laughing. She was enjoying his smile way too much.

They passed underneath the staircase and entered an open-concept kitchen/den/breakfast area that was the size of the entire house she and her family lived in back when they'd been on base in Germany.

Natural sunlight glinted off the veins of gold streaking throughout the pearly white marble countertop, and the Sub-Zero refrigerator and range were worthy of a high-end restaurant. She hoped to God he used it for more than cooking ramen.

"Okay, never mind about the tour," Taylor said as she plunked her duffel bag on a kitchen island at least twice as big as her bathroom.

"You sure?" he asked. "I don't mind."

She shook her head. "Jealousy has never been a good look on me, and I will not be able to hide it if I see any more of this house."

"If it makes you feel any better, I bought it as more of an

investment than anything else," he explained, a hint of embarrassment tinging his voice. "I only use about a third of it."

"Well, damn. Now I feel bad," Taylor said. "I didn't mean to wealth-shame."

"Is wealth-shaming a real thing?"

"You're the one trying to justify your house to someone you just met."

"Point taken."

"I'm sorry," she said, and she really did mean it. She'd heard stories of athletes who blew through the millions they earned and had to get jobs selling insurance or bagging groceries once their sports careers were over. Hell, she was only three years older than he was, but if she'd had access to the kind of money he did when she was twenty-five, investing in real estate would have been the last thing on her mind. She would have probably spent it all on Disney Vinylmation figurines.

"You have every right to be proud of this gorgeous house," Taylor added. "And I reserve the right to that tour at a later date. For now, let's talk strategy."

Jamar pulled out a high-back stool and motioned for her to take a seat at the kitchen island. "What am I getting myself into over these next two months?" he asked, taking the seat next to hers.

She unzipped her duffel and pulled out a poly folder with the Taylor'd Conditioning logo imprinted on the front. From the folder, she slid the chart she'd created and set it between them so they could both look over it.

"I usually call this the plan of attack, but you can think of it as your playbook or game plan, or whatever they call it in football."

"I like *plan of attack* better," he said. "It makes it feel as if I'm about to do battle, which I am."

"I like that attitude, Twenty-Three."

"Are you planning to call me Twenty-Three for the next two months?"

"It's that or Chicago Bears. Pick one."

"Why would I choose either of those when Jamar is so much easier?"

"I never take the easy way. Let that be a warning," she said with a wink.

He grinned. "I'll keep that in mind."

Apparently the flutter that swept through her belly had not gotten the memo that this was a no belly-fluttering situation. She cleared her throat. "Let's go over what I came up with."

After a few minutes of reviewing the various cardio drills she'd designed, he got up and asked, "Can I get you something to drink? Water? Orange juice?"

"Water is fine."

He pulled two bottles of water out of the refrigerator; then he went into a walk-in pantry and came out with a bag of potato chips.

Potato chips? Was he serious?

He reclaimed his seat and unfurled the top of the bag. Taylor took it out of his hand before he could reach for a chip.

"If you're going to get back in tip-top form, you'll have to say goodbye to these," she said. She slid off the barstool and looked around for a garbage can. There was none. "You're ruining my dramatic effect here. I wanted to toss the chips in the trash and slam the lid closed for emphasis."

"Don't throw away my chips." He rounded the kitchen island and plucked the bag from her hands. "They're organic and they're baked."

"It doesn't matter." She tried to snatch the bag back, but

he held it out of her reach. "You need to limit your complex carbs. If you're craving a crunchy snack, go for those made from lentils or white beans instead."

"I don't like lentils," he said as he retrieved a chip.

Taylor plopped her hands on her hips. "Are you seriously going to eat those in front of me? Okay, you need to decide if you're going to take this seriously. If not, I can leave. I won't have you saying in two months that I didn't do my job because *you* can't say no to a potato chip."

He dropped the chip back into the bag and held it out to her. Taylor snatched it from his hands.

"You see, *this* is why I wanted to hire you," Jamar said. "Another trainer wouldn't have had the balls to tell me off the way you just did." He dusted his fingers, as if wiping away crumbs. "I'm done with potatoes. Bring on the lentil chips."

"You have to *earn* lentil chips."

His brow arched, amusement shimmering in his dark brown eyes. "Is that how it is?"

"You wanted a drill sergeant," she said.

Taylor wiped the grin off her face before he misconstrued it as flirting. Except this totally felt like flirting. Shit.

"Wait, you do meal prep, don't you? How much to add that to what you're already providing?"

"You want me to cook for you too?"

He shrugged. "If you think it will help get me into shape."

She thought for a moment, then said, "I can prep your meals, as long as you pay for the cost of groceries." She crumpled the bag in her hand, crushing the remaining chips into inedible crumbs. She handed it back to him. "We'll start working on your diet tomorrow. Go change into your workout clothes. It's time for you to show me what you've got."

CHAPTER EIGHT

Jamar tugged a pair of running shorts on over his tighter compression shorts and grabbed a tank made of wicking material from the neat stack the cleaning service had placed in his dresser. Pulling the tank over his head, he made his way to the walk-in closet that housed more than four hundred pairs of tennis shoes, each in custom-built units that lined the walls.

He was willing to be sensible with every other aspect of his life, but when it came to his Jordans, Vans, and old-school Chucks, sensibility went out the window.

He slid a pair of white-and-gray New Balance from their cubby and brought them to the bench in the center of the walk-in closet. He loosened the laces on one shoe, then dropped it to the floor.

Jamar hung his head, braced his hands on his thighs, and sucked in a deep breath.

What was he doing, thinking he could pull off something like this? Did he really think a new diet and changing up his workout routine would make a difference? Some of the best doctors in the world had evaluated his knee, and all but one had determined that he would never run onto a football field as a professional ever again. What made him think he could defy the odds?

"Because you always defy the fucking odds," Jamar said, sitting up straight.

He'd been defying the odds since birth, when he'd spent six weeks in an incubator before his parents could even take him home from the hospital. He'd defied the odds when he'd made the varsity team at Katy High. When he'd earned his football scholarship to UT.

He wasn't the kind of natural athlete his best friend Silas had been. None of this shit had ever come easy for him. If his teammates ran five miles, he ran seven. If they spent two hours in the weight room, he stayed for an extra thirty minutes.

He put in the work and made shit happen. And he would do it again.

He stuffed his feet into his tennis shoes and jumped up from the bench.

"No more excuses," he said, reinstituting the old saying Coach Cunningham used to drill into his high school team.

Jamar went downstairs and walked into his home gym. He stopped short.

Damn.

Taylor had changed into the outfit she wore in her YouTube videos: baggy army-green pants and a camouflage print fitness bra with the words TAYLOR'D CONDITIONING in orange lettering across her not too big but not too small breasts. Her abs sported a six-pack, but it wasn't cut like his. It was soft, delicate. Delicate looked *so* fucking good on her.

She looked up from her phone and spotted him. "Oh, you're back. Good. Ready to get started?"

"Just a sec," Jamar said. He walked over to the cubby where

he kept athletic tape and a compression sleeve for his knee. His knee felt fine, but he needed a moment to recalibrate his brain after the initial shock of seeing Taylor in her workout clothes. Not preparing himself for that was a rookie move.

He slipped on the compression sleeve and returned to the custom-made, high-impact foam mat he'd had installed in the middle of the six-hundred-square-foot gym. Taylor stood in the center, her hands on her hips and her legs braced apart.

She was going to kick his ass.

He was ready for it.

Jamar clapped his hands and rubbed them together. "So, what's first?"

"You're in much better shape than most of my clients. That means I'm going to work you harder, so I hope you're prepared."

"Gimme what you got," he taunted.

Her brow quirked. Jamar knew he was playing with fire, but at the moment getting burned didn't seem all that bad.

"First, I'm going to test your endurance." She motioned to the treadmill.

He stepped up on the platform and reached for the display panel, but she stopped him.

"No. *I* control this. You run."

She started him off with a comfortable jog, the slight incline and 4.5 mph pace nothing he couldn't handle. After ten minutes she increased the speed to 6.5 mph and raised the incline by two degrees, then incrementally raised both every five minutes. By the time he crossed the half-hour mark, sweat was pouring down his face and pooling at the base of his spine. The muscles in his thighs were on fire.

"How do you feel?" Taylor asked.

He tried to speak, but words wouldn't come. Instead, he nodded. He knew his body. He could push through this.

"Give me ten more minutes at this pace," she said.

Shit. No way would he make another ten minutes. Jamar flashed five fingers.

"Okay, I'll take five," she said with a shrug. "It's only the first day."

As he continued pounding along the rubber belt, absorbing every twinge and throb that pulsed throughout his body, something changed. Instead of concentrating on the pain, Jamar used it as fuel, knowing that each step brought him closer to his goal. He closed his eyes and imagined himself back in the training facility in Lake Forest, Illinois, with its orange and navy blue walls. He heard the roar of the crowd at Soldier Field, felt their energy thrumming in his blood.

When Taylor reached for the display after five minutes had passed, he blocked her hand. He shook his head and returned his focus to that sweet spot he'd found.

It felt like home.

He ran for another ten minutes, until his legs threatened to give out on him. Sucking in shallow breaths, he decreased the speed on the treadmill to 2.5 mph. Every fiber in his body hummed like a tuning fork.

Taylor crossed her arms over her chest. "Well. That was impressive."

"That felt good," he huffed out. "That felt so fucking good. Excuse my language," he quickly added.

She waved off his apology. "I like *fuck*. Sometimes it's the only word that fits." She tipped her chin toward his knee. "How does it feel?"

Jamar bent his knee, testing the joint. "Better than ever."

He waited for a twinge or some kind of pinch, but he only felt the satisfying ache that came with rigorous exercise. A sense of calm washed over him even as excitement exploded in his head.

He could do this. He could get back in playing form. He refused to renege on the promise he'd made to his best friend.

"How about we take five minutes for you to come down from that runner's high, then move on to the next test?" Taylor asked. "I'd planned to work solely on cardiorespiratory endurance today, but this caught my eye," she said, turning to the machine with the inverted seat. "This is for both leg presses and squats, right?" She ran her hand along the brown leather backrest. "Now that I've seen all the fun toys we have to play with, I'm going to have to rethink my game plan."

After Jamar had caught his breath and gotten some water, Taylor gave the backrest of the machine a firm pat. "Hop on. Let's see if those quads are as strong as they look."

"Strongest quads you've ever come across," Jamar said as he slid into position.

She looked down at him, amusement shimmering in her eyes. "You sure are sure of yourself," she said. "Don't take it personally when I do my best to break you. I do it with all my clients. It builds character." She winked. "Give me twenty reps."

They repeated the sequence she'd put him through on the treadmill, increasing the intensity of the exercise every couple of minutes. This time, Jamar wasn't going to force himself to go any further than she pushed him.

"Shit," he said as he pumped his legs. "You don't give a person an inch, do you?"

"Do you think the players on the other teams will give you an inch? You're not paying me to go easy on you. Now move!"

Damn, that was hot. Why hadn't he anticipated how much of a turn-on it would be to have her barking orders at him?

He pressed pause on his hot drill sergeant fantasy and redirected his mental energy to contracting and extending his quadriceps. Taylor began to count down his reps, starting from ten. He grimaced with every push but made it through the end of her count.

Jamar damn near collapsed. He closed his eyes and concentrated on his breathing.

"I admire the hard work you're willing to put in, but aren't you afraid of doing even more damage to your knee, or even worse, to this?" She tapped her head. "I saw that movie with Will Smith. I know about the permanent damage multiple concussions have had on football players."

"You sound like my mom," Jamar said. "She's read every article on CTE there is."

"Can you blame her?"

He shook his head, a wry grin pulling up one side of his mouth as he thought about the numerous lectures on chronic traumatic encephalopathy he'd endured while sitting at his mother's kitchen table. She always ended them by saying that she supported his choice to play football because she loved him, but she didn't like it.

"No, I don't," he answered. "And I understand the risks that come with playing. I plan to take every precaution to protect myself."

"But why?" She gestured to the state-of-the-art equipment surrounding them. "I know it's not my place to point this out, but it doesn't look like you're struggling to make ends meet here."

No, he didn't need the money, but an extra three million in his bank account would go a long way in helping Silas's family. Jamar didn't have the energy to discuss the complicated rationale behind his push to get back into the League. He didn't know Taylor well enough to gauge how she would react to the admission that he was putting his body through all this pain because of a promise he'd made to his dead best friend. Because of the guilt he'd been drowning in for the past seven years over the role he played in his best friend's death.

But Silas wasn't the only driving force behind this. He had other reasons—less noble causes—that spurred him on. And *that* Taylor would understand.

Jamar locked the leg press into place and climbed off the machine, then went over to the cubby where he'd left his phone. He opened the browser and clicked on his bookmarks, searching through the collection of Reddit posts and message board threads he'd saved over the past year. He found one of the harshest, posted just after his injury.

He handed her the phone, showing one of the reasons he was willing to work so hard. "This is why I'm busting my ass to get back into the NFL."

He watched her as she read over the posts, her lips moving as her eyes looked at the screen.

"Ugh, why did you read the comments?" she lamented. "You never, ever, *ever* read the comments."

"Yeah, I learned that lesson the hard way, and not early enough." He shrugged. "I've gotten used to it over this past year, but it hasn't been easy, and I still go back and read over them whenever I feel myself getting too comfortable." He pointed to the phone. "Those people? They're the reason I'm pushing myself so hard to play ball again, because they think I can't do it. Revenge can be a hell of an incentive, and I can't think of sweeter revenge than signing a new contract."

She looked down at the phone and then back up at him again. A slight smile drew up one corner of her lips. "Well, if that's the case, get your ass back on that machine. We've got work to do."

Jamar did as he was told, moving from the leg extension to the leg curl machine. His quads felt as if they were in hell, but he knew the result of that burn would be worth it.

Taylor counted him down through his last five reps. "And rest," she said. "I know you said you want to go for at least five hours a day, but I think we need to gradually build you up to that."

Jamar didn't argue the point. He would need to rest his legs for ten minutes before he could take a single step.

"Tomorrow we focus on your upper body. I'll be here at nine."

"I need to push our session back to late afternoon if possible tomorrow. The running backs coach at the University of Texas asked me to join them at practice in the morning."

"Hmm." Her brow arched. "That actually sounds pretty cool. Can I come too? It'd be the perfect opportunity to see other football players at work—specifically those who play at your position. I could create a workout that's even better tailored to exactly what you need."

"What if someone puts two and two together?" Jamar asked. His gut twisted with unease just at the thought of it.

Taylor's hands went to her hips. "Do you really think a bunch of college kids will see us together and automatically assume I'm your fitness instructor? They'll more likely think we're hooking up, which would hurt my reputation more than it would hurt yours."

Jamar's head reared back. "How's that?" He didn't mean to sound so offended, but shit, he was. He didn't consider himself the bottom of the barrel when it came to hookup choices.

"Because when you get back into the NFL in a few months, you will then have to make good on the other part of our deal," Taylor said. "I don't want people to think you only chose me as your trainer because we were messing around on the side. So yeah, I'm the one with the most to lose here."

She was probably right about what people would think, which was fucked up.

Still, this whole thing made him uneasy. He didn't want to take the slightest chance of someone drawing the correct conclusion about his relationship to Taylor. But, then again, she had a point about tailoring his workouts.

After a minute, he nodded. "Okay, fine. We'll say that you're a friend who's interested in football or something."

"Not sure I can pull off that lie, but we'll see. Where should I meet you?"

"Why don't I just pick you up? We can drive over together," he offered.

"I'll text you my address." She winked, smiling the smile of someone who'd just gotten her way. She picked up her duffel and hauled the strap over her shoulder. "See you tomorrow."

CHAPTER NINE

Jamar stood on the sideline with his arms crossed over his chest as he observed the running backs conducting their drills. The crunch of shoulder pads crashing into each other played like Mozart in his ears, the rank smell of sweat like perfume to his nose. He'd missed this so much more than he'd been willing to admit.

The Longhorns' running back coach, Mark Green, had been instrumental in preparing Jamar for the NFL, so when he'd asked if Jamar could attend today's practice and give his running backs a pep talk after their hard loss on Saturday against a huge conference rival, it wasn't a question as to whether he would be here.

He knew what these guys were going through. He also knew that if they didn't put the mistakes from Saturday out of their heads, it could mess up their entire season.

"Do you see those bands over there?" he asked Taylor, pointing to the wide receivers working out on the far side of the field house. Three guys had harnesses wrapped around their feet, the ends of the thick leather bands secured into the wall. "Those are for helping to build speed. I have some, but haven't had them installed in the gym at home."

"Oh, I'll bet running against that resistance builds up core muscles too." She bumped him with her elbow. "You need to get those babies installed. I can come up with all kinds of ways to torture you with something like that." She looked over at him, a note of apology in her pained expression. "I totally didn't intend for that to sound like some kind of kinky S and M come-on."

Shockingly, his mind *hadn't* gone there. But now that she'd brought it up, he would have to work extra hard to expunge those thoughts from his head. He added them to the dozens of other inappropriate thoughts about his new fitness instructor that had invaded his brain over these past couple of days.

Jamar shut his eyes and tilted his head from side to side, working out the tension in his neck. This was frustrating as hell. Yet, he only had to consider her words from yesterday to understand why Taylor could never be anything other than his trainer. If word got out that they were hooking up, no one would take his endorsement of her business seriously. The last thing he wanted was to stifle her success.

Coach Green walked over to them, his hand outstretched. "Thanks for coming, Diesel."

"You know you can call on me whenever you need me," Jamar told him. "This is Taylor. I hope you don't mind me bringing her along. She's a huge fan of the game, especially the Longhorns."

"Hook 'em, Horns," Coach said, extending his index and pinky fingers to resemble the horns of a steer.

Taylor's eyes widened. "Umm...go team?" she replied, holding her fingers in a gesture that looked more like the Hawaiian shaka sign than the UT hand signal.

Coach Green's forehead creased in a puzzled frown.

"Why don't you bring us over to the running backs?" Jamar quickly suggested.

The moment Coach turned, Taylor caught Jamar by the hem of his shirt and pinched the shit out of his bicep.

"I'm a big Longhorns fan?" she hissed.

"Ouch," he whispered, rubbing his arm. "It was a joke."

"What did I tell you about your jokes?"

He chanced another pinch on the arm by leaning over and whispering, "You have to admit it was a little funny."

She rolled her eyes, but he could tell she was trying hard to contain her grin. She was cute even when she was pissed off.

Coach called for his players to huddle up and then introduced Jamar, even though many already knew him. Some of the seniors on the team had been redshirt freshmen back when he was still playing for the Longhorns.

When had this happened? When had he become the sage, older player young running backs turned to for advice?

Silas was somewhere up in heaven laughing his ass off right now.

Jamar stood before the players and quietly prayed that he could give them the pep talk he knew Coach was hoping for.

"I know how you guys are feeling right now," he started. "I know what it's like to eat, sleep, and breathe football, to put in so much time and effort on the practice field, only to walk away with another game in the L column."

He walked over to Carson Wallace, the backup running back who'd fumbled twice in last Saturday's game.

"My freshman year as a Longhorn, I had four games with back-to-back fumbles. I thought my season was done. But that guy"—he pointed to Coach Green—"he refused to give up on me, and he wouldn't let me give up on myself either. Put those fumbles out of your head. They're in the past. *Your* focus is on the next game, and then the next, and then the next."

He returned his attention to the entire group again.

"Losing is an unfortunate part of the game, guys. It doesn't matter if it's high school, college, or the pros, you're going to lose and it's going to suck. I know how that feels," he reiterated. "But I also know how it feels to fight your way out of a losing stretch. And that's all this is. You know how to win. And you're *going* to win. You just have to believe in your ability to do it."

Their expressions changed in real time, their heads lifting higher, their chests sticking out just a bit more. It gave him the confidence to keep going.

As he digested the look on each player's face, Jamar saw so much of himself. He'd experienced how an inspiring talk, delivered at just the right moment, could give him the boost he needed to make it through the next game.

He tried not to scrutinize the current starting running back, but it was hard not to pay particular attention to the guy who was only two hundred yards away from passing him up in the team's record books. The irony wasn't lost on Jamar that he'd been asked to speak words of encouragement to someone he would likely have to battle for a job in the not-so-distant future.

He ended his speech with an invitation for any of the guys to call him if they ever needed help, then accepted the handshake and pat on the shoulder from his old coach.

"I can't thank you enough for doing this, Jamar. Those kids needed to hear from someone like you, someone who's been on the field recently and not twenty years ago like me." Coach Green squeezed his shoulder. "Not everybody can reach players the way you just did. You've got something special there."

"Um...thanks," Jamar said, the words striking a chord he had been unprepared for. He'd come here to help out his former coach, with no expectation of getting anything in return. But he couldn't deny how incredible it felt to look into those players' faces and realize that he was making a difference.

Coach Green gave him another firm pat on the shoulder. "Shoot me a text if you can make it to next Saturday's game. I'll have sideline passes for both of you at will call."

As they walked away from the group of players, Taylor leaned over and whispered, "I was ready to pick up a helmet and run out on the field myself after listening to you."

Jamar chuckled. "I can see that. Powerhouse Powell, kicking ass and taking names across the Big Twelve Conference."

"Powerhouse. I like it." She tipped her head in the direction of Coach Green. "He was right, you know. You're pretty good at giving pep talks."

"I've listened to my share," Jamar said.

"So I guess I'll have to learn to like football if I want to build a clientele of football players," she said.

"I'll bet by the end of these two months you're going to wonder how you ever lived without football," Jamar said.

"You care to place money on that?"

He laughed at her flat tone, but his amusement swiftly dissipated at the sight of Alec Mooney approaching. His blog and podcast were lauded as the gold standard in college football. Jamar appreciated him because he was fair and didn't rely on sensationalism to get his point across. He also liked that Alec always carried around a slim notebook, as if he were single-handedly trying to bring back old-school reporting.

Still, Jamar's relationship with the media had been a bumpy one. They'd treated him as the darling of Texas football since high school, a kid who had it all: brains, brawn, and the type of easygoing personality that made reporters gravitate toward him. As a straitlaced kid from a two-parent, middle-income suburban household, he defied the stereotype that the NFL was comprised of young black men who used football as their only way out of inner-city poverty.

The media adored him, but they'd typecast Silas the moment it was revealed that his birth mother was serving time in a Texas state prison. Silas had taken it in stride. Jamar wasn't so forgiving. It didn't matter how decent and equitable Alec Mooney appeared on the outside; the fact that he was a member of the media placed him squarely in Jamar's Do Not Trust category.

"Hey, Diesel. Long time no see," Alec said as he approached. "You've been MIA lately. I figured I'd see you on the sideline of at least a couple of Longhorn games this season."

Jamar shrugged. "I haven't been able to make any games yet, but when Coach Green calls, he knows I'm here for him."

Alec nodded. "How is the knee holding up? Is Dr. Hoffman the orthopedic wizard everyone claims he is?"

"I couldn't have asked for a better surgeon," Jamar said, bending his knee.

"Hi there," Alec said, offering Taylor his hand. "Alec Mooney from Central Texas Sports Talk." Jamar was about to apologize for not making introductions when Alec added, "You were in that viral dating video a few months ago. Weren't you one of that guy Craig's girls?"

Jamar saw the way Taylor's jaw tightened and knew Mooney was in trouble. He crossed his arms over his chest and waited for the show. It promised to be a good one.

"Taylor," she said in an excessively sweet voice that signaled to any guy with half a brain that his ass was grass. "I much prefer being called by my name than to be called 'one of Craig's girls.' It's sexist as hell to refer to any woman as someone's *girl*."

Alec had the blank look of someone who'd been put in his place so soundly that he didn't know how to react.

"Umm...yeah, sorry about that," he said. "That was rude. Please, accept my apology."

That was a half-decent recovery. Jamar was impressed.

Taylor gave him one of those regal, Queen of England nods. "Apology accepted," she said, her smile more genuine this time around.

"Uh, so," Alec continued. "Are you Jamar's new trainer?"

A surge of shock calcified Jamar's muscles, rendering him numb. He'd been preparing his *we're just friends* story as an answer to what he thought was the most logical presumption people would make upon seeing him and Taylor out in public.

"What do you mean?" Jamar asked, mentally crossing his fingers and hoping that Alec hadn't made the correct leap.

The reporter pointed at Taylor with his pencil. "She—Taylor—is a fitness trainer, isn't she?" He looked to her. "I've watched some of your YouTube videos."

Fuuuuuck.

Jamar tried to play off his unease with a laugh. "Yeah, but that doesn't mean she's *my* trainer? We're—"

"C'mon, Jamar." Alec shot him a sly smile. "There's been speculation for months that you're looking to return to the League. It would make sense that you've hired a personal trainer to help you get back in playing form."

Dread raced through his veins. The one thing he'd feared the most was happening, and he had no idea how to stop it.

"I don't..." he started, but the words caught in his throat.

"Actually, we're dating," Taylor said. She grabbed his hand

and entwined her fingers with his. A radiant smile stretched across her lips, but when she glanced at him, her eyes were wide with a *Holy shit, what did I just say?* look.

"It was one of the few positive things to come out of that disastrous viral video," she continued with a shaky laugh. "I caught Jamar's eye and he was bold enough to ask me out."

"I guess there's a silver lining to every situation," Alec said. He nodded at Jamar. "If you ever do decide to make a comeback, I'd appreciate a heads-up. You have an open invitation to break the news on Central Texas Sports Talk."

"You'll be the first to know." Jamar managed to smile as he answered the reporter. The moment Mooney was out of earshot, he turned to Taylor. "What was that?"

"I don't know!" She lifted her hands in hapless frustration. "I panicked! I just said the first thing that came to my mind." She pressed her palms to her cheeks. "*Shit!* Shit, shit, shit."

Jamar sucked in a deliberate breath. It felt as if his ribs were squeezing his chest.

How had things gone so wrong, so fast? Keeping his desire to return to the League a secret should have been an easy task, yet they'd failed it in spectacular fashion. Fucking Mooney. How had he jumped to the right conclusion? How could Alec take one look at Taylor Powell and not assume that hooking up with her would be the first thing on Jamar's mind?

A knot the size of Texas twisted in his gut, but he knew what he needed to do.

"I'll catch up with Mooney and tell him the truth," he said. He started after Alec, but Taylor caught his hand.

"No. Don't do that. Not yet." She exhaled an impatient breath. "Look, we'll figure it out. For now, just...go with it."

"Taylor—"

"We'll figure it out," she repeated. "We just have to think this through."

Jamar stared at her for several moments, trying to figure out what was going on inside her head.

"Okay," he said. "Let's figure it out."

CHAPTER TEN

If Taylor thought back on the last twenty-eight years, she could probably come up with at least a dozen awkward situations she'd gotten herself into. There was that time she was caught sneaking underwear out of the boys' changing room at school—a dare she'd made with her friend Keva. And then there was the time she showed up to her very first job interview on the wrong day. *Soooo* awkward.

And, goodness, she couldn't think about her disastrous one and only one-night stand without wincing. Not only had the sex been boring AF, but she'd also woken up the next morning to find the guy's grandmother standing over the bed with Taylor's bra hanging from her fingers, opining on the kind of loose women who wore brassieres with a front clasp.

Taylor could only assume that the years had lessened the sting, because none of those previous awkward moments felt as cringe-worthy as what she now experienced nestled in the passenger seat of Jamar's SUV.

What in the world had she been thinking?

Broadcasting to a reporter, of all people, that she and Jamar Dixon were dating was the most idiotic move she'd made in months. And she'd made her share of super idiotic moves lately.

How could she possibly use Jamar as a legitimate spokesperson for Taylor'd Conditioning now? If word got out that they were dating, people would just assume he was endorsing her simply because she was his girlfriend.

Taylor clenched her fists tight enough to score the fleshy part of her palm. Even when opportunities were handed to her on a silver platter, she had to go and upend the damn thing.

Jamar cleared his throat.

"Umm, Taylor?" he said. They were the first words spoken since they'd left the University of Texas field house twenty minutes ago. "We should probably talk about what happened back there."

"Not yet." She shook her head. "I'm still trying to figure it all out. That Alec guy didn't come across as the type of person who would run and tell his friends about Vin Diesel's new girlfriend," she said. "Besides, he writes about sports, not celebrity gossip."

"It's just Diesel, not *Vin* Diesel. And Mooney's a reporter. When it comes to these guys, any news is worth sharing, especially on a slow news day."

Shit. This definitely topped her Biggest Fuckups of All Time list. Who knows where this gig would have taken her? She could have become the new fitness guru of the NFL, but instead she'd relegated herself to being Jamar Dixon's arm candy.

Nice job, genius.

Taylor refused to believe all was lost. She could not give up on this without at least *trying* to come up with a plan to fix it.

"I'm going to figure out a way to spin this," she said. "I just need some time."

She adjusted the seat belt as she twisted in her seat.

"Okay, I'm changing the subject here, Twenty-Three, so keep up. When that woman came to our table at the café the other day, she mentioned that you should consider coaching for the Longhorns. After this morning, I think maybe she's on to something."

He glanced at her with a sour expression.

"Seriously," Taylor said. "I was impressed listening to you talk to those players. And remember, I know nothing about football."

"Just because I can babble on about football for a few minutes doesn't mean I'm fit to be anyone's coach."

"You did more than just babble," she said. "You were inspiring. I could tell those players were taking your words to heart. If you don't want to be a coach, maybe you can be a motivational speaker because you really are good at it."

"You do realize if I did either of those things I would no longer need you as a trainer, right? Are you trying to talk your way out of this job again?"

"Oh, for the love of Jason Momoa! Would you stop reading the wrong thing into everything I say? I was paying you a compliment." She looked up at the SUV's ceiling and sighed. "You're a good speaker. That's all I was trying to say."

His mouth tipped up in a grin. "In that case, thank you."

"You're welcome," Taylor said with an eye roll. She pretended to look out the window so he wouldn't see her answering grin. He was exasperating. Cute, but exasperating.

A few minutes later, they pulled up to the curb in front of her apartment complex. Jamar started to get out of the car, but Taylor stopped him.

"There's no need for you to play the gentleman," she said. "I can make it to my apartment by myself."

"Doesn't matter," Jamar said, unsnapping his seat belt. He came around the front of the SUV, and even though she'd already opened her door, he held it out for her. "When I was twelve, my mom signed me up for this program on proper etiquette at our church. It's ingrained."

"Aw, that's sweet," Taylor said. "A little corny, but sweet. You're still not walking me to my door."

"Sorry." He hunched his shoulders. "Those are the rules."

"Fine," Taylor said. She should add *infuriating* to his list of qualities.

It wasn't until they started up the stairs that Taylor acknowledged the discomfort that had begun to prickle at her scalp. Who could blame her for feeling self-conscious about her little studio apartment after visiting Jamar's massive house?

When they arrived at the landing, Taylor turned to him and said, "Thanks for walking me to my door. I'll see you tomorrow."

"Are you really not going to invite me in?"

She tipped her head to the side as if contemplating her answer. Finally, she said, "Nope, I don't think so."

"Taylor, come on."

"Why do you need to come inside?"

"Because we need to decide what we're going to do about Mooney. We can't put this off until tomorrow."

She knew he was right, but goodness, she did not want to think about this right now. Of course, if she had been thinking earlier, she wouldn't have made that impulsive outburst in the first place.

She slid the key in the lock, but before opening the door, she said, "Fair warning: my apartment is the size of your foyer. No judging."

His head reared back. He looked offended. "Have I come across as the kind of guy who would say anything about the size of your apartment?"

No, he had not. Honestly, he was the most down-to-earth multimillionaire she'd ever met. Okay, so he was the only multimillionaire she'd ever met, but still...

She opened the door and led him into the apartment.

"This isn't so bad," he said.

"Hey, I never said it was bad. I just said it wasn't a mansion."

"Mansions are overrated," he said, a hint of a smile playing at the corner of his lips. "The upkeep is a bitch."

"And you think it's easy taking care of all this?" she asked with the haughtiest expression she could summon.

Jamar's smile broadened and a warm sensation fluttered low in her belly. *Shit.* She really needed to stop flirting with her client.

Taylor took off her jacket and hung it on the hook near the door. She pushed her shirtsleeves up, stuck her hands in her pockets, then pulled them out and crossed her arms over her chest. Why was she suddenly nervous?

"Can I get you a drink?" she asked.

"Sure. Water is fine." He scratched his left palm, a move Taylor already recognized as a nervous habit he relied on when thinking. Great, so now they were both edgy. This was ridiculous.

He stopped at the bookshelf that held her collection of Disney snow globes and trading pins.

"I take it you're a fan of Disney?"

"*Huge* fan," Taylor called from the kitchen. "Visiting Walt Disney World in Florida is at the top of my bucket list."

"You have all this Disney stuff and have never been to Disney World? That's just wrong."

She detected when he started moving again, the thump of his Timberland boots echoing on her floors. He reached the tiny kitchen and his steps abruptly stopped.

"Are you baking cookies?"

Taylor looked down at the bag of chocolate chips, flour, and sugar that she'd gathered from the pantry without even realizing it.

What the hell? This was not the time to stress-bake!

"No, no." She shoved the container of sugar to the side, then turned to the fridge and grabbed two bottles of water. She gestured to the sofa. "Have a seat."

After handing him his water, she perched against the arm of the sofa. She glanced at the twin bed in the corner, whispering a silent prayer of thanks that she hadn't left something embarrassing in clear view.

"So how do you think we should handle this?" she asked.

Jamar hunched his shoulders. "Contact Mooney and tell him the truth."

"You know what that would mean for you, don't you? Months of speculation and random jerks leaving snotty comments online."

"What else is there to do, Taylor?"

She jumped up and began to pace in front of the sofa. "I know that we can come up with a plan that works for both of us. Now, the most important thing for you is that no one finds out that you want to play football again, right?"

"The most important thing for me is to play football again. Period. I would prefer to keep what we're doing out of the public until I return to the League, but if word gets out..." Another shrug. "I guess I'll just have to deal with it."

Guilt twisted in Taylor's gut at the disappointment she

heard in his voice. "As someone who recently experienced a pretty awful dragging by strangers online, I can't stomach the thought of putting you through that just because I stupidly blurted out that lie."

"Taylor, if I had to list all the times I've been dragged online, it would stretch all the way up to my house in Georgetown. It comes with the territory when you're an athlete who's played at the professional level."

"That doesn't change the fact that *I'm* the reason for this particular dragging," she said, feeling even worse that he was trying to downplay her role in this.

Jamar caught her by the wrist. "Can you please sit down? Your pacing is making me dizzy."

She sat on the sofa, but then immediately popped back up again. "Wait. I have an idea. It's a little crazy, but it can work. No, it *will* work."

"What?" His apprehension was justified. At this point, Taylor wouldn't trust herself either. But the more the idea began to coagulate in her head, the more it started to make total sense.

"Hear me out," she began. "What if we stick with the dating story for now?"

"What?" His head jerked back. "You're not serious?"

Okay, so she was a tad offended by the incredulity in his tone.

"For the record, I'm a catch," she said. "But that's beside the point. Listen, if people think we're dating, we won't be confined to your home gym anymore." She put her hands up. "Don't get me wrong, it's the coolest home gym I've ever seen in my life, but I love getting outdoors too. We wouldn't have to hide out if people think you've just tagged along on workouts because I'm your girlfriend."

"I thought that was exactly what you were trying to avoid, having potential customers assume that I'm only working with you because I'm your boyfriend?"

"I know." She sighed. "I didn't say this was ideal, but it's the best solution I can come up with. If I could travel back in time and not open my big mouth to that Mooney guy, I would. But that's not happening. And, you know what? If I'm able to prove to people that I'm so damn good that I can get a guy with a busted knee back into the NFL, it won't matter if they believe we're dating."

Taylor slapped her hand to her forehead. "Oh. My. *God*. Come on, Taylor Renee! Why didn't you see this before?"

"You're addressing yourself in the third person, and that kind of shit always scares me," Jamar said. "What should you have seen before?"

"We can be the new IG power couple!" she said. She laughed at his confounded expression. "Do you spend even a second on Instagram? Because, if you do, you would know that the power couples rule Fitnessgram."

"Are you even speaking English right now?"

"Keep up, Twenty-Three. You're younger than I am; you should know this lingo." She snapped her fingers. "I need something to write on." Taylor walked over to the kitchen and grabbed a piece of mail and a pen. "We need to put together a game plan," she said, returning to the sofa. She turned the envelope vertical and wrote *game plan* at the top.

"The *a* is backwards."

She looked over at him. "Huh?"

He lifted the envelope from her hand and pointed to it. "The *a*. You wrote it backwards in both *game* and *plan*."

"It's only because I was writing too fast. Now, let me finish this." She snatched the envelope from his hands and made a list of bullet points. Once done, she turned to him, unable to stanch the smile that curled up her lips. "So this is freaking brilliant."

"You want to share?" he asked, holding out his hand.

"I'll read it to you," Taylor said. She didn't need Mr. Penmanship dissecting her messy handwriting. "This is our official dating playbook. Our overall goal is to convince everyone that we're the hot new fitness couple on the block. I'd love to come up with a couple's name, but all I can think of is TayJar."

"Please don't make me half of TayJar."

Taylor had to bite the inside of her cheek to stop herself from laughing at the desperation in his frantic plea.

"Forget TayJar," she said, tapping the pen in a chaotic rhythm against her leg. "It's not important. What *is* important is selling this story to the public so that they'll believe we're really a couple."

"And how do you propose we do that?"

"I told you, by becoming a fitness power couple. We'll convince people you're helping me develop new exercise routines for Taylor'd Conditioning. I'm known for my boot camp workouts, but I can say that I'm moving into a new genre— work out like an NFL player, or something.

"Now, in order to really sell this, we're going to have to play up the whole couples routine." She ticked items off on her fingers. "Posting pictures of ourselves together online, especially when we're working out. Maybe even making a few YouTube workout videos together. But it can't be *all* about working out," she stressed. "We're going to have to stage a few dates where I get to wear cute clothes and heels."

The furrows in his forehead were so deep Taylor feared he'd end up with permanent frown lines.

"Taylor, are you sure about all of this?" he asked. "I can clear this up with a single text to Alec Mooney."

"No, it will work. I promise." She pointed to the envelope. "If we follow the playbook, we can both get what we want. What do you say, Twenty-Three?"

He sat in contemplative silence, studying her. After several strained moments passed, he said, "I guess we're dating."

CHAPTER ELEVEN

Jamar refastened the belt on the heat wrap around his knee and flexed the muscle, trying not to wince at the sharp pinch that shot through the joint. He dialed back the flash of worry that immediately sparked, reminding himself that even an uninjured knee would ache after the punishing workout he'd put it through.

He'd left Taylor at her apartment yesterday afternoon after they'd both agreed they were too mentally exhausted to undertake the upper-body workout she'd had planned. But once he'd arrived home, his pent-up adrenaline wouldn't allow him to rest. He'd changed into sweats and took off for a four-mile run, intending to clear his head. But four miles had turned into ten as he'd mulled over the ramifications of yesterday's chance meeting with Alec Mooney. How could something seemingly harmless cause his plans to implode in such spectacular fashion?

He thought of the chaos theory he'd learned about in high school, and how the fluttering of a butterfly's delicate wings in one part of the world could result in cataclysmic consequences in another. That's what this felt like. If he'd hung around just a few moments longer to chat with Coach Green, or if he'd taken Taylor over to check out some of the equipment, there was a possibility they would have never encountered Mooney. A minor tweak in the course of yesterday's events and everything would still be on track.

He heard a car door slam and jumped up from the weight bench. His new girlfriend was here for today's workout.

He dropped his head back and chuckled at the ceiling.

If anyone questioned whether God had a sense of humor, Jamar need only point to the fact that he now had to *pretend* that he and Taylor Powell were dating. The irony of trying to pull off a fake relationship with a woman he would've dated in a heartbeat if circumstances were different wasn't lost on him.

The more he thought about it, the more Jamar was convinced this was his best friend having a good laugh at his expense. Silas had been the king of practical jokes.

He arrived at the front door just as Taylor ascended the top step.

"I'm sorry I'm late," she said, breezing past him on her way into the house. "There was a huge piece of farm equipment being carried by a flatbed truck on the interstate. It took up two lanes and had traffic backed up to the Forty-Five on-ramp." She held up two red reusable shopping bags. "I was too keyed up after everything that happened yesterday, so I spent half the night cooking your meals."

"Oh, cool. What did you make?"

"This is grilled chicken with brown rice and sautéed root veggies," she said, holding up a container. "I also have flank steak with a mushroom and spinach tart. It is divine." She cradled the other bag. "And in here are black bean quesadillas and chickpea burgers."

"Nope." He shook his head. "I'll eat the chicken and steak, but not that other stuff."

She peered at him over her shoulder as she unloaded plastic meal-prep containers from one of the bags. "Seriously, how did you get a body like that without eating vegetables?"

Jamar arched a brow. "You've been checking out my body?"

"Uh, give your ego a Xanax. I'm your trainer; it's my job to check out your body."

And just like that, his ego was now the size of the speck of dust he found on the marble countertop. He swiped at it with his thumb.

"I'm serious about those burgers and quesadillas," Jamar said. "You can take those back with you because they'll just go to waste here."

She plopped a hand on her hip, that sassy-ass attitude on full blast. "Okay, both of these are freaking delicious. They are, by far, my most popular dishes. But do you want to know what tastes even better than those amazing quesadillas? Revenge." She dragged out the word. "Now, how bad do you want it?"

Jamar cursed under his breath. "Fine, I'll eat the chickpeas."

"You will also eat crow when you're forced to admit how much you like them," she said. If she were anyone else, he would have found her triumphant grin irritating. On Taylor, it was charming.

She picked up four of the eight containers and carried them to the refrigerator. Jamar snatched up the remaining ones and brought them to her.

"Thanks," she said, taking them from him and storing them along with the others. "By the way, I'm going to need you to change out of those clothes."

He looked down at his compression leggings/shorts combo and muscle tank, his typical workout gear. "What's wrong with my clothes?"

"We're not working out today. At least not yet."

"What? Why not?"

They'd skipped yesterday's workout. He didn't want to bring up money with her, but he *was* paying her some damn good money to train him.

She closed the refrigerator and leaned back against it. Folding her arms over her chest, she said, "We need to address your nutrition."

"I said I'll eat the chickpeas, Taylor. And I threw out all the potato chips."

"Good. But if your nutrition isn't on point, all the bicep curls in the world won't make a difference. I'll bet you were taught to carbo load because carbs are fuel, right?"

Jamar shrugged. "They used to serve us spaghetti dinners before the game on Friday nights."

"I'm not surprised." She snorted. "I'm not anti-carbs or anything, but you have to be smart about how you consume them."

"So Twix and cheese puffs are out of the question?"

She rolled her eyes. "Your sense of humor is trash," she said, but then a reluctant smile drew across her lips.

He should be concerned by the amount of satisfaction he gained from the simple act of putting that smile on her face. Then again, making her laugh was the kind of thing he was supposed to do as her boyfriend, wasn't it? If he was going to play the part...

Jamar stuck his hands in his pockets and perched against the counter. "So if we're not hitting the gym today, what are we doing?"

"We *are* hitting the gym, just not yet." She folded the reusable tote bags she'd brought with her and tucked them underneath her arm. "Right now, we are going on our very first date!"

"A date?" He glanced at his Apple Watch. "At this time of the morning?"

"Trust me, when it comes to where we're going, this time of the morning is ideal. Everything is nice and fresh, and not picked over."

Nice and fresh?

Jamar winced. "Please don't say we're going to the grocery store."

"It's as if you're psychic," she said, her brown eyes bright with amusement.

"Taylor, c'mon. I *hate* the grocery store. As in, I will do anything to avoid it. Even eat kale."

"You want a long and successful career in the NFL, don't you? Then you need to learn how to shop and cook the right kind of meals for yourself."

"What if I just pay you to cook for me until I retire?"

"No." She tilted her head to the side. "Actually, that can be arranged for the right price. But what if I'm on vacation?"

"Delivery?"

She grabbed him by the wrist and pulled him toward the stairs. "A lesson in proper nutrition and how to cook easy, healthy meals will do you wonders. Now, go change."

Twenty minutes later, Jamar found himself in the produce section of the grocery store near his house. He had been here exactly one time in the year since he'd moved to Georgetown. Once he discovered grocery delivery, he was sold. Apparently, his new trainer had never heard of Instacart.

"You look like a kidnapping victim," Taylor whispered. "How are we going to convince the public we're falling madly in love if you're constantly frowning?"

"Maybe you should have thought about that before choosing a grocery store as the site of our first date, *dear*."

"Grocery stores are heaven, especially *this* grocery store. I mean, just look at the selection here!" She gestured like a game show hostess at the yards of colorful organic vegetables displayed before them. "I could spend hours in this place."

"You really need to get out more. No one should be this excited over produce."

Jamar ducked when she picked up a yellow bell pepper and made as if she was going to pelt it at his head.

"Stop making fun of me," she said with a laugh. "Remember when you predicted I would fall in love with football by the time we're done? That's the same way I'll have you feeling about vegetables."

"If you can pull off that miracle, I will—" Jamar started, but then he stopped when he caught sight of a figure just to his right. A second later he heard, "Excuse me? Diesel Dixon?"

He turned. A lanky guy with shaggy blond hair held a Texas Longhorns baseball cap and a black Sharpie out to him. "Do you mind signing my cap? I want to give it to my dad. He's been a fan since that seventy-yard TD you ran against Kansas State your freshman year."

Jamar dialed up his obligatory smile for fans. "Tell your dad I appreciate the years of support," he said as he scribbled his signature on the ball cap's stiff bill.

"Thanks a lot, man. He's going to love this." The guy walked away, clutching the cap as if it were a brick of solid gold.

When he turned back to Taylor, she was still staring in

the direction of the retreating fan. She finally looked at him, hooking her thumb toward the guy. "Be honest, it's hella awkward when stuff like that happens."

Jamar scratched the back of his head. "It was cool the first thousand times it happened to me, but after five years of it? Yeah, it's kinda awkward. Especially in grocery stores, which is why I avoid them."

She stuck her tongue out at him. "Come on, let's see if you can get through your assignment before another of your adoring fans interrupts us."

Jamar pulled up short. "My assignment?"

"Okay, Twenty-Three, I know we've only been working together for a few days, but you should know by now that there are no easy days. Ever. You've got to put in some work." She held out the green shopping basket she'd been carrying on her arm. "Your assignment is to pick out five types of vegetables that would be acceptable additions to your diet."

He grudgingly grabbed the handbasket. "Am I being graded on this?"

"Absolutely."

"If only I'd known what I was signing up for," Jamar mumbled as he ventured over to the potato bins. "So what started this obsessive love affair you have with produce?"

"I am not obsessed."

His brow arched. "You didn't see the way your eyes lit up when you looked at those tomatoes."

Her modest grin was reluctant, but Jamar still counted it as a win.

"Well, what do you expect to happen when I walk into a store and see all these heirloom tomatoes?" One corner of her mouth twisted upward. "Okay, fine," she said, her cheeks flushing a faint crimson with her admission. "I may be a *little* obsessed. It probably started back when I lived in Germany."

Her unexpected answer snatched his attention away from that alluring blush that had crept across her face.

"When did you live in Germany?"

"Much of my junior high and high school years. My dad is career Army, so I've spent most of my life living on different military bases all across Europe."

Jamar nodded, suddenly fascinated by this peek into her background. Her boot camp workouts made even more sense now.

"I've always wondered what it's like to be a military kid, living in all those foreign countries. Except for the one year I had with the Bears, I've spent my entire life in Texas."

"Texas isn't so bad," she said. "I wasn't completely sold on it when I first moved here, but it's grown on me."

"Let's get one thing straight: there is no place better than Texas. None."

"Texans," she said with exasperation.

"But did I tell a lie?" His brows arched, daring her to refute his words. "After a single winter in Chicago, I realized that I never have to live anywhere but the great state of Texas."

"Then you definitely wouldn't have liked winter in Stuttgart, Germany," she said. Her expression softened. "But I loved it. I especially loved that we were able to get the Food Network when we were stationed there. This was back when they actually taught you how to cook on the channel and didn't have a bunch of silly competition shows. I became addicted to watching *Barefoot Contessa* and Emeril Lagasse. I'd walk around the house yelling *bam!* at everything."

"Why?"

"Because that's what Emeril would say when he cooked." Her eyes grew wide. "Don't tell me you have never watched his show?"

He shook his head.

She threw her head back and sighed. "You have so much to learn, young grasshopper. Okay, I'm adding this to the dating playbook. We're going to spend an entire afternoon watching old episodes of *Essence of Emeril*."

The image of kicking back on the couch with Taylor while they watched television held way more appeal than it should for someone who was only *pretending* to be romantically interested in her. But he couldn't deny the way his pulse thumped at the thought.

Lowering his voice, Jamar asked, "How is a day in front of the TV supposed to convince the public that we're dating?"

"Not everything we do has to be for public consumption," she said. "Think of it as a practice session."

He resisted the impulse to point out that, when it came to that particular subject, he didn't need any practice. He would either sound like he was flirting or like he was an asshole. Or both.

Instead, he asked, "So what made Emeril so special?"

"It wasn't Emeril, per se. What made it special is that I usually watched it with my dad," she answered, slaying him once again with another of those subtle, yet radiant smiles. "It was our thing, you know? Every Saturday evening, Dad and I would try to re-create one of Emeril's recipes. Except we could never find all the ingredients, so we had to come up with substitutes. Believe or not, jambalaya made with bratwurst is pretty good."

"I'll take your word for it," Jamar said. The hint of wistfulness he heard in her soft laugh caused unease to stir in his gut. He hesitated a moment before he asked, "Is your dad . . . still here?"

"Oh yeah. The Colonel is alive and well. He's in North Carolina, at Fort Bragg. My entire family is there." She gestured to his basket. "Go for the sugar snap peas. They're good for snacking."

Jamar had been so caught up in her story that he'd forgotten about his assignment. He grabbed a bag of snap peas and reached for a butternut squash. He was pretty sure he'd eaten it in a soup once without wanting to dry-heave. He added collard greens to the basket.

He could have sworn he heard a tsking sound coming from her general direction.

"What?" Jamar asked.

"Nothing." She motioned for him to go ahead. "Continue."

"The added pressure of you watching my every move isn't helping here," he said as he lifted a head of cabbage from the shelf. Coleslaw counted as a vegetable, right?

"It sounds as if you're afraid you're going to fail the test."

"Not even. Don't let the jock label fool you. I got all A's in school."

"Did you really?" she asked, the teasing tone now absent from her voice.

"Well, not *all* A's," he clarified with a shrug. "But I did all right." He finished with several ears of corn that were still in the husk and a head of cauliflower, then brought over the basket. He held it out to her. "How'd I do?"

"Hmm." She peered at his choices. "You do have a few starchy vegetables, but I can live with that. The problem I

see here is that when you cook those collard greens, you're
going to want to load them up with stuff like ham hocks,
am I right?"

"Is there any other way to eat them?"

She shook her head. "You have *so* much to learn. Come on.
Let me show you how this is done. I have a recipe for a healthy
stir-fry that I guarantee you will love."

Jamar grimaced as she filled the basket with carrots, broccoli, asparagus, and other shit he hated. She picked up a slim,
purple eggplant.

"This is a Chinese eggplant. It's sweeter and less bitter than
your typical American version," she said, dragging her fingers
down the length of the vegetable.

Was she serious?

"Also, the skin is thinner, so there's no need to peel it." She
wrapped her fist around the eggplant.

"Are you fucking with me?" Jamar asked, too keyed up to
police his language.

Her brows dipped with her frown. "No. You can look it up.
The thin skin makes it easier to cook with."

"I'm not talking about cooking. I'm talking about you
giving that eggplant a hand job in the middle of Whole
Foods." He rubbed the back of his neck. "Shit, Taylor. I'm
trying to be respectful here, but come on."

She gaped at him in almost comical bewilderment, her eyes
growing wide as her lips soundlessly parted.

Fuck. He hadn't meant to say that out loud. Jamar affected
a nonchalant shrug in an attempt to camouflage the awkwardness that suddenly hung over them like a thundercloud.

"I'm not the biggest fan of vegetables," he said. "But when
I see one being molested like that, I have to call it out."

A laugh shot from her mouth. She quickly pressed her lips together, but her shoulders still shook.

"I'm sorry," she said. "That was not my intention at all. I love vegetables. I would never knowingly violate them."

"If you say so," he returned. He flashed her a sly grin to make sure she knew he was joking. He was beyond relieved that he'd managed to defuse the weird tension he'd caused. "So, am I done picking out vegetables?" he asked.

She nodded. "Yeah, I think we're good here. Time to move to another section." She tucked the basket's handle in the crook of her elbow and gestured with her head for him to follow her. She looked back over her shoulder. "You get a B minus on veggies. Now let's see how well you handle your meat."

Jamar dropped his chin to his chest.

She was going to kill him.

CHAPTER TWELVE

Taylor yanked on the bright purple metal door to Booze N' Brush, the art studio housed in a converted warehouse on the city's south side. Samiah had chosen it for this Friday's girls' night out. Taylor walked inside and spotted Samiah standing near the entrance.

"Hey, lady! Cute shoes," Taylor greeted, pointing to her friend's ballerina flats. They were bright red and covered with artful paint splotches.

"They go with tonight's theme," Samiah said, cocking her leg back like a 1950s pinup girl.

The door creaked open again, and London walked inside.

"So whose idea was it to come to this place?" she asked. Her bold yellow jumpsuit perfectly suited both London's deep brown skin tone and her in-your-face personality. "We could have just had drinks and skipped the painting."

"No!" Samiah and Taylor said in unison.

"Our mission is to find you a hobby, remember?" Samiah said. "Don't knock it till you try it. You may discover a hidden talent."

"My talent is saving lives. Isn't that enough?"

"There's nothing wrong with being multitalented," Samiah threw over her shoulder as she started for the reception desk.

"You know there's a sip-and-paint place not too far from your condo, right?" Taylor asked.

"They weren't interested in beta-testing my Just Friends app. The owner of this place is at least willing to discuss it."

That explained why Samiah had insisted they drive so far out of the way. Just Friends was designed to help people find platonic friends by matching users' interests. Then businesses could curate one-of-a-kind experiences based on some kind of algorithm Samiah's brilliant, tech wizard brain had developed.

"So this isn't about finding me a hobby at all," London surmised. "It's about business."

"Two birds, one stone. And don't pretend you wouldn't be complaining no matter what hobby we were trying out tonight."

Samiah gave her name to the greeter at the desk and the three of them were shown to their section of the cavernous studio. Each station was comprised of a medium-size canvas on a short easel, a paint palette, several brushes of various sizes, along with wineglasses and small plates of cheese, crackers, and fresh fruit.

"Hmm," London murmured as she picked up a strawberry. "This doesn't look so bad. I didn't realize it was a paint by numbers kind of thing. I can do this."

"Places like this are more about the booze and the socializing than the actual painting," Taylor pointed out. "But like Samiah said, maybe you'll discover that you actually like it." She took her seat at the easel to London's right. "Remember, *you're* the one who wanted to find a hobby."

"Yeah, well, I may need to put the hobby search on the back burner for a while," London said. "When we came up with our projects, I didn't realize I would be dealing with a

DEFCON 1–level crisis at the hospital. I don't have the brain power to devote to a hobby." She turned to Taylor. "Speaking of our projects, how are things going with—"

"Good evening." A middle-aged woman with frizzy red hair and more freckles than Taylor could count walked up to their work area. "I'm so excited for you all to join us. Now, which of you lovely ladies is Samiah Brooks?"

"That's me," Samiah said, reaching out her hand. "Are you Peggy?"

"Yes, I am. I'll be back to talk once we're done with the class. The app you discussed sounds right up my alley. Why don't you all enjoy your wine and snacks, and we'll get started on our portraits in just a few minutes."

"Psst," London whispered once the woman left. "I say we finish off the wine and snacks and then get out of here."

"Will you at least give it a chance?" Samiah said. "Sit your cute ass in that chair, pick up a paintbrush, and have some fun, dammit!"

"All right, all right." London put her hands up. "You know, you're way too mean for someone who's getting regular sex."

"Actually, she's *not* getting regular sex," Taylor said. "Daniel is out of town."

"Yes, he is," Samiah hissed. "And I am extra pissed off that I've become so addicted to his dick that my vibrator doesn't excite me anymore."

"Ugh." London shook her shoulders in an exaggerated shudder. "I never want to get to that point. Men come and go, but your vibrator is your forever friend. You gotta protect that relationship at all cost, girl."

"My vibrator stopped working," Taylor said, plucking a grape from the stem. "I think it broke from too much use."

"I'll buy you another one. Don't fight me on this," London said when she started to argue. "These days that shit is medicinal."

"I don't need you to buy me a vibrator because I have money again," Taylor said. "Umm...I said that kinda loud, didn't I?" She looked around to make sure no one had heard her singing about vibrators.

"I take it your new client came through with the funds?"

"Yes, he did. Thank God. Rent is paid and Nessie's gas tank is full!"

"I figured as much when I saw the new braids," Samiah said. "They look nice."

"That's what I was asking before the painting lady interrupted us," London said. "How's it going with the football guy? This makes a week, right?"

Had it only been a week?

Time had stretched like a rubber band since Jamar Dixon had showed up at her pop-up class last Saturday afternoon.

Taylor figured they would be here all night if she tried to recount everything that had happened to her since the three of them met for dinner last Friday, but she had to at least share this week's most important highlight, if only for their reactions.

"I'd say it's going well," Taylor drawled in an exceedingly blasé tone. "I mean, now that we're dating and all."

"You're *what*?"

Yep, that's the reaction she'd anticipated. Their simultaneous screeches drew stares from neighboring tables.

"Oh my God, if you could see your faces right now." Taylor laughed. She held up her hands. "Let me explain."

She motioned for them to come in closer and dished out an abbreviated version of this past week's events, starting with her first workout with Jamar and ending with the run-in with Alec Mooney during the Longhorns' football practice, and their decision to move forward with the story that they're a new couple.

"Do you really think you can pull off a fake relationship in this day and age with social media?" Samiah whispered.

"We can pull it off if we're smart about it," Taylor returned.

"You do realize this sounds like a romance novel, don't you?" London asked. "I mean, it's adorable, but it is *such* a romance novel. In the book, you two would end up getting married." London lifted one shoulder. "I'm just saying."

Taylor immediately dismissed London's theory. There would be no ugly bridesmaid dresses, or sugary wedding cake in her future—at least not with Jamar Dixon. Or *any* client.

She'd learned that hard lesson two years ago, when she'd made the mistake of hooking up with Chad Lewis, an asshole of a client who'd decided that once they slept together it meant he no longer had to pay her to be his trainer. She'd discovered that the only reason his best friend hired her is because Chad had told him that she would probably sleep with him too.

They'd *laughed* at her. Taylor could still hear their disgusting cackles as she confronted Chad about this idea of passing her around to his friends. No amount of positive self-talk could expunge those memories, and she hated that the experience still affected her so much.

That incident had been the catalyst behind her move to Austin. She had been so afraid that she would acquire a reputation of being open to sleeping with clients, or that Chad and his friend Brandon would put that lie out there. It had seemed like the smart thing to just get the hell out of North Carolina.

She'd also decided to put dating—and men in general—on the back burner for a while. She'd had a couple of coffee meetups and flirted online a bit, but that fateful date with Craig Walters back in August had been her first *real* date in over a year.

Maybe she should just give up on men altogether. Her track record wasn't worth shit.

"That's not happening," Taylor assured London. "*This* story ends with Jamar making it onto an NFL team and telling all of his teammates how he owes his success to his amazing personal trainer."

"Work that hustle," Samiah said, holding her hand up for a high five.

"I don't understand why you can't do both, but whatever," London said. She slid off her stool. "I need more wine."

Samiah caught her wrist. "Not yet. We're about to start." She motioned to the front of the room, where the freckled redhead stood. The woman held up a painting of a wineglass on the ledge of a windowsill. It was a completed version of the image outlined in gray on their canvases. Peggy instructed the class to "go with their heart" when painting their own version, but informed them that hers would remain at the front of the class as a guide.

"Okay, that was helpful," London said. "Now more wine." She grabbed her empty glass and went off in the direction of the table near the check-in desk that held bottles of wine and extra food.

"I don't think painting is her thing," Taylor said.

"I'll be president of Trendsetters before that girl finds an interest outside of the hospital," Samiah said.

"Hey, that may not be too far off base. At the pace you're

moving, you'll be running that company soon," Taylor remarked. Samiah had already achieved rock-star status at the tech firm where she worked in downtown Austin.

"It sounds as if I'm not the only one making big moves," she said. "This deal you made with Jamar Dixon is going to work out great for you. What about the other thing?"

"What other thing?"

"Going back to school. Have you looked into any yet?" Samiah asked.

For a moment, Taylor's confusion rendered her speechless. She'd been so busy with her new client this week that she hadn't given school a passing thought.

"I think I can scrap those plans now that I'm working with Jamar," she said. She wouldn't think about why those words left a sour taste on their way out of her mouth.

"What does one have to do with the other?" Samiah asked.

"The whole point of going back to school was to—"

"To get your degree so that you can take your fitness consulting business to the next level."

"Which will happen once Jamar gets back into the NFL," Taylor pointed out.

"But what if he doesn't?"

The earnestness in Samiah's voice caused Taylor's stomach to churn with acid and that sour taste to return to her mouth.

"No . . . no negative thinking," she stammered. She cleared her throat and tried to inject some enthusiasm into her voice. "I don't allow myself to think that way when it comes to my clients."

Samiah didn't look convinced, and why should she? Even Taylor had to admit it sounded like bullshit.

"Trust me on this," Taylor said. "Jamar is getting back into the NFL."

"Fine," Samiah said. "So let's say he *does* make it onto a team; there's still no guarantee that it will impact Taylor'd Conditioning in the way that you think it will. Anything can happen." She took a sip from her wine. "Look, I don't subscribe to the notion that everyone has to go to college. I just think, in your case, earning your degree would provide security that you don't have right now."

She knew Samiah was right, and at this moment, Taylor hated her for it. She'd had this debate with herself. She'd made the pros and cons list. And she'd discovered that it was possible for her to recognize the transformative power of a degree yet still be reluctant about obtaining one.

London returned with her wineglass and a small saucer.

"There is cheese dip," she sang, doing a little shimmy as she reclaimed her seat. "And it's good cheese, not the processed kind. I have to admit, this place is growing on me." She looked from Taylor to Samiah. "Okay, why does it suddenly feel like Thanksgiving dinner back before my parents were divorced? This kind of tension gives me hives."

"Well, *some*one is backing out on her plans to get her degree," Samiah provided.

"Damn. Already? You just decided to go back to school like a minute ago. Why are you giving up so soon?"

"I'm not giving up! I'm just...Shit," Taylor muttered. "I won't take it completely off the table, but I can't handle both school and training Jamar."

"You'll always have clients that you're training," Samiah said. "We already established that you'll have to simultaneously work and go to school."

"I *know*!" She grimaced, hating the whiny quality in her voice. "Look, I know that I'll have to work while earning my degree, but this particular client requires more attention than most. Just the thought of having to do homework after a full day of training makes my stomach knot."

"Wait a minute," London said, her eyes suddenly alight with excitement. "I just thought of something. I actually *like* school. What if my new hobby is helping you with your schoolwork?"

Taylor started to nod, until Samiah declared, "That is not a hobby. Why don't you go back to painting?"

"Forget the painting. I can't do this shit. We just got started and I'm already bored out of my mind."

"Then we'll find something else. Homework isn't a hobby."

"Speak for yourself."

Samiah rolled her eyes, then turned her attention back to Taylor. "What do you need from us? Other than us doing your homework?"

That would have been ideal, but Taylor knew if she was going to go through with school, *she* would have to do it. She didn't want an invisible asterisk stamped on her degree.

And as much as she hated to admit it, Samiah was right about the security that degree would provide.

"What I need is…time," Taylor said. "I need time to get through this project with Jamar." She looked to her two friends and decided to be honest. "And then I will really need you both to hold me accountable."

Samiah lifted her wineglass in a toast. "That we can do. Don't worry, hon. We got you."

CHAPTER THIRTEEN

Taylor grabbed a plastic storage container from the cabinet—the one that was stained from heating red sauce in the microwave—and filled it halfway with water. She placed four of the five credit cards she owned in the container and set a rock on top of them. Snapping the lid on, she walked over to the freezer and placed it next to a bag of frozen broccoli.

"There," she said, dusting her hands for good measure.

She'd used the initial payment from Jamar to cover this month's rent and to pay off one of the credit cards, with a vow that she would pay off the rest over these next two months and never get into this kind of financial trouble again. Putting the credit cards on ice was symbolic. She could still access them through apps on her phone, but she wasn't going to. She would keep one card in her wallet for emergency purposes only.

And when she said *emergency*, this time she meant a *real* emergency. No more "emergency" sales on tennis shoes or "emergency" sushi because she deserved to treat herself after a long day. She was going to start living by an actual budget, and she would not allow any stupid *you only live once* nonsense to entice her into making irresponsible choices.

Ugh. She was starting to sound like a grown-up.

"About damn time," Taylor muttered.

She took a pint of store-brand strawberry frozen yogurt from the freezer—part of her new adulting was forgoing the expensive one she usually bought—and grabbed a spoon. She perched against the kitchen counter and started eating straight from the carton.

She used the remote to turn the volume up on *The Princess and the Frog*. It had become her Saturday morning ritual to pop in the DVD and listen to it as background noise while cleaning her apartment. Until Tiana started singing "Almost There." Then it was time to belt it out like a contestant on *The Voice*. Well, whatever was the equivalent to *The Voice* for people who couldn't sing a single note in tune.

Lack of musical skills aside, when Tiana sang about how she worked real hard each and every day and now things for sure were going her way, Taylor felt that in her spirit.

"Preach, girl!" she said, waving her hand like a deaconess in church. Her hustle would pay off in the end, just like Tiana's. Except she wasn't kissing a frog.

Her phone dinged with an incoming text message. She glanced at it over on the counter and couldn't stop the ridiculous smile that instantly stretched across her face.

Hey, Drill Sergeant. Do you have a minute?

Taylor put the yogurt back in the freezer and lowered the volume on the TV before picking up the phone.

Taylor: U get 1 minute. Do u always txt in complete sentences???

Jamar: Yes. And proper punctuation. Commas are our friends.

> **Taylor:** Nerd :)
> **Taylor:** What's up, 23? U like my comma usage?
> **Jamar:** Very much appreciate the comma usage....
> **Jamar:** I know you had a bad experience going viral a few months ago, but something tells me you're about to go viral again.

A chill that had nothing to do with the frozen yogurt she just ate raced down Taylor's spine.

> **Taylor:** Y? What happened?
> **Jamar:** We've been outed.

A moment later, the link to a TikTok video appeared. Taylor clicked on it and waited for the video to open in the app. It started with an image of Jamar handing her a pineapple in Whole Foods. Whoever posted the video had added thought bubbles just above their heads. Taylor's said "best couple ever" and Jamar's had "couple envy"—as if either of them would ever think those words.

Taylor had to admit she was impressed by the editing, but as the nineteen-second clip played, she realized their covert videographer had followed them around the store, snapping pictures of them in the produce section, the deli, and at the checkout counter. It freaked her out a bit.

> **Taylor:** Oh well. It was only a matter of time. At least I look cute in all the pics. :)
> **Jamar:** Very cute.

Her stomach executed a perfect somersault. Before she could spend a single minute overanalyzing the meaning behind those two words, he followed up with another text she longed to overanalyze.

> *Jamar:* Maybe we need to go on a date that isn't at the grocery store. Give the public something to really talk about.

It wasn't as if this was coming out of left field. She was the one who'd written "several pretend dates" in the playbook sitting right there on her countertop. So why did this suddenly feel too much like the real thing?

> *Taylor:* I guess we should.
> *Jamar:* What are you doing today?
> *Taylor:* U mean besides kicking ur ass in the gym?
> *Jamar:* 😊 🏋️ 🏃
> *Jamar:* What are you doing after you're finished with my ass?

She was smiling so much that her cheeks ached, but she couldn't stop.

She wrote: this is starting to get dirty. But then she erased it. Maybe it was just her own dirty mind's interpretation. Instead, she typed: Is this how u talk to all ur girlfriends? Then she erased that too. She meant it as a joke, but what if he didn't read it that way?

> *Jamar:* What?
> *Taylor:* What?

Jamar: Those dots keep appearing like you're trying to text, but then they disappear.

Shit. Technology could be a real son of a bitch at times.

Taylor: Yes. Time to take our fake relationship to the next level. Wine and dine me, 23.

Jamar: 🍷 🍷 🍷

Taylor burst out laughing. Just then, the video hub on her kitchen counter lit up with an incoming call, undoubtedly from her mother. Her parents had sent her the device for her birthday, and they were the only ones who used it to call her. Well, her mother used it. The Colonel was satisfied with a quick Just checking on you text once every other week.

She pressed the green answer button. "Hey, Mom, what's up?"

Her mother stood at the granite countertop in their newly remodeled kitchen, unloading groceries from a cloth grocery bag. Her sensible bob cut didn't have a strand of hair out of place.

"What are you smiling about?" her mother asked.

Taylor looked up from her phone. "Nothing," she answered.

Taylor: I need to go. TTYL.

She added a heart emoji without thinking, and hit send.

"Fuck!"

"Taylor Renee!" Gail Powell screeched.

"I'm sorry!" Taylor said. "Give me a sec, Ma."

Taylor: Ignore that emoji. My finger slipped.

Jamar: You sure about that?

Taylor: YES!!!

She slumped against the counter and tried to get her accelerated heart rate back to a normal level.

"Excuse my language," she apologized again to her mother.

"I can't talk for long," her mother said in that I've-got-places-to-go-and-people-to-see tone of voice she used when in the middle of a hectic day. "What are your plans for Thanksgiving? Are you coming in the Tuesday before like you did last year?"

"Ma, I told you that I can't do both Thanksgiving and Daddy's party— Wait, is he around?"

"He isn't, but it doesn't matter. I'm convinced he knows about the party."

"How? I thought you were being careful?"

"That man knows everything," her mother said. She folded the cloth bag and directed her full attention at the screen. "If you can't afford the plane ticket home for Thanksgiving, your father and I will pay for it."

"It's not about the money." Biggest lie ever. Even with the money she was making with Jamar, she still couldn't afford those airline prices at Thanksgiving.

"I have clients to consider," she said. She had *one* client, but still. "And you know Thanksgiving is the start of my busy season. I have a ton of meal prep—" Not a lie now that she was doing meal prep for Jamar. She was working on a low-carb alternative to sweet potato pie. "I just can't take that much time off from work."

"What I'm hearing is that this is no longer a question of

you having to decide between Thanksgiving and your father's sixtieth birthday party. You've already made your decision."

Taylor hunched her shoulders. "Well, Thanksgiving comes around every year. The Colonel only turns the big Six Oh once. If given the choice, I think Dad would rather I be there for his birthday party."

"Fine, but make sure you're here for more than just a day. I don't want you flying up the morning of the party and then on the red-eye back to Texas."

Count on her mother to read her like a book.

"I won't," Taylor said. "I promise."

"Good. I have to go. The work at the office never ends."

"I wondered what you were doing home in the middle of the day," Taylor said.

Her mother's penciled brow spiked. "I could say the same for you, but I didn't."

Taylor reminded herself that her mother would see it if she rolled her eyes. "Goodbye, Mother."

She blew an air kiss toward the digital display before ending the call; then she folded her arms on the countertop and dropped her head on them.

Taylor wasn't sure there was a word in the English language that adequately represented the complex, oftentimes thorny space her family occupied in her world. She couldn't imagine loving another group of people as fiercely as she loved them, but a simple conversation with her mother left her feeling drained.

She dreaded going home to North Carolina, enduring bouts of anxiety over her family's judgmental attitudes. It usually started weeks in advance, with the apprehension steadily escalating as the date to fly home drew closer. Taylor found herself waking up in cold sweats, hardly able to catch her breath. Her skin became tight and itchy, as if something was slowly sucking the moisture from her pores.

The most ridiculous aspect of all of this was that, for the most part, she enjoyed her time at home. Last Thanksgiving she'd had the best time watching old movies with her sister, playing gin rummy with her niece, and baking pecan pies with her dad. It had been her most blissful holiday in ages, until her brother, Darwin, made a comment about one of Taylor's old friends who'd just opened up a franchise of a regional pizza restaurant. That's when the murmurs about wasting her time with that "fitness thing" had flitted around the dinner table, and her holiday had turned to shit.

She was done putting herself through that kind of turmoil. She'd learned that she could love her family from a distance. She would endure them for her dad's birthday party, because she owed it to him to celebrate this milestone in person, but she wouldn't subject herself to their thinly veiled censure any longer than she had to.

The next time she made an extended trip home, she would have some measure of success that she could shove in her brother's face. She would no longer be the Powell Family Fuckup. She would be the one everyone talked about with pride, the one her mother bragged about to the people in her law office.

She just had to completely turn every single thing around in her life.

Piece of cake.

CHAPTER FOURTEEN

Jamar's stomach clenched. His pulse beat erratically with a manic *tum thump, tum thump*. His fingers fumbled with an antique-brass cylinder as he spun the dial, struggling to decode the cipher.

"Hurry," Taylor hissed. "We have less than three minutes."

"I'm trying!" He licked at the sweat that formed on his upper lip and attempted a different combination.

"Do you want me to try?"

"I've got it," he said. Shit. Maybe he had it. He was so nervous you'd think someone's life really did depend on him solving this stupid riddle.

When Taylor had suggested an escape room for their first official "date," he hadn't considered he might develop permanent anxiety from it.

Prolonged side effects notwithstanding, tonight's date was necessary. Chatter surrounding their new romance had increased throughout the day, even popping up on a few gossip sites. Screenshots of the video of him and Taylor at the grocery store had started circulating on Twitter and Instagram, accompanied by mounds of speculation about their relationship.

Unlike Alec Mooney, the general public had not automatically jumped to the conclusion that he'd hired Taylor as his personal trainer. The consensus seemed to be that Taylor had sought him out instead of the other way around.

His new girlfriend hadn't appreciated that. She'd gone on a tirade after today's workout, raging about how women were always labeled gold diggers, and why couldn't *he* be the one who'd pursued *her* because she was "such a fucking catch."

Jamar had to agree with her on that one.

After her rant, she'd settled down long enough to recognize how this could work in their favor. The more off base the public rumors, the more likely they would succeed in keeping his attempt to return to the League a secret. Taylor had suggested they become even *more* visible as a couple as a way to feed the gossip beast, thus their jaunt to downtown Austin tonight.

Jamar should have known she wouldn't have settled for a simple dinner and movie for their first date. Instead, she had him sweating like a cat burglar about to get caught while they tried to save some fictional prisoner.

The clock on the wall began to tick louder. That wasn't just his imagination; the volume on the damn thing really had increased as the seconds ticked down. He secured the last letter on the dial and felt the pin holding the lock in place give way.

"Thank God," Taylor said. She snatched the cylinder from his hands and slid the rolled-up paper out of it. She unfurled it, then quickly handed it back to him. "Here! I'm too nervous to read it."

Jamar sighed as he took the scroll from her hand.

"Read it!" she urged.

He stretched out the scroll. "Congratulations on solving

this riddle. Your next mission is to find the one thing that has hands but cannot clap. Fail to locate it and your subject dies."

She gasped, horrified. "Oh my God!"

"Taylor, you do realize this isn't real, don't you? No one is dying."

She smacked him with the cylinder. "Get in the spirit of the game. We have to find the thing with hands." She turned to one of the many cluttered shelves in the small room. "Do you see one of those creepy dolls? This seems like a place that would have a creepy doll in it. They have hands."

"It's not a doll," he said.

"Are you looking for clues?"

He would have laughed at the panic in her voice if he wasn't still wiping the sweat from his hands after that last riddle. But his heart rate was beginning to return to a safe level. He could think with a clearer head.

"What are we looking for again?" Jamar asked.

"It says to find the one thing that has hands but cannot clap. Oh, I know! It's the clock," Taylor said. She pointed to the loud, annoying clock above the door.

Jamar reached up and grabbed it, then flipped it over. There was an envelope taped to the back of it.

She took it from him and did a little dance as she removed the envelope and lifted the flap.

"'Congratulations. You have saved your subject and earned your escape. Punch this code into the keypad to enjoy your freedom and a twenty percent discount on your next adventure to the Escape Room.'" She winced. "That's a bit tacky, but whatever."

She entered the code into the electronic keypad and stood back as the door opened to the lobby they'd first entered.

"Congratulations on escaping," the attendant who'd checked them in called from the desk in a bored voice. "Do you want to schedule your next visit?"

"No thanks. We're good," Jamar replied before Taylor could say anything.

"Not even cool," Taylor said, her eyes narrowed in annoyance. But she didn't object, which told Jamar all he needed to know about her desire to return to the Escape Room.

They exited the automatic doors and walked out onto Blanco Street.

"You have to admit that was fun," Taylor said as she buried her chin inside the collar on her jean jacket.

The night had been chilly when they left Jamar's house, but not cold enough for a heavy coat. The temperature had dropped considerably while they were rescuing their subject. Jamar shrugged out of his brushed suede sport coat.

"I will admit that we have different ideas when it comes to fun. Take that trip to Whole Foods, for example." He draped his coat over her shoulders. "But if you enjoyed yourself, that's all that matters."

She glanced down at the coat, and then up at him, regarding him with a mixture of surprise and gratitude. "Thank you," she said.

Jamar acknowledged her response with a nod and fought against playing the fool who read a thousand things into a simple *thank you*. This was fiction. Fiction being carried out with the sole purpose of convincing the public that he and Taylor Powell were a couple.

"So," she continued. "Did I hear you say tonight is all about *my* enjoyment?"

"That's how dates usually work."

"Actually, there's a better chance of a *second* date happening if *both* parties enjoy themselves."

He peered down at her, an easy grin spreading across his lips. "I'm pretty sure I'm getting a second date."

"Cocky bastard." She laughed.

"Confident, not cocky. And only with things I know are a sure bet."

"I've noticed that," she said, tilting her head to the side. "I figured all professional football players had to be conceited—how could they not be, right? You can't reach such an elite level and not be full of yourself. But you're not as arrogant as I first pegged you."

"You may want to hold off on your decision. You've only known me a week," he reminded her.

Her sharp laugh melded into the boisterous sounds of the city.

Clasping his jacket over her chest with one hand, she captured his fingers with the other and swung their hands back and forth between them as they turned onto Sixth Street. The picture of the perfect couple.

Jamar reminded himself again that this wasn't real.

But it sure as hell felt real. Especially when she smiled at him.

"Since you didn't enjoy the Escape Room, what would you have rather we do tonight?" Taylor asked.

"The Escape Room was fine."

"You're lying." She bumped him with her shoulder. "Come on. I want to know what your idea of the perfect date is."

He quirked a brow. "The PG version?"

"G-rated."

Jamar snorted. "We *really* have different ideas when it comes to fun."

She bumped him again. "Perfect G-rated date. Go."

"Um, let's see," he said, giving the impression that he was really thinking hard on this. "The tacos we had were good, even though you gave me that look when I asked for extra cotija cheese."

"I did not give you a look."

"You gave me a look."

"Well, you weren't supposed to notice the look. You were supposed to wonder why I tacked on an extra half hour to tomorrow's workout."

"Ah!" He chuckled. "Make a note. I will *always* work a half hour more for extra cheese."

"Noted," she said with a nod. "So that's your perfect date scenario? Street tacos with extra cotija?"

"I'd include a walk like this one." He nudged his chin at the nondescript gray building about ten yards away. "And two scoops of Belgian chocolate."

"Oh, Twenty-Three, you will get no argument from me this time." Taylor tugged his arm. "I never say no to Amy's Ice Cream, even when it's cold out."

"Wait a minute," he said. "How much extra time will this add to my workout?"

"You don't even want to know. Just enjoy the ice cream tonight and don't think about tomorrow's ass kicking."

The direct stares and low rumbling were apparent the moment they joined the line outside of the Austin ice-cream staple. Jamar made a mental bet with himself over how long it would take before someone approached.

"Excuse me, but didn't you play for the Longhorns a couple of years ago? Jamar Dixon?"

He lost. He thought it would take at least twenty seconds.

"Yes, I am," he answered, then stood for a picture with the woman and her two kids. That opened the floodgates. Pretty soon, he was posing for selfies and accepting praise for his time in the burnt orange and white with everyone in line. A few people mentioned his banged-up knee, offering sympathy for the raw deal he'd been dealt.

Jamar had prepared to bypass the two teenage girls, but even they asked for his picture. And, in a surprise to both him and Taylor, they asked if Taylor would join in. Turned out *she* was the star in their eyes. Their admiration for the way she, London, and Samiah had handed that Craig guy his ass—their words—in that viral video was all they could talk about.

"Well, that was fun, if a bit unexpected," Taylor said once the girls walked up to the counter. She quirked a brow, a smug, sassy look on her face. "Guess you're not the only celebrity here tonight."

Why hadn't he considered how the kind of sexy, flirtatious teasing that comes with a relationship—even a fake one—would affect him? It was too damn easy to get taken in by that mischievous gleam in her eyes and the impish smile playing at the corners of her mouth.

She was his trainer.

This wasn't a real date.

He needed to concentrate on his end goal: getting his job back.

They ordered their ice cream—two scoops in a waffle cone for him and one in a cup for her—and continued along Sixth Street.

"Were you okay with what happened back there?" Jamar asked, motioning his head toward the ice-cream shop. "I'm used to the selfies and autographs, but if it makes you uncomfortable when we're together, I know how to gently decline fan requests."

"You'd better not," she said. "I'm finally getting a taste of the fame I've always longed for."

"Have you really?"

"Nah," she said with a laugh. "Honestly, I don't know how you put up with that all the time. Don't get me wrong, I'm thrilled that I'm up to ten thousand followers thanks to TayJar taking over Fitnessgram, but I still value my privacy."

"Are we really known as TayJar on Instagram?"

"Why don't you open your own IG account and find out for yourself?"

"Not gonna happen," he said. She'd been pestering him to join the social media platform for days.

Jamar studied her as she scooped ice cream into her mouth. Her eyes closed briefly, a look of pure contentment washing over her.

"What made you choose fitness consulting?" he asked.

"Huh?"

"Your profession? Of all the things you could have been, why did you decide to torture poor, innocent people who are only trying to get in shape?"

"That is so not fair. You make me sound like some obnoxious taskmaster."

"Have you listened to yourself when we're in that gym?"

She pinched his arm. "That's enthusiasm. And to answer your question, my dad is the reason I became a fitness consultant." The light in her eyes dimmed. "Although he would probably have a heart attack if I told him that."

They moved to the side to avoid a group of teenagers who were all looking down at their phones.

"Why would knowing he's the inspiration behind your career give your dad a heart attack?"

"Because the Colonel thinks I should go to college, earn my degree, and get a real job."

"So being a trainer isn't a real job?"

She shook her head. "Not to my family."

"I've got about a dozen trainers I've worked with in the past who would beg to differ."

"You totally freak me out when you talk that way. My mom is the only other person I know who uses that phrase. She 'begs to differ' all the time."

And that was the last time she would hear him say it. He sure as hell didn't want her thinking about her mom when she was with him.

"Anyway," Taylor continued. "Maybe if I owned my own gym, my family would take my career seriously. As it now stands, I'm wasting my time with this 'little fitness thing.'"

"Ouch." Jamar winced.

"I know, right? Holidays are a blast in the Powell household." She scooped up more ice cream, but the spoon didn't find its way to her mouth. "The funny thing is, I only became interested in fitness because I was so fascinated by all the soldiers doing PT every morning. I used to love watching them, the way they all moved in unison as they performed jumping jacks and push-ups and doing that two-mile run around the base."

There were cones blocking the sidewalk at Sixth and Guadalupe, so they changed direction, walking down toward Lady Bird Lake. When they came upon Republic Square, Jamar suggested they grab a seat on a bench so they could finish their ice cream.

He wanted to ask more about her family but didn't know how without it seeming as if he was prying. Fact is, he *was* prying. He was intrigued by that hint of vulnerability he'd heard in her voice as she talked about her dad. He wanted to know what was behind it, and why someone who exuded so much confidence would allow her family to reduce her business to a "little" fitness thing. It didn't gel with the fierce, self-assured woman who barked out orders like a drill sergeant.

"Hey." He waited for her to look up from her ice cream. "Don't let them get to you," Jamar said. "Your family," he clarified. "You're good at what you do. Don't let anyone make you feel as if you're wasting your time."

"Thank you," she said, her eyes softening with a look of genuine gratitude. "I won't."

His eyes dropped to her lips.

"Don't," she said.

"Don't what?"

"Don't look at me like you want to kiss me."

"It's hard not to look at you like I want to kiss you," he admitted. "Especially if we're supposed to convince people that we're really a couple. In fact," he said, brushing back two of her braids, "kissing you should be part of the playbook, shouldn't it? Is the public really supposed to believe I would spend an evening like this with you and *not* kiss you?"

"I guess you're right," she said. The low, raspy tone of her voice resonated like a tuning fork through his body. She leaned toward him, then pulled back. "Don't lose your head here, Twenty-Three. This is all for show. Remember that."

He caught her chin in his hand and pulled her closer. "Just because it's pretend doesn't mean we can't enjoy it."

The first brush of her lips against his felt exactly how Jamar expected it would feel. Like heaven.

it's pretend it's pretend it's pretend

The mantra scrolled across his brain, but with each subtle give of her pliant mouth, his ability to decipher fact from fiction dissipated. He grazed her bottom lip, a faint testing of his tongue, challenging how far she would let him go.

He needed more from her. One clue. The barest indication. He silently pleaded for a sign that she was into this. That this wasn't just an act. That the sensation of their lips coming together, the restrained yet hungry caress, affected her too.

Just as her mouth finally opened for him, a flurry of nearby giggles broke the spell that had woven around them.

Taylor's head snapped back and they both looked toward the snickers. A half-dozen teens held their phones pointed toward Taylor and Jamar.

"Well," Taylor said with a breathy laugh. "I guess we know what we'll see on TikTok tomorrow."

CHAPTER FIFTEEN

Despite the whirl of the professional-grade blender, the light rock streaming from the speakers, and the cacophony of voices buzzing throughout the bookstore, Taylor slurped her iced coffee as silently as possible as she perused the glossy magazine covers. Her visits to the library as a shy sixth grader on base at Hohenfels Middle School had conditioned her to be quiet when surrounded by books.

She picked up a copy of *Fitness* magazine and brought it to a nearby table in the bookstore's café. But as she flipped past the full-page ads for erectile dysfunction and toe fungus medications, her thoughts meandered back to Jamar's kiss. A *fake* kiss, she reminded herself. Although, if that was fake, Taylor was ready to sell her vintage Snow White cookie jar for the chance to experience the real thing.

And that's *the kind of thinking that will get your ass in trouble.*

Determined not to let her mind tumble headfirst into the gutter, she retuned her attention to the magazine. As she thumbed through the pages, she couldn't help but roll her eyes at the headline of one of the articles: GET THE PERFECT BOOTY WITH THIS BOOT CAMP WORKOUT. Taylor recognized the flash of resentment that rushed through her for what it was: jealousy.

Her mood had a tendency to turn salty whenever she came across a piece written in that fun, hip vein. She would have been writing these features if she'd landed that job with *Modish and Melanated*, one of the hottest lifestyle sites for young black women on the web.

She pressed her hand to her stomach, warding off the sickening feeling that attacked her whenever she thought back on that day a few weeks ago.

At first, Taylor thought the email from Ashanti West, *Modish and Melanated*'s editor at large, regarding an opening for a health and wellness contributor was the universe's idea of a cruel joke. She'd just lost the homeschooling job the week before and—because life could be a *real* bastard at times—had overdrawn her bank account that very morning.

Ms. West had reached out after running across the Taylor'd Conditioning Instagram account. But when Taylor forwarded her résumé, the editor at large had replied that readers came to *Modish and Melanated* with the expectation of receiving vetted expertise and that she could not in good conscience hire someone for the position who didn't hold a degree in a field of study relevant to fitness and wellness.

That's when Taylor knew that if she really wanted to make a career out of her love of fitness, she would have to do whatever it took to make it happen, even if it meant facing her biggest fear.

She just had to find the courage to do it.

That's why you're here. Get off your ass and get that practice manual!

Taylor slapped the magazine closed and took it back to the rack. But instead of going over to the study aids section, she moved to the comics, hoping there were still copies of her favorite graphic novel series.

She used to refer to her comics as her guilty pleasure, but fuck that shit. Anything that brought her pleasure these days was welcomed and she refused to feel guilty about it.

Of course, the entire Nisekoi: False Love series was sold out, because Austin comic geeks knew what was up. She picked out a couple of other contemporary romance manga that looked promising, then tossed her empty coffee cup into the trash and took a deep breath.

It was time for her to embrace the grown-up version of herself and face her demons. She straightened her spine and marched over to the aisle marked STUDY AIDS AND TEST PREP, approaching the ACT prep guide as if it were a snake.

"Stop being ridiculous," she chided herself.

But she still didn't reach for the thick book. Instead, she retreated until her shoulders met the opposite shelf.

Closing her eyes, she dropped her head back and blew out a deep, weary breath. She needed a moment to work through the painful memories that enveloped her whenever she was reminded about what happened the last time she'd made a failed attempt at being a student. The hurt and anger, the paralyzing sense of worthlessness; it was demoralizing.

Taylor had been so sure that she'd finally gathered the courage to face the college entrance exam when she'd sat down to take it last spring. She'd spent weeks studying—well, conducting her own brand of studying, which admittedly, left a lot to be desired. Still, she'd been so sure of herself.

The morning of the test, she'd spent an hour meditating to the calming hum of Tibetan singing bowls from one of the apps on her phone. When she slid into the chair in the lecture hall a few hours later, she'd felt calmer and more confident than she ever had in a classroom. But, per her standard operating procedure when it came to anything to do with school, the weeks of preparation and positive self-talk dissipated the moment the test administrator told them to break the seal on their testing booklet.

The irrational fear she'd always faced in school had instantly sprung to life, bringing with it the debilitating anxiety that tightened her chest and made her insides feel as if she was both ice cold and fiery hot. She'd left the testing center after the first bathroom break and had ignored the follow-up emails regarding the test.

Why would she want to put herself through that again? The gig she had going with Jamar was bound to lead to the success that had eluded her in the past. It was all but guaranteed.

You thought the same thing about going viral.

She sucked in another deep breath to quell the turmoil churning in her head. Just the thought of going back to school, of sitting in a classroom and suffering through a test while some teacher breathed down her neck, made her start to hyperventilate. But if there was one thing this past year had taught her, it was that her lack of a degree had become a nearly insurmountable brick wall between her and her goals.

She took a step forward, running her hand along the ACT prep manual's glossy spine before lifting it from the shelf. She'd allowed Samiah and London to think that she'd just come up with the idea to go back to school, but it had been swirling in her head for well over a year. She'd researched the nutrition and kinesiology programs at area universities and diligently read over the course requirements to figure out how many credit hours she could carry while still working full-time. And then she'd signed up to take the college entrance exam.

That damn test. It persisted as the one barrier that stood in her way.

Actually, that wasn't entirely true. There was another obstacle that she'd done her level best to ignore over the years.

Despite her reluctance to even glance that way, Taylor's gaze traveled to the section just a couple of yards to her right, where the purple and green cover taunted her. She knew exactly where the book on common learning disorders stood on the shelf, between the one on sensory processing disorders and the one on curriculum planning for the exceptionally gifted. She'd flipped through its pages on a previous trip to this bookstore, studying the diagrams about kinesthetic learning styles and skimming the chapters on how learning disorders develop and tools for helping those who have them.

Her eyes fell shut. She tried to swallow, but it felt as if her constricted throat would never open again.

She looked down at the thick prep manual in her hands, hands that had started to sweat. She set the manual back on the bookshelf and turned away, darting from the aisle and out of the store without a backward glance.

CHAPTER SIXTEEN

As they stood at the base of Mount Bonnell, Jamar tilted his head back and stared up at the thick clouds hovering overhead.

"Are you sure about this, Taylor? It's going to storm."

She brushed off his concern with a dismissive wave. "We don't have to worry about the rain for a few more hours."

"Really? Is meteorology one of your secret talents?"

"Well, if it was a secret talent, I wouldn't tell you about it, would I, smart-ass?" She swept across her phone and held it out to him. "My weather app says the rain isn't coming until late this afternoon."

"Far be it from me to question the scientists at Apple, but this sky?" He pointed upward. "This sky is calling bullshit."

"You know what? In the end, it doesn't matter because *I'm* the trainer, so *I* make the rules. And *I* say we're hiking Mount Bonnell. We've been working together every day for nearly two weeks, you should understand this by now."

Yes, he understood her by now. He understood that she could be stubborn as hell when she wanted to be. He threaded his arms through the sleeves of his hooded running jacket, then knelt to tighten the laces on his tennis shoes.

"A little rain never hurt anyone," Taylor said as she twisted from side to side, stretching her obliques. "After all, you need to be ready no matter what the conditions are on any given Sunday."

Except when those clouds opened up, it wouldn't be a "little" rain. He'd lived in Central Texas long enough to know when a washout was imminent.

"For someone who claims to know so little about the sport, you sure toss out football facts when they suit you."

"I've been watching ESPN."

"You're lying."

"I'm totally lying," she said with a laugh. "Since you're so concerned about the rain, I'll cut out the hamstring and quad exercises I'd planned for our climb to the top. Instead, we'll make this a timed run up the staircase. Once we get to the summit, we can run the trail." She put one foot up on the third step and leaned into a quad stretch. "I brought you here because navigating that trail will help with dexterity and conditioning your knee to adapt to various playing conditions."

"You know, there's this thing called ladder drills that we could have done at the gym."

"Who's the trainer?"

He blew out a deep sigh. "You're the trainer."

"Thank you," she said with a sharp nod. "Now, my fastest time up this staircase is just under five minutes."

"Pfft. I can break that record in my sleep."

Straightening from her leg bends, she narrowed her eyes as she propped her hands on her hips. "You know, one day that mouth of yours will write a check that your cocky ass can't cash."

"Maybe," he said with a shrug. Then he grinned. "But not today."

Her growl only made him laugh harder as they started up the stairs. "Watch it," she warned. "This limestone is slick even without rain."

The roughened steps had been made smooth by decades of people pounding their way up the hill, but they were still uneven in many places.

He spotted a couple descending the left side of the staircase and nodded a greeting as they passed them down the hillside.

Taylor looked back over, and in a loud whisper, she said, "They're probably in that other car that was parked at the base of the mountain. At least we don't have to put on a show for the public."

And she considered that a *good* thing?

Guess he was the only one who counted down the hours until they could put on their show for the public. The hand-holding, the lazy grins, the longing glances, the whispering in each other's ears...He'd started to really get into their little performances, especially when they turned out like the one they'd put on a couple of days ago.

After a three-hour workout in Zilker Park Monday morning, they'd returned to the food truck park where they'd first discussed working together. Unlike their previous trip there, the area had been packed with the lunchtime crowd, which meant they had to perform their happy couple routine.

As she held his hand while waiting at her favorite smoothie truck, Taylor had leaned over and told him a stupid knock, knock joke. Jamar had refused to laugh, which only made her try harder. He returned with a silly joke one of his agent's kids had told him about a snowman and a vampire, but Taylor wouldn't bite.

It became a competition—because when it came to Taylor, *everything* was a competition—to see which one of them could make the other laugh first. She'd won, but not because of a silly one. It wasn't until she'd shocked him with a dirty joke that Jamar had cracked.

Was it all really just a pretense for her?

Why wouldn't it be? That's what they'd agreed to, wasn't it?

He was the one who'd allowed that kiss to consume him these last few days. He couldn't blame Taylor for the uneasy heaviness that had settled in his stomach. She'd kept up her end of their bargain so far. This was all on him.

As he extended his gait to reach one of the steeper steps, a sharp pinch shot through his knee.

What the fuck?

He brought his other leg up and just stood there, unsure. Anxious.

Taylor peered over her shoulder. "Hey, you tired already? I thought you could break my record in your sleep?"

Jamar looked up at her. "What?"

She stopped. Her eyes narrowed with her frown. "Everything okay?"

"Yeah, yeah," he said, waving off her concern. "I decided to let you win this one. It wouldn't be fair for me to win them all."

"Whatever," she said with an amused eye roll. When she turned to continue her climb, her foot slipped on the slick stone. She yelped as she fell forward, bracing her hands against the limestone steps to cushion her fall.

"Whoa. I got you," he said, hooking an arm around her waist. He hauled her up, her back against his chest. "You okay?"

He had to take a minute to claim some control over his senses. It felt way too good to have her body this close to his, to have an up-close-and-personal view of that tiny tattoo he'd noticed peeking from under her shirt collar. It was a butterfly.

She looked back at him. "Just get it over with."

Jamar's stomach pitched sideways. Was she asking . . . ?

"Just say it," Taylor taunted. "*I told you so.* We should have worked out at the gym today like you said."

Jamar blew out a shuddering breath. He nudged his chin forward. "We're almost there. It's too late to back down now."

He helped her regain her balance, and they continued the climb up the staircase. Once they reached the summit, he took the lead, guiding her to the wood and stone pavilion at Covert Park, the greenway that covered the top of Mount Bonnell. It wasn't until he let go of her hand and noticed the red smear on his own that Jamar realized she was bleeding.

"Hey, come here," he said, walking over to the ledge that served as a bench.

"It's nothing. I just scraped it a little."

He took her hand in his and turned it palm side up. It didn't look too bad, just a couple of surface scratches, but it had to sting like a bitch.

"Too bad it was my idea to come out here," she said. "I can't demand hazard pay if I'm the one who put us in harm's way in the first place."

"You had good intentions," he said. "Here, it shouldn't take much to clean this up." He used the bottom of his shirt to dab at the cuts.

"Let me take a wild guess," she said. "You were planning to become a doctor if you hadn't gone into football."

"A doctor? No way."

"Why not? You said you were so smart in school."

"I said I did all right," Jamar replied, knowing he was being modest. He graduated valedictorian of his high school class and magna cum laude from UT. "My degree is in marketing, which is as far from medicine as you can get."

"What did you plan to do with a marketing degree?"

"Market research. Back when I was in high school, I took a class in free enterprise. I had to write a paper on how cereal companies choose where to place cereal on the shelves and became fascinated with the concept."

"The sugary stuff at kid level, right?"

He nodded. "It's genius when you think about it."

"It is." She nudged him with her shoulder. "Too bad you won't be able to use all that knowledge. You'll be too busy playing football for many years to come."

"Hopefully."

"Not hopefully. You *will*. No defeatist attitude allowed, remember?"

"I'm not being defeatist, Taylor. I'm being a *realist*. It's a hard lesson to learn, but it's better to be prepared just in case things don't go your way."

"If you work hard enough—"

"You're still not guaranteed anything," Jamar said. "No matter how hard you work to make something happen, there's a chance that it won't. That's just life. Having a backup plan is smart."

Her expression turned contemplative, as if she were taking stock of his words. After a moment, she shook her head and said, "So, marketing? Is that what you plan to do?"

"Nah." He shrugged. "My agent thinks I should join his sports management agency. He's convinced I would be good at it."

"Well, I know even less about what sports agents do than I know about football," she said, amusement illuminating her brown eyes. "But I'm sure he's right. After witnessing your determination in the gym, I'm convinced you're the type of person who would kick ass at anything you set out to do."

Jamar couldn't conceal the stunned smile that stretched across his face. "Thank you," he said. "That's probably one of the nicest things anyone has ever said to me."

"I call 'em how I see 'em." She issued a teasing warning. "Don't let it inflate that massive ego of yours."

"You know my ego really isn't that big," Jamar said. "I'm only joking when I try to come across as this super arrogant kind of guy."

"Nooo," she said with feigned shock. She shoulder-bumped him again. "I know you're only joking. You're one of the good ones, Twenty-Three. I can tell."

The sincerity reflected in her eyes triggered a reaction better left unexplored. Jamar swallowed past the sudden knot that formed in his throat, knowing he didn't deserve her praise. She had no idea what kind of guy he was. The things he'd done. How he'd treated the person he'd called his best friend.

The simmering shame that had burned continuously in his gut for the past seven years flared to life. He quickly doused it, shoving the reminder of his long-ago sins to the recesses of his mind. He was in the process of righting his wrongs; harping on them would do him no good.

Jamar continued to gently dab at Taylor's palm with the edge of his shirt. When he looked over at her, her attention was on his face instead of what he was doing to her hand. The thumping in his veins escalated.

His gaze dropped to her mouth, flooding his brain with

the memory of how those soft lips felt against his. If someone asked him to trade the car they'd arrived in for another taste, he would toss them his keys without a second thought.

He angled toward her. Her eyes roamed over his face as she leaned forward.

But then she pulled back.

"Umm, we should probably hit the trail before the rain comes," Taylor said as she gently extracted her hand from his hold. She jumped up and walked over to the edge of the pavilion.

Jamar closed his eyes for a moment, swallowing past the knot of lust clogging his throat. "Yeah, that's what we're here for after all."

He tucked his shirt back inside his running jacket and tugged at the zipper, securing it underneath his chin.

"Is this a race?" he asked as he came up behind her.

She turned. "Of course it is—"

He took off before she could finish her sentence.

Jamar jogged along the path, dodging any protruding stones. She'd been right with her dexterity argument; the way he had to sidestep the various impediments mirrored the fancy footwork he often found himself doing on the field.

Out of nowhere, he felt a stinging slap on his ass.

"Pick it up, Dixon," Taylor said as she whizzed past him and darted down one of the narrow paths that shot off from the main trail.

He bolted after her, skirting around a huge branch that had fallen along the path. He was mindful of his knee, waiting for that twinge he'd felt earlier to return. He slowed, unsure if the pinch he'd felt just now was real or a figment of his anxious as hell imagination.

Fuck. He'd faced this before, back when he first started rehab. Every twinge sent him spiraling. He often thought the fear of reinjuring his knee was as debilitating as if he actually did hurt it.

He heard Taylor approaching and assumed an exhausted pose, resting his hands on his thighs. He'd rather her think he couldn't keep up than let on that there was possibly something wrong with his knee. He had no doubt she would demand they put an end to the workout if she thought he could reaggravate his injury.

Jamar wasn't about to stop now. He could work through this.

"Really?" she said as she came upon him. "If you can't handle this, some of my more challenging training circuits might just kill you."

He sucked in several shallow breaths, then with a wink said, "Bring it."

She burst out laughing. "You can't help yourself, can you? You can barely catch your breath, yet you have the nerve to talk trash?"

"I've been trash-talking since high school. I think it's just a part of me at this point."

He stood up straight and discreetly tested his knee, relieved when he didn't feel anything unusual.

"I don't want to imagine you in high school," Taylor said. "I'll bet you thought you were the hottest shit to ever walk the hallways."

"I *was* the hottest shit to ever walk the hallways at Katy High. You would have been all over me."

She pointed her finger at her mouth in a gagging gesture.

Jamar took a step toward her. "How much you wanna bet?"

"So damn cocky. I told you that mouth will get you in trouble."

His eyes zeroed in on her lips, his own curving up in a devilish grin. "I can think of one way you can shut me up."

Arousal and anticipation mingled in the air around them, as thick as the smell of the impending rain. The attraction that had been steadily growing between them pulsed like a quickening heartbeat.

Taylor advanced on him, backing him up until he came in contact with a tree. Her brow arched. "Are you sure you can handle this?"

"Bring it," he said again.

She braced her hands on either side of his face and leaned forward. "There's no one else here. We don't have to put on a performance for anyone," she murmured.

Jamar swallowed. "You're not going to let that stop us, are you?"

She shook her head. "No." And pressed her open mouth to his. He capitulated with a matching ardor, thrusting his tongue into her mouth as he gripped her hips.

Her mouth was hot and sweet, an intoxicating combination of cinnamon and honey and everything else that was delicious in this world. Unlike that first kiss, this was the opposite of slow and gentle. It was hard and noisy and hot and addicting as fuck.

Thunder cracked overhead seconds before the sky opened and a deluge rained down on them. Jamar ignored it, refusing to let anything deter him. He hooked his arms underneath her legs and lifted her, her legs bracketing his waist.

He'd wanted her from the very first time he saw her on that video, and nothing he'd tried had been able to abate his unrelenting need to consume her. He ran his hands up and down her back, wishing he could pull the wet shirt off so that he could feel her skin against him.

As the cold rain pelted them, Jamar drove his tongue deep, over and over again, plunging with a fervor that had them both breathless within seconds. He left her mouth long enough to trail his tongue along her neck, lapping at her rain-slicked skin, imagining the other places he wanted to explore. Holding her steady with one hand, he skimmed the other along her side, then up to her breast.

She was sheer perfection in his palm. He massaged her nipple through her damp shirt, caressing it into a point.

In the back of his mind, he knew he needed to pump the brakes. They were already so close to crossing the line between real and pretend. But how was he supposed to say no to this? How was he supposed to pull away from a mouth that occupied his every waking thought?

He would deal with the consequences later. Right now, he wanted—he *needed*—to enjoy every second of her kiss. His fingers clutched her ass, pulling her against his hardening body. The compulsion to go further, to demand more, was so strong he ached with it. If they were at his home gym, he would drop to his knees and beg her to let him strip these clothes off her.

But they were in a public park where anyone could come upon them. They wanted people to think they were a couple, but this wasn't the kind of notoriety either of them needed.

"Taylor," Jamar breathed against her lips. The soft mewl she emitted shot directly to his groin. "Taylor, let's get out of here. We need to at least wait until we're in the car."

He felt her body go rigid a second before her head jerked back, her eyes wide, shocked and disoriented.

He started to make a joke, but something in her expression stopped him. She looked spooked as hell.

"Taylor? Taylor, please don't freak out on me. It's okay."

"No." Her voice shook. "No, it isn't." She unwound her legs and slid down his body. "I can't do this with my clients. I *never* do this with clients."

"Shit," he breathed. She was totally freaking out. Her hands shook as she pulled her braids free from the band that held them at the base of her head and then tied them up again.

Jamar leaned his head back against the tree, letting the rain that had eased into a light drizzle pepper his face.

"We have to remember the playbook," she said. "Public displays of affection should only occur when performing for the public."

"Do you really still think that way?" he asked, his voice hoarse with the need still crashing through him.

One would think he'd asked if her mother had five heads and a tail.

"Yes, of course. The whole point is to convince people that we're a couple." She stretched her arms out. "Do you see any people here?"

She ran her palms down her face and growled. "I *knew* this would happen. Even though I promised myself this would *not* happen."

"What wouldn't happen? The two of us kissing? That's part of your playbook."

"Don't get cute with me, Twenty-Three. You know what I'm talking about. Look, you're hot, okay? You are *so* fucking hot, and if you were not my client, I would be climbing you like one of these fucking trees. But you *are* my client, and I can't go there with you."

He pushed away from the tree. "There's nothing wrong with the two of us—"

"No!" She cut him off. "Just stop, Jamar. I can't. *We* can't." She broke eye contact for a second before looking at him again, her eyes imploring him to understand. "The only way this will work is if we stick to our original game plan. None of this is real. It's all a charade, a way to cover up the lie I told that reporter, okay?"

The trembling plea in her voice caused a sharp pang to twist through his gut. It was so fucking unfair. Why insist on sticking to this fake relationship story when they both wanted it to be more?

Jamar ached to ask her this very thing; instead he said, "Yeah, okay. You're right. It isn't real."

They were both telling a lie.

CHAPTER SEVENTEEN

Taylor reached over and lifted a sambusa from the compostable takeout container on Samiah's coffee table. The spicy lentil-stuffed puffed pastry was by far her favorite of the half-dozen dishes they'd ordered, although everything she'd eaten tonight had surpassed her expectations. Kudos to London. Taylor doubted she would have ever tried Ethiopian cuisine had her friend not suggested it.

Loud, popping sounds rang out from Taylor's phone.

"What the hell was that?" London screeched.

"Sorry." Taylor laughed. "My niece is sending me a text. She's a firecracker, thus, the ringtone." She opened Fredericka's text message and felt her stomach twist. "Oh, shit," Taylor groused.

"Something wrong?" This from Samiah.

Taylor turned her cell phone so they could both see the screen.

"My niece just sent a video of me and Jamar huddled up together on a bench downtown Saturday night." She flipped the phone back and looked at the screen. "You gotta admit, we're a cute couple."

Another text message came through.

Auntie Jesamyn wants to know what's going on.

"Oh, of course they would use the fifteen-year-old to dig up dirt," Taylor said. She looked up from her phone and explained, "My entire family knows that Freddie can ask me for anything and I'll never deny her, so my sister has recruited my brother Darwin's daughter to get the details. They're so transparent."

Taylor sent Freddie a quick text, letting her know that she'd explain later, then set the phone facedown on the coffee table. "I should have been better prepared. I knew I couldn't keep this thing between me and Jamar from my family for long."

"Were you *trying* to keep it from them?" London asked.

"Not really. I just... I don't know... thought if I didn't mention it, they possibly wouldn't find out? I know, I know," she admitted before either could say anything. "I should know better after that whole viral video thing with Craig." Taylor hunched her shoulders. "I'm not good when it comes to lying to my family, okay? Especially when it comes to my mom and dad. Back when I was a teenager, I used to tell them beforehand that I was going to sneak out of the house, because I knew they would find out anyway."

Samiah and London burst out laughing.

"It's true," Taylor said. "Most of the time they stopped me, but after a while they just told me to be careful and lock my window when I snuck back in." She shook her head. "I'm not sure Dad would be so understanding about me willfully deceiving the public. He's like... frighteningly honest. Like, if McDonald's puts an extra McNugget in his six-piece, he'll drive back and give them fifty cents to cover the cost."

"Damn, that's hard-core." London chuckled as she tore off

a piece of the spongy flatbread and used it to soak up some curry. "Do you think Jamar would have a problem with you telling your family the truth?" she asked before popping the food in her mouth.

"It wouldn't be fair of me to even ask," Taylor said. "I'm the reason we have to go through with this whole fake dating nonsense in the first place. The fewer people who know this thing between us isn't real, the better."

Maybe she should remind herself of that every once in a while. Maybe then she wouldn't allow him to feel her up in the rain while kissing the ever living fuck out of her.

Taylor seesawed between being completely vexed with her raging horniness and being upset that she'd put an end to their kiss. She should have followed his lead—no, screw that! *She* should have been the one leading *him*. She should have dragged him to the car and finally satisfied her curiosity about how those powerful thighs of his felt against her hands. And against other parts of her.

Kissing him had been a monumental lapse in judgment, but if she was going to feel *this* guilty, she should have at least gotten an orgasm or five for her trouble. Instead, she'd stayed awake nearly all night stressing about what would happen when she walked into his home gym this morning.

In the end, nothing had happened.

After a brief awkwardness Taylor had plowed ahead with their workout, deciding it was best to ignore what happened up on Mount Bonnell. Jamar's barely concealed frustration signaled that he wasn't fully on board with her plan to forget it, but he kept his objections to himself.

Taylor picked up her phone again and put it on silent. Then she placed it facedown so that she wouldn't be tempted to answer any further texts from her niece. "I'll figure out what to do about my folks," she said. "I've taken enough of our time tonight. What's going on with you two? Is Daniel still out of town?" she asked Samiah.

"He was home for one day before flying off again. Thankfully he'll be in Virginia only a few days, and when he gets back, he'll work out of the San Antonio office for the next six months. At least that's what we're hoping." She picked at the himbasha, the Ethiopian sweet flatbread they'd ordered for dessert. "It's true what they say—absence really does make the sex *so* much better. I may send Daniel away every now and then just so we can have return-home sex."

"I can't stand you right now," London said.

Samiah laughed, but Taylor wasn't so certain London was joking.

"What's the deal with the hospital?" Samiah asked her.

"Yeah," Taylor said. "You never finished telling us about the drama happening there. Why are you ready to strangle everyone in the administration office?"

London rolled her eyes. "Wait." She reached for the pinot noir. She refilled her wineglass, then took a healthy sip before continuing. "I need fortification before talking about it."

"Damn, is it that bad?"

"It's that bad." She nodded. "The hospital is being sold."

Taylor was openly dumbfounded. "I . . . I didn't know someone could buy a hospital. Is it like buying a house?"

"Believe it or not, there isn't much difference. And the problem with privately owned hospitals is that all too often the priority shifts to shareholder profits instead of patient care."

"That's gross," Samiah said. She brought her own glass to her lips. "Don't get me wrong, capitalism is my jam. It's the reason I'm able to afford this condo. But no one should profit off sick people. Especially sick children."

"Yeah, that's some comic book villain–level shit right there," Taylor said.

"I'm willing to fight for my patients," London said. "Literally. I will bitch-slap the first slick-tongued, suit-wearing asshole who comes into my operating room and tries to spew bullshit about cost-cutting measures." She took another gulp of wine before gazing out the floor-to-ceiling windows. When she spoke again, her voice was tight with anger. "Hedge fund managers and shareholders don't have to look a parent in the eyes and tell them that their eight-year-old's brain tumor is inoperable. Until one of them has to go through *that* particular hell, they can't tell me a damn thing."

London's distress was palpable, unlike anything Taylor had ever witnessed from her. It was a stark reminder of the burden her friend shouldered. Sure, Taylor had her own troubles—she *had* been days away from possibly having to sleep in her car at one point—but it was nothing compared to the pressures London had to contend with. Sick kids trumped everything.

"If anyone can win this fight, it's you." Samiah leaned over and clinked London's wineglass with her own. "Give them hell, my friend. Based on everything you've told us, they deserve it."

"Yeah, lady. Give 'em hell."

Taylor wouldn't badger London about her boyfriend project anymore. She recognized that her friend needed an outlet to vent her frustrations more than she needed a hobby these days.

"Oh!" London exclaimed, jumping up from the sofa. "Before I forget. Someone left these in the break room at the hospital."

She unsnapped her mustard-yellow Tory Burch clutch and pulled out a business card. "Don't take this the wrong way, but based on past conversations, I thought maybe you'd want to give it a try." She handed Taylor the card.

"Who is the Debt Defeater?"

"Someone who helps you defeat debt," London said. The *duh* was silent. "I checked out the website. Apparently, they help you negotiate down your debt. It couldn't hurt."

Taylor was tempted. She was *so* tempted. But she could hear the Colonel in her head, scolding her about shirking her obligations and not holding herself accountable. If there was one thing that had been drilled in her head from birth, it was that you took responsibility for your actions.

"As much as I would love someone to just wipe away my debt, it wouldn't be right," she said. "I accumulated those bills fair and square, and I made some shitty business decisions along the way." She shrugged. "I have to deal with the consequences. At least the money I'm making with Jamar will pay off most of it."

"Sixteen thousand will only pay off *most* of it? So you weren't joking before when you said you were twenty thousand in debt?" London asked. She held up her hands. "Not that I'm judging."

"It kinda sounds like you're judging," Samiah said.

"It's okay." Taylor laughed. She could do that more easily now that she had a clear path to digging her way out of this hole she'd been in for the past few years.

"I already told you guys about signing up for that coupon site. Well, because my rates were so reduced, I started putting things on credit cards. Then I bought all that merch to give away as 'free' advertising, but I didn't get nearly the number of clients I thought I would."

"Well, what about the money from YouTube?" Samiah asked. "I thought you said going viral over that mess with Craig sent a bunch of people to your YouTube channel? Don't you make money based on the number of views you get?"

"Yeah, about that...Did you know when you're self-employed you have to pay your income taxes every three months?"

"It's called estimated taxes," London said.

"I wish someone had clued me in. I didn't even know I had to pay taxes on the money I made from YouTube."

"Girl, you don't play around when it comes to the IRS," Samiah said.

"I know that *now*, but only after meeting my archenemies: penalties and interest."

"Shit, Taylor," London said. "No wonder you've been stressed. Maybe you should try hooking up with your fake boyfriend after all. You know, for medicinal purposes."

"As if I need an excuse to hook up with him," she said.

"Wait a minute now," Samiah said, sitting up straight. "What are you not telling us?"

"Nothing," Taylor lied. But what was the point in *not* telling them? In about three seconds it would look as though she were storing maraschino cherries in her cheeks. Stupid blush.

"Fine, okay. Maybe something happened," she admitted.

"Did you already sleep with him?" London asked.

"No!" Taylor screeched. "May I remind you both that I am a professional? I cannot sleep with a client, no matter how much I want to."

"So you admit you want to," London said, as if she'd uncovered some big secret.

"Have you seen her client?" Samiah asked.

"Exactly! Have you *seen* him?" Taylor said. "Of course I want him. I want to screw him until his dick falls off. Then I want to put his dick back on and screw him again. But I can't, because I'm a fucking professional."

She picked up the wine and took a swig straight from the bottle.

"Honey, did you buy that vibrator like I told you to?" London asked.

"Yes, I bought a new vibrator," Taylor said. "And to answer your question, no I did not sleep with my client. But I did kiss him. And it wasn't a fake kiss to go along with our fake relationship. It was a *real* kiss. With tongue. And my legs around his waist. And I can't stop thinking about it." She slapped her palm to her forehead. "I don't know what I'm going to do."

"So why did things stop at a kiss?" Samiah asked.

Taylor threw her hands up in the air. "Didn't I just explain this? He's a client!"

"You know," London drawled, swirling the wine that remained in her glass. "This has been a really enlightening conversation. I'm learning things about myself that I never considered. For example, I never saw myself as an amoral person. I mean, come on, I save the lives of children for a living. But, I have to admit, you're a better person than I am, Taylor Powell. I would be fucking that man every chance I got. Screw being a professional."

Taylor covered her face with her hands. Peeking through her fingers, she looked to Samiah and asked, "Are you going to be the voice of reason here?"

Samiah lifted her shoulders in an apologetic shrug. "I'm totally dick-whipped, so my advice would be the same. Screw being a professional."

Taylor growled. "You two are absolutely no help," she said, pushing herself up from the floor. "But thanks for the Ethiopian food, I guess."

"You're leaving? It's only— Oh, shit, it's almost ten," London said, looking at her phone. "I need to get out of here too. I have two consultations scheduled before nine tomorrow morning."

They cleared the food from the coffee table and divided the leftovers into take-home containers. Samiah put her arm around Taylor's shoulder as they followed behind London to the door.

"I know we weren't much help tonight when it comes to advice," Samiah said. "But I applaud you for being so principled about this."

Taylor tried not to roll her eyes. Unless principles became a magical cure for horniness, she wasn't sure they did her much good.

CHAPTER EIGHTEEN

This shit is not working."

Jamar peeked out of one eye, then quickly shut it again. He forced himself to remain in the massage chair, pressing his head back against the mechanical balls made to mimic thumbs. He still saw a massage therapist monthly, but for the time between his sessions, the therapist had suggested he set up a "tranquility room."

He'd ordered an obscenely expensive massage chair, along with a commercial-grade aromatherapy diffuser that misted lavender, rosemary, and other shit that was supposed to relax him. He'd even had mood lighting installed, thin LED strips that ran along the crown molding, casting off colors he manipulated by remote control based on the ambience he wanted to set.

None of it was working today.

It would have helped if his "Soothing Sounds" playlist hadn't filled the room with the sound of gentle raindrops. The moment he heard them, his mind immediately went back to that secluded spot at the summit of Mount Bonnell and the feel of Taylor's body pressed against his. He felt her hands cradling his face, her hard nipples against his palms as he massaged her breasts through her wet T-shirt.

How was he supposed to relax when every molecule in his body craved her, when her taste still lingered in his mouth? How was he supposed to continue with this pretend relationship after getting a glimpse of what the real thing could be like?

"Fuck," Jamar whispered. He should have told Alec Mooney the truth from the very beginning. Just two weeks into this fake dating scheme and they were already in too deep to call it off.

His phone rang, startling him. He set the phone to Do Not Disturb while in his tranquility room, so the only people who got through were those he deemed worthy enough to have on his favorites list.

Jamar smiled at the name on the phone. Andrea Cannon, Silas's older sister by three years. She was one of the few people he *always* had time for.

"Hey, Drea. What's up?"

His smile faded as he listened to her share that her grandfather had gone into the hospital. He could tell she was trying to keep her tone even.

"I'm on my way," Jamar said.

"That's not necessary, Jamar. I just wanted you to know about Big Silas."

"Okay, thanks for calling," he said. He hung up the phone and immediately started for his room. As if he would sit here doing jack shit while Silas's grandfather lay in a hospital bed.

He grabbed his leather duffel and threw in some clothes, along with a Dopp kit embossed with the Hill Sports Management logo.

He called Taylor as he bounded down the stairs.

"I was just about to call you," she greeted, answering after the first ring. "I finished the last of your meal prep. I should be there in about an hour."

"Hey, I'm sorry, but I'm going to have to cancel our workout for today and tomorrow," he said. "I need to go home—to Katy," he clarified.

"Is everything okay?" Concern colored her voice.

"I'm not sure. A close..." How could he describe Silas's grandfather? He wasn't just a family friend. He was so much more than that. "The grandfather of a really close friend is in the hospital. I need to make sure he's okay."

"Do you want me to come with you?"

Her question sent a wave of gratitude through him. That she would even offer meant more to him than he could describe right now. But accepting her offer meant having to tell her about Silas, and he wasn't ready for that. Not yet.

"Thanks, but I'll be okay on my own," Jamar answered. "I may even be back tonight. According to my friend's granddaughter, he'll be out of the hospital soon. I just want to be there, to make sure he's okay. I'll let you know when I'm back."

"Okay," she said. "Are you driving?"

"Yeah. I can usually make it home in two and a half hours, even less than that if I push the speed limit."

"How about you *not* do that," she said in a warning tone. "Be safe on the road. I hope everything is okay with your friend."

"Thanks, Taylor."

For a minute, he thought about reversing course and accepting her offer to join him. But that would create an entirely different set of questions he wasn't up for fielding right now.

His mom had asked about Taylor the last time she called, after several of her coworkers and friends sent her links to the online chatter that had popped up over the past couple of weeks. He'd avoided the third degree by suggesting that his and Taylor's relationship wasn't as serious as the Internet was making it out to be. If he showed up in Katy with Taylor in tow, Jamar would have some serious explaining to do.

He climbed into the Range Rover, then spent the drive in silent prayer that Big Silas was okay.

A sad smile pulled at the corner of Jamar's mouth. Big Silas had been like a surrogate grandfather to him. He'd treated Jamar no differently than he treated his own grandson, who he'd raised along with Silas's sister after their mother was sent to prison for life for killing their father.

Silas was the stereotype the media loved to perpetuate.

He and his sister had spent their early years with heroin junkies for parents, who would leave their two young kids for days at a time. Once he was granted custody, Big Silas had scraped together whatever he could find to take care of his grandchildren. It hadn't been easy for a disabled vet with emphysema and little income coming in from side jobs, but he'd made it work. It had taken Jamar far too long to realize just what his mom was doing when she sent Silas home with so many leftovers on the frequent nights when he would join them for dinner.

While most kids with after-school jobs spent their paycheck on the latest pair of Air Jordans or Madden video game, Silas used his to buy groceries and toilet paper. When they would talk about what they would do with the money from their first big NFL contract, the first thing Silas spoke about was fixing up his grandfather's house, because he knew Big Silas would never move into a brand-new one.

After he signed with the Bears, Jamar made sure that small two-bedroom house on the outskirts of Katy was renovated before he bought his own house. He'd vowed to Silas on his deathbed that he would take care of his grandfather and sister. He even put money on Rashida Cannon's books at the maximum security prison in Gatesville every month, because he knew Silas would want him to take care of his mother too.

Despite Taylor's warning, Jamar made it to Katy in just over two hours. He pulled into a parking spot at the VA clinic on Westgreen and went straight for the information desk. He was directed to a room down the hall.

His heart dropped when he walked in and found the bed empty.

"God, please no."

"Jamar? What are you doing here?"

He whipped around to find Andrea stirring coffee in a foam cup.

"Drea, how is he? *Where* is he?"

"They took him to get X-rays," she said. She set the coffee on the rolling tray that was against the wall, then turned to Jamar, enveloping him in a hug. She slapped him on the back of the head. "Why did you come all the way here? I told you he would be okay."

"I had to see him with my own eyes," Jamar said. He gave her a squeeze before releasing her. "What happened?"

Drea rolled her eyes as she picked up her coffee. "Well, first, he cut himself trying to open a can of tuna. And then, as he was looking in the bathroom cabinet for something to use as a bandage, he fell." She took a sip, then set it back down. "They don't think anything is broken, but it's possible that he bruised a couple of ribs."

She walked over to the bed where the red and black plaid flannel shirt Big Silas wore all the time lay crumpled against the thin pillow. She picked it up and started to fold it.

She was stalling.

"What is it?" Jamar asked.

"The doctor thinks he needs round-the-clock care," she said, releasing a deep sigh. "His home health nurse has been a godsend, but she's only there for a few hours a day. It's a good thing this happened *before* her visit, because if it had happened after, he would have spent the entire night on the bathroom floor. I had already called to do my daily check on him before starting my shift, so I wouldn't have even thought to call until tomorrow." She closed her eyes and shook her head. "I think about what could have happened and it just . . ."

"Don't think about that," Jamar said. "We'll get him in a facility that can offer him round-the-clock care, or if he still doesn't want to leave the house, we can hire a live-in nurse to look after him."

Andrea placed the shirt on the bed and then folded her arms over her stomach. "Look, I know you've made this pledge to Silas, but I can't ask you to pay for long-term care for my grandfather."

"You're not asking," Jamar said.

"Jamar—"

"I mean it, Drea. He may not be my grandfather by blood, but he is in every other way."

She shook her head, a somber smile pulling at her lips. "You're just as stubborn as my brother was."

"Wrong. I'm *way* more stubborn than Silas was."

"I can't argue with that," she said with a laugh. She made her way back to where he stood, just inside the door to the small hospital room. "He would have been so proud of you," Drea said, kissing his cheek. "Thank you for always being there for us."

The weight of her words settled heavy in Jamar's chest.

Money wasn't at the top of his list of reasons for wanting to return to the League. Fulfilling his promise to Silas that he would have the career they'd both dreamed of and shoving crow into the mouths of those haters who counted him out following his knee injury both ranked higher. But Jamar couldn't deny that a new NFL contract would go a long way in helping to take care of both his family and Silas's family for decades to come.

This quest to make it back into the League wasn't just about him; it was about all the other people in his life that he wanted—needed—to provide for. Drea's words drove home just how stupid and irresponsible it was to get caught up in all these feelings for Taylor. He'd hired her for a reason, and she was damn good at her job. He would not allow his overexcited dick to mess things up. Too many people were counting on him.

Just then, the door swung open and Big Silas was wheeled into the room by a harried-looking nursing assistant. Jamar got another earful from him about making the drive from Austin, but then he and Drea spent the next half hour laughing as Big Silas regaled them with the latest stories of him and his dominoes buddies.

The nurse came in carrying two small plastic cups. She scanned the hospital bracelet, then explained each medication as she handed the tiny cups to Big Silas.

"Radiology will be here in about ten minutes to take you up for your CT scan."

"It looks as if they have everything under control here," Jamar said once the nurse left the room. "I should probably head over to see my folks." He shoved one hand in his pocket and rubbed the back of his neck with the other, preparing himself for pushback.

He glanced at Drea, who stood with her arms crossed over her chest.

"So...umm...Big Silas," Jamar started. "As I was driving in, I noticed that new place they built out there on Bartlett Road. The one with the nice fountain in front."

"That old folks home?" Big Silas asked.

"It's called an assisted-living facility," Drea said.

"I don't care what *they* call it. *I* know it's an old folks home. Now why you bringing it up?"

Jamar raised his hands. "I was just saying how nice it is. You know...with the fountain and everything."

This conversation had gone a lot differently in his head. He looked to Drea, waiting for her to back him up. She just stared at him, her eyes teeming with *I told you so*.

He stared back at her and tipped his head toward her grandfather.

"We don't have to talk about any of this now," Drea said as she unfolded the plaid shirt and draped it across Big Silas's bony shoulders. "I'll stay at the house for a few days once they spring you loose from this place."

Jamar nodded in agreement. He would call Drea once he was back in Austin and they would come up with an alternate game plan. Maybe they could convince him to give the live-in nurse a chance.

Once Jamar was assured that things were all good with Drea and Big Silas, he left the VA clinic and headed for his parents' house, or as he tended to refer to it: home. That seven-bedroom house he lived in back in Georgetown was the kind of place he'd always dreamed of living in. He'd paid cash for it, snatching it up for what his real estate agent considered a steal at five million. It was spacious and professionally decorated and had every bit of luxury he could ever hope for.

But it was the simple two-story ranch-style house with the basketball hoop attached to the garage that would always be home. He'd offered to buy his parents a new place when he made it to the NFL and had felt no small bit of relief when they'd turned him down. This house provided comfort when he needed it. His old bedroom remained a sanctuary that he could return to when he yearned for peace and quiet.

Although they wouldn't allow him to do too much to the house, Jamar had convinced his dad to let him add on the woodworking room he'd always wanted. This past summer he'd built his mom a "she shed" that his dad now complained about because she spent too much time in there.

He pulled up to the house, happy to find both their cars parked in the driveway. They weren't expecting him home for a few weeks yet—not until Thanksgiving. It would be fun to surprise them.

He used his house key to let himself inside.

"Hey," he called. "Anybody home?"

His question was initially met with silence, but then he heard, "Jamar?"

The panicked lilt to his mom's voice sent him racing to the kitchen.

Jamar made it to the arched entryway and stopped short. He wasn't sure if he wanted to burn his eyes out or go to his old room and cry.

His mom sat atop the kitchen counter, her skirt hiked up. She held her unbuttoned shirt tight over her breasts. His dad was bare-chested, his pants and belt gathered at his ankles.

"What are you doing here?" they yelled at him.

"Dying inside," Jamar answered.

He pivoted and started for the front door. He wasn't mature enough to accept the fact that his parents had sex. He would never be fucking mature enough for that.

"Jamar, come back here," his mother called.

"That's okay," he called over his shoulder. "I'll see you guys at Thanksgiving."

"Boy, would you get back here!" His mother caught him by the arm. She still held her shirt together with her fist.

Jamar squeezed his eyes shut. "Please button your shirt. God, I'm never surprising you guys again," he said. He went into the living room and plopped down on the sofa, propping his elbows on his thighs and cradling his head in his hands.

"You've got to expect to see some things you may not want to see when you come sneaking up on empty nesters."

He groaned. "I don't want to hear this."

His dad came into the room, his belt buckle still flapping. "What are you doing here?" he asked. "Why didn't you call?"

"I will be asking myself that same question for the rest of my natural-born life," Jamar said.

He told them about Big Silas's medical scare. They then informed him that they'd booked a last-minute cruise out of Galveston that was leaving the Monday before Thanksgiving.

"So you won't be here for Thanksgiving? When were you going to tell me?" Jamar asked.

"Today," his mom answered. "After I finished thanking your dad for the cruise. That's what you interrupted."

"That's it, I'm out." He pushed up from the sofa.

"Oh, stop." His mom laughed. As if *any* of this shit was funny. "You really need to lighten up," she added.

So now he was a prude. Great.

He hugged them both goodbye and left the house, wondering why mind bleach wasn't an actual thing.

For the entire drive home, all Jamar could think of was how messed up it was that his fifty-year-old dad was getting laid more than he was these days.

CHAPTER NINETEEN

W hat if it was wrapped in bacon?"

Jamar sat back in his chair and casually traced his finger along a crude drawing of the Longhorns emblem someone had carved into the table's scarred surface.

"Nope," he answered, failing to suppress his grin.

"Bullshit!" Taylor's indignation was genuine as she held up her fork. "You're telling me you wouldn't eat this if there was a thick, crispy, perfectly cooked slice of bacon surrounding it?"

"Regardless of what most people think, bacon doesn't make everything better. I would not eat a brussels sprout, even if it was wrapped in bacon."

"You don't know what you're missing," she said, slipping the fork in her mouth.

"I don't mind not knowing everything, especially when it comes to those little baby cabbages."

She rolled her eyes in that way Jamar had come to expect when she couldn't force him to see things her way. Sometimes he only pretended to have an opposing view in hopes of eliciting that pout. He fucking loved that pout.

It killed him that she had yet to acknowledge their kiss on

Mount Bonnell. He'd lost count of the number of times he'd had to stop himself from forcing the issue this past week, but what would he say? *I know we agreed that this whole dating thing was just a ruse, but you're funny, and you sincerely care about other people, and you're hot as fuck, so why don't we just forget about pretending?*

Yeah, that would go over *real* well.

Taylor stabbed another brussels sprout and pointed it at him. "You never told me about Hou—"

Her words were drowned out by an eruption of cheers.

Jamar glanced at the fifty-two-inch flat screen mounted above their table and discovered why. He took a long pull on his beer, washing down the mix of longing, nostalgia, and jealousy that collected in his throat as he watched UT's running back eat up yardage on his journey to the end zone.

The foot stomping and overall chaos from the people surrounding them caused the walls of the Tavern, one of Austin's oldest sports bars, to vibrate with unrestrained excitement. As with the previous three touchdowns, a host of fans came up to Jamar and Taylor's table to offer high fives.

He reminded himself that interacting with the public— having them see him out with Taylor—was the main reason they chose to come to this bar to watch one of the most anticipated games of the season. Though tempting, asking Taylor to move to one of the more secluded tables would defeat the purpose of their being here.

"I guess the Longhorns did something good," Taylor said once the volume in the sports bar had returned to just below jackhammering at a rock concert decibels. She propped both elbows on the table and leaned toward him. "As I was saying, you haven't mentioned your trip to Houston. Is everything okay?"

"It is now," Jamar answered. "Well, except for the fact that I walked in on my parents in an...umm...compromising position on the kitchen counter. I'll never be the same again."

"Oh, God, no. That is the worst! It happened to me when I was eight. My mom said they were wrestling, so I ran in the bed and joined them. Needless to say, it didn't end well. And I'm sorry to confirm it, but you're right, you will never be the same."

"I'm trying to put the entire ordeal out of my mind."

She barked out a laugh. "Good luck with that."

"You're having too much fun at my expense," Jamar said.

"I'm laughing *with* you," she said. "So what was the point of your trip to Houston, other than an impromptu visit to surprise your parents that went horribly wrong? I thought it was an emergency. You sounded...I don't know...unsettled when you called to cancel our session."

"I was a lot unsettled," he said.

He glanced up at the screen just in time to see Texas Tech's kick returner get clobbered in a bruising tackle. Jamar winced, recalling with painful clarity how it felt to have 260 pounds of muscle crashing into him at twenty miles an hour. That was one thing he *didn't* miss about football.

"A friend—no, more than just a friend," he corrected. "A man who is like a grandfather to me suffered a fall and ended up in the emergency room. He's the grandfather of my best friend from high school."

"Silas Cannon?" she asked.

Jamar's shoulders stiffened with shock. How did she know about Silas?

As if she'd heard the question in his head, she continued. "My friend Samiah is from the Houston area. She told me about your friend Silas and, well, what happened to him. You should have told me," she said in an accusatory tone. "I had to find out the full story from Google."

"Or you could have called or texted me," he said with a casualness he didn't feel. He was still trying to process the fact that she knew about Silas and hadn't said anything. "In the future, if there's anything you want to know, that's all you have to do. I'm a much better resource than Google."

"I don't think so," she said. "Google is how I discovered that you ran track in high school. You should have told me that too."

"It sounds as if Googling me is now a favorite pastime for you."

She laughed. "Don't flatter yourself, Twenty-Three. After witnessing the way people go crazy over you, I had to find out what all the hype was about. It was obvious that I was missing something."

"Ouch." He slapped a hand to his chest as if covering a wound. "You know, as my trainer, you can do a slightly better job at pumping up my ego instead of taking a sledge-hammer to it."

"You hired me to build up your muscles, not your ego." The amusement glittering in her eyes dimmed as her soft smile sobered. "I'm sorry about your friend. It must have been so hard to lose him."

"He was my brother in every way but blood," Jamar said. "I know there are things I may face in the future that would possibly be harder than losing Silas, but it's hard to imagine them."

It wasn't lost on him just how rare it was to talk about his Houston ties with anyone. He recognized the shift it signified in how he regarded Taylor. He'd never discussed Silas in even the most superficial way with any of the women he'd dated in the past.

Of course, none of his past relationships had been deeper than those kiddie pools they sold at Target, but this revealed a lot about what was happening between them. He felt...comfortable with Taylor. More comfortable than he'd felt with anyone else in so long.

"Anyway," Jamar continued. "Big Silas—that's what everyone calls Silas's grandfather—he needs round-the-clock care, but he's stubborn as hell. Silas's sister, Andrea, is looking into hiring a full-time nurse." He caught her gaze and did his best to communicate how important this was to him. "I want to make sure Big Silas gets the best care possible, not just right now, but for the rest of his life."

Jamar could tell the exact moment she caught the meaning behind his words. She nodded, then reached for his hand, lacing her fingers through his.

To anyone looking at them, they would appear to be a normal couple on a date, sharing a relaxed smile as they held hands. He rubbed his thumb back and forth across her wrist, sending a silent message of gratitude for the way she just sat and listened as he talked about people she didn't even know. It meant so damn much to him.

After several more moments passed, she gave his hand a reassuring squeeze before letting it go.

"So this game we're watching, what's so important about it?" she asked in a voice that was meant for others to hear.

"Texas versus Texas Tech? The honor of winning the Chancellor's Spurs trophy? You're kidding me, right? Even if you don't follow college football, you can't live in Austin and not understand the importance of this game."

She hunched her shoulders. "Sorry to burst your bubble, Twenty-Three. I've been here almost two years and I have no idea what any of it means."

Jamar ran a hand down his face. "I still have so, so much to teach you."

The server came around with a second round of drinks for them. Jamar started to order more wings, but Taylor stopped him.

"I can't eat any more."

"You sure?" he asked.

She looked up at the server and said, "Thanks. We're good with the drinks." Once the guy had left the table, she looked over at Jamar with a sly smile. "You think you're slick. I know you were just trying to prolong your splurge meal."

He pointed at his chest. "Me? Never."

She rolled her eyes as she lifted the laminated menu from the condiment holder in the center of the table.

"I'll agree to dessert, but only if we split it."

Jamar observed the way her lips moved as she read over the menu, even though she wasn't speaking loud enough for him to hear. This wasn't the first time he'd noticed her doing that.

"Hey, have you—"

"Looks like we got ourselves a star in the house," a brash, inebriated voice called from somewhere nearby. "None other than Diesel Dixon. That is you, isn't it, Diesel?"

He glanced in the direction of where the voice had come from. There was a group of guys sitting two tables over, dressed head to toe in Texas Tech red and black.

Shit.

He was hoping this would be a case of quickly appeasing a

couple of tipsy fans with an autograph or two, maybe a couple of selfies. But these guys didn't want his autograph.

"You here living out your glory days, Diesel?"

Taylor hooked a thumb toward the table of four. "Who's that?"

Jamar made a cutting gesture with his hands. "Nobody. Don't worry about them."

Several of the other fans in the sports bar had turned their attention from the TV screens. Jamar knew he needed to defuse the situation before this got out of hand.

"Don't worry about these guys," he said loud enough for those at the surrounding tables to hear. He infused amusement into his voice in an attempt to convey an air of joviality he wasn't really feeling.

"Yeah, Diesel was all big and bad when he played for those Longhorns," the guy continued, his words slurred. "The boys in the NFL showed you what *real* football is about, ain't that right? How's that knee treating you?"

Taylor twisted around in her seat.

"Taylor," Jamar warned, but it was too late. Poor bastards.

"Has your skinny ass ever even played football?" she asked the mouthy one. "Why don't you just shut up and watch the game."

There were murmurs of agreement from some of the other patrons.

The guy cackled. "Oh, you got your girl fighting your battles for you?"

"I don't need—" Jamar started, but Taylor talked right over him.

"He knows that I can kick your ass with one hand while I finish eating my cheese fries with the other. Why should he waste the effort?"

The guys at the table burst out laughing, but Jamar wasn't willing to take a chance that their good-natured ribbing wouldn't turn ugly. He stood and made another attempt to lighten the mood.

"I'd watch what I say around her if I were you," Jamar said with a laugh. "Not only could she kick your asses, but she would have fun doing it." He threw a hundred-dollar bill on the table. "Let's get out of here, Taylor. Maybe if the Raiders had come to play, it'd be a game worth watching."

Jamar did his best to ignore the table of heckling Texas Tech fans as he and Taylor headed out of the sports bar. He reminded the offended Longhorns faithfuls to ignore the guys. The last thing anyone needed was a brawl to break out.

Breathing a sigh of relief once they exited the Tavern, he glanced over at Taylor and grinned.

"You really were ready to kick some ass, weren't you?"

"Hell yes," she said. She hooked a thumb back at the sports bar. "Is this the kind of bullshit you've had to put up with since you got hurt?"

He shrugged as he opened the door of his SUV and helped her into it.

"Usually guys aren't that drunk this early in the day," he said. "But, yeah, I get some version of that at least once a month."

"How haven't you landed yourself in jail on an assault charge!"

"You're cute as hell when you're angry on my behalf," Jamar said.

"I don't want to be cute. I want to go back there and kick that guy in the face." She caught his arm before he could close the door. "This shit just became personal. If it means shutting up assholes like the ones we just had to deal with, I'm ready to do whatever I have to do to get you on a football team."

"It sounds as if I'm going to have to suffer even more in the gym because of these guys."

"In the gym *and* out of it," she said. "It starts tonight with our survivalist training."

Jamar winced. She'd asked him to join her for some lost-in-the-woods-type experience she wanted to develop for Taylor'd Conditioning. Even as he'd agreed to tag along, he knew he'd live to regret it.

"Are we still doing that?" Jamar asked.

"You bet your ass we are," Taylor said. "Get ready to rough it."

CHAPTER TWENTY

The last fading rays of sunlight cast dappled shadows on the leaf-covered ground of Pace Bend Park. Taylor led the way through the uneven terrain, trying her best to avoid unwelcome surprises left by the critters who called this densely forested patch of land home.

She'd considered a number of local parks for tonight's adventure but had settled on this one in Spicewood because of its primitive campsites that would give them the "roughing it in the woods" experience she was going for.

She and Jamar had veered off the marked trail a good half mile back. They should be nearing the innermost area of the park soon.

"Let's stop for a second," Taylor said. "I need to get my bearings." She reached into one of the zippered pouches on her backpack and pulled out her compass.

"Is that a compass?" Jamar asked.

She laughed at the incredulity in his tone. "Why do you sound so surprised?"

He slipped his phone from his pocket, swiped his thumb across the screen, then held it up to her. "Not sure if you know this, but these cool little computers that fit in your pocket? They come equipped with a compass."

"Ha ha, smart-ass. What if that cool little pocket-sized computer doesn't have cell service, or worse, what if you lose it? Knowing how to use an actual compass can be a lifesaver." She studied the compass and confirmed that they were still headed in the right direction. "Remember, the whole point of this exercise is to be a survivalist. At least that's what I'm hoping people will sign up for."

Taylor had convinced him to join her on the test run of the survivalist camp experience she planned to offer on Samiah's Just Friends app. She'd been honored when her friend asked her to put together a curated experience for Taylor'd Conditioning.

They continued their hike, maneuvering around the remnants of a dank, crumbling log. Fallen leaves carpeted the earth, their crunch seeming to get louder as darkness fell.

"We'll need to pick up the pace if we're going to make it to the campsite before the sun goes down," Taylor said.

"Tell me," Jamar called from just behind her. "Did you consider how cold it would be before you decided to do this?"

Taylor raised her voice to be heard above the crunching pine needles underfoot. "Survivalists don't get to pick the weather on the night they get stranded. The point of this exercise is endurance. I'm building this for those people who want to put themselves to the test. Who want to see just how far they can push themselves, and then push a little more. And have fun while doing it."

"Maybe I should pull up my Dictionary app and show you the definition of *fun*. Something tells me you still don't know what that word means."

"And something tells me that you're still a crappy comedian."

"Admit it. My jokes are growing on you."

"I will not admit to any such thing," she said, unable to mask the amusement in her voice.

The fact is, *he* was growing on her.

For the hundredth time, she fought the urge to suggest they end this ridiculous game where they pretended they didn't want each other. She only had to say the word. There wasn't a doubt in her mind that Jamar would be ready, willing, and able to pick up where they'd left off on Mount Bonnell.

She wouldn't have to rely on her vibrator and the memories of that afternoon for relief. He would give her the release her body so desperately craved.

She ignored the hot, growing ache in her belly and continued on their hike.

Using the compass, she navigated them to the spot she'd picked out to spend the night. Because of an ongoing drought, they were not allowed to use the fire rings, so they would have to make do with thermal blankets and their sleeping bags.

Taylor unrolled the blankets from her backpack, then unhooked the bag that held her tent, which Jamar had carried strapped to his back. When he tried to help her, she shooed him away.

"I appreciate the chivalry, but I want to prove that I can do this."

"You plan on getting lost in the woods?"

"Does anyone *ever* plan on getting lost in the woods?" She looked back at him over her shoulder. "You are not getting into the spirit of this. I'm extremely disappointed."

"You're right. I'm sorry," he said. She thought he was sincere until he added, "Should I go chew on some tree bark or find some bugs for dinner? That's the kind of stuff they eat on *Survivor*, right?"

She pitched a skinny tree branch at him. "Smart-ass."

His rumbling laugh sounded even louder in the quiet of the forest.

She refused to give him the satisfaction of laughing with him as she watched him out of the corner of her eye. He unpacked his knapsack and cleared away some of the larger branches that had fallen to the ground.

She should be happy that he'd agreed to camp out with her this cold November evening. It was more than any of her past boyfriends had ever done.

Except Jamar *wasn't* really her boyfriend. He wasn't her significant anything. He was a client—a client whose dick had been pressed up against her as he kissed her against a tree, but still just a client.

Taylor stifled a groan.

She excused herself and went in search of the waterless toilets placed throughout the campground. According to the map, there was one about thirty yards from their campsite.

When she returned, she found Jamar sitting on a fallen tree that had no doubt served as a couch to many campers in the past. He was bundled up in his thermal blanket with . . . was that . . . ?

"Is that a heater?" Taylor asked.

"You said we wouldn't be able to start a fire. You didn't expect me to sleep out in forty-degree temperatures without some form of heat, did you?"

She guessed that was a bridge too far.

"Is this thing battery operated?" she asked.

He nodded. "I had Amazon overnight it." He patted the downed tree. "Come on. It's warm."

She was about to tell him no, but then a brisk wind blew, rattling the trees overhead and cutting through her jacket like a sharp knife. She skittered over to his sofa log and huddled in beside him.

"Okay, yeah, this is much better," she admitted.

"Told you." He pulled her in tighter. "Now, if we *really* wanted to warm up, I've heard body heat is the best kind of heat."

"That's such a weak come-on." She laughed. "It's a good thing you're rich and adorable, because your flirting game is trash."

"It's the best I can do with a tree knob jabbing my ass." He turned the dial up a notch on the heater. "And what's up with calling me adorable? Adorable is for koala bears."

"Sorry." She hunched her shoulders in apology. "It's not my fault you're adorable. Take that up with your parents. You know, when you can look them in the eye again."

"That's not funny."

Taylor bit her bottom lip in an effort not to laugh, but she couldn't hold it in. "I'm so sorry. I promise to never tease you about it again. Unless you end up with a new little brother or sister, then all bets are off."

"That was brutal," he said, doubling over as if she'd punched him in the gut. "If I didn't think I'd get lost on my way to the car, I would leave you out here."

"No you wouldn't," she said. "That was the last one. I will never bring up that subject again." She held up her pinky finger. "I swear."

"I don't believe you. Get that old stank finger away from me."

Now *she* was the one doubling over. Taylor laughed until her sides hurt. The fact that his face remained stoic just made her laugh harder.

"You done?" he asked.

She wiped tears from her eyes. "I am," she said. She was

relieved to see the hint of a smile playing at the corner of his mouth.

"So, what do we do out here in the wilderness?"

"That's what we're supposed to figure out, although I'm not sure we're doing the best job of it. True survivalists wouldn't have a tent, or a heater, or a backpack full of turkey jerky, protein bars, and wine in a can."

"You have wine? Crack that shit open."

Taylor hooked the toe of her hiking boot under the strap of her backpack and dragged it closer. She unzipped it and pulled out two cans of cabernet and a bag of pistachios.

"This is only a trial run, so it's not as if we have to do everything the people who sign up for the experience will do. I just wanted to get a feel for the area."

"I think you wanted to get me out here in the wild so you could have your way with me," Jamar said.

"Your jokes are still corny, but you *are* getting better at flirting," she said. "As for the survivalist workout, I think the three-mile hike, along with having to put together a shelter—with materials that I'll bring in ahead of time, of course—and foraging for food will be enough. That sounds like fun, doesn't it?"

"There you go again with that twisted idea of fun. Your family must love when it's your turn to come up with the holiday activities."

"Yeah, as if they would ever allow me to do that," Taylor said with a snort.

The amusement faded from his expression. "Why wouldn't they?"

She shrugged. "They just wouldn't. I'm kind of the black sheep, so when it comes to family fun, I'm usually not consulted."

"What did you do? Try to force them to eat kale too?"

"Ha," she deadpanned. "You're still not funny."

"Come on. You have to give me credit for that one."

"Nope."

"Well, at least tell me why you're the black sheep of the family."

"You don't deserve the story."

He caught one of her braids and brushed it along her cheek. "Please, my life will not be complete until I hear how you earned the title of the Powell Family Black Sheep. I'll bet it was joyriding. You probably took the car out for a spin every chance you got."

"I did," she confirmed with a laugh. "But my reign as the black sheep began long before that. I probably was five years old."

"You became the black sheep of the family at *five*?"

"Will you let me tell my story, please?"

He motioned for her to continue. "I promise not to interrupt again. Unless you say something that's completely outrageous, like you being labeled the black sheep of the family at five years old. Because that's a pretty messed up thing to do to a kid."

"No one treated me like a black sheep when I was five, but that's when the foundation was laid. It started when my mom decided to go to law school." She tucked her braids behind her ears. "How much do you know about military life?"

"The only people I know who are active duty are a couple of classmates from high school. I'm not close to them or anything."

"The thing most civilians don't realize about military life is that it can be just as hard on the families of service members as it is on those who are serving, whether in wartime or peacetime."

"Is there even such a thing as peacetime? Seems as if we've been in one war or another for as long as I've been alive."

"That's true," she said ruefully. "My dad has served in most of them. He received a Bronze Star and continues to dedicate his life to the military. But he would be the first to say that he didn't reach that level of success on his own. While he was off fighting wars, my mom was taking care of the family while moving from one military base to another.

"For most people in that situation, the idea of obtaining a law degree would feel impossible. But not for my mom. She earned her degree and never missed a beat."

"I guess those are some extremely high standards to live up to."

"I'm not sure 'extremely high' is adequate to describe just how hard it is to measure up to those standards. She's Wonder Woman, but with just a little more wonder to her. My brother and sister are in a competition to see who will reach Gail Powell status first."

"What do they do?"

"My brother is a lawyer, of course. You only have to be in his presence for five minutes to know that nothing brings him more joy than arguing that he is right on just about every subject."

"He sounds like a bucket of laughs," Jamar said in a flat tone. "What about your sister?"

"Jesamyn. She's an architect. She's a lot more mellow than Darwin, but her analytical brain is always running at full speed. It's intimidating to even start a conversation with her." She gave him a playful nudge with her elbow. "I think you would do okay, though. She can be a bit of a snob, so she would automatically think you're a dumb jock. I'd love to see you go head-to-head with her while watching *Jeopardy!*"

"You think I'd have a chance?"

"I think you'd give her a pretty good run for her money," Taylor said. "And when she discovers that you *aren't* a dumb jock, she would spend the next hour talking your head off. Me and Chester—that's my brother-in-law—have this special signal we send to each other when Jesamyn gets going. You see, Chester is of average intelligence like me, which is probably why I feel more of a kinship with him than with my blood relatives."

"Average intelligence? I think you're smarter than you let on."

"Hey, I'm not saying that I'm a dummy or anything," she said. "But I know I'm no Einstein either."

"Einstein had an IQ of one sixty. Less than one percent of the world's population is an Einstein."

"And probably less than that can rattle off Einstein's IQ and the number of people who share it," Taylor pointed out. "And there's nothing wrong with being average. Did you know that Walt Disney never went to college? He took a few night classes at the Art Institute of Chicago while in high school, but he didn't get a degree. I'll bet people considered him average before he created Oswald the Rabbit and changed the entertainment industry forever."

Jamar reached over and captured her chin with his fingers. They were warm after being tucked inside his jacket pockets.

"I repeat, there is nothing average about you," he said. His eyes fell to her lips and Taylor forgot how to pull air into her lungs.

"Taylor." His voice was a whisper. "We have to eventually talk about that kiss and what it means."

Her head snapped back. "No, we don't."

"Taylor—"

She shrugged off the blanket and stood. "I need to gather firewood."

"We're not building a fire," he reminded her.

"Then I need to go to the bathroom," she said as she took off for the toilets again.

Let him think she had a tiny bladder, or irritable bowel syndrome, or whatever.

You are such *a coward!*

Fine, so she was a coward. She'd wear the label this one time if it meant evading talk about that kiss. Taylor knew she'd have to face the implications of it sooner or later, but she was willing to do all she could to avoid it for as long as possible.

She walked around for twenty minutes, collecting twigs and other kindling that could be used to start a fire if they really were stranded in the forest. If Jamar asked why she'd been gone for so long, she could use the excuse of wanting to give clients a more authentic experience by gathering fire-making materials.

She returned to their campsite to find an orange and gray tent that resembled a space pod set up near the downed tree sofa. Jamar was nowhere in sight, but he had unfolded her army-green tent and laid it on the ground, its metal poles and stakes strewn across it. Was this his way of telling her that she was sleeping in her own tent *and* she had to assemble it herself?

Taylor was upset at just how upset she was. Sure, she'd told him that she wanted to do this on her own, but it was the principle of it. He was her pretend boyfriend, for crying out loud!

"Hey, you're back," he said.

She whipped around and tracked him with her gaze as he made his way to the orange tent.

"I did try to put yours together, even though you wanted to do it yourself. But it was too complicated." He hooked his thumb at his tent. "I had this overnighted from Amazon too. It's even bigger than I thought it would be, and only about the size of a roll of paper towels when it's stored away."

"Hmm, how nice," Taylor said, walking to her tent.

"Where are you going? I'm not sleeping in this tent by myself. Body heat, remember?"

"So you want me in there with you?" Taylor asked.

He gave her a look that said, *What do you think?*

The rush of relief and exhilaration she felt was so annoying. She wasn't supposed to *want* him to want her.

Taylor took a step toward the tent, then stopped. "I shouldn't have to say this, but I'm saying it anyway. Nothing is happening in there except for sleep."

"Is talking allowed?" he asked.

Smart-ass. "It depends on what you want to talk about."

"Fine, Taylor. Can we please just go in there before the hypothermia sets in?"

"It's not even that cold out here," she said. Once again, the elements chose that moment to prove her wrong as a stiff breeze whipped up the leaves around their feet.

Taylor grabbed her thermal blanket and scrambled inside the tent's arched opening. Jamar crawled in behind her, bringing the battery-operated heater.

"What now?" Taylor asked.

"I would tell you my suggestion, but I don't want an elbow to the gut," he said as he arranged his unzipped sleeping bag on the floor of the tent, making a bed for them. He stretched hers out on top of it.

"I know what we can do," he said. He slipped between the sleeping bags and turned down the top edge so that she could get in. "I have season two of *Stranger Things* on my phone. We can watch that."

"Don't you need Wi-Fi to stream TV shows?" She held both hands up. "Please don't tell me you brought a Wi-Fi hub."

"I did, actually, but we don't need it. I downloaded it to my phone." He patted her side of their makeshift bed. "Come on."

Taylor knew she should feel more reluctance at crawling underneath the covers with him, but the fluffy sleeping bags looked too inviting for her not to do it. She settled in next to him, taking care not to brush against him. He immediately negated her efforts by shifting over a few inches so that their arms touched from shoulder to wrist.

Halfway through the first episode, Taylor said, "I'm not sure this is the best thing for me to watch while out in the woods alone."

"Except that you're not alone," he said, his eyes bright with amusement.

"Don't go getting any ideas, Twenty-Three." She scooted even closer to him and wrapped her arm around his. "This is for heat and just in case I get scared. That's it. Nothing else."

"Whatever you say," he replied. "Will there at least be a good night kiss?"

"No! Absolutely not."

Because Taylor knew she wouldn't want to stop at a single kiss, not when they were both snuggled up against each other with the entire night stretching in front of them.

CHAPTER TWENTY-ONE

Taylor reached over to the coffee table in Jamar's living room and picked up the touch-screen display panel that controlled everything, from the room's temperature, to the lights, to the television. She glided her thumb along the screen, bringing the temperature up a couple of degrees. Then she set the electronic tablet back in its cradle and returned her attention to her laptop.

"Where in the hell is it?" Taylor growled as she clicked through the five billion tabs open on her browser, searching for the article on ligament tears she'd run across this morning. One of these days she would learn to bookmark websites she wanted to revisit.

"Finally," Taylor said as she clicked onto the article without bookmarking it.

Ever since the run-in with those drunken assholes at the sports bar Saturday afternoon, she'd turned into a woman on a mission. If Jamar thought she'd worked him hard before, he wasn't ready for the nightmare she was about to unleash. She would do whatever it took to ensure he was in the best form possible when he tried out for those NFL teams.

From the extensive research she'd done on his knee surgery,

Taylor now understood how lucky Jamar was that he could even walk. He'd undergone a massive amount of physical therapy after the operation. Yet, because of the severity of the injury and the threat of reinjuring himself, he was still considered a huge risk for any team to undertake.

But there was still a chance, and that's all that mattered. All she needed was the slightest bit of hope.

She'd just clicked on another video uploaded by an orthopedic surgeon when she heard Jamar approaching. She twisted on the sofa to find him walking toward her with a huge smile on his face and a casserole dish in his hands.

"I finally found a brussels sprouts recipe I like. Try it." He held it out to her with the enthusiasm of a kindergartener presenting his teacher with a finger-painting. He was as adorable as one too.

Taylor was bowled over by the memory of waking up next to him in that tent Sunday morning, his arms surrounding her, the front of his body flush against the back of hers. She didn't know exactly when the spooning had occurred, but if things were different between them, Taylor would be just fine waking up that way for the next few decades.

Don't go there.

She attempted to ignore his cuteness and those memories as she surveyed the dish. There was twice as much cheese as brussels sprouts.

"You could eat this if today was a cheat day—by the way, you're out of those for the rest of the week," she reminded him. "But unless this is a healthy vegan cheese, it won't work with your diet."

"I'm not eating fake cheese."

"Well, say goodbye to these cheesy brussels sprouts." She

grabbed at the casserole dish, but he stretched it aloft, just out of her reach.

He gestured at the screen with his chin. "What are you watching?"

"I've been doing more research on your injury."

"Hmm...that looks like my orthopedic surgeon, Dr. Hoffman," he said.

"I know. He's pretty fancy," Taylor said.

"Yeah. The League wanted me to have the best care money could buy."

"So, was it Dr. Hoffman who told you that you would never play football again?"

"Actually, Dr. Hoffman was optimistic about my chances," he said as he lifted a brussels sprout from the casserole dish.

Taylor snatched it from his fingers and popped it in her mouth. "Damn, this *is* good," she said. She patted the sofa next to her, encouraging him to sit. "Come on. We'll just add more time to today's workout. And if Dr. Hoffman was so optimistic, why aren't you playing?"

"Because it was the team's doctor who made the final call. Micah and I have talked about it—Micah is my agent," he clarified as he sat down. "And we both think that it has more to do with the team doctor thinking I wasn't worth the risk if I were to suffer a second injury. He was looking toward the future. That's his job. At the end of the day, he has to do what's best for the team."

Taylor shook her head. "It's crazy to me that a world-renowned surgeon can declare you fit to play, yet no team will sign you."

"The NFL is a different kind of beast. What makes sense in everyday life doesn't necessarily fly when it comes to professional football." Caution clouded his voice. "I'm mentally preparing myself just in case this doesn't work out as planned. I know you don't like to talk about failure, Taylor, but I have to be realistic."

The compulsion to reject his words was automatic, but she stopped herself. He knew how the NFL worked better than she did. He'd told her once before that he could train as hard as possible, yet still fail to make it onto a team because of circumstances outside of their control. She would keep her objections to herself if this is what he needed to do in order to deal.

But she would also make damn sure he was as physically prepared as he could be. If he didn't make a team, it wouldn't be because she fell down on the job.

"I've been studying everything I can about what happened to your knee and developing a plan of attack that's even more detailed than before," Taylor said. "Those guys at that sports bar pissed me off. I hate, hate, *hate* that you have to put up with that kind of bullshit, and I want to personally feed them crow when you run onto an NFL field next year." She pointed to the legal pad on the table. "This is our new game plan."

He reached for the pad, but she snatched it up before he could.

"Hold on. Let me check a couple of things first." She started reading over the notes she'd written. After a minute or so, she looked up to find Jamar staring at her with a curious frown. "What?" she asked.

"Have you always done that? Mouthed your words?"

"Huh?"

"When you read? I noticed it at the restaurant the other day when you were looking over the menu. You were reading aloud—under your breath, but still aloud."

Taylor's defenses immediately went up. "So?"

"It's just an observation." He was quiet for a moment as he set the casserole dish on the coffee table. "Umm...Silas used to do the same thing. He said hearing the words spoken aloud helped him to comprehend them better than just reading the text."

Well, that made sense to her. "I don't understand what the big deal is," Taylor said.

"It's not a big deal. When we were in about the tenth grade, Silas was diagnosed with a learning disorder. It changed the way teachers—"

"We can go over your game plan later," she said. She set the legal pad on the coffee table. "We need to get going. I booked us for an hour at this new CrossFit gym in the city. If we don't leave now, we'll be late."

Taylor could tell by his pensive expression that he wanted to say more. She stared into his eyes, imploring him to drop it.

After a moment, he nodded and, in a subdued voice, said, "I'll meet you outside in ten minutes. I'll follow in my SUV so that you don't have to ride all the way back up here once we're done."

An hour later, Taylor's biceps burned like liquid fire as she counted down the last five hammer curls before instructing Jamar to stop.

"Holy shit," she said. "We're both going to pay for this in the morning."

She set the twenty-pound kettlebell back into the rack, then rubbed it down with a sanitizing wipe. She pulled a few more from the plastic container and did the same to the rest of the surfaces they'd touched during the high-intensity full-body circuit Jamar had just completed. This boutique CrossFit gym had been on her radar for a while now, but none of her previous clients had been willing to spend the money they charged to rent the space to nonmembers.

As much as she appreciated Jamar's personal gym, getting the chance to work him out on the gymnastic rings, rope-climbing wall, and monkey-bar rig was worth putting on a public show. Not that there was anyone here to watch the performance.

She'd chosen this particular place because they offered an exclusivity option on certain days of the week. They had two hours to themselves, and Taylor was going to make the most of it. They would both be exhausted by the time they were done.

She continued wiping down the surfaces, observing Jamar out of the corner of her eye as he replaced the athletic tape around his wrists and ankles.

Taylor had always considered herself a forearm kinda girl. Well-defined forearms on a man were her kryptonite. But Jamar's powerful, chiseled thighs made a convincing case for switching to the leg camp. Watching the way his inner thigh flexed as it peeked out of the hem of his shorts had her wanting to take a bite out of it.

You cannot bite your clients, Taylor Renee.

Maybe repeating those words in her mother's voice would help curb the unholy thoughts ravaging her brain.

"Doubt it," she murmured under her breath.

All it took was one simple kiss in the rain to fully embrace the idea of hooking up with her client. Not that there had been anything simple about that kiss, but did it warrant the constant ache it had set off in her pants? No!

Well, maybe.

After a week of pretending as if everything was normal, acting as if that kiss hadn't changed *everything*, Taylor was ready to climb the walls. Okay, fine. She was ready to climb *him*. But she wouldn't do either. She would be a professional and handle this like an adult. She and Jamar needed to air this out if she had any chance of surviving the remaining month with her sanity intact.

He finished taping up his ankles and jogged over to where she stood next to the free weights.

"Are you ready to get back to it?" he asked. "We're doing kickboxing next, right?"

"Um, yeah," Taylor said. She moved the ten-pound dumbbell back to its correct position, then started for the freestanding punching bag. After a couple of steps, Taylor stopped and turned. "Wait."

"Whoa." He caught her by the shoulders to prevent himself from running into her. "Watch yourself."

Taylor began to peel his fingers from her bicep before he quickly released her. She cleared her throat. "We need to talk about it. I'm *ready* to talk about it."

"About?"

"The kiss," she clarified. "We need to discuss it and stop pretending it didn't happen."

His brow arched a fraction as he took a step back, giving her space. "I agree," he said. "But for the record, I never said that we should pretend it didn't happen."

"I know," she said. She gestured to him. "Well...talk."

"Me? What do you want me to say? That I'm sorry we kissed?" He shook his head. "I'm not. That I don't want it to happen again? I can't say that either, unless you're okay with me lying to you."

A ball of angst rolled around like tumbleweed in the pit of her stomach.

Did you think this would be easy?

"I guess what my dad says is true," she said with a nervous laugh. "Don't ask a question if you're not ready for the answer."

"What did you expect me to say, Taylor?"

"I don't know. Maybe I *did* want you to lie. It would make things easier."

"No, it wouldn't." He looked over both shoulders before leaning forward and saying in a muted voice, "People already think we're a couple. If we both want this, why shouldn't we go ahead and follow through?"

"Because it doesn't matter what other people think." She crossed her arms over her chest, cradling her elbows in her hands. "I won't deny the attraction. We both know it's there. But I can't date you and work for you. It's a line I'm not willing to cross."

"So how do you explain that kiss?"

"That was...It was a one-time thing. I'd love to call it a mistake, but—" She shook her head. "I can't. It wasn't a mistake. But that doesn't mean it can happen again."

"Even though we both want it." He didn't frame it as a question, because there wasn't any question that, if circumstances were different, they would both be open to sharing so much more than just a kiss.

"It's not something I'm willing to even discuss." After a heartbeat, she added, "Not yet."

His brows peaked. "Yet?"

Taylor pulled her bottom lip between her teeth. She could only hope she didn't live to regret dangling this small bit of hope, but an all-out rejection of there ever being anything between them was too harsh to bear.

She lifted her shoulders in a hopeful shrug. "My contract ends in a month."

"So that's our only option?" He expelled a gruff, exasperated laugh. "Working together and being together—like, *really* being together—are mutually exclusive?"

"Yes," Taylor said with an emphatic nod. "That's the way it has to be, Jamar. Once we cross that threshold, lines get blurry and it's...it's just not something I'm willing to do." She lowered her voice, even though they had the gym to themselves. "Things are messy enough with this pretend dating thing. If we decide to explore a more..." She paused, trying to come up with the right word. *Intimate? Real?* "A *personal* relationship," Taylor continued, "it will have to wait until after we're done with our professional one."

A muscle flexed in his jaw as he chewed over her words.

"What if I don't want to give you up as a trainer?" he finally asked.

Taylor's head jerked back, her eyes narrowing. "Are you considering hiring me for longer than our original two-month agreement?"

"Why don't you answer my question first?" He stayed her with a hand. "Wait, no. Don't answer it." He pressed the heels of his palms against his eyes, then dragged both hands down his face. "You're right. *Fuck.*" He returned his gaze to her, his eyes fraught with frustration. "We shouldn't blur the lines."

"We shouldn't," Taylor said, as much as it pained her to admit it.

He huffed out a laugh. "You want some irony? I spent the entire drive here mentally rehearsing how to tell you this exact thing, how I couldn't allow what happened on Mount Bonnell to let me lose focus of my goal." He shook his head. "My trip back home put a lot of things into perspective for me, Taylor. I have *so* much riding on this. Not just me, but people I care about. I can't allow anything to distract me."

She folded her arms, grasping her elbows in her hands. "So? What does this mean?"

"That I'm back to taking cold showers that don't work worth a damn," Jamar said.

"They totally don't," Taylor agreed. She paused for a moment, then continued. "You mentioned possibly keeping me on as your trainer even after our agreed upon two months. Were you serious?"

"I would be a fool not to," he said. "I had high expectations when I hired you, but did I think I would be able to crush an agility drill this early into our training? Hell no. That's all you. The fitness regimen you created is as effective as anything the trainers I worked with both in college and the pros ever put together. If I get back into the League, I'll need to maintain this level of conditioning, which means I'll need you long-term."

Taylor tried not to completely lose her shit, but her chances of spontaneously combusting from excitement were pretty high.

Calm down!

She needed to adopt Jamar's more realistic approach to this whole thing. It wasn't a guarantee that he would make it back into the League, so she shouldn't get ahead of herself here.

Yet, Taylor felt the anxiety over having to take that college entrance exam melting away in real time. If he hired her as his full-time, long-term fitness coach, she would no longer need to put herself through the agony of getting her degree, not if she negotiated a rate similar to what he was paying her. Hell, she would even continue with the free meal prep. He could never fully understand what this promise of job security meant for her.

At the same time, Taylor had to acknowledge the ache of what might have been. Having an end date to their professional relationship had left a door open to them possibly exploring something real. If Jamar decided to keep her on the payroll, it would essentially close that door.

You can't have it both ways, Taylor Renee.

Life was a hodgepodge of tough choices pitted against even tougher choices, and no one ever said you were guaranteed to like either.

"When I agreed to work with you, I never thought of these eight weeks as a job audition, but I guess that's what they are," Taylor said.

"I never considered it that way either. But, then again, I had no idea you would not only meet my expectations, but surpass them."

"Thanks." Her lips twisted in an apologetic grin as the reality of what they'd silently, yet mutually decided settled between them. They both knew what had to be done, just as they both wished things could be different. "So, are you ready to try your hand at kickboxing?"

Jamar nodded, obviously taking his cue from her. "Are you going to take it easy on me? I've never done kickboxing before."

"I told you once before, you didn't hire me to go easy on you."

She walked over to the wall where boxing gloves in various sizes hung from silver hooks. She grabbed a pair from a hook and slapped them against his chest.

"Glove up. It's time to get back to work."

CHAPTER TWENTY-TWO

Jamar could only conclude that it was the need to burn off the absurd amount of built-up sexual frustration that had him kicking the ever-loving shit out of this punching bag. He backed away, then studied Taylor as she demonstrated an inside crescent kick, lifting her knee and swinging her leg in a fluid arch. Witnessing the power in her shapely legs—in her entire body—was the biggest turn-on.

How was he going to survive working with her indefinitely without losing his mind? He'd convinced himself that sticking to their fake relationship was the only way he could focus on his primary goal, but he now realized that it didn't matter if the relationship was fake. His attraction to her was 100 percent real; there was no way of overcoming that particular distraction.

"Okay, now you try it," Taylor said.

Jamar snapped to attention. Drawing his body into position, he followed her instructions, striking the bag with the side of his foot.

"Double jab," she barked.

He struck out with a one-two punch, reveling in the satisfying thud of the glove connecting with the bag. He knew several former teammates who swore by kickboxing as a form of training, but Jamar had never been drawn to the sport. He hadn't known what he'd been missing out on. The precision that went into hitting the bag at just the right angle appealed to the perfectionist in him.

"I don't care what you claim, you won't convince me that this is your first time kickboxing," Taylor said.

"I promise you, it is," Jamar said. He'd taken flack for his drive to be perfect over the years, but if it meant wowing his hot fitness instructor with his quick-learning kickboxing skills, he'd take all the flack in the world. "I've only seen it done, but never tried it." He tilted his head to the side. "You know, with all the trash-talking you were doing earlier, I expected this to be a lot harder. This is nothing."

She plopped her gloved hands on her slim hips. "Oh really?"

It was so easy to get her riled up.

He shrugged, playing up his nonchalance. "I'm not saying it hasn't been a good workout. It's just not the challenge you made it out to be."

"That's because I was taking it easy on you, in case you hadn't noticed."

"I didn't hire you to take it easy on me. Isn't that what you said?"

Her eyebrows hiked. "Hmm...I guess it is."

She strolled around him in a slow circle, her gaze traveling from the top of his head to his feet, sizing him up. It was on the tip of his tongue to ask her if she liked what she saw, but flinging around sexual innuendo wouldn't help when it came to sticking to the rules they'd just laid out for each other. It was a pity, because flirting with her was so damn much fun.

"Are we done for the day?" Jamar asked.

She snorted. "You wish." She snapped her fingers. "Pay

attention." She placed two front kicks to the middle of the bag and followed them with a roundhouse. "Your turn."

He mimicked her actions, hitting the bag in the same spots she had. It progressed in that fashion for ten minutes, with her executing increasingly difficult moves and ordering him to repeat the sequence. Jamar found himself having to hide his huffing. Taylor wasn't even winded. She was a beast when it came to this shit.

"Okay, so that was a good warm-up," she said.

"Warm-up?"

"Oh, you thought this was the workout? Nah, boo. That was playtime."

She continued with another series of strikes to the punching bag followed by power kicks. As Jamar performed a straight kick to the bag, a sharp pain shot through his knee.

"Fuck!"

"What's wrong?" Taylor asked. "Is it your knee?"

"No, no." He bounced lightly on the balls of his feet, trying not to grimace when another twinge resonated from the joint. If he told Taylor about the little tweaks he'd started experiencing in his knee, she would blow things out of proportion. She'd probably insist he call Dr. Hoffman. And she would definitely pause their workouts.

He couldn't afford a break in his training, not without the risk of falling behind. His knee would be fine. It was nothing he couldn't handle.

"I think I have a blister forming on my foot," Jamar said. "It stung when I made contact with the bag."

"Do you want to call it a day?" she asked.

"No way. I'm not letting you off that easy," he said with a teasing grin.

"Oh yeah? Here's one for you." She struck the bag with a jab, then an uppercut, but when she followed it with a twirling back kick, she let out a howl like an injured animal before crumpling to the floor.

"Taylor!" Jamar rushed to her side.

She rolled around on the rubber flooring, clutching her ankle and writhing in pain.

"Shit! Where does it hurt? Do you think it's broken?"

"I don't know." She grimaced. "I don't think so." She stretched out her hand to him, signaling for him to take it. "Here, help me up."

He walked behind her and hooked his arms underneath hers. "Can you stand on your own?" he asked as he lifted her from the floor.

"I think so—" she said, but she cried out the moment she tried to do so. She would have slumped to the floor again if he hadn't been there to catch her fall. "I guess that's a no," she gritted through clenched teeth.

"We need to get you to a hospital."

"No!"

"Hey, is everything okay here?" It was the guy who'd checked them in at the start of their session. "I saw that fall you took. It looked pretty bad."

"No worries. I'm fine," Taylor told him.

"I've got her. Thanks," Jamar said. He turned his attention back to her once the attendant left. "What do you mean no? You need to get an X-ray. Your ankle's probably broken."

"It's not broken. And I don't need to go to a hospital. I just need some ice." She pointed to a padded bench. "Help me over there."

He held her upright as she limped toward the bench,

emitting a tiny yelp with every step she took. She was one of the toughest people he'd ever met; for her to openly show such discomfort meant she was in excruciating pain.

"This is ridiculous. Let me take you to the ER, Taylor."

"Okay, I know this concept may be a little hard for you to grasp as a super-rich football player, but it costs money to go to the hospital. And, yes, I have Obamacare, but the deductible is sky-high. I'm not wasting money on an ER visit just so some doctor can tell me to put an ice pack on my ankle and pop a couple of Aleve!"

Jamar closed his eyes. Damn, but she was stubborn. "I'll pay the bill. The only reason you hurt yourself is because I goaded you."

"You have a point," she groused. "This is your fault."

"And I take full responsibility. Now let me make up for it by taking you to the hospital." He went to stroke her ankle, but she flinched before he could touch it.

"I guess I should say yes since I'm about to burst into tears from the pain."

Jamar cursed under his breath. "Do you think you can get in my SUV, or should I call for an ambulance?"

"Maybe not your SUV." She bit down on her bottom lip and nodded toward the duffel bag she'd brought in with her. "We'll take Nessie. My keys are in the zippered compartment in the front."

"You named your car?"

"This is not the time for judging," she hissed. "Just get the keys."

He retrieved the keys from the black duffel. "A *Princess and the Frog* keychain?" he asked.

"Again with the judging?"

"I'm not judging." He needed to quit while he was ahead. "I'll get the car. Give me just a minute."

He had to adjust the seat before he could get in. He slipped behind the wheel of her little Nissan Sentra, but when he tried to close the door, he grabbed nothing but air.

"Where's the door handle?"

Jamar had to stop himself from immediately calling his favorite auto dealership. It was not his place to buy her a new car, no matter how much she desperately needed one.

He brought the car around and found Taylor waiting for him at the entrance, assisted by the gym attendant. Together they guided her into the car's back seat. Jamar wadded up a jacket and placed her swelling ankle on it to keep it elevated.

"I have a friend who works at Travis County Hospital," she said. "I'm texting her now."

When they arrived, a woman Jamar immediately recognized from that viral video was waiting outside the ER. She ran to the car and opened the back door before he could get to it.

She briefly glanced Jamar's way. "What happened here?"

"I was showing off," Taylor said from inside the car. "Jamar, this is London. London, Jamar. And despite whatever he says, this was *my* fault. I tried to do a fancy kickboxing move and fell on my ass. I'm really hoping it isn't broken—not my ass, my ankle."

"You're lucky you didn't break your head," London said.

"That's too hard to break." Taylor laughed, then winced as they helped her into a wheelchair. "I really can't afford a broken ankle."

"I told you—" Jamar said.

"I'm not talking about the bill. I'm talking about not being able to work."

"Let radiology have a look at it," London told her. "It'll be okay."

Jamar watched as Taylor was wheeled past the waiting area and through double doors. He slumped into a hard plastic seat, rested his elbows on his knees, and covered his face with his hands.

"If you're embarking on a guilt trip, don't."

He looked up at her friend standing over him. "It's pretty hard not to feel guilty," Jamar said.

"Look, I've only known that chick for a few months," she said, pointing toward the door where they'd taken Taylor. "And I know how impulsive she can be. You didn't do that. *She* did that."

"Only because I pushed her," Jamar said.

"Or because she's strong-willed, hardheaded, and takes unnecessary risks," London retorted. She pulled a phone from the pocket of her long white lab coat. "I need to let Samiah know what's going on."

As she walked away with the phone to her ear, Jamar remained in the uncomfortable waiting room chair, suffocating under the guilt weighing down on him. He'd known the more he pushed Taylor, the more she would push right back. Until she pushed too far.

He didn't even consider what effect this could have on her work until Taylor mentioned it. He could pay her hospital bill, but what if she'd permanently damaged her ankle? If there was one thing he knew about, it was career-ending injuries.

If she couldn't work, what would she do?

He could ask that same question of himself. What would happen if he took a blow to the knee that permanently knocked him out of commission? How would he support his family or Silas's family? What kind of spokesperson would he be for Taylor'd Conditioning?

If there even was a Taylor'd Conditioning after those doctors got through with her back there.

Jamar squeezed his eyes shut.

He *had* to figure out a way to make this up to Taylor. Although he had no idea how.

CHAPTER TWENTY-THREE

Taylor swiped through the selfies she'd forced Jamar to take with her before leaving the hospital three days ago, and posted another to her Instagram account. Just because she was laid up with a bum ankle didn't mean their fake relationship had to suffer.

She set the phone on the coffee table and went back to her comic book. As she flipped through the latest in the Nisekoi: False Love series—big ups to London for scoring her a copy—she absently reached for the bottle of kombucha Samiah had placed on the coffee table before she left to run errands. Her pull on the straw was met with nothing but air.

"Well, shit," Taylor said, squinting at the empty bottle.

She gingerly shifted her propped foot on the pillow, trying to decide if it was worth the trouble to hobble to the refrigerator on those stupid crutches.

Her ankle had turned from a bluish red to a deep, dark purple, but at least it was no longer the size of a cantaloupe. Now it was only a grapefruit. And the persistent throb had lessened to an on-again/off-again ache, so yay her.

Taylor cut her eyes to the vial of prescription pain pills the ER doctor had prescribed and pointed her middle finger at it.

Every single pill was still in the bottle. She'd popped a couple of the ibuprofen she kept in her purse for cramps—because there wasn't a person out there tough enough to handle cramps—but that was the extent of her medicating. A measly little ankle sprain wasn't enough to keep her down.

She repositioned her leg and winced.

"Dammit," she hissed. Mental toughness only went so far. Three days later and this still hurt like a bitch.

After being fitted with a plastic ankle brace in the ER, she had insisted that she was capable of taking care of herself, but neither Samiah nor London would hear of it. Instead of driving Taylor to her apartment, Samiah had brought her to her condo.

Thank goodness for stubborn friends. Samiah's help had been a godsend over these last few days. Of course, it didn't matter where Taylor was physically—whether holed up in this apartment or her own, she still had far too much time to dwell on the seriousness of what she now faced.

She had banked her entire future on being able to make a living teaching people how to live healthy, fulfilling lives. She had never, not once, anticipated what would happen if she couldn't do this job.

She hadn't considered herself lucky as she rolled around in pain on that rubber floor, but Taylor now recognized just how fortunate she'd been to have only suffered a grade 1 sprain. She could have easily broken her ankle and been dealt a prognosis a million times worse than simply staying off her feet for the next couple of weeks. Her injury had forced her to ask a question she had only allowed to live in the very far-off corners of her mind.

How would she support herself if she could not work as a fitness instructor?

"Stop being an ableist dick," Taylor muttered.

There were double-amputee fitness instructors who could kick her ass in the gym. She could still do this job even if her ankle never healed, but this still brought home the danger of having all her eggs in one basket.

Taylor's breath hitched, panic overwhelming her as she accepted that she had no plan. She had zero fallback options. The few things she'd done in the past, like driving for rideshare services or scoring the occasional meal prep job, weren't enough to sustain her. Her recent brush with the possibility of having to sleep in her car was suddenly all too real.

She swiped at the stupid tear that rolled down her cheek.

God, she hated this crushing sense of helplessness. She *wasn't* helpless, dammit. She had options; she was just too damn afraid to explore the one alternative that was a surefire way to improve her prospects.

"Shit," Taylor cursed, angrily wiping her cheeks.

If there was one thing the Colonel had taught his children, it was that you never allowed fear to get the best of you. But fear had made Taylor its bitch these past few months. Even now, the thought of taking the college entrance exam stole the breath from her lungs. Yet, it was nothing compared to the sheer terror of finding herself without a viable way to make a living.

This sprained ankle had done so much more than just sideline her for a few weeks. It had put her future in stark relief. She could not count on pop-up fitness classes or the hope that views of her YouTube videos would provide enough income to live on. As of yesterday, she couldn't even count on earning money from her clients, because she no longer *had* a client.

The decision to end their working relationship had not been a mutual one. Jamar contended that she could coach him via FaceTime or Zoom, but Taylor didn't feel right continuing as his fitness instructor when she could no longer be there to provide adequate, one-on-one training. She offered to provide ongoing guidance as a friend, but she would not work as his paid trainer.

And then he'd completely negated her attempt to do the right thing by insisting he pay the balance of her consulting fee. They went back and forth, sending and returning the payment through Apple Pay before he pulled a fast one on her. He'd sent the money to Samiah, knowing she wouldn't allow Taylor to return it.

Taylor was grateful, of course, but it felt as if she was taking advantage of his generosity. Or, more accurately, of his guilt, since he continued to maintain that her injury was his fault.

Yet, even with that huge lump sum payment from Jamar, which had thankfully allowed her to pay off two more credit cards and stash away enough money for the next couple of months' rent, Taylor could not ignore her current reality. Just a few days ago, she'd thought she had it made. When Jamar disclosed that he wanted her to continue as his trainer indefinitely, the pressure to go back to school had all but evaporated.

Now it was back and more suffocating than ever.

"I can't believe it's come to this," she murmured.

Taylor covered her face with her hands and gave in to the tears she'd been fighting for days—for months. Fuck, for all her life! This shroud of dread had begun the day her first-grade teacher had handed her a multiple-choice test and shushed her for not reading the words silently. But it wasn't enough for her to just *see* the words—she had to *hear* them in order to grasp the meaning.

Taylor thought back on what Jamar had said about his friend Silas. She'd skimmed books on learning disorders during past trips to the bookstore and, after some serious mental gymnastics, had grudgingly accepted that she could identify with a number of the listed common signs.

But if a learning disorder *was* behind the difficulties she'd faced all this time, how could she have gone through twelve years of school without being aware she had one? How had everyone missed this? Her parents? Her teachers? No one had recognized that she learned differently from other kids?

She rested her head on the sofa cushion and let the tears continue to flow.

She had no idea how much time had passed when she felt Samiah gently shaking her shoulder. She opened her eyes to find her friend staring down on her, concern etched across her face.

"Have you been crying?" There was both concern and accusation in Samiah's voice. "Does your ankle hurt? Do you need more painkillers?" She rounded the sofa and reached for the bottle, but Taylor stopped her.

"No, I'm fine." She lifted herself up, taking care not to jostle her ankle. "I'm just...I—" She couldn't hold it in. Once again, the dam broke, sending tears cascading down her face.

"You *are* crying!" Samiah rushed to her side and perched on the arm of the sofa. "What's going on?" she asked as she wrapped one arm around Taylor's shoulders.

Taylor's first instinct was to brush off her concern, but maybe talking it through with Samiah would help. She needed to talk to *some*one other than herself about this stuff.

"Do you promise not to judge?" Taylor asked. Samiah's pursed lips and stiff jaw were answer enough for her. "I hate school," she said. "I mean, I really, really *hate* it."

"I've gathered that from past conversations," Samiah answered.

"But what if this"—Taylor gestured to her ankle—"had turned out to be worse than a sprain? What if I couldn't conduct classes or do one-on-one training?"

"Have you—"

"And I know I can still do a lot of things without a college degree. A degree is *not* an indicator of a person's ability to be successful."

"No, it—"

"And comparing myself to you and London has *got* to stop. Not everyone is destined to be a doctor or a computer brainiac. Or a lawyer or an architect like my brother and sister."

"Who said you—"

"A person's occupation does not define them. It's not a measure of how good a person they are. Well, except for London's job, but who the hell can compete with someone who saves the lives of sick kids? I can't—"

"Taylor!" Samiah screeched.

She jumped, slapping a hand to her chest.

"Sorry for yelling," Samiah said. "But being polite wasn't getting me anywhere."

"Sorry." Taylor grimaced. "I've kinda been holding all of that in for a while."

"Yeah, I could tell. You do realize this isn't some competition, right?" She took Taylor's hand in hers. "Your decision to go back to school shouldn't be about competing with anyone else. You have to do it because you believe it's what's best for you." Samiah pointed to her chest. "I'm ready to cheer you on, Taylor, but only if this is what you really want."

"You will never hear me say that I actually *want* to go to school," Taylor said. "But I want the things that having a degree will provide. I guess I have to decide if I'm willing to do what it takes to make that happen."

Samiah waved her fists in the air. "This is me with my pom-poms."

Taylor sensed her old fears and uncertainties creeping up on her, but she couldn't deny the other feeling that began to take root. For once, the terrifying panic she experienced at the thought of going back to school had legitimate competition: hope.

CHAPTER TWENTY-FOUR

As she hoisted her foot up another step, Taylor was grateful she'd thought to watch those YouTube videos about climbing stairs with crutches. She was an asshole for ever taking for granted her ability to walk up this one flight unassisted. She'd never do it again.

But it was worth this arduous effort for the chance to sleep in her own bed. She missed her little postage stamp of an apartment.

Okay, so she would give up this apartment in a hot minute to live in Samiah's gorgeous high-rise condo, but there was something to be said for having your own space and not feeling like a freeloader. And even though Samiah hadn't said anything, after five days at her friend's place, Taylor felt as if she was on the verge of outstaying her welcome.

Especially after Daniel unexpectedly returned home early from a job out of town. She refused to stick around and listen to sex noises coming from Samiah's bedroom. Or, even worse, prevent Samiah from being able to make any sex noises because she felt uncomfortable getting busy with her cute boyfriend while a houseguest slept in the next room.

When she finally made it to the landing, Taylor noticed a slip of paper hanging from the clip next to the door where the property manager left notes for residents. She unfolded the flyer and had to struggle not to lose the breakfast taco she'd picked up on the way home.

YOU MUST VACATE BY TOMORROW was printed in bold and all caps across the top.

"What the hell? I paid the rent!" Taylor screeched.

But as she read further, she realized this wasn't an eviction notice. Disbelief rendered her motionless.

Toxic mold had been discovered in the HVAC systems of several buildings in the complex, including hers. By order of the county health department, all affected buildings were required to be treated. Residents must vacate their apartments for the next three weeks.

"You mean I paid rent only to have to leave this damn apartment anyway?"

According to the note, the property management company would provide a stipend to cover the cost of living at a nearby hotel. At least she would have a place to stay, but still...

She entered the apartment and made her way to the sofa. Moments after she sat, there was a knock at the door.

"Shit," Taylor hissed underneath her breath. "One minute."

She used a single crutch to make her way to the door. She opened it to find her downstairs neighbor, Rob, holding a foil cake pan wrapped in cellophane.

"I figured it was time I returned the favor," he said. "It's store-bought, but still pretty good."

"Aw, Rob, thank you," Taylor said. A store-bought cake wouldn't give her the satisfaction of baking from scratch, but she appreciated the gesture.

"Did you hear about the mold?" Rob asked.

"Yeah, there was a note waiting for me when I got here. I guess I'll see you in three weeks," she said.

Rob brought the cake into the kitchen for her before leaving. Taylor was tempted to serve up a huge chunk but eating her feelings would do her no good right now. She had to figure out what to do about her sudden homeless state.

When she returned to the sofa, her phone chimed with a FaceTime call from Jamar.

"Hey," she answered with a heavy sigh.

"Damn. Did you get a dog and have it die on you while I wasn't looking?"

"I would laugh at that, but it wasn't funny," she said. She held up the paper. "I have to leave my apartment."

"What? Why?"

She read the note to him.

"At least they're paying for a hotel," Taylor said. "Unfortunately, it's not a very nice one. I've passed it a couple of times when I had to take an alternate route through the not so nice part of town to get home."

Jamar was silent, his face unreadable.

"What?" Taylor asked.

"Huh?"

"You're thinking," she pointed out.

"Yeah, I do that from time to time."

"Smart-ass." She snorted. "Care to share?"

He paused for a moment, then asked, "Why don't you stay here?"

She was sure she'd heard him wrong. "Excuse me?"

"I have the room. In fact, I have *seven* rooms, along with a pool house that's basically a private apartment. You can stay there if that makes you more comfortable."

Oh, he was not playing fair. That pool house was ten times nicer than her little studio.

"Jamar, I can't."

"Why not?"

"Do you want me to list the reasons why this idea is straight up banana pants? How much time do you have?"

"What does banana pants even mean? I swear, it's like you speak another language." He chuckled. "Look, I already know what you're going to say."

"Really? Why don't you tell me?"

He held up a hand, ticking items off with his fingers. "You're going to say that we haven't known each other long enough for you to move into my house. You're probably also going to point out that it would be unprofessional."

"Damn, you're pretty good at that. That's *exactly* what I was going to say, because both are true."

He was shaking his head. "Either of those would be good excuses if you were still my fitness instructor, or if we would be living under the same roof. Since we already established that you'll stay in the pool house, and since you *fired* me as a client, none of that matters."

"I did not fire you. We agreed to terminate our working relationship." She paused, then asked, "You would really let me stay in your pool house? Rent-free?"

"Hell no. You have to cough up some cash if you want to stay here. Of course, rent-free." He didn't even give her a chance to call him a smart-ass this time. "It would make up for you not allowing me to cover your hospital bill."

"Except that you *did* pay it," Taylor pointed out.

"It would make up for the grief you gave me over covering your hospital bill," he amended.

She rolled her eyes at his attempt to be sarcastic.

Taylor knew she should be grateful for his offer. She *was*

grateful. *Extremely* grateful, especially if it meant she could pocket the money the property management was providing for lodging. But Taylor also knew she would be remiss if she didn't point out the staggeringly obvious elephant in the room.

"Jamar, have you thought about the...uh...complications that could..." She was about to say *arise*, but that probably wasn't the best word to use in this particular conversation. *Come* was even worse. "That could occur if the two of us live so close to each other?"

"I only thought about that after I'd already asked you," he admitted. "Look, I know ignoring this...this attraction between us may be difficult, but I can control myself."

"Yay for you," she muttered. "Maybe you can teach me how to do it."

She felt his deep chuckle through the phone. It sent a tingle through parts of her body that had no business getting tingly.

"I think we can *both* control ourselves enough to make this work," Jamar said. "And think about it this way. You staying here makes it easier to pull off the idea that we're dating. Maybe the Instacouples crowd will report that we're getting serious."

"Oh, my parents will just love to hear that I've moved in with a man after dating him for less than a month."

"Do your parents know about us? I mean the part about us dating? Supposedly dating?"

"I assume they do, even though neither have asked me about it. My niece texted me one of the videos of us that's been circulating."

He hesitated a moment before asking, "Do you want to tell them the truth?"

"Would you be okay with that?"

"Maybe. I guess. Just ask them not to say anything if TMZ comes calling."

Taylor burst out laughing. "I'm imagining my dad's face if he saw me on TMZ." She shook her head. "I don't think we need to say anything. Let them think I scored myself a hot football player."

His brow rose. "So is that a yes?"

Taylor considered all the reasons why she shouldn't take him up on his offer, the most obvious being that it was the height of unprofessionalism to be reduced to bunking on a client's couch—no matter how nice the couch or that it came with its own kitchen and bathroom. Or that he, technically, wasn't a client anymore.

The *real* issue was whether she could survive the constant state of horniness she would be forced to deal with if she agreed to this.

For the two thousand dollars she would pocket by not having to stay in a hotel? Hell yes! She just had to make sure she packed her new vibrator.

Great, now the thought of using her vibrator with Jamar just a few yards away made her horny enough to have to use the damn thing right this second. She really should say no to this.

Yet, Taylor found herself saying, "Okay."

"Okay?" It was obvious by the sheer surprise in his voice that he'd expected her to turn down his offer. Relief swept across his face. "Okay," he repeated. "I'll be there to pick you up in an hour."

"Make it two hours. My ankle is doing much better, but I'm still moving like a sloth. It's going to take me a while to get my things together."

"Don't. I'll pack for you when I get there."

Oh, sure. She could only imagine his reaction when she

asked him to throw in an extra set of batteries to go along with the hardware she kept in the drawer of her bedside table. That wouldn't be awkward at all.

"I'm not helpless. I can pack my own bag," Taylor said. "And, Jamar?"

"Yeah?"

She smiled. "Thank you."

He smiled back. "No problem. I'll see you in a bit."

The minute she ended their video call, she rang Samiah and London and said, "Okay, ladies. I need to talk."

"Have you come to your senses?" Samiah asked. "Daniel can be there to pick you up in a half hour."

"I'm moving in with Jamar," Taylor blurted.

"What!" Samiah shouted.

"Girl, I was joking when I talked about you two getting married," London said.

She explained the situation with her moldy apartment building and that she would be staying in Jamar's pool house.

"Rent-free?" London asked. "This sounds like the perfect setup for you. What's the problem?"

"The problem is that I want to ride him like a contender at the Kentucky Derby," Taylor said.

"Again, what's the problem?"

Taylor rolled her eyes. "Come on, Samiah. You're my voice of reason. Am I making a mistake here?"

"I don't know about this one, chick. It is an ideal setup. You just have to make sure you're ready for whatever happens."

"My suggestion is that you don't just *let* it happen," London said. "Go there knowing what you want and *make* it happen."

Again, Taylor rolled her eyes. But the more she thought about it, the more intriguing she found London's advice.

CHAPTER TWENTY-FIVE

Taylor sat in the cushioned rattan armchair and tracked Jamar's movements as he moved from one area of the pool house to another. He'd been at this for the past twenty minutes, pointing out every available feature. He picked up the electronic tablet from a stand on the coffee table and swiped his finger across the screen.

"This controls everything from the lights to the television to the thermostat, just like the one in the main house. You've used it before, right?" He pressed something, and the ceiling fan started to twirl lazily above them. With another swipe, taupe window shades began to lower inside the double-paned floor-to-ceiling windows that spanned the side of the structure that faced the Olympic-size pool.

"It's all pretty easy to operate," he said, reversing the window shades with another swipe of his finger. "If you need help, just call. I'm...you know...right there." He hooked a thumb toward the main house.

"I will," Taylor said. She started a mental countdown to see how long it would take him to find something else to point out.

He snapped his fingers. "Oh, and converting the sofa into a

bed is pretty easy too. You just pull this out." He tugged on a metal bar Taylor hadn't even noticed protruding unobtrusively from the bottom of the sofa. He glanced over at her wrapped ankle. "Actually, it's probably better if you call me to pull it out for you when you're ready to go to bed."

Oh, of course. Because having him inhabit her space just before she slipped into bed would be no problem at all. He must be delirious.

"I think I can handle it," Taylor said.

"Well, okay, then." He shoved his hands into his pockets. "Um, about dinner. I plan to heat up the quinoa and grilled chicken you made for me. There's two of them in there. I can bring one for you."

She scrunched up her nose. "Actually, I'm not a fan of quinoa."

"So why are you making me eat it?"

Taylor waved off his indignation. "Because it's a healthier alternative to rice. Now, I'll take the green chili enchiladas if you have any of those left."

He shook his head, a rueful grin on his face. "I'll check." He took a step toward the sliding glass door but then turned back to her. "The bathroom. It has fresh towels, but if you need—"

"I'll call you," Taylor said, biting the inside of her cheek to stop herself from laughing. One thing she had not counted on was Jamar Dixon being outrageously adorable when flustered.

She stood and, using one of the crutches—even though she was pretty sure she didn't need them anymore—started for the kitchen.

"Where are you going?" Jamar asked.

"To get a glass of water."

"I can do that for you."

"I can get my own water, Jamar." But by the time she traversed the half dozen or so yards to the kitchen, he was already filling a glass from the refrigerator's dispenser. He held it out to her.

Setting the crutch to the side, Taylor grabbed the glass from him and took a sip.

"You do realize that I will have to do some things for myself, right? I can't call on you for every little thing."

"Except that you can. I told you to call me if you need anything."

She rendered a slow, deliberate perusal from the top of his head to his feet. In a warning voice, she said, "You need to be careful about the offers you make."

Despite the twirling ceiling fan, the temperature in the room seemed to rise by a dozen degrees. Jamar took a step toward her, a spark of heat flashing in his eyes.

"When I say anything, I mean...*any*thing."

There was no mistaking the meaning behind his words.

They stood there staring at each other, a silent, seductive ribbon of awareness wrapping around them. Her gaze dropped to his chest, then came up to his full lower lip. He pulled it between his teeth and her heart started to beat triple time.

"What do you need, Taylor?" There was a hint of challenge in his voice.

She set the glass down and grabbed hold of his shoulders, drawing him to her. Without another word, she crushed her lips to his, *taking* what she needed.

She warned herself to slow down, but then completely ignored her own advice. She didn't want slow. She wanted them naked and sweating as quickly as possible.

Jamar pulled the ponytail holder from her hair, causing her braids to cascade down her back. Capturing the back of her head in his palm, he held her steady as his tongue pushed past the seam of her lips with a possessiveness that made her nipples grow tight.

Taylor splayed her fingers wide over his muscles, marveling at the topography of his chiseled chest. The man was a work of art. Every curve and contour felt as if it were carved out of stone.

"Taylor," he rasped against her lips. "What are we doing?"

"I'm not explaining it to you, young buck."

He pulled his mouth away from hers, his breaths choppy. "I'm serious. We said we wouldn't do this."

Yes, they had. And not even an hour into her stay she had his tongue down her throat.

But, dammit, she *wanted* his tongue down her throat. She wanted *more* than his tongue down her throat.

"Look, I know what we said, but it isn't realistic. We both know that we want this. Common sense demands that we satisfy that want. It's called 'let's get it out of our system' sex."

"You just made that up."

"I did not! Look, we do it this one time so that we both don't spontaneously combust. And then we're done."

"And you think one time will be enough? It doesn't work that way, Taylor."

She huffed out a laugh. "What? You think I'm gonna get dick-whipped after one time?"

The grin that curled up the corners of his mouth was impossibly wicked. "It's happened before."

Taylor narrowed her eyes at him. If she didn't want him

so bad right now, she would put his cocky ass out of his own pool house.

Yeah, that wasn't happening. At least not until he gave her the orgasm she'd been dreaming about for these past few weeks.

"Are we doing this or what, Twenty-Three?"

He shook his head. "No, I don't think so. What if you end up regretting it? *You're* the one who initially said we shouldn't go there, remember?"

"I also said the minidresses-over-jeans trend would make a comeback. Sometimes I say stupid shit."

"I don't even know what that means."

She ran her hands down her face in exasperation. "It means you should forget what I said before and fuck me, okay! It's not a hard concept to grasp, Jamar."

"Interesting choice of words."

She pointed to his crotch and the bulge straining behind his zipper. "That says it all."

"Don't worry about this," he said, pulling at the front of his jeans. "I can take care of this."

"Really? So is that what we're doing? We'll each go off to our separate corners and masturbate? Because that's what I'm going to do if you walk out of here without getting me off."

His head fell back. "Why would you put that visual in my mind?"

She tugged on the hem of his shirt and brought him to her. "You don't need the visual in your mind when the real thing is right here."

His nostrils flared with the intense look he leveled at her. "Just remember, this was your idea."

She pulled her bottom lip between her teeth, trying and failing to hold back her grin. It was hard not to gloat when she knew she was going to get her way. She let out a squeak when he reached down and scooped her into his arms. He set her on the counter and dove straight for that spot between her jaw and collarbone.

"How does that ankle feel?" he asked as he trailed his tongue along her neck.

"Forget the ankle. Worry about this."

She grabbed his hand and moved it between her legs. He released a desperate moan as he cupped her and pressed upward, the heel of his palm grinding against her.

Taylor braced her hands behind her and dropped her head back, all her thoughts focused on the hand between her legs. He slipped it inside the waistband of her running pants and brushed his thick forefinger against her clit.

She gasped, pressing forward, needing way more than just his finger there.

"Tell me you have some condoms in here somewhere?"

"In my wallet." He reached into his back pocket and pulled out the wallet. While he fished inside for the condom, she helped him with his jeans, unbuckling them and jerking the zipper down. The imprint of his dick pressed against his dark blue boxer briefs.

Mercy.

She tugged at his jeans, but he moved her hands out of the way and pulled both the jeans and boxers down his hips.

Taylor took a moment to appreciate the sheer fucking beauty of his erection.

"Stop staring," he said as he rolled on the condom. Once he secured it in place, he pulled her to the edge of the counter and spread her thighs wide enough to wedge his hips between them.

"Remember," he said. "Your idea."

"I take full responsibility," she said. Then she sucked in a slow breath as he eased inside of her. Instinctively, her thighs spread wider, making more room for him as he began to move with measured strokes. Taylor closed her eyes and concentrated on the luscious feel of him, the delicious friction causing all manner of sensations to flutter through her.

Reminders of past mistakes she'd made—of that time she'd been intimate with a client—tried to creep into her psyche, but she batted them away. This was different. Jamar was different. It was an insult to compare him to anyone from her past.

He shoved her T-shirt and bra up over her breasts and captured one of her nipples in his mouth, sucking hard as he continued to drive into her with deep, unrelenting thrusts. The strength and heat of him, the overwhelming power of his body; it was too much.

His fingers dug into her sides, his firm grip holding her steady as he pumped harder and faster. Taylor was spellbound by the sight of their bodies connecting in such an erotic, primitive way. A tortured groan climbed up from her throat as the first tingling of impending release started to build low in her belly.

The orgasm hit her out of nowhere, sending a sensual spiral of pleasure shooting from her core to every part of her body. She clutched Jamar's shoulders and rode the wave of sensation that washed over her, savoring the intense satisfaction suddenly flooding her system.

She felt him stiffen before he came, his arms shaking with the force of his release. Their harsh breaths echoed throughout the kitchen as they both absorbed the aftermath of the last ten minutes.

Taylor tried to hang on to the lingering euphoria, but

reality seeped past her defenses, casting an unwelcome light on what they'd just done.

"I told you."

Her eyes popped open at the sound of Jamar's raspy voice. "Told me what?" she asked.

"That you would regret this."

"I don't," she assured him, although she wasn't sure if she was being honest with him or herself.

His heavy sigh was filled with resignation, which told her that he wasn't buying her denial.

"So where do we go from here?" he asked. "Do we try to pretend this never happened, or can I mention over morning coffee that you're the best sex I ever had?"

"Is that a thing we're doing? Morning coffee?"

"That wasn't the important part of the question, Taylor."

"Okay, so I guess it's something we need to discuss," she said. "Where do *you* think we should go from here?"

He looked pointedly at her breasts. "Don't expect coherent conversation from me when you're sitting there like that."

Taylor pulled her bra and T-shirt down to cover herself, as if that mattered when they were both still naked from the waist down.

"Better?" she asked before purposely brushing the back of her hand across his semi-erect penis.

"Stop," he said with a hoarse groan. He leaned forward and tucked his head against her neck, inhaling deep before taking a step back. "Living here with you is going to be the hardest fucking thing in the world."

"Was the pun there intended?"

He leveled her with a look that clearly said he was not amused.

"I'm sorry," Taylor said. "Are you still okay with me living here?"

"I'm not that much of an asshole. I wouldn't ask you to leave just because I'm going to go half crazy thinking about you sleeping so damn close by."

"Did I mention that I sleep in the nude?"

"Taylor."

"It was a joke!" She ran her hand along his rib cage. The sleeveless T-shirt he still wore was damp with sweat. "If it makes you feel any better, I'll be just as hot and bothered as you'll be."

"Not sure that makes me feel better." He tilted his head to the side. "Okay, maybe it makes me feel a little better. Misery does love company."

He hooked his hands underneath her knees and lifted her off the counter, placing her gently back onto the floor. After pulling up his own underwear and pants, he helped her into hers. Then he braced his hands on either side of her and stared into her eyes with an intense, probing look.

"If I invited you to come into the main house, what would be your answer?"

She knew she couldn't do that. He knew it too. It would cross a line that was even bigger than the one they'd just crossed.

"I can't," she said.

He didn't speak; he just gave a resigned nod before backing up.

"Not that you don't already know this, but if you need anything . . ." he said.

"I know where to find you."

She watched as he left through the French doors and took

off across the small patch of stone that connected the main house to the pool house. Taylor closed her eyes and leaned back against the kitchen counter—the kitchen counter where she'd just gotten laid.

She wouldn't obsess over what just happened. He was no longer her client. He was her fake boyfriend, for goodness' sake! If you couldn't smash your fake boyfriend in his pool house, what was the point of having one?

And now that they'd both satisfied this itch, they could peacefully coexist until her apartment was mold-free. They could even have morning coffee.

You did the right thing.

Maybe.

CHAPTER TWENTY-SIX

In a typical month, Jamar spent approximately twenty minutes sitting at the desk in his office, however long it took to handle the few bills that weren't set up for automatic payment. Being surrounded by the trophies, plaques, game balls, and other memorabilia from his playing days that decorated the room put him in the shittiest mood.

Not this morning. He'd discovered a dozen different tasks that could only be done in this particular room. His agent had asked him weeks ago to autograph some eight-by-ten photos from his rookie season. They would be auctioned off at a fundraiser to benefit several schools in the Chicago area. After repeated "you got those pics" texts from Micah, Jamar suddenly felt a burning need to finally get to signing them.

He huffed out a laugh as he tapped the Sharpie cap against his lips. Of all the bullshit excuses he'd drummed up, at least this one would benefit a good cause.

There was only one *real* reason for his sudden affinity for this room: the vantage point from behind his desk gave him the best view into the window of his pool house's kitchen. He only caught the briefest glimpse of those dark burgundy braids piled atop Taylor's head when she passed in front of the window, but it was enough to ignite an explosion of flashbacks to the things they'd done to each other against that kitchen counter yesterday.

Jamar tossed the marker on the desk and ran both hands down his face. He was turning into a Peeping Tom. It didn't matter that he was peeping on his own property.

He'd gone back and forth, questioning just what in the hell he'd been thinking to invite Taylor to live here. They weren't under the same roof, but what difference did that make when it took him exactly thirty-eight seconds to walk from his living room to the pool house? Thirty-eight seconds to get to the place where she now slept, bathed, *lived*.

The fact that they were no longer trainer and client obliterated the one barrier that stood in the way of them being together. *Really* being together. Not just a one-time hookup or this pretend dating ruse they had going on. There was nothing stopping them from starting a real relationship.

Except Taylor didn't seem to be interested in more than what had transpired between them in his pool house yesterday. She wanted him, but not in all the ways he wanted her. So he had to settle for sitting behind his desk and reminiscing about the way it felt to have her legs wrapped around his waist while he explored every inch of her mouth.

And wishing there could be more.

There *couldn't* be more. Not right now. He *knew* that, just as he knew he could never be satisfied with those few rushed minutes he'd had with her yesterday. Why did he allow it to end so damn soon? Why hadn't he carried her to the sofa and spent hours bringing her more pleasure than either of them could handle? Then spent even more hours whispering in her ear all the ways they could be perfect together if they gave themselves the chance.

The way she laughed at his jokes, even while claiming that she didn't find them funny. The way she listened so intently when he talked about the most mundane things. That couldn't be totally fake, could it? She had to feel something more for him than she was letting on.

Jamar's phone chimed with Micah's ringtone. The FaceTime app on his computer joined in a second later.

"Hey, man, I was just about to call you," Jamar said as he leaned back in his chair. "I need the address of the school where I'm supposed to mail those autographed pictures." He squinted at the screen. "Wait a minute. Are you in your home office?"

"Shocking, isn't it?" his agent drawled.

"Did your wife and kids recognize you?"

"Not really. My youngest keeps calling me Uncle Kyle," Micah said, referring to his twin brother, who was the other half of Hill Sports Management.

"As long as Rhea doesn't call you that," Jamar laughed, speaking of Micah's wife.

His agent laughed along with him, then took a drink from the mug on his desk before continuing. "Is that what you were calling about yesterday?" Micah asked. "Those pictures?"

"Uh, not really," Jamar said.

It had been less than twenty-four hours since he'd left that voicemail for Micah, but it felt like an eternity. It had been just before he'd called to check on Taylor and upended his entire world by inviting her to live with him.

But Taylor's presence didn't alter his reason for contacting his agent. In a way, she *was* the reason behind this call that Jamar had been putting off for weeks. Her ankle injury had brought things into perspective for him. He recognized the precariousness of her line of work, and how her livelihood could be snatched away as quickly as his football career had been taken from him. He wanted to be a success story for her, a shining example that she could broadcast to the world.

He'd vacillated over when to tell Micah about his decision to make a return to the NFL. He wanted to get a feel for how things were progressing under Taylor's training program before bringing his agent into the mix. Jamar knew his body, and he knew that if he didn't feel as if the work he'd done this past month was going to get him where he needed to be that he wouldn't even bother telling Micah.

He was ready to tell him.

You sure about that?

He immediately silenced that bitch-ass voice in his head. Those twinges he'd felt in his knee were more than likely phantom aches. It wasn't enough to derail his plans, not when he still had so much riding on them.

He was ready.

His body felt stronger, but even more important than that, his *mind* felt stronger. He believed in his ability again. The endurance he'd managed to build up these last few weeks had him more confident than he'd felt since that fateful Thursday last year when he injured his knee.

"I called yesterday because I need something from you," Jamar said.

"Oh yeah? What's that?" Micah asked, his body leaning out of the field of vision as he reached for something to the right of his desk.

"I need reassurance from my agent that I have a fighting chance at getting my old job back. I want to return to the League."

Jamar couldn't remember a time he'd seen Micah Hill speechless. He stared at the screen in confusion, as if he were trying to decide if he was looking at an actual person or an alien pod.

"You want to play football again? In the NFL? With a shattered knee?"

"You do remember that I had several surgeries to repair that shattered knee, don't you? I'm stronger, Micah. I can do this. I've been working toward this since I started rehab. Last month I hired a trainer and—"

"Wait, wait. You hired a trainer? Since when?"

"I just said last month. Are you listening to me or what?"

"I keep my ear to the ground. I haven't heard a single peep about you working with a trainer."

"That's because she isn't part of the normal NFL circuit."

"She?"

"Yeah, she. And she's brilliant."

Understanding dawned in Micah's eyes. "This is that girl you're dating, isn't it? The one from that video. Rhea texted me a screenshot of an article she found on some gossip website with the two of you eating ice cream. At the time I thought it was ridiculous that anyone would care who you were eating ice cream with, but it looks as if I need to pay more attention to those gossip sites."

"Yeah, about that," Jamar said. "We're not really dating. It's just a front because I didn't want it to get out that I was working with a trainer." He told him about the episode with Alec Mooney during the Longhorns' practice.

"Well, your plan is working. Rhea's been trying to come up with a name for you. She liked Jamaylor more than TayJar."

Jamar couldn't help but laugh. "I don't understand the

obsession with celebrity gossip, but if it keeps the press occupied, they can call us whatever they want, as long as I can keep
my plans under wraps until the end of the regular season. I
figure I'll have a better chance with a team that doesn't make
the playoffs. That's where you see the most roster moves."

"And this is where I come in," Micah said.

Jamar nodded. "I want you to send invites to attend a
private workout where I'll go through the battery of tests used
at the Combine." He ran a hand down his face. "Look, Micah,
I know it's a long shot. It's not as if I'm expecting to be a
starter or anything."

"Not so fast. Maybe you *can* start," Micah said.

His head flinched back. "What do you mean?"

An eruption of laughter came from somewhere in the
distance.

"Give me a minute." He stood. A moment later, Jamar
heard a door close. "There's a *Fortnite* competition taking
place in the living room," Micah said when he reappeared.
He reclaimed his seat and took another sip from his mug.
"I wasn't going to say anything because I honestly thought
you were done with the League, but I've been hearing a few
rumors lately."

"You've gotta give me more than that, Micah. What kind
of rumors?"

"Have you been keeping tabs on Demario Simpson at KSU?"

"It's hard not to," Jamar said. "Every sports magazine out
there has him as the top running back prospect this year.
What about him?"

"I hear that he's rethinking entering the draft early and
may stay another year in school."

Jamar drew in a sharp breath. "How sure are you?"

"As sure as anyone can be." He shrugged. "Who knows, it may just be rumors." He paused, then added, "But maybe it isn't. It wouldn't be the first time a top college athlete decided to give all agents a heart attack by sticking in to earn his degree.

"And that's not all," Micah continued. "Van Johnson is planning to retire this year."

"Bullshit," Jamar retorted.

"He is. That last concussion scared the hell out of his wife. She's worried about CTE, and based on the rumor mill, she gave him an ultimatum."

"She has a right to be worried," Jamar said.

He didn't blame Van for leaving early. The brain disorder was always at the forefront of his mind. But the running back's decision made it even more important that he should do what he could to get back in the game. Van's exit created a space for him. And if Demario Simpson decided to sit out the draft, that was yet another starting running back who would not be taking up a spot on a team's roster.

After talking with Micah, one thing was abundantly clear: If Jamar was going to make a return to the NFL, this was his year to do it.

CHAPTER TWENTY-SEVEN

Taylor stood before the Keurig K-Mini, mindlessly twirling the wooden carousel of coffee pods as she obsessed over how to approach today. The day *after*.

Her instincts were telling her to treat it like any other day. Just pretend that everything was normal. Well, as normal as it could be when she was already pretending to be in a relationship with a client.

A former client, her brain reminded her.

"Oh, shut up," Taylor snapped.

Telling herself that she and Jamar weren't technically working together anymore had served as a convenient excuse for playing naked Tetris on the kitchen counter, but with every decision she made, consequences followed. More often than not, those consequences turned out to be excruciatingly *in*convenient.

And, yet again, she found herself staring down the barrel of another decision. Hide out in the pool house like a coward, or be an adult and have coffee with the man.

"I don't even like coffee," Taylor said, giving the carousel a final, brutal twirl.

She gingerly made it back to the couch—without the aid of

crutches, thank you very much—and stored the bed away. After pulling her braids into a topknot, she went into the bathroom and added extra moisturizer to her face to combat the dry, early winter air. She grabbed her favorite fleece pullover from her bag and tugged it over her head. The black letters that spelled out ARMY were so worn you could barely make out the word.

Taylor stopped with her hand on the handle of the French door. She took a deep breath, then another.

"It doesn't have to be awkward," she reminded herself.

It was sex. Really good sex, but still. It. Was. Just. Sex.

It didn't change anything between them.

She left the pool house. Wisps of smoke coming off the heated pool lent an eerie haziness to the morning as she crossed the walkway to the main house. She went to the side door that led to the gym and punched in the key code Jamar had provided her. Her stomach dropped for a moment when she noticed a figure in the corner, but it was only the foam dummy he'd ordered to practice his defensive blocking.

Remember, everything is normal.

Fixing her face into a neutral expression, Taylor headed to the kitchen. She found Jamar leaning against the counter, one hand wrapped around the handle of a coffee mug, the other in the pocket of his gray sweatpants.

Fuck. Me. How did he make simple sweatpants and a T-shirt look so damn good?

He stared at her from across the kitchen. "Good morning," he said.

Everything is normal.

"Good morning," Taylor answered. Who in the hell did that squeaky voice belong to? That was *not* a normal voice. She coughed, then asked, "Is there coffee?"

He nodded and gestured to the coffee machine. With its frothing nozzle and the whole coffee beans ready to go through the built-in grinder, it made the one in the pool house look like a relic from the Middle Ages.

"There's also kombucha in the fridge. I had groceries delivered this morning because I know you prefer that to coffee."

Well, hell. How was she supposed to resist screwing him on the kitchen counter again when he went and did stuff like that?

Stop searching for excuses for more kitchen sex!

"Thank you," Taylor said. She walked past him on the way to the refrigerator and caught a familiar whiff of spicy orange and sandalwood. She didn't know if it was his cologne or body wash, but it made her nipples pebble into sharp, painful points. She'd smelled that scent all night, it invaded her sleep, seeping into her dreams.

"You don't have your crutches," Jamar remarked with a hint of surprise.

"My ankle is doing much better," she said as she grabbed a bottle of her favorite lemon and ginger kombucha. The fact that he'd stocked the fridge for her made her heart skip twice.

"Are you sure you're not pushing yourself to do more than you should?"

"I won't be running marathons anytime soon, but I think I can manage to get around on my own. I promise I'll grab the crutches if I feel the slightest twinge. I'm not a complete fool."

Taylor was almost certain she saw him flinch at her words. Before she could question it, he said, "I told Micah about what we've been doing."

Her mouth dropped open. "About what we did in the pool house?"

"About you training me," he clarified.

"Oh," Taylor said. "Oh, of course." The meaning of his words sank in. "Oh," she said again. "So does this mean you're ready to make your intentions to return to the NFL public?"

He vigorously shook his head. "Not yet." He took a sip of coffee, then set the mug on the counter beside him. Shoving his other free hand into his pocket, he hunched his shoulders and continued. "I just thought it was time to bring Micah into the fold. It will be his job to set up the workout for teams when I'm ready to showcase my skills."

"Okay. That sounds good." She wrapped her hand around the bottle cap, but didn't twist it open. She just continued to stand there like Bambi caught in headlights.

After several uncomfortable moments ticked by, Jamar asked, "So, about what we did in the pool house. Are we just not going to talk about it?"

She uncapped the kombucha and took a much too generous sip. The spicy, fermented drink hit her throat like liquid fire. Jamar came over and patted her back.

She put a hand up. "I'm okay." She coughed again, then finally said, "Um, not talking about it was kinda my plan."

He dropped his head back and groaned up at the ceiling.

"Taylor, come on. We can't just pretend nothing happened."

"Why not? We're great at pretending. It's sorta our thing."

"I'm not pretending," he said. "Not this time. Not anymore." His intense stare burned a hole straight through her. "How am I supposed to act like nothing happened when all I can think about is how it felt to be inside of you yesterday?"

Goodness. Why didn't he just light a match directly to her Fruit of the Looms?

"Don't say things like that," Taylor pleaded.

"Why not? It's true."

"Because sex wasn't part of the playbook."

"Forget the playbook!" He ran both hands down his face, then up and around his head. "Are you going to stand there and tell me you've been faking this the entire time? Has it all been just an act?"

A simple yes would put an end to his interrogation. She could put this subject to bed right here, right now. But despite this ruse they'd been engaged in for the past month, lying never came easy to her.

"It doesn't matter one way or the other," Taylor insisted. "We've gone over all of the reasons why this can't be anything more than what it is."

"You didn't answer my question."

"Don't do this," she all but begged.

"No." He closed the distance between them. "I'm not letting you off the hook this time. I want you to be honest with me. Am I the only one who's feeling this?"

She closed her eyes. "Jamar."

"Tell me, Taylor. *Tell me.*"

It was the fierce plea in his voice that wouldn't allow her to deny him a second longer.

"No," Taylor said. Her throat ached as she pushed out the word, a hoarse whisper heavy with implication.

She caught him by the forearms and gently but firmly pushed him back a few inches.

"I need to explain why this is so hard for me." She opened her eyes and stared into his. "And don't you judge me when I do."

"When have I ever judged you? Other than for the vegetables you try to feed me."

She managed to chuckle despite the tightness pulling at her throat.

"I know we're technically not trainer and client anymore. And, honestly, the status of our working relationship shouldn't even matter after weeks of the public believing we're a couple. But the truth *does* still matter to me."

She released another fortifying breath before continuing.

"Back when I was still in North Carolina, I moved from Fayetteville to Charlotte because I figured being in a larger city would help me to grow my business. It did. I picked up several regular clients very soon after I started Taylor'd Conditioning." She cleared her throat. "One of those clients was pretty damn fine. Like, Michael B. Jordan fine."

"That doesn't impress me," he deadpanned.

"Well, it impressed the hell out of me." She laughed. But then she sobered. "He soon became more than just the hot guy I was training. I hadn't considered the implications of sleeping with a client. It didn't seem like a big deal. But it changed everything. The moment we slept together, it was as if something switched, and I went from being his paid fitness coach to the chick he called when he needed a workout, either in bed or at the gym.

"When he hadn't paid me after a couple of weeks, I sent him an invoice. He actually called me up and laughed over the phone. He had the nerve to say he didn't think I would want him to pay me because it might make me feel like a prostitute."

"Motherfucker." His harsh whisper sliced through the air like a blade.

"That's not all," Taylor said with a humorless snort. "The worst part is that several of his friends tried to hire me as their trainer, because that asshole told them that I would probably sleep with them too."

"Mother*fucker*. Please tell me you beat the shit out of him, Taylor. Lie to me if you have to."

"I wish I could," she said. "I was *so* embarrassed. And I was horrified at the idea that I had developed a reputation for sleeping with my clients. What happened with Chad was one of the reasons I moved to Austin. I needed a clean start."

"Of course his name was fucking Chad," Jamar spat. "Taylor, you have to know I would never do anything to make you feel—"

"I know," she said, not even giving him a chance to finish. "I would never compare you to Chad, but letting go of those feelings? Opening myself up to that again? It's not easy, Jamar."

"Will you ever be able to do it?" he asked. "The fact is you're *not* my trainer anymore. There's nothing preventing us from turning this pretend relationship into the real thing."

He was right. It scared her in so many ways, but she wanted this to be real just as badly as he did.

Taylor had tried so hard to ignore what she was feeling, but why deny it any longer? What was standing in their way, other than her refusal to acknowledge that she was falling for him?

Her heart thudded in her chest as the fragile control she had over her ability to resist him crumbled at her feet.

"Okay," Taylor said. She looked up at him and nodded. "Okay."

"What does that mean?"

She pulled her bottom lip between her teeth. "It means that even though the couch in that pool house is pretty comfortable, I think your bed would be better."

His forehead fell against hers as a shuddering breath escaped his lips. "We can go there now."

"We cannot," she said with a laugh. "You need to hit the gym."

"You're not my trainer. You can't boss me around anymore."

She quirked a brow, waiting for him to catch up. She recognized the moment he did.

He grimaced. "You're my girlfriend."

"Which means I can boss you around whenever I want to." She reached down and slapped him on his perfect ass. "Get that workout done. Then you can take me on our first *real* date."

He pressed his lips to hers in a quick, fierce kiss, then left her standing in the kitchen. Taylor slumped against the marble countertop, a charged buzz thrumming through her veins.

"I guess it's time to update that dating playbook."

CHAPTER TWENTY-EIGHT

W hy did I agree to let you pick the place for our first real date? Remind me never to do that again."

Jamar did his best to maintain a straight face as he asked, "You don't like golf?"

Taylor cut her eyes at him as she picked up a driver and walked to the platform overlooking the driving range. Colorful circles of various sizes dotted the greens, each signifying a target for players to score points.

He'd specifically chosen this place with the hopes that she had never picked up a golf club in her life. Ever since that first pop-up workout at Zilker Park, he and Taylor had been engaged in a friendly competition, and he was just enough of an asshole to admit that he finally wanted to beat his girlfriend at something.

His girlfriend.

Damn, he liked the sound of that.

Sitting at the pub-style table in their private bay, Jamar draped an elbow over the back of the barstool and looked on as Taylor positioned her feet, using the yellow footprints on the artificial green turf as guides. She moved up a couple of inches, then back a couple of inches. She shifted her hands on the club's grip, then shifted them back into the previous position.

He rubbed the spot between his eyes. They would be here forever.

Finally, she swung the driver back and smacked the golf ball. It sputtered off the tee and took a nosedive off the platform.

"All that dancing around and *that's* what you give me?" Jamar asked. "I see why you don't like golf. Your swing is pathetic. Stay right there."

He hopped off the barstool and rounded the table, lifting a lob wedge from the collection of clubs on his way to the platform.

"First of all, you're using the wrong club." He pointed to the LCD screen, which displayed the targets for their current game. "You're aiming for yellow. It's the shortest target on the entire green, so you want to hit with a lighter club. And when you do hit, use a softer touch."

He handed her the wedge, then stood behind her. Wrapping his arms around her front, he moved her hands into position on the grip.

She looked over her shoulder. "Do you think I don't know what you're doing?"

"Teaching you to play golf?"

"Sure you are," she said. She wiggled her hips, her ass brushing against his crotch.

"You're trying to get us in trouble," Jamar whispered in her ear.

"We're supposed to play the part of the happy couple, remember?"

"We're no longer *playing* a part. Remember?"

"Oh yeah." She tilted her head to the side. "For some reason it doesn't feel all that different. What does that say about us?"

"That neither of us are very good actors," Jamar whispered, skimming his lips along her exposed neck. He pressed a kiss to the spot behind her ear and said, "Now get your mind out of the gutter and pay attention."

He cocooned her with his body, enclosing his hands over hers and guiding her through the swing. The ball missed the target, but at least it made it onto the green.

"I think you purposely made me miss so that you can rack up a higher score," she said in an accusatory tone.

Jamar gestured to the screen. He was ahead by three hundred points. "I can finish out the game for both of us and you still wouldn't catch me," he pointed out.

One corner of her mouth twisted upward. "Just so we're clear, this is the *last* time we play golf."

"Nah-uh." He shook his head. "It's golf from here on out, baby."

"You're ridiculous," she said with a laugh. She jutted her chin toward the table. "Our wings just arrived."

He followed her back to the table where the table attendant had just set down two orders of hot wings. She'd nixed his order of nachos, rebuffing the notion that she was no longer in charge of his diet now that she wasn't his trainer.

He'd attempted to order them with the sole purpose of getting her riled up. Now that he was down to the final three weeks before his tryouts, he wasn't taking any chances. He'd ordered his chicken wings baked and naked, not wanting to put anything into his body that would undermine the work they'd done.

"Are you sure this is enough for dinner?" Taylor asked. "I'm sure there are a couple of low-carb options we can order." She picked up the menu, but then lowered it so she could look at him. "I'm about to read the menu. And, yes, I will likely say the words out loud. Do you have a problem with that?"

She said it jokingly, but there was an edge to her voice that made Jamar wonder if her warning was really all in good fun.

"Do *you* have a problem with it?" he asked. He caught the way her jaw tightened. Before she could speak, he asked, "Were you ever tested for a learning disorder?"

"Your choice of topic when it comes to date night conversations leaves much to be desired," she said. "Usually, you pick a subject that will help you get laid later on. This ain't it."

"I'm not worried about getting laid. That's a lie," he quickly interjected. "But some things are more important than getting laid. When you were in school, did anyone ever mention testing you for a learning disorder?"

After several long moments passed, she finally shook her head. "No."

He studied her for some time, debating whether or not to press the issue. She was right, this wasn't the best time or place for this discussion, but if he had to wait until Taylor was ready to talk about this, he would be waiting forever.

"I told you about Silas's struggles before his diagnosis," Jamar started. "But I didn't mention how much it changed his life after his condition was identified. It made all the difference for him." He rested his hand on her forearm. "There's nothing wrong with having a learning disorder; it's just a different way of processing material."

"I know there's nothing wrong with it," Taylor said. She took a breath. "I've wondered about it," she finally said, her voice subdued. "I've read up on a few, and . . . look, I know that having a learning disorder is nothing to be ashamed of. But you don't understand the kind of family I come from. They're the most ridiculous overachievers you'll ever meet." She looked at him and rolled her eyes. "Never mind, I forgot who I was talking to."

"Hey, don't lump me in with your family!"

"Excuse me? What are you trying to say about my family?"

Jamar put his hands up. "You just called them ridiculous overachievers!"

She pointed a finger at her chest. "*I* can talk about them because they're *my* family. *You* can't. Make sense?"

It didn't, but continuing down this rabbit hole wouldn't get to the heart of what he was most concerned about.

"You said that you've wondered about it. Are you saying you've wondered about whether or not you have a learning disorder?"

She nodded. "A few years ago, I ran across this made-for-TV movie. It was a family drama about divorce or something, but one of the kids had a learning disorder. I recognized myself in some of the things he did, and I thought about how different school may have been for me if I'd had some indication that this was my issue."

"All I can go on is what I witnessed with Silas," Jamar said. "It made all the difference."

"I get that," she said. "Take science, for example. I love science. Like, *really* love it—especially biology. Learning about how all the parts of the body worked together? It's amazing when you think about it." She shrugged. "I just wonder how much more I would have enjoyed my science classes if I didn't have to spend so much time rereading the same passages over and over again."

"Silas would complain about having to do that," Jamar said.

A sad smile drew across her lips. "I just thought I didn't like school," she said. She sucked in a deep breath, then released it. "I guess I'm ready to accept that I have more in common with that little boy in the movie than I was willing to admit. If I can get a formal diagnosis, I think it will help with my decision to enroll in college."

Jamar's head jerked back. "College?"

"Yeah." She nodded. "I want to go back to school and earn my degree. Wait, no. I don't *want* to go back—I *need* to go back." She sighed. "Okay, I *want* to. Did they still have PE when you were in school?"

She gave him whiplash with the way she jumped from one subject to another.

"What does that have to do with you possibly having a learning disorder or wanting to go to college?"

"Because it's one of the reasons I want to go back," she said. "Not too long ago, I almost had a job teaching physical education to kids in this homeschool consortium in Bee Cave. Now that I think about it, it was a blessing in disguise that I didn't get that job, because if I had, we never would have met, but I still kinda wanted the job."

"It fell through?"

"Yeah. Because I don't have a degree." She laughed. "I was sooo pissed at the parents who run the consortium, but they have every right to want someone who is certified to teach their kids.

"The thing is, after I started researching homeschooling and, well, just schools in general, I discovered that many school systems throughout the country have done away with their full-time PE programs because of budget cuts. Then I asked myself, what if Taylor'd Conditioning could fill that gap?"

Jamar frowned. "I'm not following. Would you go around to different school districts teaching phys ed?"

"Not by myself. There would be freelance fitness instructors working under the Taylor'd Conditioning umbrella." She turned to him, her eyes bright with excitement. "I have this five-year plan, which is huge for me because I tend to plan things out maybe a week in advance. I guess it's my friend Samiah's way of rubbing off on me. But, anyway, in this plan, I go back to school and I start building my empire. I want to create a business model that allows schools to hire instructors part-time, the same way the homeschool consortium wanted to hire me. It would provide schools the opportunity to bring physical education back into the curriculum without having to hire full-time staff."

Jamar was at a loss for words. She'd just laid out one of the most ingenious entrepreneurial ideas he'd ever heard.

"That's . . . brilliant," he finally said.

"I *know*," she said. "As much as I hate the thought of sitting in some lecture hall, I have to get my degree in order to make this happen."

"I have no doubt that you can make this a reality, Taylor. Once Silas began using the tools they taught him, he became as unstoppable in the classroom as he was on the football field." He took her hand in his, brought it to his lips, and kissed it. "I have a feeling it would be the same for you."

Her eyes sought his, as if looking for reassurance.

"I've been thinking about maybe signing up to take the college entrance exam next month," Taylor said, her voice cracking slightly. "I probably need to practice more, but I figure if I sign up for it, then at least that's one step in the right direction."

"Just tell me what you need from me," Jamar said. "I've got you."

CHAPTER TWENTY-NINE

Taylor layered another slice of turkey breast onto her open-face sandwich before adding a dollop of cranberry sauce on top. She wasn't even all that hungry, but there was something about Thanksgiving that made her want to eat all the things. She sliced the sandwich down the middle and grabbed an extra fork from the drawer, hoping she could convince Jamar to help her eat it.

They originally had plans to spend Thanksgiving with London, Samiah, and Daniel, but at the last minute Samiah and Daniel decided to drive down to Houston to celebrate the holiday with her family. And London had texted that she was being called in to perform an emergency surgery.

Taylor still wasn't sure how Jamar felt about their Thanksgiving for two, but as for her, she had much preferred today's quiet, chill vibe over the stressful holiday she usually experienced with her family.

She'd been able to enjoy the meal they'd ordered last minute from a local grocery store—which Jamar had insisted they eat in his formal dining room because it was tradition—without that cloud of anxiety hovering in the air. And now she was looking forward to relaxing on the couch in a tryptophan-induced daze while suffering through whatever football game was on television.

She carried the turkey sandwich and two bottles of apple juice out of the kitchen. She was moving less awkwardly now that she was no longer wearing the ankle splint, but she still took care as she made it from the kitchen to the living room.

"I know we just ate like two hours ago, but Thanksgiving means turkey sandwiches," Taylor said. She plopped down next to him on the couch and frowned at the home improvement show on the television. "Why aren't you watching the game?"

"How do you know there's a game on?"

"Even *I* know that Thanksgiving means football. My dad, brother, and brother-in-law always cram together on the couch in my dad's man cave, screaming at the TV." She gestured at the seventy-five-inch LCD above the fireplace. "Why don't you have it on?"

Taylor sensed his reluctance as he switched from the home improvement show to the game.

"What's going on here?" she asked. "For someone who's trying so hard to get back into the NFL, you don't seem all that interested in it."

"It's not the game," he said. "It's *this* game in particular that's hard for me to watch." He looked over at her, one corner of his mouth tilted up in a sad smile. "I was hurt in the Thanksgiving game against the Lions."

"Oh," was all Taylor could manage. Why hadn't he said that before she goaded him into switching the channel? "We don't have to watch," she said, but he didn't seem to hear her. He'd focused in on the television screen, and if the intensity in his eyes was anything to go on, his attention would remain there.

Taylor sat through a stretch of interminable, tension-filled silence before deciding she couldn't take it anymore.

"Do you want to talk about it?" she blurted.

"What? The game?" he asked, motioning to the television.

"Not this game. The *other* game. The one where it happened." She gestured to his knee. "Maybe talking will help."

He sat back on the couch and stretched his arms across the back of it.

"There's not much to talk about," he said. "I mean, other than the fact that watching this right now makes me want to lose my Thanksgiving dinner."

"Jamar—"

"I'm joking," he said. "Honestly, Taylor, I'm fine. Watching it just... it just brings back some not-so-good memories."

She paused for a moment. After debating whether to say anything, she decided to go for it. "Did you see someone after you got hurt? Like a therapist?"

"The League mandates it. If he were here right now, my therapist would say that I'm still taking time to digest dealing with my injury and that it's okay not to be okay with it just yet.

"But I *am* okay, Taylor. Really," he said, which told Taylor that she wasn't doing a good job of schooling her features. "I didn't mean to make a big deal out of it, but this is the first time these teams have played since I got hurt and I guess I just wasn't as prepared as I thought I'd be. It's still so damn raw."

"Of course it is," she said. "Are you sure you don't want to change the channel?"

He shook his head. "I'm good."

He wrapped his arm around her shoulders and gathered her close. As she nestled against his chest, Taylor fully processed the surrealness of the moment. Never did she think when she'd blurted those words to Alec Mooney that just weeks later she and Jamar Dixon would be in an *actual* relationship.

She fought hard to keep thoughts of Chad Lewis from creeping into her head. The only thing Jamar had in common with that asshole was that they had both started out as clients. There was no rational reason for her to think that her relationship with Jamar would turn out the way things had turned out with Chad.

She returned her focus to the game, but then her stomach started to sour for a different reason. This game was violent as hell. She flinched with every noisy collision between the players.

A few minutes later, Taylor twisted around to face Jamar. "Okay, I have a question. It's a bit intrusive, and even though you have every right to tell me that it's none of my business, I would really appreciate an answer."

"What do you want to know?" he asked in a strained voice, as if he would rather be in a cage with actual lions and bears instead of just watching them on TV if it meant he didn't have to address her question.

"Why are you trying to get back into the NFL? I know you want to take care of Silas's family, but is football really the only option? Couldn't you maybe sell this house and move into a place with only five bedrooms and a regular-sized pool? It seems as if football has caused you nothing but pain. I don't understand why you want to return."

"The joy football has brought me far outweighs the hurt.

Every hard hit, every bruised rib, every piece of skin I've left on the turf has been worth it."

"How can you say that?"

"Because of the friendships. The camaraderie." He pointed to the television. "Those men were my brothers. They were family. That's why it was so hard when I lost it all."

Jamar paused for several moments before directing his attention to the game. He pointed at the screen.

"It was fourth down and eight yards to go. Common sense says you pass the ball, but the offensive coordinator drew up a running play. Coach knew it was risky, but he had enough confidence in me to put the ball in my hands—to put the *game* in my hands. Everyone thought it would work."

"But it didn't," she surmised.

He shook his head.

"What happened?" Taylor asked, knowing his explanation would be meaningless to her. But she sensed he needed to talk through this.

"The Lions drew up a blitz," he said. "Somehow, they read the play. The defensive lineman—a fellow Longhorn who I played with at UT and who was one of my best friends on the team—caught me on the right side. I never saw him coming."

His eyebrows pinched together, his grimace reflecting genuine pain. Taylor could see the effort it took for him to swallow.

"I let everyone down," he said, his hoarse whisper sounding like two pieces of sandpaper being rubbed together. "I knew within seconds that I wasn't walking off that field—that I would have to be carted off." He looked over at her. The sorrow in his eyes was soul-crushing. "There were only two days in my life that have ever been harder: the day Silas died and the day we put him in the ground. It's as if something in me died those days, as if I lost a physical piece of myself."

"Do you think playing football again will give you back something you lost?" she asked in a quiet voice. "It won't bring Silas back."

"No, but it's the thing that connected us," he said. "But, you know, this is about more than Silas. This game has been at the center of everything for nearly all of my life. There's a picture of me on the living room mantel as a baby. I'm dressed in a throwback Houston Oilers jersey and holding this tiny football. Then, when I was five years old, my dad signed me up for peewee football, and I've played every year since."

"No wonder it's so hard for you to walk away."

"I just wasn't ready." He closed his eyes. "I can't accept the way my football story ended, Taylor. After all those years, all the work I put into making it onto an NFL team, to have it all snatched away from me like that?" He shook his head. "I want to write my own ending. I want to go out on *my* terms, not because of some freak hit to my knee.

"I don't know if I'll last longer than a season or two, but the next time I leave football, I want to walk away standing tall. Does that make sense?"

She nodded. "It does. Have you talked to your parents about this?"

"Yeah," he said. "Mom and Dad called before they left for their cruise. I told them about the real reason I hired you as a trainer. I can tell that my mom's worried about me playing football again, but they both gave me their blessing. They know how much this game means to me."

"I've watched you push yourself to the limit and beyond

nearly every day for the past five weeks," Taylor said. "You deserve to leave football on your own terms. I hope you get the opportunity to make that happen."

He leaned forward and pressed a kiss to her lips. "You've given me the best chance. I just have to make sure I don't mess it up."

"Have you talked to Micah about scheduling the team workout?"

"Yeah." He nodded. "I was going to wait until after the season ended, but he doesn't think I should wait that long. If I get signed by a team, it's likely to be one that doesn't make the playoffs, so what's the point in waiting. Micah suggested I do it the second week of December."

"Wow, that soon?" She shrugged. "Well, at least I'll be back from North Carolina by then."

He reared back. "You're going to North Carolina?"

"I didn't mention that?" Taylor asked. "It's my dad's sixtieth birthday. Mom is throwing a huge party for him—which he will absolutely hate every minute of—but he lives to indulge her whims." She looked up at him. "Do you want to come with me?"

Before he could answer, she shook her head and said, "You know what, forget I said that. Exposing you to my family would be cruel."

"They can't be that bad."

"My brother is an asshole, Jamar. Like, his picture should be in the dictionary next to the word."

"If that's the case, I *have* to come with you. I've never met the textbook definition of an asshole before."

She laughed. "You're not missing much."

"Let me come with you." He ran his fingers along her cheek. "I can use the distraction."

She frowned. "From what?"

"Next week is the anniversary of Silas's accident," he said quietly. "People say it gets easier, but that's a lie. Every day is a hard day, but there's something about the milestones that hit differently. His birthday and the day he died are the hardest days of the year for me."

She cupped his jaw, brushing her thumb across his cheek. "If you think it will help, then yes. I'd love for you to join me."

He lifted her hand and pressed a kiss to the center of her palm.

"Thank you."

CHAPTER THIRTY

Are you ready?"

Taylor jumped at the sound of Jamar's voice coming from just over her shoulder. A sudden burst of panic flared to life in her belly, but she managed to quell it before it could grab hold of her.

After turning him down several times last night and this morning, Taylor had finally accepted his offer to help her prepare for the college entrance exam. Jamar had braved the Black Friday shoppers, driving to the bookstore to pick up a practice test booklet. He would read the questions aloud to her, just as the proctor would do if Taylor qualified for testing accommodations.

She fixed a smile to her face before turning to face him. "I'm as ready as I'll ever be."

She followed him into the dining room, where he'd already set the test booklet and two sharpened pencils at the head of the table.

She did her best to tame the butterflies in her belly at the sight of the testing materials. Sweat formed on her palms as a rapid thud began to pound in her chest.

"Breathe," Jamar said.

She looked into his eyes and instantly felt better. His gentle, encouraging smile put her at ease.

"Remember, we're just looking for a baseline here. This will give you a picture of where you stand with the benefit of testing accommodations," he said. "Let's just see how it goes."

She nodded and sat at the dining room table, but then she popped back up. "Those bananas we bought last week are super ripe. Maybe I should bake some banana bread before they go bad."

He clamped his hands on her shoulders and guided her back into the chair. "No baking. It's a *practice* test. There's no need to be nervous."

"You're right. I'm ready."

"Okay," Jamar said in that calm, steady voice. "How closely do you want this to mimic the actual testing session?"

"What do you mean?"

He held up his phone and showed her the screen. "Are we doing this with the timer or without?"

Panic began to rise again, but she stanched it.

"With the timer," Taylor said. "That's one of the things that has always made me nervous. I need to learn how to control my anxiety while under the clock."

"Just remember that extra time to complete tasks is another accommodation given to students with certain learning disorders. We'll stick to customary time limits, but there's no need to freak out if we have to tack on a few extra minutes, okay?"

She nodded. "Yes. Okay." Taylor sucked in a deep breath and slowly released it. "I'm ready," she said again.

Jamar read the instructions and, a minute later, gave her permission to open the testing booklet. The first section was English, her least favorite subject.

Her eyes traveled across the page as Jamar began with the

first passage, which required her to choose alternative meanings for underlined words and phrases. She barely heard the words. She was too preoccupied with thoughts of the answers that would follow.

A familiar sensation began to take hold of her. Her hands started shaking as the air suddenly escaped from her lungs. She tried to pull in a breath, but it felt as though her chest were shrinking and expanding at the same time. A sharp, overwhelming surge of panic flushed through her bloodstream.

"Taylor. Taylor, take a breath." Jamar knelt next to her chair and grasped both of her hands. "It's okay," he said, his soothing voice washing over her like a reassuring, calming rain. He kissed the backs of her fingers and rubbed her hands between his warm palms. "What brought that on?"

"I don't know." Her voice cracked. "I just...The thought of having to come up with all these answers brings on this...this terror."

"It's *one* answer, Taylor. You're taking this one question at a time. Don't worry about the next one until we get there." He kissed her hands again. Brief, gentle pecks that melted her heart. "Do you want to continue?"

She closed her eyes for a moment. When she opened them, she nodded. "Yes. I'm not quitting. Not this time."

Taylor sensed his hesitation, but he stood, picked up the test booklet again, and continued with the passage. She wasn't sure if it was his low, comforting voice or knowing that he was there to talk her down if she went too close to the edge, but her confidence began to grow with each question she conquered. They completed the English, then the Math sections. Jamar assured her that it was okay to take a break before they tackled the Reading and Science portions.

By the time she was done, nearly five hours had passed. Taylor felt as if she'd just completed a triathlon. Sweat made her shirt stick to the small of her back. Her arms hung at her sides, her limbs too heavy to move.

Jamar took the seat just next to hers. He produced a Sharpie seemingly out of thin air and slid over her answer booklet.

"What are you doing?" Taylor asked.

"Scoring your test."

"Don't do that!" She reached for the booklet, but he snatched it before she could grab it.

"What's the point in taking the test if you don't know what you scored?"

"This isn't about the score," she said. "It's about whether I could get through the test without losing my shit. Mission accomplished."

His brow arched.

"Okay, mission semi-accomplished. At least I finished this time."

"Yes, finishing is very important. But the score still matters, Taylor. This wasn't only about you getting through the test— it was about finding your baseline, remember? Let's just see how you did."

"Fine," she said. She pushed up from the table. "But I can't sit here and watch while you do this."

She went into the kitchen and grabbed the bunch of bananas hanging from a hook above the fruit bowl. She tore one off and peeled it as she paced from the edge of the kitchen island to the refrigerator. She was sure she could hear the seconds ticking away on the microwave's clock as she waited for Jamar to finish.

She'd mashed five bananas and measured out all the dry

ingredients for banana bread by the time she heard Jamar's footsteps. She went to stand near the sink, preparing for the worst. When he appeared in the entry to the kitchen, Taylor knew she was about to receive bad news.

"Well?" she asked.

"Your raw score in science was a twenty-eight out of forty, so that's good. The others, not so good," he said. He held the score sheet out to her.

Taylor took it and read over his markings.

"A sixteen overall?"

"Yeah. That places you in the bottom third, percentage-wise."

She looked up at him, a smile breaking out over her face. "The last time I took this test, I scored a twelve." Taylor laughed at the way his eyes grew wide. "Don't look so spooked. I know this isn't the best score, but it's honestly so much better than I expected."

She was giddy with the relief spreading through her. She wrapped her arms around Jamar's neck.

"Thank you for doing this," she said. "And for not letting me run away."

He settled his hands at her waist. "You're welcome."

She lifted her lips to his and captured his mouth. What started out slow and gentle quickly turned manic and brutal. Heat shot through her veins as Jamar relieved her of her clothes, pulling the sweatshirt over her head and unclasping her bra with one hand.

Taylor stood in the middle of his kitchen in jeans and flip-flops, and nothing else. As he trailed his tongue along the slope of her neck, his hands caressed her breasts, kneading them, pinching her nipples until they tightened to the point of pain.

He released her hair from the clip that held her braids, letting them fall down her back. Then he pushed his hands through her hair, holding her head steady, his tongue plunging in and out.

Old insecurities tried to creep in as his lips trailed down her neck, across her collarbone, along the shallow valley between her breasts. Taylor shoved them out of her head.

Jamar wasn't like any of the men she'd dated in the past. Everything he did came from a place of respect for her, from wanting to help her. Not from what he could take from her.

She heard his low groan a moment before he closed his mouth over her left nipple. He flicked at it with the tip of his tongue, the friction setting off an explosion of pleasure between her legs.

"Wait," Taylor said. She pushed at his chest.

His breaths soughed in and out. "What's wrong?"

"I'll be damned if we do this on a kitchen counter again. If you're going to fuck me, you're going to fuck me in a bed."

She grabbed him by the wrist and started for the stairs.

CHAPTER THIRTY-ONE

Oh, wait! I love this part!"

London hopped up from her chair and raised the volume on the television. She started to sway from side to side as TLC's "Creep" streamed from the soundbar.

They'd agreed to get together for a Saturday movie night at London's since Samiah and Daniel had only returned from Houston this afternoon. They'd chosen *Waiting to Exhale*, the ultimate in Black Girl Magic cinema.

The volume had been muted for much of the movie, but it was turned up when it came to a part they all wanted to watch. They'd replayed the scene when Bernadine throws her cheating asshole of a husband's things out of the house and sets it all on fire three times already.

London pointed at the television. "Those four are the original squad goals."

"Yeah, but I wouldn't want their man problems," Samiah said. "They all had messed up relationships."

"True dat." London laughed, reclaiming her seat and picking up the skein of yarn she'd been working with since they started tonight's crafty girls' night in.

"I thought you didn't like knitting?" Taylor asked. "You're a pro at this."

"This isn't knitting—it's crochet," London corrected her. "I'd forgotten how relaxing it is."

"So you've done this before," Samiah said in an accusatory tone. "That's why you picked up on it so quickly."

"It was years ago. This lady at church taught us during vacation Bible school back when I was in like the eighth grade. I thought I'd forgotten how to do it, but I guess it's like riding a bicycle." She held up the swatch of uniform, deep purple stitches. Taylor had to admit she was impressed.

"So is crocheting easier?" Samiah asked, her attention focused on the needles and yarn she'd been struggling with for the past hour. Her forehead creased in concentration as she unsuccessfully tried once again to cast on. "Why is this so hard?"

"Uh-oh," London said in a singsong voice. "Someone has found something she isn't good at."

"I've only been trying for an hour," Samiah said. "Just wait."

"She's going to drive herself crazy trying to prove she can knit," London said. "This is the problem with perfectionists."

"Takes one to know one," Samiah gritted through clenched teeth as she concentrated on her knitting.

London took a sip of wine before pointing her crochet hook at Taylor. "How did the practice test go?"

Taylor hadn't been prepared for the quick change of subject. Unbidden, erotic scenes of what happened *after* her practice test sprang to mind, but she forced them from her head as she turned her attention to London.

"It was better than the last time I took it, but still not great."

She told them about her freak-out at the beginning of the test and how she was finally able to relax and get through it once Jamar calmed her down. She also told them her score, because she knew she didn't have to worry about these two judging her.

"I know it's not the best, but considering that I scored a twelve the last time, I'm super excited."

"You should be. A four-point improvement is huge," London said. "I'm sure nerves had something to do with it. If you continue practicing, you're going to raise that score."

If she could guarantee that each practice test would end the way yesterday's had, she could be talked into taking one every day of the week and twice on Sundays.

"The thing is, I think I have a learning disorder," Taylor announced. "And maybe an anxiety disorder too. Although the anxiety may just be a by-product of the learning disorder."

"Test anxiety is pretty common," Samiah said. She looked to London. "Is it the same thing as a learning disorder?"

"It's considered more of a symptom," Taylor answered. "I've read up on it. To be honest, I've kinda suspected that this was my issue for a while, but I ignored it because that seemed like the easier thing to do."

"What changed?" London asked.

"Jamar," she answered honestly. "His friend Silas, the one you mentioned a while back," she directed at Samiah, "he had a learning disorder. Jamar noticed that I was doing some of the same things that Silas used to do."

"You should get a proper diagnosis, especially if you suspect you have an anxiety disorder in addition to a learning disorder," London said. "There's nothing wrong with seeing a therapist."

"Who said there was anything wrong with seeing a therapist?" Taylor asked.

She shrugged. "Well, I know how the black community can be when it comes to mental health. My grandmother thought anyone with depression just wasn't praying hard enough."

"Mine too," Samiah said.

"You don't grow up as a military kid without seeing a therapist at least once in your life," Taylor said. At least that had been the case for her. "I started having nightmares during one of my dad's deployments back when we lived in Germany. I was a regular at the Family Life Center for much of the seventh grade."

Yet her issues with school had never surfaced in any of the therapy sessions she'd had on base. She'd never considered the anxiety that gripped her whenever she sat down to take a test to be anything other than a normal reaction to a scary situation.

Why hadn't she made that connection? Why hadn't anyone else? She'd attended a half-dozen schools through her elementary, junior high, and high school years, and no one— not a single teacher, counselor, *anyone*—had suspected that there was an issue.

All these years she'd thought school just wasn't her thing, that she was wired differently from all the other people who managed to get through a typical school day without suffering panic attacks.

The fact is, she *was* different from those people. She just never realized that the thing that made her different was treatable.

"I have to wait until after my dad's birthday party," Taylor said. "But I'm going to look into scheduling an appointment for an evaluation once we get back from North Carolina."

"We?" London asked, her brows arching. "You mean the fake boy toy is meeting the parents?"

"Umm…about that," Taylor said. "I don't think I can call him a fake boyfriend after the multiple orgasms he's given me this week."

Samiah and London both gasped, then screamed, "Bitch!"

Taylor burst out laughing. "It kinda just happened," she said. "Actually, that's not true. I didn't want to admit what I was feeling, but I really do like him," she said. And she realized she meant it.

"I knew it," London said. "Didn't I call it?" She pointed her crochet hook at Taylor. "If you even try to put me in a cotton-candy-pink bridesmaid gown, we're fighting. I'd prefer this color," she said, holding up the deep purple rectangular swatch she'd crocheted.

"There will be no bridesmaid gowns," Taylor said. "We've only been dating for a few days. I mean *for real* dating."

"You two make a cute couple," Samiah said. "But how will this affect Taylor'd Conditioning?"

"I don't know that it matters anymore. When we first started this whole pretend dating thing, the deal was that Jamar would become a spokesperson for Taylor'd Conditioning once he makes it back into the NFL, but who knows what Taylor'd Conditioning will even look like in another year, or once I earn my degree?"

There were so many unknowns.

"I kinda just want to enjoy being with him right now and figure the rest out later. Does this mean that I'm breaking the promise I made for my boyfriend project?"

"You're still working on what's important to you," Samiah said. "That was always the goal."

"Oh, for fuck's sake!"

Taylor and Samiah both startled at London's exclamation.

"What's wrong?"

"Do you have to go to the hospital?"

London shook her head. "No. It's the manager of the banquet hall we booked for my upcoming class reunion. Every other week there's some kind of issue." She let out a frustrated sigh. "I told the committee not to go with this guy. He was an asshole from the first time I contacted him."

"I would ask how reunion planning is going, but I guess I already have my answer," Samiah said.

"I'm honestly ready to run away from everything," London said. "Between the hospital buyout, this class reunion, and my mother's new boyfriend—yes, you heard correctly. My sixty-year-old mother gets more dick than I do—I'm just...I'm done."

"You know what you need?" Samiah said. "You need sex."

"Do you expect a prize, Captain Obvious? Of course I need sex. That's no big secret."

"No, I mean you need sex *now*."

"She's right," Taylor said. "It does the body good."

"Stop bragging," London shot back.

"Here's what you do," Samiah said as she tossed her knitting needles on the coffee table. "Find the sexiest man at that hospital and have a one-night stand."

"You don't even need to go through all the drama of a date," Taylor said. "Just tell him you want to bone and do it."

London gave them both the stink eye, but then she said, "I can't have random sex with someone I see every day. If I'm going to have a one-and-done, it has to be with someone I won't see again."

"But it can't be a complete stranger because that shit just isn't safe," Samiah said. "Someone reliable has to vet him before you hook up with him."

"Agreed," London said. She looked over at Taylor. "Your boy toy have a football player friend with a granny porn fetish?"

Taylor and Samiah burst out laughing.

"I don't know and I am not asking," Taylor said.

"Whatever," London groused. "I doubt even a one-night stand with a young, hot football player will help at this point." She lifted the yarn and crochet hook. "But all is not lost, ladies. I think I've found myself a new hobby. Well, an old hobby turned new."

She reached over and grabbed her wineglass. Raising it to them, she said, "I'm calling tonight a success."

CHAPTER THIRTY-TWO

The growing sense of apprehension in Taylor's stomach on the flight from Texas to North Carolina intensified as the plane's wheels touched down on the tarmac. She had to remind herself that she loved her family and they loved her. Their judgmental comments were a result of that love for her.

Why are you making excuses for them?

The truth was that she had never fit in with her family.

She already regretted bringing Jamar with her. Would her brother denigrate her in front of him? Would her mother regale him with embarrassing stories from Taylor's teen years?

She squeezed her eyes shut. This was a disaster in the making. She felt it in her bones.

Just get through the weekend.

The flight captain's voice came over the loudspeaker, letting the passengers know that it would be a few more minutes before they could pull into their gate. Taylor released a deep sigh. She could use a few more minutes before facing the inevitable.

"You okay?"

She looked over and saw concern in Jamar's eyes. He reached across the armrest and captured her hand, lacing their fingers together.

The small gesture sent a wave of gratitude flooding through her. How could she regret bringing him when his presence brought such comfort? This man who she'd only known for six short weeks—who had entered her life as nothing more than a client—had come to mean so much more.

After they pulled up to the gate, they deplaned from the first-class seats Jamar had insisted on buying—his Thanksgiving present. As if Thanksgiving presents were a thing.

Taylor thought they would take an Uber to her parents', but after retrieving their luggage from baggage claim, Jamar motioned for her to follow him to the rental car desk. That's when she discovered he'd already booked a car for the weekend.

"When did you do all this?" she asked.

"Before we left Austin this morning," he said. He held up his phone. "Remember what I said about this cool little pocket computer? It can do all sorts of things."

"Couldn't leave that smart-ass attitude in Texas, could you?"

"It travels well."

She rolled her eyes as she followed him to the rental car lot where a silver Lincoln MKX crossover awaited them. Taylor issued directions as Jamar navigated the SUV off the lot and onto the highway toward Fayetteville.

The familiar sights brought her an unexpected sense of peace, contributing to the tangled mass of emotions swirling in her belly. North Carolina had been her first real taste of stability. She couldn't help feeling an affinity for the place where her parents had finally settled their nomadic family. She liked knowing she could come back here.

She also liked knowing that she could easily hop on a plane and flee if necessary.

After about an hour of driving, the GPS's flat voice

announced their arrival at her parents' home in the town of Spring Lake. The split-level brick house looked like many of the others on the quiet, residential street—something Taylor had always resented. After the monotony of base housing, she'd wanted her parents to buy a house with some character. The irony of the square box of a studio apartment she'd moved into wasn't lost on her.

Her brother-in-law's F-150 was parked on one side of the driveway. A black Mercedes coupe so new it still had temporary tags occupied the other half. It no doubt belonged to Darwin. Her brother loved to show off his prizes, as he liked to call his cars.

Jamar parked the Lincoln at the curb, just past the mailbox. The door to the house opened at the same time Taylor climbed out of the SUV. A second later, her dad appeared. He wore creased black slacks and a heather-gray sweater. It was so typical of the Colonel. His "downtime" wardrobe was what others would consider business casual.

Taylor wouldn't have it any other way.

She raced over to him and wrapped her arms around his broad shoulders. It didn't matter how often they butted heads, nothing could ever take away that initial joy she felt at seeing her dad safe and healthy.

"How's my little Taylor Renee?" he said, kissing the top of her head.

"Just fine, Daddy," she said, giving him an extra squeeze. She leaned back so she could look up at him. "Feeling old yet?"

"I don't turn sixty until tomorrow," he said. He pinched her side. "Why are you so skinny? I know Texas barbecue isn't as good as what you get here in North Carolina, but you can stand to eat a little more meat, girl."

"Ha ha," she deadpanned.

Her dad tucked her against his side, keeping one arm firmly around her. With the other he extended his hand to Jamar.

"I'm Colonel Powell," he said.

"Jamar Dixon," Jamar said, shaking his hand.

"Oh, I know who you are," her dad said. Taylor stiffened. This could go one of two ways. "I'm a Packers fan, but I keep up with the Bears," her dad finished.

Thank God. It went the non-apocalyptic way.

Jamar's brow arched. "A Packers fan in Panthers country? If you don't mind my asking, how did that happen, sir?"

Oh, good one, Twenty-Three. Tacking that *sir* on at the end would definitely score him some brownie points with the Colonel. Taylor knew those impeccable manners of his would come in handy.

"I was stationed at Fort McCoy, Wisconsin, a long, long time ago. It's halfway between Green Bay and Minneapolis. My drill sergeant was a Vikings fan, which explains why I hate them to this day."

"That also explains why so many of *his* soldiers probably hate the Packers," Taylor said. She gestured to the shiny black coupe in the driveway. "I see Darwin bought himself a new toy."

"The hell he did. That's mine," her dad said. "A man only turns sixty years old once."

He took Taylor's bag from Jamar and led them inside.

A couple of years ago, her parents undertook a massive renovation, tearing down walls and going with an open-concept design that left the living room, dining room, and much of the kitchen visible from the foyer. Taylor spotted her mother sitting at the dining room table with her niece, Fredericka.

They were tying gold ribbons around little black boxes, which Taylor surmised were the party favors for tomorrow night. The fact that they were making the favors out in the open also meant that her father knew about the party. There was no need to pretend that she'd flown all the way from Austin for a small family get-together.

Taylor went straight to her mother and gave her a hug. She turned to Fredericka and signed *Hello, Beautiful. I've missed you.* Her niece signed back *I've missed you too. I like your hair.*

"Don't you dare offer to dye her hair," her mother told Taylor. "You know your brother won't let you."

"It won't matter if we do it before he finds out." Taylor signed the words as she spoke them.

She motioned Jamar over and made introductions, and then spent ten minutes relaying questions Freddie had about football and how many cities he'd traveled to while playing. Her niece suffered from a severe case of wanderlust and didn't hold back when it came to her displeasure at never having left the United States. She maintained that the one time she visited her grandparents and aunt in Germany didn't count since she was still a baby at the time.

"There are finger foods in the kitchen," her mother said. "I'm sure you two are hungry after traveling all day."

Taylor guided Jamar to the kitchen and took down two plates. When she turned back to him, he was staring at her with a mixture of wonder and appreciation in his eyes.

"What?" Taylor asked.

"You never mentioned you're fluent in sign language," he said.

"It's not as if it ever came up in conversation," she said.

"I don't understand how you ever thought you weren't

college material, Taylor. Every day I learn something even more remarkable about you."

An infusion of warmth filled her chest and then spread throughout the rest of her. Taylor closed the distance between them, cupped his face in her hands, and placed a kiss on the tip of his nose.

"Do you know those are, by far, the nicest words that have ever been said about me while standing in this particular kitchen? If my parents weren't just a few yards away, I would strip your clothes off and do all kinds of nasty things to you right this second."

Jamar closed his eyes and released a guttural sound from deep in his throat. "Please don't say things like that while we're here. I want your dad to like me. That will never happen if he notices me walking around his house with a hard-on."

"Hmm, no, I don't suspect the Colonel would take too kindly to that," Taylor said. She slipped one hand from his jaw and trailed it down his chest and torso. "But you have to admit there's something exciting about the thought of getting caught."

He sucked in a breath. "Don't."

Just then, the front door opened and Darwin, along with his wife, Rebecca, entered the house. At the exact same time, Jesamyn and Chester came through the side door that led to the backyard. The volume of the chatter in the house quadrupled. It also put an end to any clandestine sexy times in her parents' kitchen. That was probably a good thing.

They all flocked to the great room, and for the first time in ages, Taylor didn't feel an overwhelming urge to escape. The finger sandwiches, chips and dip, and cocktail wieners her mom had prepared lasted all of ten minutes, so the Colonel ordered pizza, which they ate while relaxing on the sofa and in the comfortable armchairs Taylor instantly declared were the best pieces of furniture in the house.

Jamar fell right in with her family, charming her mother and sister-in-law, and as Taylor had predicted, going toe-to-toe with Jesamyn on every topic, from politics to climate change to the winner of the best picture at the Oscars this year. He cemented his place in the Powell family when he joined Freddie in learning a new dance on TikTok, then convinced her dad to join them.

Taylor laughed so hard she could barely catch her breath. But as she observed the jovial scene from the comfort of her plush armchair, she became increasingly uncomfortable with the sense of envy that began to take root. Was she...jealous?

Don't be ridiculous.

The idea that she was anything but happy to see Jamar getting along so well with her family was laughable.

And yet...

Taylor couldn't understand how he could seem so at ease with people he just met, while she walked around in a constant state of self-doubt whenever she was near them. Then again, it wasn't all that difficult to understand how he was able to fit in. He'd matched wits with her sister and talked sports with her dad and brother. He fit in better with her family than she did.

She reminded herself that her family welcoming Jamar into the fold was a good thing. She wanted them to like him. Taylor forced a smile that she wasn't really feeling and tried her hardest to suppress her resentment.

As the evening progressed, her dad made a pot of his famous hot chocolate and directed everyone to carry their mugs outside to the stone fire pit he'd had installed. When

Jesamyn brought a bag of marshmallows for toasting, Taylor had to take a mental step back to make sure she was at the right house. Everything seemed *too* perfect.

And then her brother ruined it all.

Sitting in one of the Adirondack chairs circling the fire pit, Darwin said, "Did I mention that Caleb Mitchell started at our firm this past week? That's yet another one of Taylor's classmates who's gone on to do big things."

Taylor spun around in her chair and glared at her brother. "What is that supposed to mean?"

Darwin's eyes grew wide. As if she would ever buy that innocent look from him. "It means that we just hired Caleb Mitchell at the firm," he said.

"Why do you have to be such an asshole, Darwin?"

"Taylor." Her mother's strident tone rankled. Why in the hell didn't she say anything to her son?

"He's so transparent," Taylor said. "You know he only brought up Caleb so that he could compare him to me."

"No, I didn't," Darwin said. "I was making small talk."

"By pointing out that one of my classmates is now a fancy lawyer at your fancy law firm?"

"Look, if you're feeling some kind of way about Caleb's success, that's on you."

"Oh, screw you." Taylor tossed her wooden skewer into the fire pit and stood. "I'm tired, and I need a shower." She looked to Jamar. "Where are the suitcases?"

"I put yours in your old bedroom," her dad called from his chair on the other side of the pit. "The young man's is in the spare room, where he will be sleeping."

Taylor didn't even attempt to argue. She'd known better than to expect her parents would be okay with her and Jamar sleeping in the same room. She went back into the house and upstairs to her old bedroom, her anger at Darwin's attempt to belittle her intensifying by the minute.

Once in her room, Taylor hefted her carry-on onto the bed and unzipped it.

There was a knock at her door.

"Taylor?" came Jamar's voice.

"Come in," she called. She continued with her unpacking, taking out the jumpsuit she planned to wear to tomorrow night's party.

"Are you okay?" Jamar asked, leaning against the closed door.

"I'm fine." She sighed. "What you witnessed down there was par for the course when it comes to my brother."

"Umm." His forehead creased as he rubbed the back of his neck. "Taylor, I'm trying to figure out what your brother said that caused you to go off the way you did."

"Excuse me?" She tossed the gym shorts she usually slept in back into the open carry-on. "You're trying to figure out what he said? Did you not hear what he said about Caleb Mitchell and his fancy new job?"

Jamar held his hands up. "I don't understand how you took that as a slight against you."

"'Another one of Taylor's classmates doing big things'?" she said, doing an exaggerated impersonation of Darwin's voice.

"Is Caleb a classmate of yours?"

"Yes."

"Don't you think it's a pretty big deal that he got hired as a lawyer?" Jamar said. "It seemed to me that's all your brother was pointing out."

His words felt like two swift punches to the gut. Taylor took a step back and crossed her arms over her chest.

"Is that how you saw it? Well, given that I've known Darwin my entire life, and not just for a couple of hours, I may have a better handle on how to read between the lines when it comes to my brother."

"Taylor, I—" He reached for her, but she stepped out of his grasp.

"I'm going to take a shower and then I'm going to bed," she said, grabbing her T-shirt and shorts from where she'd tossed them in the open suitcase.

"It's not even eight o'clock yet," he said. "What am I supposed to do for the rest of the evening?"

"You seem to get along with my family better than I do," she said. "I'm sure you'll be just fine."

She pushed past him on her way out the door, not bothering to answer as he called after her.

CHAPTER THIRTY-THREE

As he stood outside Taylor's bedroom, Jamar couldn't tell if the faint strip of light that beamed on the hallway's wooden floors came from the sun or from the ceiling fan light. He didn't want to wake her if she was still sleeping, but the thought of her lying in bed brooding over the way things ended last night made his stomach turn.

Sucking in a fortifying breath, he knocked on the door. "Taylor?"

He didn't have to keep his voice down. The rest of her family was already awake and eating from the buffet-style breakfast someone had laid out downstairs.

The activity in the kitchen had woken him just after seven this morning. As far as Jamar could tell, the room he'd been assigned had once been a small office or maybe a den that had been converted into an extra room for guests.

He knocked again. "Taylor?"

A moment later, the door swung open and Taylor appeared on the other side. He couldn't read her flat expression, but he erred on the side of her still being upset with him.

"Umm, hey," he said.

"Hey," she murmured. She opened the door wider, an invitation to enter.

Jamar stuffed his hands into his pockets as he followed her inside. She cut across the room, settling near the chest of drawers, but something stopped him from going farther than the few tentative steps he'd taken just inside the door.

He shifted his weight from one foot to the other, unsure of where to start. He hated this feeling, not knowing where things stood between them. There was one thing he *had* learned in the past twelve hours—just how much Taylor Powell had come to mean to him in this short time. The intense regret over how their night had ended was just one indication. How he ached to hold her right now was another. He *needed* her.

"Look, Taylor, I know I screwed up last night by sharing my...umm...my unsolicited opinion, but—"

"Stop," she said, holding up a hand.

Jamar's throat grew intensely tight. One of the worst-case scenarios on the massive list of worst-case scenarios he'd dreamed up last night was Taylor demanding they go back to pretending they were dating for the rest of the weekend and then dumping his ass as soon as they returned to Austin.

She'd walked him through the complicated relationship she had with her family, had opened up about how inadequate she felt when compared to them. And in her eyes, he'd sided with her family—with her archenemy of a brother—over her. Could he really blame her for her hostility?

"I...um." She glanced at the bed, the chair in the corner, out the window. She released a deep breath and continued. "I was mad at Darwin and took it out on you. I shouldn't have."

It took Jamar a moment to process her words.

She finally directed her gaze to him. "Things were going so well last night that I let my guard down around Darwin. I knew better than to do that. The two of us have always gotten along like expensive taste and bad credit." She hunched her shoulders. "Like I said, I shouldn't have taken it out on you."

Jamar was almost afraid to ask, "So does this mean we're okay?"

She stretched out both her hands, capturing his and bringing herself into him. She lifted her face to his and placed a kiss on his chin.

"We're okay," she said.

The sudden release of tension made his limbs go weak. He still had so many questions about her outburst at her brother, but he didn't want to chance a repeat of what happened last night. He wasn't in the right headspace for navigating that tricky conversation.

"Taylor, can we maybe, I don't know, go for a drive or something? I just need to get away for a bit to clear my head." He paused for a moment before he said, "Today is kind of a rough day for me."

He saw the moment that understanding dawned.

"Of course," she said with an emphatic nod. "Let me change into something warmer."

She went over to the chest of drawers and grabbed a dark blue sweatshirt from the second drawer from the top and pulled it over the plain white T-shirt she wore. When she turned around, Jamar frowned at the letters across the front.

"Navy?"

She stretched out the hem, looking down at the shirt. "I bought it to piss off my dad." She hunched her shoulders again. "I can be a bit of an asshole."

She grabbed one of those ties she used for her hair and pulled her braids together, securing them at the base of her neck.

"Let's get out of here," she said. She took him by the hand as she led the way out of the bedroom. "We can take a tour of Fayetteville. It's a pretty cool town with interesting architecture, if you're into that kind of stuff."

He was into anything that included her, especially on a day like today.

As was the case on this day for the past eight years, his first thought when he woke up this morning was that call from Drea, asking him to get to the hospital. He selfishly wanted— no, he *needed*—Taylor to help take his mind off those horrible memories.

"Have you had breakfast?" she asked over her shoulder as they made their way downstairs.

"I'm not really hungry," Jamar answered.

Once in the kitchen, she went straight to the walk-in pantry and came out with two squares of aluminum foil. She piled scrambled eggs and bacon inside two biscuits before wrapping them in foil; then she grabbed two bottles of orange juice from the refrigerator.

"I'm going to show Jamar around town," she called to her mother.

"Make sure you're back in time for our pre-party toast," her mother said. "We're doing a private one here at the house first."

The front door opened, and Darwin walked in. Taylor took Jamar by the hand and exited through the side door just off the kitchen.

"I'm not up for a fight," she said, handing him one of the biscuit sandwiches and a bottle of juice. "You may get hungry later," she explained.

Taylor handled driving duties since she knew the area better than he did. She unwrapped her biscuit and placed it on her lap, eating with one hand while steering with the other.

Jamar appreciated the quiet. He appreciated her innate understanding that meaningless chatter would do him no good right now. He needed to just exist for a moment. To come to terms with what today signified.

They headed down Highway 210, straight into the heart of the city. She took him past the U.S. Army Airborne & Special Operations Museum so that he could see the unique, modern architecture of the building's entrance, and then on to the historic downtown area.

"Are you up for a walk?" Taylor asked.

"A walk or a hike? I've known you long enough now to know a walk is never just a walk."

Her lips tipped up in a rueful smile. "A little of both. The Cape Fear River Trail is nearby. It's beautiful, even at this time of the year. Peaceful. I think you'd enjoy it."

He captured her free hand and placed a kiss on the back of it. "That sounds perfect."

Ten minutes later, she pulled the Lincoln into a parking lot surrounded by near-leafless trees. They maintained a comfortable silence as they set out on the trail, strolling along a wooden platform that snaked through the bare forest, walking underneath a covered bridge and past several gurgling streams with short waterfalls. Growing up in one of the flattest parts of Texas, Jamar rarely saw this side of nature.

A couple of joggers ran past them, but for the most part, they were alone. Taylor had been right. It was peaceful. It was exactly what he needed today.

After about twenty minutes, she finally spoke.

"Do you feel like talking about it?" she asked.

"I'm not sure there's anything to talk about." He shrugged. "Eight years ago today, the driver of a pickup truck hit my best friend head-on as he rode his motorcycle. A simple story with a tragic ending."

Several oppressively heavy moments passed before Taylor quietly asked, "Was Silas an experienced rider?"

"He'd only had the bike for about a year," Jamar said. By some unspoken agreement, they slowed their steps. Jamar backed up against the weathered railing and plucked out a yellowed leaf caught between the grooves of the wooden slats. He twirled it between his fingers.

"I still remember the day me and Silas picked it up. He'd saved up for that bike all summer until he was finally able to buy it from a junkyard outside Houston. We took his grandfather's old Chevy to get it. I was scared the damn bike would fall apart before we ever got it back to Katy." Jamar huffed out a laugh. "But he fixed it up, and by the time school started, he had it running. Big Silas wouldn't let him take it to school, but as soon as class let out, he was on that bike, tearing up the fields near his grandfather's house."

"Fields? Isn't Katy pretty suburban?"

"Yeah, but Silas lived with his grandfather out in the country. The only reason he got to attend Katy High School is because a friend of his grandmother's allowed him to use her address. The administration knew he didn't live in the district, but he was too good of a football player for people to say anything.

"Sometimes I wonder if Silas would have been better off going to Morton Ranch High. It's possible we would have never met, which would have been better for him."

He heard Taylor's sharp intake of breath. "Why would you say something like that? He was your best friend."

"He was." Jamar swallowed. The lump in his throat had grown bigger in the last couple of minutes, to the point that it felt as if he'd choke on it. "And he lost his life because of it. Because of me."

Taylor vigorously shook her head, her wide eyes bright with dismay. "Don't say—"

"It's true," Jamar forced out, the words like acid on his tongue.

A familiar, punishing weight pressed against his chest, a crushing millstone he accepted as his penance for the role he'd played in his friend's tragic death. For the hardships his actions had caused Silas's family to endure all these years.

He should stop right now. Taylor wasn't his therapist. She wasn't some trash dump here to accept all his garbage.

But keeping this inside was slowly killing him. He needed someone to hear him, to allow him to finally unburden himself of the suffocating guilt he'd harbored for so long.

She took his hand and squeezed it. "Jamar, talk to me. That's what I'm here for."

His eyes fell shut as a staggering wave of gratitude crashed over him. How did she know exactly what he needed?

He swallowed several times before he could speak.

"On the night—" His voice still broke. He cleared his throat. "On the night of the accident, the Katy Tigers were playing our biggest rival. There were so many fans there, including scouts from some of the top NCAA programs in the country.

"I had my best game of the season, possibly of my entire high school career. Silas had an amazing game too." Jamar huffed out a humorless laugh. "But then he always did. That was the problem."

Taylor's forehead creased in confusion, as he knew it would.

"The town had dubbed us this amazing duo, but Silas was the real star. He would never admit it, because I'll be damned if you could find someone more humble than him, but he was a beast on the football field."

"I think you're the one being humble," Taylor said. "I've read enough articles about you to know that you were one of the best players in the country."

"Silas was better," Jamar said. "He just was. But in *that* particular game—our homecoming game—I was on fire. I'd scored three of our five touchdowns, but we were still trailing by four points with only twenty-three seconds left in the game. Twenty-three seconds to go, my football number. It was meant for me."

"What happened?" she asked.

"Coach drew up a running play, but our quarterback bobbled the snap before he could get it to me. One of the linebackers for the other team recovered the ball, but then out of nowhere, Silas knocked it out of his hands, grabbed it, and ran it in for the game-winning touchdown."

"But that's...um...that's a good thing, isn't it?"

Still holding on to her hand, he reached over and snagged another leaf that had been caught in the weathered railing.

"I guess it's a good thing if you're in it for the team and care about more than just yourself," Jamar said. He studied the veins of the leaf. "The way I saw it, it was Silas showing me up yet again. I can still remember the celebration once time ran out. Everyone was chanting his name, and I just stood there, fucking hating him."

The words felt like razor blades coming out of his mouth, but he'd held on to this truth for too long. Now that he'd started, he couldn't stop.

"Some people are born natural athletes, and some have to bust their asses to get up to that level. That's how it was for me and Silas. I'm not saying he didn't work hard, because he did. But there was just something about him that made his game look effortless. I resented that I had to work *so* much harder, and yet I still didn't measure up." He swallowed. "And that night, when I'd *finally* had the chance to stand out, once again Silas swooped in and stole all my fire."

"You were in high school," Taylor said. "Kids are like that in high school. You're selfish and stupid and it's totally understandable, Jamar. But I still don't get why you think Silas is dead because of you."

"Because it *is* because of me," he said.

Jamar scrubbed a hand down his face, wishing he could scrub away the last ten minutes. Why hadn't he listened to his gut and kept his mouth closed? Why didn't he consider how Taylor would view him after she learned the truth about him?

But it was too late to take it back. If he didn't follow through, he risked her jumping to her own awful conclusions. Although Jamar couldn't think of anything worse than the truth.

He cleared the self-contempt from his throat and continued. "As I said, it was homecoming night. So of course there were parties going on everywhere after the game. A bunch of us from the team had already decided which party we would go to first, but instead of going, I decided to just drive around.

"When I didn't show up for the party, Silas started texting.

For over an hour he kept calling and texting and calling and texting, and I just ignored it." His voice broke again. "He left one final voicemail, saying that he was worried and that he was going to come look for me." Jamar blew out a breath. "I ignored that one too."

He let the leaf fall from his fingers, studying it as it flittered to the wooden trail and landed softly on the bed of crushed leaves already there.

"The next call I got was from his sister, Andrea, asking me to come to the hospital because Silas had been in an accident. He died a few days later."

"Oh, Jamar," she whispered, reaching for him.

His first instinct was to pull away, but he allowed her to take his hand. He needed the comfort, craved it. He'd been alone with these thoughts for too damn long.

He used his free hand to pull his phone from his pocket. He swiped his thumb across the screen and scrolled through his old voicemails.

He hit play.

His stomach lurched at the sound of Silas's voice, the layer of panicked concern blanketing the words as he pleaded with Jamar to pick up the phone. A heavy silence hung in the air after the ten-second recording ended.

"I play this whenever I find myself starting to enjoy life too much," he admitted.

"Goodness, Jamar. Why would you do that to yourself?"

"Why shouldn't I? Why should I get to enjoy any of this after what I did to him? The other driver was found to be at fault, but Silas never should have been on the road. He should have been at the party. If I'd only answered one text, even if it was just to tell him I wasn't coming, he would still be here.

"And you know what's *really* fucked up? Everyone felt *so* bad for me. The entire town knew how close me and Silas were, so they treated me like I'd lost a brother, not knowing that I'm the reason my brother is no longer here."

"Jamar—"

"He would still be here, Taylor. He would be playing in the NFL—he was one of the top prospects in the nation." Jamar closed his eyes, but he couldn't hold in the hot tears that began to stream down his face. "He had no idea that we were in this one-sided competition, that I used him as this twisted kind of motivation. He deserved so much better than me."

Jamar felt the soft pad of her thumb swipe at his cheek.

"I'm not going to tell you that it wasn't your fault, because you've spent too many years believing that it is."

"Who else's fault would it be? He left the party to look for me!"

"Who's to say Silas wouldn't have had an accident on his way home from the party, no matter when he left?" she countered.

"You think I haven't tried to tell myself that lie? That I haven't tried to convince myself that this was Silas's fate and it would have happened no matter what?" Jamar shook his head. "It's bullshit. He's dead because of *me*. You can come up with however many excuses you want to, but it doesn't change anything."

"Do you know what else won't change anything?" she asked. "You playing this 'what if' game. What have you gained by blaming yourself all these years?" She cupped his jaw in her palms. "You need to ask yourself what would Silas want for you. Based on what you've told me about him, he wouldn't want you holding on to this pain, Jamar."

She tilted his face down to meet hers, and with exquisitely gentle care, pressed her lips to his. The unearned compassion shattered the tenuous hold he had on his emotions.

Jamar could do nothing to stop the tears that rolled down his cheeks, so he let them fall. Even as he lost himself in Taylor's delicious kiss, he allowed the seemingly endless, cleansing tears to run their course. He could only hope that healing would eventually follow.

CHAPTER THIRTY-FOUR

Taylor stood before the mirror and slipped on the Tiffany earrings her parents had given her for her sixteenth birthday. She checked the pins in her hair, making sure they were secure enough to hold the braids in the updo she'd fashioned for tonight's party.

There was a short knock on her door before it swung open. Freddie signed for her to hurry up and come downstairs.

Taylor signed back, *In a minute*.

Knowing Freddie wouldn't leave without her, Taylor grabbed the gold wrap that she'd bought to go with her black sequined jumpsuit and a small matching clutch. She gave herself a final once-over in the mirror before following her impatient niece downstairs.

Her entire family had assembled in the great room. Everyone was decked out in black and gold, the official Army colors, and the official colors for tonight's celebration. She spotted Jamar standing near the fireplace and damn near tripped over her own feet.

Other than in pictures online, this was her first time seeing him in a suit. She had not been ready. The tailored jacket hugged his chiseled shoulders and tapered down to his waist.

He'd paired it with a cream-colored shirt and black-and-gold paisley tie. Forget being a snack, this man was the entire freaking buffet.

She headed for him, but when she walked past where Darwin sat on the edge of the sofa, her brother reached out and grabbed her by the wrist.

"Wait a minute," Darwin said.

Taylor noticed Jamar take a step forward, but she held up a hand.

"What?" she said to her brother.

Darwin looked around, then tilted his head toward the dining area. "Come with me," he said, heading into the room and not bothering to see if she followed. Arrogant ass.

"What?" Taylor asked again.

"I wasn't comparing you to Caleb yesterday," Darwin said. "At least I wasn't trying to. If it seemed that way, I'm…I didn't mean for it to seem that way."

Taylor wasn't sure what was happening right now, but it was possible her brother was trying to apologize. Maybe she should warn the rest of the family that the world was coming to an end.

"Rebecca and Freddie thought I was insensitive yesterday," Darwin continued. "I didn't mean to be."

Of course Rebecca and Fredericka were behind this.

She considered simply accepting his unvoiced apology, but figured she could at least own up to her part in last evening's episode. She was so used to Darwin adding a negative spin to everything she did, her knee-jerk reaction was to respond antagonistically, often without taking the time to digest his words.

"Maybe I was a bit *too* sensitive," Taylor offered. "I'll be the first to admit that, where you're concerned, I tend to react somewhat irrationally."

"You *over*react," he said, his voice losing the tiny thread of contriteness it had held just a minute ago.

"I'm justified, asshole," Taylor shot back. So much for them turning over a new leaf when it came to their relationship. "God, I swear, Darwin."

He stuck his hands out, his shoulders practically meeting his ears as he tried to defend himself. "You said it yourself. I was just agreeing with you."

He was *such* an asshole.

"Can we please just come to an understanding?" Taylor said. "Whenever you get the urge to offer your opinion about *anything* concerning me, don't. It's as simple as that."

"I'm just trying to—"

"Don't."

Taylor heard her dad clear his throat from somewhere just over her shoulder. "Do you two care to join us for this toast?"

"Sorry, Daddy," Taylor said. She turned to her brother and hissed, "See, now you've pissed off the Colonel on his birthday."

"Taylor," her father said.

"My fault, Dad," Darwin said.

Darwin motioned for her to go ahead of him. Taylor pinched his arm, but then she took his hand and held on to it as they made their way back into the great room. She gave his hand a squeeze before releasing it.

She loved him. She didn't like him most of the time, but she would always love him.

She went over to Jamar and grabbed hold of the hand he offered.

He pressed a kiss near her ear and whispered, "Everything okay?"

She nodded, but before she could voice a response, her mother began her toast. Taylor felt tears welling in her eyes as she listened to her mother honor her dad's sixty years on this earth and over forty years of service to his country. Was it any wonder why she had a reputation for flaying her opposing counsel like a fish? The woman was a brilliant orator.

Once done with the private family toast, they filed out of the house and into their respective cars.

"What happened with your brother?" Jamar asked as he eased into the caravan behind her dad's new car.

"It's all good," Taylor said. "For a minute I thought Darwin had turned into a normal human being, but he's still an asshole. All is right with the world."

"I guess that's good to hear," he said with a chuckle.

"I honestly wouldn't know how to deal with him if he was pleasant," she said. She leaned over and pressed a kiss against his neck. She whispered against his skin, "I saw how you were ready to tackle him for me. Normally, I'd find that kind of stuff annoying because I'd rather fight my own battles, but I have to admit that was pretty sexy, Twenty-Three."

He glanced away from the road long enough to give her a quick kiss on the lips. "You help me slay my dragons, and I'll help you slay yours."

"Mutual dragon slayage. That's definitely going in the playbook."

He reached over and caught her hand, lacing his fingers through hers. "I think we need to revise that playbook when we get back to Austin. Some things have changed since you first came up with it."

"Such as?" Taylor asked.

"All those end dates have to go." He brought her hand up to his mouth and kissed the back of it. "I don't want this to end."

Her heart lurched in her chest, a mixture of excitement, anticipation, and fearful hope surging through her.

"I don't want it to end either," Taylor said in a soft voice.

They pulled in next to Darwin's car at the Iron Mike Conference Center on Fort Bragg. When they walked inside, Taylor couldn't contain her gasp. The decorator had transformed the banquet hall into a tasteful, sophisticated tribute to the Army, with black and gold silk bunting and tablecloths, and a dance floor that had the Army's emblem projected onto the center of it. It was the perfect setting to celebrate her dad's birthday.

As the guests started to file in, Taylor braced herself for the good-natured ribbing about Colonel Powell's "wild child" from her parents' friends. She'd expected at least a few questions about the viral video with Craig, but instead found herself fielding multiple inquiries about her relationship with Jamar. Her date, to his credit, took it all in stride, even signing a few autographs.

"I don't appreciate you being more popular than I am at my own dad's birthday party," she said, resting her head against his chest as they rocked back and forth to an old ballad from the '70s.

"That's because you're doing this celebrity dating thing all wrong."

She looked up at him. "How should I be doing it?"

"You should use me to get stuff out of people." He tipped his head toward a group of men standing near the open bar. "Take that guy who came over about a half hour ago."

"The one with the Bluetooth speaker hanging from his ear like it's 2005?"

"Yep, that one. He would have paid fifty bucks for my autograph and a selfie. Easy."

Taylor burst out laughing. "No way!"

"No doubt," Jamar said.

"First of all, what makes you think that? And secondly, why would you charge someone for an autograph?"

"*I* would never charge someone for an autograph. I was only pointing out that *you* could if you wanted to play my celebrity to your advantage. And I know he'd do it because he has a Chicago Bears tie pin and phone case, and he's come over to talk to me three times already tonight."

"Well, next time I'll set up an autograph booth," Taylor said with a laugh. She hooked her arms around his neck. "For now, I'll bask in the knowledge that every woman—save for my mother, of course—is jealous that I'm here with you."

His brow arched. "Even your sister?"

"Hell yes. Chester is all right, but he's no Diesel Dixon."

She felt his deep chuckle reverberating through his chest.

As they swayed to the music, Taylor tried to figure out exactly what she was feeling. It took her a moment to recognize it as contentment. She couldn't remember the last time she'd experienced anything close to this, especially when surrounded by people who never missed the opportunity to throw some of her ill-advised teenage antics in her face.

Being cocooned in Jamar's embrace provided a sense of peace she desperately needed, his presence making this trip home not only bearable but also enjoyable.

The party lasted until midnight, with much of the crowd remaining until the very end. Taylor was beyond relieved to learn that the same company that had furnished the decorations was in charge of cleaning up the mess now that the festivities were over.

Her mother had planned a postparty brunch for tomorrow, but Taylor and Jamar's early afternoon flight out of Raleigh would require them to leave by nine in the morning. Which was why they said their goodbyes to both her sister's and brother's families, then followed her dad's car back to the house.

Taylor and Jamar got caught by a red light, so her parents arrived home a few minutes before they did. The two were making their way up the walkway, holding hands like a couple of teenagers, when Jamar turned the Lincoln into the driveway. The Powells waited at the door for Jamar and Taylor to join them before entering the house.

Her dad wrapped his arm around Taylor's shoulder and gave her a squeeze. "Although I would have liked to have you home for Thanksgiving as well, I'm happy you chose to come for the party. Tonight was pretty nice, wasn't it?"

"The most fun I have had in ages," Taylor said. She stood on her tiptoes and kissed his cheek. "Happy birthday, Daddy."

She gave her mother a kiss and bid both her parents good night. They headed toward their downstairs bedroom, leaving Taylor and Jamar to linger in the quiet stillness of the empty great room.

"You had a good time tonight," he said.

"I did. Did you?"

"Yes." He nodded, then added, "Well, except for your sister-in-law stepping on my foot a dozen times during the Cupid Shuffle. If I can't run the forty during my tryouts, it's probably because she broke my little toe."

"Oh no," Taylor laughed. "I noticed you wincing a few times tonight. You should have told me. I would have rescued you."

His amusement faded, a somber, pensive expression taking its place.

"No," he said, the sudden rasp in his voice sending pin-pricks of unease down Taylor's spine. "That's um . . . that's not why I was wincing. And it's not why I won't be able to run the forty-yard dash."

She frowned, her anxiety ratcheting up even more as he took her by the hand and led her to the sofa.

"You're scaring me," Taylor said.

"Don't be," he said. "There's nothing for you to be scared about. Me, on the other hand . . . yeah, I'm a little scared."

"Would you please stop with the vague bullshit and tell me what's going on!" She glanced toward her parents' bedroom, then lowered her voice. "Tell me," she said.

He rested his elbows on his thighs and clasped his hands together. Releasing a deep breath, he finally said, "A few weeks ago, I felt something in my knee."

Her stomach dropped. "Something like what?"

"It started as a pinch, but the ache has gradually progressed." He tapped his fingers against his lips, then looked over at her. "I'm scared my knee won't hold up."

"How long has this been happening?"

"Since Mount Bonnell," he said. "Maybe a little before."

"Jamar," she said in a fierce, accusatory whisper. "Why didn't you say anything?"

"You know why, Taylor. Because you would have stopped the training."

"Of course I would have stopped. I've read nearly everything there is to read about your injury; I know how devastating it would be if you suffered another blow to your knee. There would be no coming back from that kind of damage, Jamar."

"I know," he said. "I just have so much riding on this."

The agony in his voice tore at her heart, but this could not be up for debate.

"It's not worth it. Nothing is worth you permanently injuring yourself. You *have* to know this." Taylor cupped his jaw in her hands. "I'm so sorry this is happening, because I know how hard you've worked. But you can't do this to yourself."

She leaned forward and rested her forehead against his. In a pained whisper, she asked, "Do you think Silas would want you to put your body in jeopardy because of him?"

"It's not just about Silas," he said. "I told you, it's about me leaving on my own terms."

"So if you make it through that tryout and onto a team, what makes you think you wouldn't get carted off the field in the very first game? That's the risk you're willing to take?"

His eyes fell shut, the corded muscles in his neck constricting as he swallowed. His anguish was a tangible thing in the room.

Taylor squeezed his hand, her soul aching for him. She wished more than anything that she could fix this, but some things just weren't meant to be. This was one of them. She had to get him to see that his health was more important than playing football again.

But before she could conjure up a new argument, he said, "I'll call Micah in the morning, before we leave for the airport. If I can't get through a line dance, I sure as hell won't get through any team's training camp."

The relief that crashed through her took her breath away. She should feel guilty, knowing how hard this was for him. But all she could feel was the tension ebbing from her body.

Still holding his hand, she rested her head against his shoulder. There were no words, no platitudes she could utter that would make this better for him. All she could offer was her presence and hope that it would be enough.

CHAPTER THIRTY-FIVE

They sat in the silent darkness until the clock on the mantel read a quarter past one.

With a reluctant sigh, Taylor slowly lifted her head from its resting spot. "We have to wake up early."

"I know," Jamar said.

"We could just sleep here on the sofa," she offered.

"We could." There was a thread of amusement in his voice. "Except that I'm afraid of what your dad would do to me if he found us together while on his way to the kitchen for his late-night snack."

"The Colonel does not snack," Taylor said with a soft laugh. "If you heard someone last night, it was more likely my mom."

"In a way she's even scarier than your dad," he said. "She's got that super nice thing going, but I can tell she's the kind who would eviscerate anyone who crosses her or her family."

"And she would do it with a smile," Taylor confirmed as she pushed herself up from the sofa.

Jamar stood as well, recapturing her hand in his. "I now see where you get your badassness," he said with a wink.

There was zero urgency as they made their way to the staircase, neither one wanting to say good night. Once there,

Jamar trailed the back of his finger along her cheek, his deep brown eyes brimming with want as he stared into hers. He tipped her chin up and lowered his head, pressing a kiss to her lips that was tender and sweet and perfect. It set off a cascade of warm tingles down her spine.

Taylor encircled him in her arms, running her hands along his sides and around his back. "Are you sure you don't want to spend the night on the couch?"

Jamar let out a deep breath and took a step back. "You should go up to your room."

"You're probably right," she murmured. Taylor cupped the back of his head and tugged, kissing him again.

"Good night," she whispered against his lips.

"Good night," he returned.

She started for her bedroom, not letting go of his hand until she'd climbed four of the steps. Once she reached the second-floor landing, she looked down to find him still lingering at the bottom of the staircase. Their gazes caught and held, the same longing she was feeling reflected in the depths of his eyes.

See you in the morning, Taylor mouthed.

He nodded and gave her a short wave.

Taylor slipped into her bedroom before she gave in to the temptation to go back downstairs. It was only a few hours until she would be with him again, yet her body still mourned the loss.

She grabbed her pajamas and went into the bathroom. Bracing her hands against the pedestal sink, she stared at herself in the mirror.

"How did you let this happen?" she whispered. She hadn't just fallen—she'd fallen *hard*.

A secretive smile curved up the corners of her mouth. Who knew a hard fall could feel so good?

She took out the bobby pins and hair tie that held her updo together, covered her hair with a shower cap, then got into the shower. But the cascade of hot water did nothing for her. A shower wasn't enough. She needed Jamar. And she knew he needed her just as much.

Dressed in a T-shirt and pajama shorts, Taylor slipped out of the bathroom as quietly as possible and padded barefoot down the stairs. She went through the kitchen to the spare bedroom, finding the door slightly ajar.

Jamar sat on the edge of the bed. He was shirtless, the corded muscles of his eight-pack gleaming in the light from the bedside lamp. He still wore his pants, although he'd loosened the belt buckle and unzipped them.

When he hooked his thumbs in the waistband and started to stand, Taylor took it as her cue to invite herself in.

"I'll do that for you," she said softly.

He froze. Hands at his waist, eyes wide with surprise.

"What are you doing—" he started, but she put two fingers against his lips, silencing him.

She moved his hands out of the way and took over, shoving both his pants and the black boxer briefs down his legs. She knew what tonight had done to him, the disappointment at realizing he would have to give up his dream. She wanted to provide whatever solace she could.

Flattening her palm against the center of his chest, Taylor pushed him back onto the bed, then got down on her knees and pulled his pants and underwear the rest of the way off.

"Tay—"

"Shhh," she whispered. She braced her hands on his thighs and dipped her head, running her tongue along the side of his hardening erection.

He released a groan straight out of a porno flick.

"Shhh," Taylor murmured again as she sucked on the head. She closed her eyes and swallowed more of him, taking half his length into her mouth before drawing up again. Jamar pumped his hips, thrusting upward as she once more lowered her head.

Need thrummed through her veins, the spot between her legs demanding attention. Instead of using her hands to sate the pleasurable ache pulsing from her center, she wrapped both her fists around his dick and began to massage him. She rubbed with increasing pressure, moving her lips up and down his length.

"*Fuck!*" He gasped. He caught a fistful of her braids in his hand before clasping the back of her head and guiding her strokes. He slid the other hand inside her shirt and captured a breast, using his fingers to torment her nipple. Every pinch and tweak sent a jolt of electricity straight to her clit.

"Taylor." Her name came out on a choppy breath. "I'm close."

He tried to pull away, but she gripped his thighs, holding him still. She sucked faster, harder, relishing the knowledge that she could provide a brief escape from tonight's painful revelation.

She felt him stiffen moments before hot liquid rushed into her mouth. She continued to suck, not releasing him until she was sure he was completely spent.

Jamar fell back on the bed, his chest heaving with his labored breaths. He leveled up on his elbow and looked at her with half-lidded eyes. "You're not finished, are you?"

Taylor shook her head. "Nope. Not even close." She slipped out of her clothes and climbed on top of him. Grabbing his wallet from the bedside table, she slapped it to his chest and said, "Condom."

He fumbled with the wallet, but within seconds he'd removed the disc from the package and rolled it on. Moments later he was inside of her, his hands at her waist, his hips lifting to meet her downward thrusts. Taylor held on to his shoulders as she rocked back and forth, quickening her pace until pure, explosive pleasure erupted throughout her body.

She landed on his chest in an exhausted heap of satisfaction. Feeling blissfully drained, she was unable to move the few inches it would take to lie on the mattress instead of on top of him. She refused to budge; she was exactly where she wanted to be.

Jamar ran his hand along her hair, lifting one of her braids and wrapping it around his finger. "I can't believe you did this in your parents' house," he whispered.

Taylor released a breathless laugh against his chest. "Believe me, I've done worse in their house," she said.

"Such as?"

"I once smoked weed in my bedroom. My mom would consider that to be worse than giving my boyfriend a blow job. My dad?" She tilted her head to the side. "Let's just say he wouldn't approve of either one."

"So you really *were* the wild child?"

"It's all relative. The 'wild child' in the perfect Powell household is just your typical teenager in any other family." She traced her finger along his chest, drawing swirls across his well-defined pectorals. "I meant to say this earlier." She looked up at him. "Thank you."

"Me? For what?"

"For being here with me. I haven't felt this . . . this *at ease* with my family in . . . " She shook her head. "I don't know. Probably forever. Having you here as a buffer, it allowed me to enjoy my time with them without the constant anxiety I usually feel."

Several moments passed before Jamar said, "At the risk of ruining what has been a surprising and extremely pleasurable end to my evening—"

"Don't ruin it," Taylor warned.

"I have to. This has been on my mind since yesterday."

She lifted her head and narrowed her eyes at him. "What is it?"

"I still don't understand why you went off on your brother the way you did. I know you said that you two get along like oil and water, but it seemed as if you were looking for something that wasn't there."

"You're right," she said. "You are ruining it." She started to get up, but he clasped his hand against the small of her back.

"Can you hear me out?"

"I'm pretty sure I don't want to hear whatever you're about to say," Taylor told him. "But fine." She folded her hands over his chest and rested her chin on top of them. "Psychoanalyze me."

"I'm not psychoanalyzing you. Well, maybe a little," he said. "I just think that you've gotten so used to expecting your family to think the worst of you, that you automatically view whatever they say through that lens. Based on the way you described them, I was prepared to meet a bunch of ogres, but your family is great. Okay, your dad's a bit intimidating, but even he's not as scary as I thought he would be."

"I never said they were ogres," she said.

"But do you think you've been fair to them? I haven't seen anyone in your family judging you or talking down to you this weekend."

"Look, I know what you're getting at," she said.

"Do you?"

"You think this has something to do with my learning disorder."

"Your undiagnosed learning disorder," he corrected her. "But, yeah, possibly. Now, this is *really* going to sound like I'm psychoanalyzing you, but I think it's possible that you've projected what you feel about yourself onto your family. They're not the ones who see you as the black sheep, at least not from what I can tell."

Taylor pinched his side. "I'm going to start calling you Doctor Phil instead of Twenty-Three."

"Don't put too much stock into my bullshit pop psychology," he said. He trailed the pad of his thumb down her cheek. "I just don't want you selling your family short."

It would have been easier for Taylor to write his analysis off as bullshit if she hadn't had similar thoughts over the years. Convincing herself that she was a normal, everyday slacker in a family of perfectionists had given her the green light to ignore her suspicions about why she'd always had such a hard time in school.

Maybe she *had* been unfair to them. Maybe when her dad referred to Taylor'd Conditioning as her little fitness thing, there was more affection in his tone than she gave him credit for. Maybe it was more concern than censure she heard in her mom's voice when she asked about how things were going.

Taylor considered how different it would feel if the next time she walked into this house, she felt relaxed instead of anxious. If she could enjoy her family without the fear that she was being judged. She felt the stress ebbing from her muscles just at the thought.

She laid her head flat on Jamar's chest, but then jerked up. "What time is it?" Taylor asked.

Jamar reached over and grabbed his phone. "Just after three," he said.

"Oh, shit," Taylor said, pushing up from the bed. "I hate to come and run, but I need to get back to my room before the Colonel finds me in here. He's always awake by four a.m." She pulled on her T-shirt and shorts, then leaned over and pressed a kiss to Jamar's mouth. "See you in a few hours. Remember, we need to be out of here by nine."

She backed out of the room, quietly shutting the door behind her. Rounding the dividing wall, she stopped short at the sight of her mother leaning a hip against the kitchen island, her silk bathrobe cinched at the waist, a satin bonnet covering her hair.

Her arched eyebrows indicated that any excuse Taylor tried to come up with would be pointless. How many times had she been the recipient of that same look after being caught sneaking into the house as a teenager?

"Um, hey," Taylor said.

"At least I like this one," her mother said. "He's more respectful than any of those boys you dated in high school." She patted the stool next to her.

Taylor would rather walk over a bed of LEGOs in her bare feet than chat with her mother while the effects of an orgasm still hummed through her blood, but life didn't always give you the options you wanted. She walked to the other side of the island and climbed onto the barstool. Her mom lifted aluminum foil from a plate, revealing several slices of leftover birthday cake. She grabbed two forks from the cutlery drawer and handed one to Taylor.

"Why are we eating cake at three a.m.?" Taylor asked.

"Why not?"

Taylor shrugged and nodded as she took a bite of dark chocolate cake with buttercream frosting, her dad's favorite.

"For the record," her mother said. "I don't have a problem with you and Jamar sharing a bedroom. That's your father."

"Can we pick a different topic, because..." Taylor waved her hands in a cutting motion before stabbing at her cake again.

"Okay, how are things going with work?" her mom asked. "You never mentioned what happened with that homeschooling job."

Oh, God, please, just bring on the LEGOs.

Taylor chewed excessively slowly, giving herself time to decide how to respond.

"It sorta fell through," she finally answered. "It all worked out in the end, though. If I had taken on the homeschool gig, I wouldn't have had time to work with Jamar."

Her mom gestured toward the guest bedroom with her head. "How serious is this?"

Taylor decided to be honest. "It's pretty serious," she said. She pulled her bottom lip between her teeth and in a hushed voice said, "I think I'm kinda falling in love with him."

Her mother's brow arched. "Kinda? You sure about that?"

The cake she'd just swallowed felt like Mount Rushmore as it went down her throat. How long had her mother been in this kitchen?

"It wasn't supposed to happen," Taylor admitted. "We were only pretending to be together."

She told her about their agreement to pretend they were dating, and how her feelings had gradually changed from fake to the real thing.

"Oh, I know what happened," her mother said. "You played yourself."

"Oh my God, Ma! You have *got* to stop hanging out with Freddie! And I did not play myself."

Okay, so maybe she *had* played herself. How foolish had she been to think she could feign a relationship with Jamar Dixon and *not* fall for him?

"So what comes next?" her mother asked. "If you're no longer working as his trainer, can he still function as the spokesperson for your business?"

"What do you think?" Taylor asked. "If you were in the market for a fitness trainer, would knowing that I once worked with Jamar Dixon entice you to hire me?"

"I would hire you no matter who you worked with, but then again, I'm biased." She winked, slipping the last bite of her cake into her mouth. "Mmm... I'll need you as a trainer if I don't get the rest of this cake out of the house."

"Just say the word. I'll give you the family discount," Taylor said with a grin.

She sat silently as her mom rinsed her plate in the sink, then slipped it in the dishwasher. Taylor had cautioned herself against bringing up this topic before she left Austin, but now that she had her mother alone, it seemed like the right time.

"Mom, when I was in school, did you ever suspect that I maybe had a learning disability?"

Her mother swung around, a puzzled frown furrowing her brow. "No. Why would you think that?"

"Well..." Taylor shrugged. "I don't have to tell you that school has never really been my thing. But I never understood *why* it was so hard for me. It's something that has bothered me for a long time."

"And you think it's because of a learning disability?"

"Possibly," Taylor said. "I've been reading up on it. And then Jamar noticed some similarities between me and a friend of his who was diagnosed with a learning disorder in high school."

She gave her a more detailed explanation of Jamar's suspicions, and how first seeing it in Silas helped him to recognize what Taylor was doing.

"Oh, Taylor." Her mother walked over to her and took Taylor's hands in hers. "I would say that I don't know how I could have missed it, but that would be a lie. I *completely* understand how this could have happened. I was so busy in school myself." She ran her hand over Taylor's hair, then settled it on her cheek. "I am so sorry, baby. I should have done a better job at paying attention."

"I'm not blaming you, Ma. It was easy enough for it to go unnoticed." Taylor covered the hand that cupped her cheek. "The important thing is that I'm now aware that this is potentially an issue. I have an appointment for a formal assessment this coming Tuesday." She peered up at her mother. "I'm hoping to enroll in school for the winter semester so I can start working toward my degree."

"Taylor Renee," her mother whispered. She pressed a kiss to Taylor's forehead. "I am *so* proud of you." The admiration in her voice wrapped around Taylor like a warm blanket.

"Thanks," she said. She could barely speak past the emotion knotted in her throat. "I'm proud of me too. I'll let you know how things go after the evaluation."

Her mother jutted her chin in the direction of the guest bedroom. With mischief crinkling the corners of her eyes, she said, "Let me know how things go with that too."

CHAPTER THIRTY-SIX

Jamar leaned back in his office chair and pressed the heels of his hands to his eyes. The pounding in his head had lessened to a dull ache, but he could feel it ratcheting up again. If he had to listen to his agent bitch for another second, he was going to hurl the computer through the window.

"Micah, you don't understand."

"Damn right I don't understand. Do you know how many strings I had to pull to make this workout happen? A lot of fucking strings, Jamar!"

"And I appreciate it, but—"

"I don't want your appreciation. I want your ass at that training facility so you can show these scouts you're ready to play. For weeks you've been talking about all the work you're putting in, how you've been training for hours and hours every day. Was that all bullshit?"

"No!" Jamar sat up in his chair and glared at the screen. "I've been busting my ass in that gym. I've worked harder for this than I've ever worked in my life."

"So why the hell do you want me to call this workout off just days before it's supposed to happen? I have reps from a half-dozen teams—teams I had to convince to come here because no one believes you're ready to play ball. I promised them that this wasn't going to be a waste of their time. I put my reputation on the line for this, Jamar. Not just *my* reputation, but Hill Sports Management's."

As he listened to Micah rant, Jamar fiddled with the face mask on the mini Longhorns football helmet he kept on his desk, anything to avoid looking at the computer screen and the disappointment he knew he'd find staring back at him.

"I know you have a lot riding on this too," Jamar said, swallowing past the thick layer of guilt coating his throat.

"Yeah, I do. Which is why I deserve an explanation," Micah said. "What's behind this change of heart? How'd you go from being willing to put everything you had into returning to the League to all of a sudden backing out? I thought this is what you wanted?"

"I did," Jamar said. "You know I want this." He paused before spilling the truth. "I just don't think my knee will be able to hold up."

"You said it was strong—"

"I *know* what I said. I thought it was, but I'm not so sure anymore."

"I expected more from you," Micah said. "You've always been straight with me, Jamar. When you say you're going to do something, you do it. Have you thought about how this will look once the rest of the football world finds out about it? They're going to think you chickened out."

Jamar sat up. "How would it get out? I told you to have the teams sign an NDA."

"A nondisclosure doesn't mean shit in the age of Twitter. Do you think this story won't leak like a fucking sieve if I have to go back and tell these scouts 'Oh, never mind, he's decided he's not up to playing after all.' Give me a fucking break, Jamar! You know how this business works!"

He did know, which was why he went to such lengths to keep his plans a secret. This is exactly what he'd feared would happen.

He'd been denigrated by nearly every blogger and podcaster in the sports world. The message boards were filled with faceless assholes who thought they had the right to criticize him. They went on and on about his downfall from being the most exciting rookie in years to a has-been in the span of a few games. He'd endured their ridicule and had vowed not to be fodder for any more of their stories.

"This is why I didn't want it to get out," Jamar said in a strangled whisper. "I knew the backlash would be brutal if I failed."

"Jamar, have you thought this through?" Micah asked. "Why don't you take a day or so to reassess. The workout isn't until Friday."

"Taking a day or so won't make that twinge in my knee go away," he pointed out.

"Has a doctor seen your knee?"

"It's *my* knee. I don't need a doctor to tell me that something isn't right. I can feel it," Jamar said. "Even if I did manage to get through the workout, I honestly don't think it would hold up past training camp."

"Will it hold up past the workout?" Micah asked.

Jamar cut him an incredulous look. "What does that matter?"

"Hear me out," Micah said. He placed his elbows on his desk and tapped his fingers against his lips. "It won't be easy, but there's a way that you can still save face, even if you never play another down of professional football again."

Jamar hated to admit just how high up saving face was on his priority list. There were so many more important things he should be concerned with, yet his mind chose to focus on all the naysayers who'd called him a has-been, and how humiliating it would be to admit they were right. If Micah had devised a strategy that would help Jamar avoid that, the least he could do was hear him out.

"How do you propose I do that?" Jamar asked. "You don't think those team reps will be eyeing my knee like an eagle?"

"It doesn't matter what the reps think. All you have to do is convince the *public* that you can still play. The key is to spin it in a way that makes the teams the bad guys here."

Jamar shook his head. "I don't know about this, Micah. There are no bad guys here, just bad luck. I got hurt. It happens. It's taken me a long time to come to terms with it, but I now understand that no one is to blame."

"Fine. You're enlightened. You'll still be dragged like a rag doll on Twitter if we cancel."

"How do you think you're going to stop that?" Jamar said. "You still haven't explained how I can save face by going through with this workout."

"We'll open the workout to the media."

"I told you—"

"*Hear me out*," Micah repeated, holding up his hands. "I know you wanted it to be private, but that does you no good. Let the people see how far you've come. Give *SportsCenter* a few shots for their highlight reels. You make some key catches, add a little razzle-dazzle to a few runs, and you're set. We can still hold it at the facility on UT's campus, because that coming-full-circle shit is ratings gold.

"And then, after all is done, we'll say that you decided not to take any of their offers because it wasn't enough money to make it worth your while." He dusted his hands off. "Easy."

Jamar leaned back in his chair, physically recoiling at the blatant dishonesty in Micah's plan.

He shook his head. "Something about this just doesn't sit right with me."

"Are you kidding? It's the perfect solution."

"Knowingly deceiving the teams? Putting them through the expense of coming here when I know I won't be signing anything? *That's* your perfect solution?"

"Are you the team accountant now? Why do you care how much they're spending? Besides, the only in-person scouts we'll have are from Dallas, Houston, and New Orleans. These guys don't care about the money. They see it as a free trip to Austin."

"I don't like it," Jamar said.

"Fine, we make it all virtual. I can call the teams right now and tell them to cancel their flights and tune in to the livestream. How does that sit with your damn conscience?" Micah asked. "And before you give me any more of that bullshit about how this isn't fair to the team owners, I want to make one thing clear. None of them are going to offer you what you're really worth. The best you could have hoped for is five million for three years. Being that you have me as your agent, I could get you another half mil or so, but with the way the League's set up these days, even *I* can only do so much.

"We can make it so that it looks as if you're walking away from them, and not the other way around. Trust me on this," Micah pleaded. "Remember, these are the same people who gave up on you. You don't owe them anything."

Jamar chewed his lower lip and tried to ignore the uneasy feeling roiling in his gut.

Even if he removed his aversion to deceiving the NFL teams from the equation, did he really have enough confidence in his knee to put it through that hellish battery of endurance tests? Was it worth the risks?

The better question: Was it worth the reward?

He considered all that he would gain if he signed on to Micah's plan. The naysayers wouldn't have any ammunition for their attacks, not if he showed them that he'd gotten back into playing form. More importantly, it would give him the chance to showcase Taylor's work. He would give her all the credit and make sure it was understood that without her help, he would never have gotten through any of this.

Still, he couldn't shake the feeling that it was wrong to hold this workout under false pretenses.

Unless...unless he *didn't* hold it under false pretenses.

He could be up front with the teams from the outset. Or even if he waited until the end of the workout, he could immediately level with the scouts, let them know that he would not be entertaining any offers. If all it cost them was an hour of watching him perform the drills via a video stream— that wouldn't be so bad, would it? Not if it meant holding up the end of his bargain with Taylor.

And, at the end of the day, he was still leaving the game of football on his terms. Even better, he could convince himself that he'd given all that he could to make the dream he'd taken away from Silas a reality.

He would eventually figure out what to do about Big Silas's care. Maybe he could do as Taylor had suggested and downsize. Between the sale of the house and the couple million he had in the bank, he could take care of his family, Silas's family, and Taylor, and still live comfortably until he figured out his next step.

He could do this. This final test, this final stand, would be enough. It *had* to be enough.

"Okay," Jamar said, the word coming out in a raspy whisper.

"What was that?" Micah asked.

He spoke up. "I said okay. If it's all virtual . . ." He paused. "If it's all virtual, I'll go through with the workout. Hell, try to get even more teams to tune in if you can."

"Excuse me?"

Jamar jerked around at the sound of Taylor's voice. His eyes never leaving hers, he said, "Um, Micah, I'll check in with you later." He clicked the computer mouse, ending the FaceTime call.

"So you're not canceling the workout? Even though, by your own admission, you could barely dance on Saturday night?"

"Don't jump to conclusions, Taylor. It's not what you think."

"Really? So what is it? Based on what I just heard, not only are you planning to go through with this, but you want even *more* teams there."

"It is *just* the workout," Jamar said. "I'm not playing football again, even if I'm offered a contract." He explained his plan to her, underscoring how it would provide him with the opportunity to end his football career on his own terms.

"This will benefit you too," Jamar pointed out. "It'll be streamed live. The entire sports world will see the job you've done training me."

"Do you really think I care more about my business than about you permanently injuring yourself?"

"But this is what you wanted. This was our original deal."

"I don't care about our original deal! What I can't figure out is why you don't care about yourself?"

"It's one workout, Taylor! An hour of me going through a few drills, and I'm done."

She paced back and forth, from the edge of his desk to the trophy display case. "All it takes is a bad landing when you perform the vertical jump, and just like that"—she snapped her fingers—"your kneecap is dust. It's gone, Jamar. And for what? For me?"

She stopped her pacing and stood before him, crossing her arms over her chest. "Or is it to show some stupid bloggers that you're not the washed-up athlete they say you are? To prove to yourself that you can still play? Well, guess what, you *can't*. It's time you accept it."

Her words ripped at the thin barrier he'd built around his pride, raking over barely healed wounds. His jaw ached with the effort it took to temper his rising anger.

"I could still play if I wanted to," Jamar said.

"My God." She sighed up at the ceiling. "You can't," she said. "I don't care what you've told yourself, nothing is worth this kind of risk."

"How the fuck do you know what's worth it to me!" Jamar snapped.

She jumped back, her eyes wide, her mouth falling open.

Jamar ran both hands down his face. Shame over his outburst gnawed at his conscience, but she didn't understand. She could *never* understand.

His shoulders slumped with the weight of despair that washed over him. "You just don't get it," Jamar said. "This is bigger than me."

Her furrowed brow flattened into a thin line as awareness slowly traveled across her face.

"This isn't about you proving anything," she said, awe lilting her voice. "This is guilt. You still think you owe this to someone who's been dead for eight years."

"Don't," Jamar warned. "You know nothing about this, so don't act as if you do."

Anger and hurt flared in her eyes. Her body shook with it.

But then a calm seemed to take over her, and Jamar found that more alarming than her rage.

"You know what?" she said, her voice sharp as cut glass. "You do what the hell you want. But don't expect me to stick around and watch."

With that, she turned on her heel and stalked out of the room.

Jamar told himself to go after her. If he let her leave this house without talking this through, it would be the biggest mistake he could ever make.

But the concoction of fury, anguish, and fear flowing in his veins wouldn't allow him to take a single step.

She was wrong. This wasn't about guilt. It was about him doing what he had to do in order to be able to look himself in the mirror.

He would fix this with Taylor. He would figure out a way to make her see that he was doing this, in part, for her. Because he cared about her. For now, he just had to get through the damn workout.

CHAPTER THIRTY-SEVEN

A crisp breeze carried the delicate scent of flowers. Several birds landed on the spindly, leafless branches of the tree overhead, their sharp chirps piercing the stillness of the afternoon.

His hands shoved deep into his pockets, Jamar squeezed his fists tight as he stared down at the charcoal-gray headstone. The sun reflected off the flecks of silver speckled throughout the polished stone, making it seem as though there were dancing lights embedded in the hard slab.

How long had it been since he'd arrived at this gravesite? An hour? Two? He'd lost track of the time, yet in all the minutes that had ticked by since he'd gotten here, Jamar still couldn't put voice to what he wanted to say.

What words of apology would ever suffice?

He stared at the block letters and numbers etched into stone and experienced that odd feeling of disassociation that had occurred the few times he'd visited this memorial. In some ways he was still unable to accept that Silas lay here, even after eight long years. If only he could talk to him one last time. If only he could tell him how sorry he was, and beg for his forgiveness.

But that would never happen.

He would never hear *I forgive you* from Silas. All he could do was hold on to the belief that his best friend would extend to him the grace and compassion he'd shown so many times while he was alive. It's the only way Jamar would gain a semblance of peace.

Shame tore through him for admitting, even to himself, that he sought forgiveness, that he wished for peace. He didn't deserve either.

But he couldn't go on like this. He ached for the tiniest shred of absolution from the guilt that had plagued him for so long.

"I wondered if I'd find you here."

Jamar twisted around at the sound of Andrea's voice. She stood several yards behind him; the carpet of mowed grass must have silenced her footsteps. She held a cellophane-wrapped bouquet in one hand and a package of Chips Ahoy! cookies in the other.

Jamar pointed to them. "His favorite."

"Yep," she said with a sad smile. "He ate five every night with a glass of milk."

"With ice in it," Jamar said.

"With ice." She chuckled. She examined the blue package as if someone else had put it in her hand. "I used to come here once a month and eat cookies while I talk to him, but I haven't been here since his birthday back in July. I hadn't even realized it had been that long until this morning."

She traveled the rest of the way to the gravesite and set the unopened cookies on top of the slab.

"I can move these," Jamar said, reaching for the dozen white roses he'd placed in the stone vase built on top of the headstone.

"No, that's okay. I'll just lay these here. The roses are nice."

Jamar swallowed and nodded. He stared at the flowers, because he didn't know where else to look. The guilt that stuck to him like a second skin intensified. Acknowledging the misery he'd caused Silas's family ate at his gut.

"When did you get to town?" Drea asked.

"Just before noon," he said. "I wasn't sure if I was going to make the trip. I hadn't planned on it. You know I don't really like coming to this graveyard."

"I know," she said. "But I'm happy you did. The anniversaries are never easy." She tipped her head to the side and peered up at him. "So what's this I hear about you holding some event for NFL scouts tomorrow?"

He frowned. "You know about that?"

"I don't live under a rock," she said. "It's all anyone is talking about. The local newscast ran a story during their sports segment, and at least twenty people sent me the link to your agent's tweet when he announced that you would be doing this virtual workout because you're thinking of playing again."

Jamar rubbed the back of his neck. "If I tell you something, do you promise to keep it to yourself until tomorrow?"

Drea nodded.

"I'm not doing this so that I can get on anyone's team. I won't give any of them the opportunity to even make an offer."

"Why not?"

"Because the chances of me getting through even a single NFL season without injuring myself are slim to none," he admitted. The words tasted like acid on his tongue.

"So why are you going through with the workout at all?"

"I need to show everyone just how far I've come in my recovery. You see, I made this deal with my trainer that I would endorse her fitness consulting business."

"You mean your girlfriend," Drea said.

"Yes, she is my girlfriend," he conceded. Although Jamar wasn't sure how true that was anymore. "But that's beside the point. We made this bargain before things became serious between us. And there's more to tomorrow's workout than the promise I made to Taylor. I want to make this happen for Silas.

"That's what's so damn hard about finally accepting that I'll never play again. It feels as if I'm letting Silas down." He shook his head. "I didn't want much, Drea. Maybe another year or so, something more than the half season I got to play. It just wasn't enough time to live out that dream the two of us had."

"You were lucky, Jamar. There are so many who would give anything for the half season you got to play professional football. And I'm not talking about Silas," she added. "I'm talking about others who get to live long lives but never get a taste of what you had in those few games you *did* play in."

"Yeah, I know that," he said. "I just wanted a little more time. I wanted the chance to leave on my own terms."

"I know how hard it was when you were hurt and had to leave the game." She clamped a hand to his forearm and rubbed back and forth. Then she pinched him. "But that's still no reason to scare me like that! What in the hell were you thinking!"

"Ouch!" His eyes snapped to hers. "What was that for?"

"That was for you nearly giving me a heart attack," she said. "I never liked the fact that you and Silas played football. I would sit in the stands and hold my breath through the entire game. I did that for years, Jamar. All through high school, while you were at UT, and then with the Bears. I finally get some peace and you go ahead and do this!"

"I was doing it partly for you and Big Silas," he said.

"Why? Because of your ridiculous belief that you're in some way responsible for taking care of us?"

"It's not ridiculous. I am respon—"

"You're not."

"Yes, I *am*," he said. "I owe it to Silas. Eight years ago today, I sat beside him in that hospital room and I made a promise. I told him I would take care of all of you."

"Silas would never want you to jeopardize your own health for our sake—for anyone's sake. And I sure as hell wouldn't want you to do that either. Seeing you carted off a field once was more than enough for me." She looped her arm in the crook of his elbow and leaned against his side, resting her head on his shoulder. "I much prefer you like this, living a long, safe, and healthy life."

Guilt sat like the Rock of Gibraltar in his throat. Her brother should be living a long, safe, and healthy life too.

"It was my fault," he whispered.

Time stood stock-still as the words hung in the air. It was his voice, but Jamar could have sworn someone else had spoken. How else could he explain what had just come forth from his mouth?

"The accident," he clarified, now that the words were out there. "It was my fault."

"No, it wasn't," Drea said.

"Yes, it was. You don't—"

"I *know*, Jamar," she said, her voice soft yet insistent. "I know." She let go of his arm and moved a couple of steps closer to the grave. "I have Silas's cell phone. I've had it since that night. It miraculously survived the crash."

Shock siphoned the air from his lungs. Shame assaulted

him—hot and burning. She'd known all this time? She'd known and had never confronted him?

"I saw all the text messages he sent you that night, and how you never replied." She ran her fingers over the engraved letters. "I wondered if maybe you didn't have your phone on you, or if you'd had it on silent? But when I saw how guilty you looked at the hospital that night, I realized you'd purposely ignored him." She looked up at him. "I still don't know why. I've wanted to ask you so many times over the years."

"I'm so sorry," Jamar whispered, his throat on fire as he tried to get the words out. "Drea..."

"I'm not asking for an explanation anymore, because it doesn't matter. It doesn't. You were the brother he never had, Jamar. And there is nothing on this earth that you could have done that Silas wouldn't have forgiven." She lifted her shoulders in a helpless shrug. "So I forgave you too. I forgave you a long time ago."

He couldn't speak. For the life of him, he could not utter a single word.

"You have to stop blaming yourself. He wouldn't want that. That's how I stopped blaming you, because I knew my brother's heart, and I knew he would *never* want you to carry this guilt with you."

"How?" Jamar had to work to clear his throat. "How can you not hate me, Drea? How can you ever stop blaming me when you know he'd be alive if not for me?"

She stalked over to him and cupped his jaw in her palm. Jamar didn't realize he was crying until he felt her brush the tears from his cheek.

"I could *never* hate you. Ever." She wiped another tear. "I don't know whether Silas would still be alive if you'd answered his calls, and neither do you. That truck could have hit him at any time. Even if he'd left at midnight, or whenever that party ended. We will never know, and it's not our place to question what fate had in store for Silas."

Her words mirrored Taylor's so closely that Jamar heard them in Taylor's voice. But just as it had done with Taylor, his mind refused to allow those words to absolve him from his guilt.

"I stopped blaming you when I finally accepted that no amount of blame would bring Silas back. You can go on blaming yourself, but what will you gain from it, Jamar? How does it honor Silas if you spend the rest of your life punishing yourself?" She squeezed his arm. "You're the closest thing I have to a brother, and I need you to be here for a very long time." She gestured to the headstone. "There are better ways to honor Silas than playing football. He was more than just football, and so are you."

His eyes roamed over her face, over those features she shared with her brother. The broad, flat nose with a smattering of freckles. Sharp, pronounced cheekbones. Deep-set brown eyes.

Eyes that held forgiveness.

"And you don't have to worry about Big Silas," Andrea continued. "I've handled everything. Between his VA benefits and supplemental insurance plan, his round-the-clock care is paid for. The only person you have to take care of is *you*." She gave him a peck on the cheek. "Silas would want you to be happy. You need to find what would make you happy and embrace it."

Jamar knew what would make him happy. Or rather, who.

He closed his eyes and breathed in a heavy sigh. He'd

messed up so damn badly when it came to Taylor. What was he going to do? How was he going to fix this?

He didn't deserve her forgiveness, but that didn't mean he wasn't going to fight for it anyway. He just had to figure out how.

He had so much to figure out. About Taylor. About this workout. About *everything*.

"Jamar?"

He opened his eyes.

"Stop overthinking," Andrea said. "Life isn't as complicated as you're making it out to be." She pressed a finger to the center of his chest. "Let this, and *only* this, guide you. You got this."

Jamar nodded, the corners of his mouth tilting up in a wan smile. "Yeah, I got this," he said. He wrapped her up in a gentle but fierce hug and pressed a kiss to the side of her head. "I couldn't have chosen a better big sister if I tried. Love you, Drea."

CHAPTER THIRTY-EIGHT

Taylor increased the volume on *The Princess and the Frog* as Ray the firefly started to sing about Evangeline, the evening star that he was convinced was his long-lost love. This part got her every single time. Poor Ray, putting all his hopes and dreams in an unattainable object that would never be what he needed it to be.

"You and me both, Ray," she muttered. "You and me both."

She reached for her phone, then quickly set it back, face-down, on the sofa. She'd done so unconsciously, but she was determined to break the habit of automatically picking up her phone whenever her mind wandered. Especially on a day like today, when she was actively avoiding social media.

Despite muting everything to do with football, she'd continued to catch tidbits about the biggest story in sports. It seemed as if the entire freaking Internet had gone wild after Hill Sports Management tweeted their announcement about "some big news" regarding Jamar "Diesel" Dixon. The chatter surrounding his attempt at a comeback had reached levels that made the viral video with Craig from a few months ago seem like nothing.

Taylor refused to be a witness to any of it. If Jamar thought performing for cameras was more important than his health, well, that was his prerogative. She decided it would be better for *her* mental health if she stayed off social media and avoided live TV for the next twenty-four hours. She would watch Tiana, Naveen, and the rest of the bayou crew on repeat as she strategized her own future.

Taylor grabbed the packet of materials she'd received from the assessment center. For the first time in forever, her initial reaction to the thought of going back to school was not accompanied by mind-numbing dread or baking a pan of brownies. She still wasn't all that enthusiastic about the idea—she doubted she would ever feel excited by the thought of sitting in a classroom. But there was an optimism flowing through her that she hadn't experienced in far too long.

This was a new journey, and she was eager to take that first step.

Taylor had been all but certain before ever walking through the doors of the assessment center that she would be diagnosed with an LD, as the diagnostician had referred to it. But she hadn't expected to get a possible ADHD diagnosis as well.

Now that she'd had a couple of days to research it, she realized that she fit the textbook definition of someone who suffered from attention deficit hyperactivity disorder. The constant restlessness, the abundance of energy, the inability to concentrate on one thing for any period of time; they were just a few of the many checkboxes she ticked off under the list of common symptoms.

During her assessment, both the diagnostician and the psychologist who sat down to discuss her diagnosis with her suspected she'd had the conditions all along. Because of the frequency with which she'd switched schools as a kid, she'd just fallen through the cracks. Her hyperactivity had been written off as her being a tomboy, and her underperformance on tests blamed on a lack of self-discipline.

It was reassuring to learn the true cause behind the issues that had plagued her for so long. The road ahead wouldn't be easy, but at least she finally had a map to help navigate it.

She felt...hopeful. As horrible as these past few days had been since walking out of Jamar's house, it had also been an awakening, giving her the motivation she needed to get serious about school. She'd started looking at area college programs again. And because karma had to prove that it was always the baddest bitch, the kinesiology program at Southwestern University in Georgetown—just minutes from Jamar's house—seemed to be the perfect fit.

Taylor's throat tightened as the sense of foreboding she hadn't been able to shake flared up yet again.

She'd fought so hard to subdue all thoughts of him—a wasted effort if ever there was one. On a scale of one to five, her anxiety hovered at about one hundred.

What if he slipped while running the forty-yard dash or that tricky shuttle run? Those short sprints between the orange cones were hell on the knees.

It was *his* knee. He'd made his choice. It was no longer her concern.

It would be great if she could communicate those sentiments to the ball of trepidation rolling around in her stomach.

Her phone rang. She flipped it over to find London's picture staring back at her. As she answered the call, there was a simultaneous knock on the door.

"It's us. Open up," she heard London say both through the phone and the front door.

What are they doing here in the middle of the day?

Taylor flung her head back and sighed up at the ceiling. She should have anticipated this after sending that vague text yesterday, telling them that she would be skipping tonight's girls' night out. Especially after avoiding all their other texts this week.

"Come on, Taylor! It's freezing out here!"

She pushed herself up from the sofa and made it to the door.

"Why aren't you both at work?" Taylor asked by way of greeting.

"Hello to you too," London said. "Are you going to let us in? That cold front moved in this morning and now my ass is literally frozen."

"Do I *have* to let you in?" Taylor asked.

London and Samiah both gave her that look—the one that said she had two seconds to start acting right before she got her butt handed to her.

Taylor stepped out of the doorway and flung her hand out. "Fine. Come in," she said.

They both entered, making her tiny studio feel that much smaller. London held a cloth shopping bag and Samiah had a tray of something.

"Sorry I haven't replied to the group texts lately. I haven't been in the mood to talk," Taylor said. "Or to do anything social, to be honest."

"Yeah, we gathered that," London said. She pulled a paper sack from the bag. "Thus the wine."

"And the charcuterie board," Samiah said, holding out a platter with artfully arranged fruit, crackers, cheese, meats, and olives. She brushed past Taylor and went into the living room. "Oh, we're watching...cartoons," she said as she set the platter on the coffee table. "I guess that's"—she looked to London, concern creasing her forehead—"good?"

"Don't read too much into it. I watch this movie at least once a week," Taylor said. She picked up the remote and turned off the TV.

"So where are we in the breakup process?" London asked. "Are we wallowing, or are we still in the angry, 'fuck that guy and the horse he rode in on' stage?"

"I hope we're in the eat our feelings stage, because I skipped breakfast," Samiah said, removing the plastic lid from the platter.

"I'm not in any of those stages," Taylor said as she grabbed paper cups and napkins from the kitchen and brought them over to the coffee table. She pointed to the literature from the assessment center. "I'm moving forward and looking toward the future."

"Ooooh, you had your evaluation." Samiah lifted one of the pamphlets from the coffee table. "How did it go?"

"It'll be another week before the diagnostician provides the formal report, but I already feel more confident after talking with her. I can do this," Taylor said, unable to squelch her excitement now that she had people to share it with.

That's what these two did for her. They were her sounding board, her support system; they would never understand just how much they'd come to mean to her.

"Ah, I get it. You're in the 'all right nah, look at you' stage," London said with a finger snap. "It's what we're all striving for, girl. Good for you."

Taylor lowered herself to the floor and sat cross-legged on the side of the coffee table opposite the sofa. She helped herself to cheese, crackers, and a cup of wine. If someone told her just an hour ago that she would be anything but pissed at such an interruption, Taylor would have called them a liar. But this is exactly what she'd needed today.

"Hey, did either of you see the trailer for the new Beyoncé special on Netflix?" Samiah asked. She picked up her phone and swiped across the screen. "It dropped on Twitter earlier today."

Taylor shook her head. "I'm avoiding social media. I haven't looked at Twitter or Instagram since yesterday. I was forced to go on Facebook to post about my pop-up yoga class tomorrow morning. I can use some students. Hint, hint."

London stared directly at her as she bit into a green olive. Based on that raised eyebrow, Taylor figured she shouldn't count on her friend to show up tomorrow.

"Turn it to ESPN," Samiah said, still looking at her phone. She pointed at the television. "Turn it on now!"

"No." Taylor shook her head. "I'm avoiding TV too. Especially ESPN."

"Jamar canceled his workout. He's giving a press conference right now."

"What!" Taylor picked up the remote and stabbed at the power button. "What channel is ESPN?"

"I don't know!" both London and Samiah screeched.

As she scrolled through the channel guide, stark terror seized her chest. God, had he been hurt? Is that why he'd called it off?

"Is there anything explaining why he canceled it?" Taylor asked.

"No, just a tweet from that Alec Mooney guy. He posted a picture of the empty parking lot at the UT practice facility. It says 'Micah Hill of Hill Sports Management announced that

Jamar Dixon's scheduled tryout event would no longer take place.' His follow-up tweet says that Jamar will be making a statement instead."

What could have caused him to call it off at the last minute like this?

After what seemed like endless scrolling, Taylor finally found ESPN. She involuntarily flinched at the sight of Jamar sitting at a white folding table; various pieces of football equipment were assembled behind him. He was reading from his phone.

"—wasn't the easiest decision, but it was the right one to make. Going through with this workout would have put me at risk for an even more substantial injury. I decided it wasn't worth it. I now know that I don't have anything to prove to anyone. Including myself."

A rueful smile crossed his lips. "To say my professional football career didn't last as long as I wanted it to last is the ultimate understatement, but I will eventually learn to live with that. Millions of young men who strap on their shoulder pads on Friday nights would give anything to experience what I did for those few short months with the Chicago Bears. I will always be grateful and count myself as one of the lucky ones.

"But today is about more than my football career. This is about the future. As many of you know, I lost my best friend, Silas Cannon III, during our senior year at Katy High School. If he'd had the chance, I have no doubt that Silas would have made it all the way to Canton, Ohio, and the football Hall of Fame. Even though the game meant a lot to him, Silas's family meant more. Helping people—especially those who just couldn't seem to get a fair shake in life—meant more to him."

Jamar folded his hands on the table.

"Today, as I announce my official retirement from professional football, I want to also announce my plans to launch the Silas Cannon III Foundation, which will focus on supporting kids with incarcerated parents. I know this is a cause that my best friend would approve of.

"As I bring this statement to a close, I want to take a minute to thank everyone who had a hand in bringing me to this point in my life. My parents, my agent, my coaches and former teammates, the physicians and specialists who took care of me, the Cannon family, and Taylor Powell of Taylor'd Conditioning Fitness Consulting."

"Oh, shit," London gasped.

"Shhh..." Samiah whispered.

Jamar looked up from his phone and stared directly at the camera.

"My biggest regret in not being able to work out for you all today is that I won't be able to showcase the strides I've made in my recovery thanks to Taylor'd Conditioning. Its owner is one of the toughest, most talented, and most qualified fitness professionals I've ever had the pleasure of working with. If I *had* made it back into the League, any success I enjoyed would be thanks to her.

"Taylor'd Conditioning has my wholehearted endorsement." He paused for a moment, then said, "And Taylor Powell has my whole heart." He stood. "Thank you for your time today," he finished, and then he walked out of the camera frame.

None of them said anything. They all just continued to stare at the television until London broke the silence with a low whistle.

"I don't know about you, but I'm ready to marry his ass," London said.

"What do I do?" Taylor asked. "Do I call him? Do I wait for him to call me?"

Samiah hunched her shoulders. "I don't know. Maybe wait?"

"But what if he doesn't call?"

"Of course he'll call," London said. "The man just told the entire world that you have his whole heart. That's the sweetest thing I've seen since this one's boyfriend had us tacking sticky notes all around the botanical gardens. I hate both of you right now."

"Save your hate," Taylor said. "At least until Jamar calls."

A niggling trace of uncertainty lingered, preventing her from fully giving in to the hope that had bloomed like wildflowers within her chest.

"If he calls," she amended.

CHAPTER THIRTY-NINE

With her ankles resting on her thighs, Taylor interlaced her fingers and pressed her palms together.

"Breathe in," she instructed in a soothing voice. She sucked in a cleansing breath and tried not to wince as the sharp gust of cold air cut through her.

Hot yoga seemed to be all the rage these days, but maybe she was in the midst of creating an entirely new trend: freeze your ass off yoga. She should embrace the goose bumps popping up along her forearms.

There were at least a dozen more suitable places she could have held this pop-up yoga class, but she needed to be here in Zilker Park and she refused to change the location. She hadn't expected anyone to sign up after that cold front blew in yesterday, but to her surprise there were six brave souls willing to endure the elements of this chilly morning.

An even bigger shock, Samiah and London were counted in those six.

Their presence calmed her nearly as much as the asana yoga poses she'd guided the class through. Her mind and body needed this today.

"Stretch your hands to the sky," Taylor guided, lifting her

hands over her head. "And now back to your center." She brought her palms together in the resting pose. "Another breath in. Feel your chest expand. Then push out everything that's troubling you. Let the wind take it."

She opened her eyes and glanced out at the class.

She was pretty sure London had fallen asleep. Her head was bowed low, her chin on her chest. Taylor couldn't be upset. London had warned her this might happen.

She took the class through several more poses before bringing their session to a close.

After thanking them for joining her and passing out business cards, she walked over to where London and Samiah were rolling up their mats.

"Did you enjoy your nap?" she asked London.

"It was perfect," she answered with a dreamy sigh. "Exactly what I needed before starting the marathon of surgeries I have today." She tipped her head toward Samiah. "I'm happy she convinced me to come with her."

"So am I," Taylor said with a laugh.

"Have you gotten a phone call yet?" Samiah asked.

Taylor shook her head.

"It hasn't even been twenty-four hours," London said. "Maybe he's still working up the nerve to call, or he's meeting with lawyers to set up that foundation, or he drank away his sorrows over having to retire and he's too hungover to use a phone. He'll eventually call." She hefted the mat strap over her shoulder. "My shift starts in an hour, so I need to get out of here."

She gave them both quick hugs before taking off in the direction of Strafford Drive where she'd parked.

"She's right, you know," Samiah said. "Not about the hangover, although she may be right about that too. Lord knows he has reason to get drunk. But I think if you give him time, he'll call." She clamped a hand on Taylor's shoulder and gave it a squeeze. "I need to get going myself. I have to go into the office."

"On a Saturday?"

"Gotta make sacrifices if I'm gonna be the boss one day."

"You got that right." Taylor held her hand up for a high five. "Gimme some."

Samiah obliged, but then her eyes grew wide and a smile drew across her face.

"You've got company," she said.

Taylor turned in the direction she indicated.

Her breath caught.

Jamar leaned against the front of his parked Range Rover, feet braced apart, hands stuffed in the pockets of his tan corduroys. Taylor fully embraced the longing that swept through her. She'd spent most of the past week avoiding any mention of him, but ever since yesterday's press conference, her heart fluttered like hummingbird wings within her chest just at the thought of him.

"Told you," Samiah said. She gestured to several students from the class who still lingered. "Why don't you finish up with these folks and then *you* can go to *him*? And you'd better text us to let us know how things go," she added.

"I will," Taylor said. "I'll see you Friday night."

"It's next Saturday, remember? We're getting together for Daniel's birthday."

"Oh yeah, right," she said. "I knew that. See you next Saturday."

As Taylor fielded questions about yoga poses from the two women who remained, she was hyperaware of the fact that Jamar stood less than thirty yards away. She didn't have to look over her shoulder to know that he'd started walking toward her. She felt him in her bones.

"How much do you charge per hour as a personal trainer?" asked the woman with curly brunette hair.

"I'm sorry, but I won't be taking on any new clients for a while," Taylor answered. "I will continue to hold classes like this one. Keep an eye out for announcements on my Facebook page and Instagram account."

"I will! This class was great, although I'd rather be somewhere warmer."

So much for her new yoga trend.

"We'll definitely be indoors next time," Taylor said.

The smiles on both women's faces grew wider as they looked past Taylor and waved.

"Hi! I'm a big fan, Diesel," the brunette said.

"Thanks," he answered.

The deep timbre of his voice caused more goose bumps to pop up along her skin. Taylor kept her back to him, even after the two women withdrew from the area she'd commandeered for this morning's class. She needed a moment to gather herself.

"Taylor," he called.

Anxiety knotted in her stomach as she turned to face him.

He still had his hands in his pockets. Any passerby who saw him would presume he was the epitome of relaxed and unbothered, but she noted the strain in his broad shoulders, the lines marring his forehead and bracketing his mouth.

"Hey," she said, her heart pounding steadily against her rib cage.

"Hey," he returned. He nudged his chin in the direction of the two women who'd just left. "Did I hear you say you aren't taking on any clients?"

"Not anyone new." She picked up her yoga mat and rolled it up so that she'd have something to do with her hands. Tucking it underneath her arm, she said, "A couple of my old regulars contacted me. I'll be working with them and offering a few pop-up classes here and there, but I don't want to take on too much."

"Because of your ankle?" he asked. "Is it healing properly?"

"My ankle is fine," Taylor said. She straightened her shoulders, any vestiges of modesty floating away on the wave of pride that swelled in her chest. "I don't want to take on any new clients because if I do as well as I *think* I will do on the college entrance exam in a few weeks, I'll be starting classes full-time when the winter semester begins."

A small smile lifted one corner of Jamar's mouth. "You registered to take the exam."

"And I requested testing accommodations: extra time to complete the test and a proctor to read the questions out loud."

"Good." He nodded, his throat undulating as he swallowed.

Intolerably tense moments ticked by as they stood there facing each other. Disquiet filled the space between them, a cloud of unspoken words weighing heavy in the air.

"Did you see the press conference yesterday?" he asked.

"Yes. I think the foundation is a wonderful way to honor Silas's memory."

"Yeah, I think so too." He glanced at the ground, then brought his eyes back to her. "I'm sorry, Taylor," Jamar said, the words exiting his mouth on an achingly soft whisper. "I know sorry isn't enough. There's no excuse for the way I spoke to you the day you left, especially because you were right."

Her brow arched. "Was I?"

"I was never going to accept a contract from any team. I'd made that decision while I was still on that call with Micah.

But it was irresponsible for me to even consider going through with the workout after feeling that pain in my knee."

"Were you the one who called it off?" she asked.

He nodded. "I had Micah contact the teams yesterday morning, about an hour before the livestream was supposed to start."

"What made you cancel it?"

"It's like you said, it wasn't worth the risk. Knowing I wouldn't play ball, no matter the outcome of the workout, it just didn't make sense to put my body through that." His gaze caught hers and held it. "I realized performing for those teams wouldn't give me the one thing I've truly been seeking: Silas's forgiveness."

Taylor pulled her trembling bottom lip between her teeth, her throat tightening with empathy over the anguish she heard in his voice.

"Everything else I said I wanted, it was all bullshit," Jamar said. "This was about Silas. It's always been about Silas, about me trying to make up for what I stole from him. I've always known that in here," he said, tapping the center of his chest. "But when you pointed it out that day in my office, it just . . . it hit me in a way I wasn't ready for."

"Hurting you was not my intention," Taylor said, but then she stopped. Shaking her head, she admitted, "That's a lie. I *did* want to hurt you. I was *so* furious that you let Micah talk you into going through with that workout. I didn't think past my own anger. I should have, and I'm sorry."

"No, I needed to hear it," he said. He cast his eyes downward and toed a thin branch that had been carried by the wind. "I found out that Andrea, Silas's sister, has known this whole time that Silas left the party to look for me. She knows that I ignored his calls that night, yet she doesn't blame me for what happened. I figure if Drea can forgive me, maybe one day I'll be able to forgive myself. I'm not there yet, but I'm working on it."

He lifted his head and looked at her, his imploring eyes full of remorse and longing.

"But I'll *never* forgive myself if I've messed up things with you, Taylor."

The aching tenderness in his voice shattered her. She reached for him.

Jamar captured her hands and brought them to his lips, pressing a firm yet gentle kiss to the backs of her fingers.

"I've spent the past eight years existing, but not really living. I didn't think I deserved a life. I definitely didn't deserve happiness." His mouth tipped up in the barest smile. "And then one day I came to this very park and found you, and my entire life changed.

"You showed me what it means to be happy, Taylor." He bowed his head and with an anguished plea said, "Just tell me what I have to do to make this right, and it's done. I'll do anything. *Every*thing. As long as I don't have to let you go."

A fierce rush of emotion surged through her, its intensity so powerful it took her breath away. Taylor captured his face in her hands and tilted it up so she could look at him.

"Damn you, Twenty-Three. How dare you make me cry in public," she said with a tearful laugh. She ran her thumb over his lips before brushing her own against them. "You don't have to do anything more," she whispered. "Because I'm not letting you go either." Taylor rested her forehead against his. They stood there for several moments before she said, "Now that you won't be spending five hours in the gym every day, what are you going to do with all your time?"

He squinted as if contemplating. "Hmm...I think I'm going to Disney World. Care to join me?"

EPILOGUE

Taylor rested an elbow on the red-and-white-checkered tablecloth and peered out at the sea of bodies moving with the cowgirl leading the Texas Two-Step. The crowd had been boisterous all night, but the energy level had spiked once the live band took to the stage.

To no one's surprise, several patrons had come to their table, seeking an autograph, picture, or both from their favorite Longhorns running back. Taylor doubted she'd ever get used to it, but as she looked over at Jamar—who was in an animated conversation with Daniel—she knew it was worth it. She would happily put up with the interruptions from random strangers if it meant being with him.

"Hey, Taylor," Samiah called as she reached into the basket of sweet potato fries they'd ordered as an appetizer. "What were you saying about that website? Have they had a change of heart?"

"Not exactly," Taylor said. "The editor at *Modish and Melanated* contacted me yesterday to discuss the possibility of me writing a few featured articles for the site. It's not the job I wanted, of course, but I figure it's a way for me to get my feet wet and remain on their radar."

"Don't forget the most important part," Jamar chimed in.

He took a pull on his bottle of Shiner Bock. "Once she earns her degree and expands Taylor'd Conditioning into a world-dominating fitness empire, having some articles written on a nationally known website will look pretty good in the brochures."

"Oh, I like the way you think," Taylor said, kissing him on the nose.

London rolled her eyes and groaned. "Lord, save me from yet another nauseatingly sweet couple."

"I know," Taylor said. "We're disgustingly sweet. You should try to find—"

"Wait." London cut her off, holding up a hand. "Was that a yeehaw? Did I just hear a genuine yeehaw? Whose idea was it to come to this place?"

"The birthday boy's." Samiah laughed. "Daniel's been in Texas all these months and has never been to a honky-tonk."

"I've lived here all my *life*, and I've never been to a damn honky-tonk." London pointed a cheese-stuffed jalapeño at Daniel. "You'd better be happy it's your birthday, Dimples, and that the food is good. Otherwise I'd be out of here."

"You're not enjoying this?" Daniel gestured at the memorabilia covering nearly every inch of wall space. "This would impress the hell out of country music fans."

"Of which I am not," London said.

"You should keep an open mind," Taylor teased. "I'll bet a place like this would be great for the class reunion you're planning."

"Ha ha. You're so funny," London deadpanned. She pushed back her chair. "I need to boot-scoot my way to the bathroom."

"Don't sneak out the back door," Samiah said.

"I make no promises," she called.

Taylor noticed quite a few heads turning as London strutted toward the restrooms. If she was still on the hunt for a random hookup, she'd have no problem finding a list of willing candidates tonight.

She turned back to Jamar and found him grinning at his phone.

"I want to laugh too," Taylor said.

He turned the screen to her. It was a picture of a skinny black man with a pout worthy of a two-year-old who'd just had his favorite toy taken away.

"Big Silas is not happy with his live-in nurse," Jamar said.

"I thought you said he agreed to it?"

"He agreed to a nurse, but he didn't realize that nurse's name would be Darrell."

She burst out laughing. "That is so cruel. That man thought he'd have a cutie taking care of him."

"I'm sure Darrell is both a handsome and competent nurse."

"Your jokes are getting better," she quipped. "Hey." She bumped him on the shoulder. "You think your knee can handle a few twirls on the dance floor?"

The band had switched from the upbeat two-step number to a slow country ballad.

He pushed his chair back and stood. "Only one way to find out."

Taylor quickly got up from her seat and took him by the hand. "We'll be back," she called to Samiah and Daniel.

She waved at London as she passed them on her way back to the table, a fresh drink in her hand.

The crowd was happy to make room as their beloved Diesel Dixon made his way onto the dance floor. Taylor leaned her head against his chest while they rocked back and forth to the sad love song.

"You know," he whispered into her ear, "you're not the only one who got a call yesterday."

She lifted her head to look at him. "Who called you?" she asked, her brow arched in inquiry.

"The son of my old football coach at Katy High School. He was just hired as the athletic director at a school in Round Rock."

"What did he want with you?"

"He wanted to know if I was interested in an assistant coaching job."

Her eyes widened in surprise. "High school football?"

"Maybe," he said with a shrug, but the excitement sparking in his eyes told her all she needed to know. He wanted this. "I'll have my hands full getting Silas's foundation off the ground, but by the time football season rolls back around, the foundation will be in the hands of the administrator.

"And that's not all," he continued.

He let go of her hand and reached behind him, pulling something from his back pocket.

"What's this?" Taylor asked before recognizing the brochure for Southwestern University that she'd picked up when she visited the campus.

"I'm thinking of checking out their Education Department. I know I have the marketing degree, but a second degree wouldn't hurt, especially if I join the coaching staff at that high school."

A slow smile drew across Taylor's lips. "Are you saying there's a possibility we're going to be college sweethearts?"

He grinned. "I know it wasn't part of our dating playbook, but it's not as if we haven't revised it before."

She wrapped her arms around his neck and linked her fingers behind his head.

"I think it's time we throw that playbook out the window, Twenty-Three. We don't need it anymore. We've got this."

Don't miss London's story,

COMING SUMMER 2022

READING GROUP GUIDE

BOOK CLUB
DISCUSSION QUESTIONS

1. The fake dating trope is a popular one for romantic comedies. Do you find them believable? Have you ever encountered a real-life fake dating story?

2. Taylor had several reasons for not wanting to date Jamar, including not wanting to cross the boundary between instructor and client. What are your thoughts on couples whose relationships began in a professional capacity?

3. How do you feel about Taylor's relationship with her family, especially her brother? Do you believe she was fair to her family?

4. Jamar took it upon himself to care for his family, Silas's family, and Taylor. How did you feel about Jamar's instinct to take care of everyone? Where do you think this comes from?

5. Was there anything about Taylor's or Jamar's journey that you connected with on a personal level? If so, what was it?

6. Did your opinion of the characters change at all during the course of reading *The Dating Playbook*?

7. Was there a particular scene that stuck with you? If so, which scene was it and why do you think it resonated with you?

8. How did you feel about the way the book ended? Did Taylor forgive Jamar too quickly? Was she justified in being upset with Jamar's decision to go through with the workout?

Q&A WITH
FARRAH ROCHON

Girlfriend support is such an important theme in your books. How do you keep up with your "squad," and what do you most like to do when you get together?

I'm lucky enough to have several "squads" in my life and I cherish each of them. I consider my sister and cousins as my very first squad. We called ourselves "The Golden Girls" because we found gold paint in a shed at my grandparents' and decided to build ourselves a clubhouse and paint it. I learned the true meaning of sisterhood back then, and I've carried those lessons into other friendships throughout my life.

Another of my squads was formed almost twenty years ago, when I stumbled upon an online bulletin board for one of my favorite authors. Although we were brought together through books, those women have become an integral part of every facet of my life. I've been there for weddings, the birth of their children, and sadly, the passing of one from breast cancer. Through it all we've remained an extremely close bunch.

The squad I rely on the most these days is my close-knit group of writer friends. In addition to our private Facebook group where we offer encouragement and the occasional dose of tough love, we also get together for a writer's retreat every year at a beach house in Destin, Florida. With a job as isolated as writing, it's important to have friends you can call on who understand what you're going through.

What would be the project you'd focus on, in the same way Samiah developed her app and Taylor her studying?

If I had time to focus on a project of my own, it would be starting a travel agency that focuses on all things Disney! I love helping people put together the perfect Disney vacation, either at the parks or on a Disney cruise ship. To spend all day curating these magical experiences would be a dream come true.

In what ways are you and Taylor alike?

To be honest, I originally thought I had nothing in common with Taylor. She's fifteen years younger than I am, a fitness guru, and while I do have a positive outlook on life, it's nothing compared to Taylor's tendency to look on the bright side. However, during the course of writing *The Dating Playbook*, I discovered that I have so much more in common with Taylor than I ever imagined. Taylor's drive and determination reminded me of my early days as a writer. Becoming a published author wasn't seen as the most practical career path. Like Taylor, I experienced my share of rejection, but I didn't allow it to deter me from following my dream.

Why was it important for you to write a character with a learning disorder? What kind of research did you do for Taylor?

Taylor's learning disorder is based on the daughter of a dear friend (who happens to be named Taylor). Like *my* Taylor, my friend's daughter was not diagnosed until well after she'd finished high school. She was always a good student, but she had to work extra hard in every class throughout high school, college, and nursing school. Her story is one of strength and resilience. She was the perfect model for Taylor.

As I prepared notes for writing this story line, I interviewed a school speech pathologist who specializes in learning disorders and did extensive online research. My goal was to make Taylor's character as authentic as possible by exploring the doubts an undiagnosed learning disorder can create, but also not allowing it to define her as a person.

Like Jamar, you also recently lost one of your best friends. Were you able to channel some of your grief into his character? Did the changes in your life shape the book in any way?

I lost my older sister—my only sister—halfway through the writing of this book. She was my very best friend and losing her knocked my entire world off its axis. It took months before I could even look at *The Dating Playbook* again, because I knew I had to face that aspect of Jamar's story line.

I learned that I had never experienced true grief before. I've lost family members and suffered a deep sadness, but there is nothing that has ever come close to the raw pain I've endured since losing my sister. I truly believe this loss allowed me to empathize on a deeper level with Jamar's grief journey. There were many tears cried as I worked through some of the scenes that explored Jamar's loss of his best friend, Silas, but I stuck with it and hope it makes for a better story.

What was the most interesting thing you learned when writing *The Dating Playbook*?

The fascinating world of "Fitnessgram" is, by far, the most interesting thing I discovered while writing this book. There are fitness instructors who have created an entire world for themselves on Instagram, with hundreds of thousands of followers. The entrepreneurial spirit of these fitness gurus is inspiring.

Who's your favorite football team and what's your favorite game-day snack?

I am a lifelong New Orleans Saints fan, much to my uncle's chagrin. He's a thirty-five-plus-year veteran of the NFL and has coached for more than a half-dozen teams. I love him dearly, but I refuse to cheer for any other team. It's the Saints all the way. As for game-day snacks, nothing beats a nice bowl of gumbo while watching my Saints.

BONUS SCENE

In the very beginning of The Dating Playbook, *readers learn that Taylor has gotten herself into a heap of financial trouble. Unfortunately, many of us can probably sympathize with her. In this scene that never made it into the book, Taylor is suffering through the hard task of choosing personal items to sell in order to earn some extra cash. It gives some insight into Taylor's journey of personal growth and her effort to become more responsible.*

Taylor fought back the bile rising in her throat as she stared at the clothes and jewelry arrayed over her unmade bed. She'd spent the past half hour trying to decide which ones to upload to the app she'd been using to sell some of her things. It was only on the rarest occasion that she treated herself to what one would consider a luxury item. Having to part with any of them was more traumatic than she had anticipated.

Each item held special meaning. The bomber jacket she'd brought back from Germany was her only connection to the group of girlfriends she'd made there. It conjured fond memories of Saturday afternoons spent in the mall near the base, always with a parent or one of their older siblings nearby.

The Manolo Blahnik pumps were her only pair of fancy

shoes. Period. Most of her shoes came from the low-end section of DSW's clearance rack or Target. She'd bought these under duress, after much badgering by her best friend Keva, who insisted that the champagne satin pumps were the only shoes Taylor should even consider wearing to her wedding. In the end, Taylor was happy she'd bought them. She felt powerful in these shoes. As if she could rule the world simply by slipping them on.

She picked up the platinum diamond-stud earrings from Tiffany's. Most of the time they remained in that signature blue box, mainly because she didn't go anywhere that warranted wearing two-thousand-dollar earrings. She'd priced similar items on the site and knew she could get anywhere from eight hundred to twelve hundred dollars for the pair.

But she couldn't do it.

She'd come up with a dozen practical reasons for selling these earrings, but when weighed against the significance of what they meant to her, she just couldn't bring herself to part with them.

The shoes. She would sell the shoes. She'd last worn them on her date with Craig. She didn't need any reminders of him.

After uploading several pictures of the satiny pumps to the website, Taylor left her tiny bedroom and walked over to the closet just to the right of her front door. She'd put this off long enough.

She dragged out the tattered cardboard box, cursing as the tear on the side ripped a little more. It was time for her to take inventory of her remaining Taylor'd Conditioning gear.

She wasn't sure which choice had been the worst, giving this stuff out so freely or buying it in the first place. When she thought about the thousands of dollars she'd sunk into the T-shirts—both unisex and female cut—baseball caps, bandannas, crop tops, backpacks, headbands, and wristbands? What in the heck had she been thinking?

She shoved the box toward the sofa and cleared the junk mail from the ottoman that did double duty as a coffee table. She counted out twenty-two T-shirts, eighteen caps, seven crop tops, and fourteen wristband and headband sets. She didn't have to count the backpacks; she already knew there were only eight left. She'd stored them underneath the other gear. At nearly thirty bucks apiece, they were now reserved for clients who stuck with her for more than three months.

Maybe if she'd been a bit more stingy, using this stuff as incentive for folks to stick around, she'd have more than a handful of clients.

Taylor rolled her eyes.

The promise of a free T-shirt and baseball cap wasn't enough to entice the number of clients she needed to get herself out of this mess. The time for recriminations had passed long ago. It wasn't as if she could go back and get her gear from the dozens of people who'd happily taken the free stuff and hadn't bothered to call her back.

Oh, God. That thought was *way* too reminiscent of those early days when her family moved back to the States. The ability to date boys who didn't live on the same Army base as her had been an awakening. She'd gone boy crazy, giving away far too much of herself without getting anything in return.

"At least you've learned your lesson in that arena," Taylor muttered.

She grabbed an envelope from the pile of junk mail—a credit card company offering her a credit line increase. She snorted. They must not have gotten the memo. She flipped the envelope over and jotted the list of remaining inventory; then she neatly packed everything back into the box. Before closing it, she picked up a set of wristbands, thinking she'd offer them to the client she was meeting with later today.

"God, you are *so* bad at this," Taylor said with a sigh, tossing them back into the box. She'd already given Bonnie a T-shirt, baseball cap, and bandanna. She was like a child trying to buy the affection of an absentee parent, so grateful for any crumb of loyalty she received from clients.

She just never expected it would be so difficult for her business to gain traction. She blamed it on naïveté, and that irrepressible penchant she had for always looking on the bright side, believing that if you remained positive, only positive things would come your way.

She'd started small, with only a few YouTube videos and Instagram posts. As her follower count increased and the views on YouTube grew, the more confident she became in her ability to do this full-time. She'd seen so many fellow fitness instructors who were killing it; she just *knew* she would crush it too. Especially when she came up with the brilliant idea to play up her Army brat background and specialize in boot camp–style workouts.

Her videos hadn't taken off the way she'd expected, but Taylor figured she'd hit gold when that clip of the three of them chewing Craig out at that sushi restaurant had gone viral. London and Samiah had abhorred the notoriety, but Taylor soaked it in.

For weeks following the incident with Craig, she'd been inundated with inquiries, and the views on her YouTube channel had spiked. But most of the people who'd contacted her for consultations hadn't really wanted a full-time fitness and nutrition coach. In the end, she'd garnered three new clients who'd actually turned out to be legitimate.

"So much for going viral."

Taylor plopped down on the sofa and took out her phone. She skimmed through her Gmail account, then switched over to Facebook.

She rolled her eyes at the sight of the familiar orange-and-white logo of the Texas Longhorns avatar. The person behind the YourFavorite23 account was one persistent SOB. The messages came like clockwork, one every three days, with someone claiming he or she was willing to pay top dollar for her services as a personal fitness instructor.

As if she hadn't heard *that* a hundred times since the video with Craig went viral. She was so over these lunatics. She refused to entertain messages like this one.

But she needed to make some money. And fast.

She clicked over to her business Facebook page and posted a message:

> Boot Camp circuit training pop-up. 3pm tomor-
> row. Zilker Park. Only $10.

If she managed to convince at least five people to sign up, maybe she would be able to eat something other than ramen for dinner this week. It was a big ask, but she wanted to stay positive.

ACKNOWLEDGMENTS

My dearest Tamara,

Never in a million years did I imagine that I would dedicate a book to your memory. You are and will forever be so much more than just a memory.

You are my big sister, my staunchest cheerleader, and my very best friend.

When I reflect on my career, I see your handprint on every significant milestone. I remember the day you put that copy of LaVyrle Spencer's *Separate Beds* in my hands, opening my eyes to the wonder of the romance genre. And when you loaned me one of your precious Judith McNaught novels and changed my life forever. I'm not sure you ever knew how consequential those moments were, how consequential you were. I owe all of this to you.

You have been with me for every step of this amazing journey. You were the first person I called after getting "The Call," and the one I had to share every achievement with, no matter how big or small. It is impossible to envision living in a world where I cannot call on you, yet that's where I find myself.

My life will never be the same. How could it be, and why would I ever want it to be the same if you're not here? But I am determined to live every single day in a way that will honor you. Because, as always, everything I do, I do it to make my big sister proud.

Until we see each other again...

With all my love,
Farrah

And we know that in all things God works for the good of those who love him, who have been called according to his purpose.

—Romans 8:28

ABOUT THE AUTHOR

Farrah Rochon, *USA Today* bestselling author of *The Boyfriend Project*, hails from a small town just west of New Orleans. She has garnered much acclaim for her Holmes Brothers and New York Sabers series. When she is not writing in her favorite coffee shop, Farrah spends most of her time reading, cooking, traveling the world, visiting Walt Disney World, and catching her favorite Broadway shows.

You can learn more at:

FarrahRochon.com

Twitter @FarrahRochon

Facebook.com/FarrahRochonAuthor

YOUR
BOOK
CLUB
RESOURCE

VISIT
GCPClubCar.com

to sign up for the **GCP Club Car** newsletter, featuring exclusive promotions, info on other **Club Car** titles, and more.

 @grandcentralpub

 @grandcentralpub

 @grandcentralpub